FIRE AND POWDER

FIRE AND POWDER

HANNAH BOGGS

Library of Congress Control Number: 2020920510

ISBN: 978-1-7359647-0-6 (HB)
ISBN: 978-1-7359647-1-3 (PB)
eISBN: 978-1-7359647-2-0 (e-book)

To my Mom and Dad,

without them, you wouldn't be

reading this book right now.

"... And in their triumph die,

like fire and powder,

Which, as they kiss, consume ..."

~ William Shakespeare

PROLOGUE

LAST SEPTEMBER

With every great empire, there is a simple formula: rise to power; conquer; and the fall. The fall typically doesn't happen just after all the conquering takes place; quite often many years later sometimes even hundreds of years—but the fall always comes. It is inevitable and nothing can stop it because it's the law of nature.

In Odette's case, her fall came only a couple of months after her reign. And what a fall it was.

A once beautiful garden laid out beneath her window; the grass yellowed by the summer heat, the flowers wilting with the coming of autumn. The last light of the day touched the dying garden and filtered through a lonely window, warming Odette as she looked out.

Reluctantly, she pulled away. The gardens would be there tomorrow and the day after that, but summer wouldn't.

Summer was traditionally a time when teenagers were *free*, with no expectation or chains holding you down. A painful reminder of something Odette was not.

A small patch of sunlight shone on the vanity. Unconsciously, Odette moved to sit there, seeking out the comfort the light brought. If she shut her eyes, she could pretend she saw houses or mountains in the patterns dancing over her eyelids. She could pretend she was anywhere else than the mansion.

Something softly rustled behind her, breaking the cocoon of peace she'd created. Her hair felt like it stood on end.

The warped image of a shadow man appeared in the mirror. On his head were two distinct horns nestled where his hair should have been. There was no face. (At least, that's what she told herself, because if she stared long enough, she would see something horrendous.) It was his true image, Odette learned not that long ago, the mirror revealed.

Thorn spoke, his voice closer than she anticipated. "It is time."

Her breathing stuttered to a halt. She shifted so she no longer had to look at him. It couldn't be *that time* already.

Odette forced herself to laugh and leaned into the mirror to inspect herself. "Oh, Thorn? Is it dinner ready?"

Another step. Thorn's dark head towered above her. "You know my meaning, Odette. You have put this off long enough."

"You're wrong." Odette stopped her primping and met his warped gaze in the mirror. "It hasn't been long enough. It will never be long enough."

"So, you *can* hear." Thorn's voice was as soft, contemplative, and a little amused. His head bobbed in the reflection for a moment as he came closer. "I thought you had gone deaf."

Odette laughed humorlessly. She waited for him to join in; but he didn't. There were times when they could joke with one another; yet those times were far behind them now. Obviously, he wouldn't be easily swayed this time.

"Listen to me—"

Odette cut him off. "No. I don't want to, Thorn. Not yet, please. I'm not ready yet."

Thorn held up his hand, quieting her "You cannot barter your way out of this. You have had your time, now you have to fulfill your end of the bargain."

She turned to face him. The real Thorn was nothing like the shadow version in the mirror. When she'd first met him, his hair had been pure silver, reflecting his skittish and subservient nature. It began to change after the twins were locked away, slowly darkening as he regained his confidence. On his face he wore a mask, which covered the mutilated half of his face; an eyepatch covered his blind eye.

"I can't. I won't." Odette crossed her arms over her chest, her resolve firm. "Have you forgotten what they did? It wasn't just me they hurt—it was you too."

"I haven't forgotten."

How could he? Every time someone looked at him with disgust, he was reminded of the disfiguration of his human vessel; the scars he covered with a mask, and his blind eye, a painful reminder of his enslavement.

"Then *why?*"

Thorn's expression hardened. There was no denying, when he wanted to, he could be terrifying. Sometimes Odette would forget he wasn't human, until she was painfully reminded.

"You know why. I am bound to serve the Mages name until they are no more. It is my duty to protect them." The sun finally set, and darkness filled the room. "And I cannot protect you unless you are one of them."

Unconsciously, Odette reached behind to where her special, silver jewelry box sat. With a simple touch, the ring seared onto her left ring finger, pulsed upon sensing its mates.

Thorn extended a hand, waiting for her to give him the box.

The power made her hair feel odd in an irritating way. She wished she could scrub at it until the annoying hum just beneath her skin would leave, but she knew well enough there was no way to get rid of it. She was stuck. At least, Odette thought, she was stuck in a place where she had the advantage.

"I can't." Thorn's jaw clenched from her defiance. "I won't," she pressed.

He sniffed, raising his chin. "There will be consequences."

Odette pulled away from the jewelry box and slapped his outstretched palm away. "Why are you trying to give them power over us? Do you know what he'll do to me once he gets that back? What *they'll* do?" Tears bubbled up in her eyes, but she would not cry. She couldn't afford to.

"It does not matter."

The room grew colder, like he was trying to choke out the last of the warmth. Perhaps it was only Odette's fears, but Thorn was a powerful being. She had only seen a sliver of his power before, as most of it was under lock by the Mages'. And yet ... Thorn was not under any real surveillance, not since Odette deemed, he should oversee his own person. It would be a lie to say she was as strict as the twins. She hadn't once thought of keeping him reigned in.

The shadows encased the room wholly, plunging it into blackness. The windows were blotted out by opaque shadows. The only source of light was Thorn and his glowing eye.

"You have failed to do what you promised."

Odette fell against the vanity, and the wood dug into her ribs painfully. "Why are you forcing me to do this, Thorn? I thought you were my friend?"

Slowly Thorn revealed more of himself in the dark. An ethereal silver light came from nowhere but himself. His face turned towards her; his brows furrowed.

"My allegiance lies with the Mages'." The words were painful to hear, and yet he didn't let up. "You ... you must know I want to help you, Odette; but my hands are tied.

You have not married Grayson and my power can only stretch so far for you now. It was a different matter when that man was holding you prisoner. You said you would marry Grayson. It has been too long.

"They call me, and I have to serve them. If you do not give them back, I'll have to hurt you." His voice sounded defeated, but she didn't know what to believe anymore. She thought he was a friend, but a friend wouldn't force her to do something as awful as this.

This was really it. There was no more bartering for more time; there was no more pretending she could avoid it. Thorn was right, she had to give their amulets back.

Briefly, Odette considered running away again. She'd tried a handful of times before, knowing the day would eventually come when she had to free the twins, and every time Thorn stopped her.

A morbid thought crossed her mind. *If I did go, Grayson would come for me. Even after everything I've done, he would come.*

Odette wished the ground would open and swallow her up. Once more, she tried; hoping luck would be on her side. "Thorn—"

"You need to do as you promised; otherwise, I will be your enemy."

And, just as soon as the darkness came, it receded. The sudden light was harsh and revealed too much of herself. Odette would have preferred he kept her in the dark.

Thorn frowned pityingly as he stared at her where she now crouched on the floor. She could almost believe he was the same Thorn she had grown to be friends with, but there was a lingering fear. She couldn't trust anyone.

"I need you to give them the amulets back. I don't want to hurt you." Thorn's hand extended again, pleading. "Please, Odette."

Her bottom lip quivered as she stared at his hand. "You're in control of your own actions. We can keep them away."

"I am a servant to them." Thorn's sadness was difficult to place. It seemed fake, like he was trying to lure her into a false sense of security. He sighed, realizing she would not take his hand, and drew it back to his side. "I am sorry, Odette."

She couldn't breathe. This was how it ended for her. The one person whom she believed to be a friend in this horrible place was no more than a monstrous pawn.

Thorn stepped to the vanity and bent over her.

Being next to Thorn was frightening and cold that came with him was like an arctic blast. It was the kind of deep cold that lingered with you for hours after, turning your fingers and toes blue. She had only been this close to him a few times before, but never did he exuded this much power.

Odette squeezed her eyes shut tight and readied herself. She wouldn't show fear. She would pretend she wasn't crying. No blow ever came. She peeked at him with one eye and saw him still standing there, jewelry box in hand. A blue glow emanated from the inside of the box, shining through the cracks and keyhole.

This was a fate worse than death.

"You have to marry him," Thorn said. "It is the only way I can extend my protection to you. Things ... things don't have to go back to the way they were. I will be on your side."

He laid a hand on her shoulder hesitantly. She flinched. It was like a block of ice. "How can I trust you? You'll be on their side no matter what."

The glow highlighting his face dimmed. "I *am* bound to them. This is something I cannot change. It is up to you what you believe ... I promise you. I will do everything I can in your best interest."

But she couldn't believe him. Even if she married Grayson, one day it would come down to Thorn choosing between those he was bound to or her. No amount of promising could break the supernatural chain that bound Thorn to them.

I

ODETTE

Odette was certain she would pass out. Her heartbeat so loud, it had to be audible. The thudding echoed in her ears like a war drum, going faster and faster; louder and louder, until it drowned out everything else. She had experienced stage fright before, she was no stranger to it, but this wasn't stage fright. This was fear.

Before this, if she messed up while dancing, the worst would be the internal shame because she knew she could do better. However, the consequences for messing up the Magical Mages Twins Magic show could be death.

How she allowed them to rope her into doing their show, she'd never know.

Thorn stood behind her, adjusting the feathers of her costume so they lay just right. He stepped back, giving her a once over, and then asked, "Comfortable?"

Odette made a *what-do-you-think*, type of face and the man conceded with a bowed head. She turned to the side and caught her reflection in a mirror.

Heavy stage makeup covered her face. The costume was a ridiculous feathery leotard. Her eyes dropped to her stomach, where a small, somewhat visible, baby bump pushed through the costume spandex.

"It's time to go," Thorn said.

Odette broke free of her spell and faced him once more, finding him closing an old-fashioned pocket watch. "Are you sure I can't hang back a little longer? It's not like they need me to be *right there.*"

"They might not," he agreed, "but Grayson wants to see you."

Of course he would, and Thorn had no right to refuse. Odette huffed, "It's not like he's gonna know I'm there."

Grayson would be focused on the show, not on her. He might've hated being a performer, but he took the job seriously.

Thorn gave no indication he agreed and motioned for her to follow. Odette glanced around the dressing room once more before stepping into the labyrinthine halls of velvet.

The Tent of Mystery was a large purple-and-silver tent as tall as it was wide. Only half of the Tent was utilized for the auditorium, with a decent size stage but a small audience capacity. Tickets were expensive but well worth the price of admission.

Because what many did not know, this magic was *real.*

On stage were the Magical Mages Twins. They were legends, having commanded the attention of the nation from a young age. They had everyone under their spell, being as charming and polite as they were.

Oh, if only they knew.

Greer Mages stood front and center, finishing up her infamous knife trick. She twirled the last blade between her fingers, goading the audience. "One more?"

The crowd's answers overlapped one another as they shouted.

Greer smiled a Cheshire cat grin and turned her attention towards the Spinning Wheel of Terror. Though Odette only saw the back of the Wheel, she knew who was strapped to it. Grayson Mages, her husband.

Greer stood towards the side, the final knife twirling between her fingers, focusing on the volunteer like a predator does its prey. With swift precision, the female magician did a half-pirouette, her arms arcing above her head for dramatic flair and then in one fluid motion threw the blade. The knife was little more than a silver blur in the air.

Grayson didn't flinch. He had been on that Wheel countless times and Greer couldn't have hurt him with those knives even if she wanted to—they were illusions. But this said nothing about Greer's actual knife throwing skills. She was good.

Thunderous applause filled the tent's small space, equal in adoration for Greer's performance and Grayson's resilience. Greer helped her brother down, a self-satisfied smirk on her lips as Grayson stood (a little wobbly) and bowed.

The Wheel was pushed aside as they made room on the stage for the next act: Odette's act.

Sensing her unease, Thorn patted her shoulder, but she didn't find comfort in it. Moments later, Grayson emerged with a tall, hard steel safe that towered above them, probably seven feet tall, and brought it to rest near the edge of the wings.

Maybe Odette would've been more agreeable to participating if she hadn't witnessed what they were capable of doing. What they could still do.

She took a step back, knocking into Thorn's chest. He rested his hands on her shoulders, steadying her.

"*It's going to be fine,*" he whispered.

"*You can say that*" she bit back, looking up at him. "*You're not the one they're dragging in there.*"

Thorn gave her arms a gentle squeeze. It might have been comforting if Odette wasn't aware, he was tasked with keeping her from running. "*I thought you trusted me?*"

"For this next trick," Greer projected, strutting across the stage until she was front and center. "We will need a volunteer."

Hands shot up, excited voices chanting their own name or the names of their neighbor. Greer shot Grayson a sly look, as if to say *hey-it's-your-turn,* and he reluctantly moved from his position by the elongated safe. For a brief second, he turned his gaze to the left wing, meeting Odette's eyes. Then, he vanished. The crowd roared!

When he reappeared, there was a young girl holding his hand, maybe seven or eight, and he situated her in the middle of the stage with Greer. Odette's stomach turned. She didn't like the idea of either of them being near a child, and she found herself taking a small step forward.

Something about seeing a child on stage with them seemed perverse. She wanted to go to the little girl and shield her from the twins; but Thorn's grip kept her grounded.

"This is a disappearing act—have you ever wanted to disappear?" Greer asked the little girl. She nodded; her eyes wide with innocence. "Now, you can. What we're going to do is put you in that impenetrable box and lock it tight so *you* can't get out and *we* can't get in. Then, with magic, we'll make you vanish."

She should have been scared, but the awe of it masked any alarms blaring in the back of the little girl's mind. Odette could feel and hear it all. It frustrated her. Why couldn't she see what they really were? But the little girl looked up at Greer with the utmost admiration and followed her directions to enter the ginormous safe. She didn't even flinch when it slammed shut.

Grayson threw a tarp over the box and the twins began to circle it, performing a fake routine they had worked out weeks ago at practice. If they wanted to, the little girl would be out of the box by now, but they liked the theatrics.

"And now, we're going to make her disappear."

Odette felt Thorn's hand on her shoulder, and then she was plunged into dense darkness. The air was heavy and thick with the scent of dust. Odette reached forward, but her arms couldn't extend because there wasn't much space in the box. Her steel casket.

Nothing could be heard from inside the safe, but her own deafening heartbeat.

Odette tried the breathing technique Dr. Short—her former therapist—had taught her. It was the only helpful thing the woman ever taught her she could remember.

And then, without warning, the door swung open wide. The scent of burnt wood and powder hung in the air. A hot spotlight from above swung down and centered on her in the box, and the audience applauded.

At the same time, in one of the back rows, a spotlight fixed on one of the audience members. Odette squinted; the bright light was harsh compared to the total darkness she had been in only moments before. As her eyes adjusted, she could see they were focused on the little girl, now free from the safe and looking stunned.

A hand reached into the safe and Odette flinched. She didn't want to leave the box—leaving meant she had to go through with the rest of the show, with Greer's *accidental* slip-ups. She couldn't prove Greer would hurt her on purpose, because tricks went awry all the time, but Greer seemed to slip-up more than a little. But Odette mechanically took Grayson's hand without another thought.

Both the twins were looking at her, their mouths stretched into smiles that would make anyone uncomfortable. She gingerly stepped out of the safe with

Grayson's assistance and he presented her to the crowd with a flourish.

"Ladies and Gentlemen, our lovely assistant, Ms. Odette!"

The three of them bowed in unison. Coming out of the bow, Grayson still holding Odette's hand, pulled it close and pressed a chaste kiss to the back of it. Odette turned her head to the side; she didn't want to look at him.

He let go, but the contact remained on her skin. He brushed her hair behind her ear; hand trailing down her spine. He stopped when he reached her hip and pulled away, his professionalism returning.

Holding her breath, Odette allowed herself to be put through the motions. Things they had all rehearsed tirelessly over the past several weeks. Simple tricks at first; levitation, the Zig-Zag Girl, (leaving Odette dizzy and a bit disproportionate); and the Hoops. They were amazing tricks, but they were nothing compared to the finale the Twins had planned.

Tricks lined up one right after the other and all executed with practiced precision. Odette couldn't mess up if she wanted to. She felt as though she was on autopilot and invisible strings moved her like a marionette. She always hit her mark. Always landed safely.

Odette's eyes wandered to the wings, but Thorn was no longer there. Her courage withered. A sharp jab from Greer drew her back into the present. The female magician gave her a meaningful glare—Odette couldn't lose her head like that.

In a hail of fire, Greyson re-appeared on stage, his own stunt ended, and the audience went wild. He acknowledged them with a curt nod, mouth moving but his words were lost. They all adored him.

Greer turned her back to the crowd. The pair of them were positioned off to the side, awaiting their cue, all sorts of props surrounded them. The finale had come, and it was Grayson's job to set the stage.

"For our final illusion we would like to introduce something new. Something never before seen" Greer announced. "Something so new even our assistant has not seen it."

"*Ready to drown?*" she hissed. One hand laid over her mic so no one would hear. "*I hear it feels like you're burning from the inside.*"

Odette might have snapped back, but she was acutely aware of the brightness of the lights on her face. The audience would see any and every tick of her face. Odette planted herself firmly where she stood and said nothing but smiled like she had been telling her a joke. On the inside, her heart thudding painfully in her chest.

It's only a trick, she reminded herself, *they won't let you get hurt ... They can't.*

Again, her eyes darted to the wings, but Thorn had yet to reappear. The velvet curtain swayed with the movement on the stage, creating the illusion someone was behind them, watching silently; however, it was nothing more than a dark abandoned corner. She swallowed thickly. Had he really left her? No, he was still around here *somewhere*. He had to be; Thorn was always present during the shows.

Grayson stalked along the front of the stage and gestured to the glass tank, which rose from the floor via a trap door, dry ice billowing around the bottom to create the illusion it was floating.

The smoke washed over her shoes. The fog seemed, to Odette, to be chains made of smoke that tethered her to the stage.

"Once she is fully submerged, she will have a limited amount of time to escape," Grayson explained, projecting his voice toward the audience, "or our lovely assistant will *die*."

Gasps and cries of awe filled Odette's ears. The finality of his words struck her odd—if she didn't know any better, she would have thought he was okay with this, when in fact he was more likely to be against it than she was.

It's all pretend, Odette reminded herself.

Greer was instantly beside her and placed her hands-on Odette's shoulders, pushing her toward the glass tank. It was barely as tall as she was but was wide enough, she could lay flat on the bottom and not touch either side.

Unlike the classic water tank trick, there were no safeguards, no oxygen tank and no secret key. Odette was at their mercy.

Grayson joined them in front of the tank with a cheap-looking straight jacket in his hands and motioned for her to hold out her arms. She fought an urge to spit at him, maybe it would have taken that pitying look out of his eye.

Odette raised her arms, her jaw clenched tight. He slipped the rough costume piece over her and from behind, Greer began to buckle. Grayson took her hands and wrapped them around her torso so Greer could fasten her completely.

He was too close. As a rule, Odette always tried to keep him at arms-length; however, tonight, he dared to break her unspoken rule. The feathers on his cape prodded at her and she could see the dark black kohl he had applied to his eyes before the performance, enhancing his unearthly blue eyes.

Greer pulled the two of them apart and led Odette to the back of the tank. A set of roll-away stairs latched onto the side. She looked at the railings warily, and began to climb, her legs shaking beneath her. Not knowing what to expect.

Once she reached the top, she stopped—noticing movement in the wings. Odette turned; her brows furrowed. It was Thorn, standing as if he'd been there the whole time.

She frowned, nervously shaking her head at him. *Where had he gone?*

Thorn placed a finger to his lips.

"Odette." Her head snapped up. Grayson, with his arms out in a hammy gesture, nodded to her. "If you would."

She tried to read his mind or his body language to spot some sign of reassurance, but nothing.

Reluctantly she put one foot in the tank. Instantly, her shoe filled with icy water and she was pulled downward.

Caught off guard she slipped, and with no way to catch herself, Odette found herself instantly submerged.

Water shot up her nostrils and pierced her ears. Odette reached the bottom quickly, weighed down by the weight of her shoes and ballooning skirt. She pushed off the bottom— the lid wasn't closed yet; she could still reach the surface.

Odette breached the water's surface for a moment, inhaling as much air as she possibly could. Then, something slammed against her nose. Odette lost her footing and sank back to the bottom and the tank went dark.

Suddenly, this didn't seem like a magic trick, but a flashback to a day in the swimming pool where she had nearly died, thanks to Greer.

Greer, Odette grit her teeth. She was going to get it when Odette got out of this.

Odette fought against the straight jacket; her arms tight against her back. She pushed against the straps, but nothing moved. It was as if the buckles had been welded together.

She slammed her feet against the side glass, kicking with all her might. Just this *once*, could her amulet work? She kicked the glass over and over, but it did nothing.

Odette tried to push up to the top once again, but this time, there was no air. She was met with a smooth leather surface, and no amount of pushing made it move.

Black spots appeared before her, her heart pounding painfully in her chest. If they didn't get her out of there soon, she would drown. Wasn't that what Greer had said?

Where was Grayson? She felt her lungs spasm and the cold water hit the back of her throat.

Suddenly, as if the world had been sucked out from beneath her feet, Odette was no longer in water.

Greer threw off the cover with a flourish. The audience waited with bated breath to see what would happen. The tank was empty—Odette was gone.

Greer's smile faltered, only for a moment, but she recovered. "While you all were so preoccupied with a tank full of bubbles—" The stage lights spun to the back row where Grayson and Odette would be sitting, but Grayson sat alone.

Grayson seemed confused and his eyebrows pushed together. He didn't look at anyone in the crowd, but he straight at Greer. Her throat tightened and she shook her head. If Grayson didn't have Odette, she had no idea where she was.

Off in the wings, Thorn watched the chaos unfold in silence before vanishing. The gentle sway of the velvet curtain was the only evidence anyone had been standing there. In the corner, a sopping wet straight jacket.

II

GRAYSON

Grayson's chest heaved rapidly. He couldn't breathe or even think. He hadn't felt this kind of fear since he was a child.

The show ended abruptly, much to Greer's displeasure but Grayson knew she would get over it. Even if she didn't, Grayson didn't care. His world was crumbling all around him and he felt like he was being smothered by the rubble.

Odette was *gone*. She vanished from the tank on her own, one of the most advanced things to do with their magic.

The tent was searched first, of course; but it was a bust. If she were there, the twins would have felt it. Odette could never hide very well and though the tent had many hiding places the only people found were a couple of stragglers looking for a restroom.

Grayson didn't linger. He searched all possible locations she could have gone: her old house (now nothing but ash);

the church; the cemetery, more specifically, her parents' graves; and the lighthouse (also, nothing but rubble); but, there was no sign of her. No trace she'd even been to those places in the last week.

Wherever she went, it wasn't around town.

Grayson parked his car haphazardly on the driveway. He couldn't make himself get out—it felt like leaving his car meant giving up, leaving Odette. He rested his head on the steering wheel and closed his eyes.

She could be in the city, he thought. He hadn't tried there and it was as good a place as any to hide.

Grayson adjusted himself in his seat, ready to tear off into the night again when the porch light caught his eye. Thorn stood on the front steps. His sorry expression told Grayson everything.

His vision clouded over, and a searing heat shot through his veins. Grayson didn't remember coming inside but suddenly he was. He could hear screaming; the sound was foreign and strange, only for him to realize it was his voice.

After what seemed like an eternity, the mind fog lifted, and Grayson found himself in the middle of his own destruction. He was in Odette's room, which was once as pristine as an ornamental dollhouse. However, now ...

Odette's vanity had been thrown clear across the room and flipped over on its back. The small bits and baubles that decorated the top were now scattered across the hardwood in broken fragments; its mirror smashed in hundreds of little pieces.

The sheets on the bed had been torn off, the pillows were busted. Clothes from her closet were scattered and ripped; trinkets he bought her, smashed; and her curtains torn down from their rod and shredded like tissue paper.

Grayson released a shaky breath he had been holding, his rage shrinking until his anger was replaced by despair.

Grayson hissed as he ripped off his feathered cape, throwing it in with the remnants of Odette's room. He then undid his tie and the top few buttons of his shirt. It truly felt as if he would choke from this stifling feeling if he didn't do something.

He set a chair upright and sat to inspect the damage he had done to himself. Cuts on his knuckles. Rivulets of blood poured between his fingers and down on some of her clothing. Otherwise he was unscathed.

He could feel something heavy settle in his stomach - something worse than her oppressive presence, scolding him for what he had done to her room. It was loneliness.

Grayson sniffed and wiped his damp eyes on his sleeve. No, he couldn't cry. He wasn't weak. Grayson reasoned, throwing a fit wouldn't help him find her. He needed to shove these emotions down and focus on what was important. Those emotions inside of him were too dangerous for anyone to see. *Especially* Odette.

Why would she go? Odette was smart enough to know he left no bad deed unpunished. She was smart enough to know he would tear the world apart to get her back where she belonged—so why?

A couple feet away, something caught his eye. He bent down and picked up a photo from a broken frame he smashed in his rage. It was one of Odette and her parents. Grayson looked at the faces of her parents with indifference. Obviously, an old pic she printed from her phone. Everything from her parents' home, burnt to ash. He ensured it.

Grayson ran a thumb over the image before tossing it back onto the floor. Was he thinking of this all wrong? Had they finally pushed Odette over the edge?

No. Ever since the fire, Grayson made Thorn monitor Odette for signs of suicide. If anything questionable came up, he would have been told. Thorn had a fondness for her, as much as Grayson hated to admit it. Thorn would do anything to guarantee Odette remained happy. They had some kind of bond, and Grayson didn't know how deep it went, but he hoped the servant knew his place.

He slammed his fist into the wall, hard. What more could she want? He let her punish him by taking away his powers so she might hurt him like she'd been 'hurt'.

They both *moved on* with their lives, forgive and forget. They were married. They were in love and starting a family! Why? *Why?!*

There was a knock on the door. His head snapped upright, jostling a tear on his cheek he didn't know was there.

Grayson's lips peeled back in a snarl and grabbed the nearest item—a book—in a white-knuckled grip before hurdling it. "LEAVE!"

The book smashed hard into the wall, leaving a small dent where the spine connected with the paint. There was a pause. Had they left? No. The door opened and shut within the same second.

Greer.

"I don't think that attitude will bring her back," Greer stated, her eyes flicking over the mess of the room. "This is what, the third time you've done this? No wonder ..." Greer continued to mutter things under her breath as she stepped over the remnants of the room.

Grayson clenched his fists, the shredded skin burning hot with the need to hit something again; possibly her.

"Have you even *tried* calling her?"

Scoffing, he grasped at the floor beside him. "Do you think I'm an idiot? Of course, I called her!" Grayson tossed Odette's smashed cell phone to his sister. "I found it when I returned to the mansion. All it did was ring."

She looked it over, mildly interested, dropping it into a pile of smashed glass on the floor.

"This is really inconsiderate of her, you know?" said Greer, breaking the quiet. "Disappearing like this when I'm about to go through my *disposal* ..."

His sister continued to talk about some little morbid project she had in mind but Grayson's attention had already split from the conversation.

Where could she have gone? Odette was a novice at using magic, she knew nothing beyond what she'd witnessed. If she managed to make herself disappear, a difficult feat even for an advanced magician such as himself, she couldn't go far.

"No one knows she's gone," said Grayson.

"They know something's up. You should've kept the show going, ending like that only draws suspicion." Greer picked up a shirt of Odette's and pinched it between two fingers. Her nose wrinkled and she tossed the garment on the floor with the rest of the garbage. She perched herself on the edge of the bed. "Have you talked to Thorn about it?"

"He says she isn't here."

"He could be *lying*."

"Why would he lie?"

Greer shrugged. "You know they're close. He could have helped her. Maybe he isn't telling you everything he knows."

The urge to smack her was strong. Grayson didn't like it when she told him what to do, even if she made a valid point. His knee bounced on the floor as he curled and uncurled his fist. "I am positive Thorn is loyal enough to not do something so ... treacherous. But doubt bloomed in the back of his mind. As if she could sense it, Greer pursed her lips, sizing him up. She had an unfettering ability to make the smallest doubts grow.

"He wouldn't, Greer," he said again, stronger this time.

"*Alright*," Greer lifted her hands, conceding from the argument far too easily. She narrowed her eyes. "You've been crying."

Grayson bristled. "I have not—"

"Your eyeliner is streaking. You've been crying." Greer huffed and pushed her hair back. "She isn't worth it, you know. All she's been is trouble since she came here."

"Shut up." Grayson scrubbed at his face vigorously with his sleeve. "Odette has no worth. She's priceless ... She's just confused."

His sister scoffed. "Whatever. You've disposed of your pets for much less than this. I don't see why she is any different."

"Because she is my wife!" Grayson could feel something bubbling up inside of him. It was dangerous, like a void in his chest sucked up all of his unwanted emotions. That void was about to become a volcano.

"She's a fad."

"She is my family!" Greer recoiled as though his words had slapped her. *Finally*, he thought. "And she is more of a family than you have ever been to me. She understands me. She cares for me deep down, and I just have to make her remember that."

Grayson sat back, eyes smiling even if he did not. For once, Greer was silenced. Her look of despair was greatly satisfying to him. He had only truly gotten such a reaction out of her a few times before, so seeing it was something to savor. After all, she should feel remorseful and guilty. She should feel like her whole world is crashing down on her. It was only fair.

Greer's hands tightened around her show skirt. "I just ... want to help you."

Help? Grayson couldn't help but laugh bitterly. He briefly wondered if she had offered her help in a similar fashion to his Odette. He scoffed and turned away. Odette was too smart to accept help from a serpent like her.

"Get out, I'm not interested in your *help*." He spat out the four-letter word with such venom Greer flinched. "Go torture your boy some more, I don't think he's scared enough."

Greer stood and her emotions melted away to the cold shell of a human he was so familiar with. She sniffed and jutted her chin out. "You know, if Odette had spent more time locked away like Skylar, maybe she wouldn't have—"

"GET OUT!"

Grayson jumped up from his chair and slammed his hand hard against the wall. Something cracked but he wasn't sure if it came from his bones or the wall. Greer didn't have the right to speak about *his* wife. Not after everything she put her through.

The whole house seemed to rattle with the force of his hit. He was seconds away from ringing her neck, which he knew she wanted. She wanted a reaction out of him to show the kind of monster she helped create.

Greer stepped back. "Fine."

His eyes flicked towards the door and it swung open violently, sounding like a thunder crack throughout the room, leaving a hole in the wall.

Anger flashed across Greer's face. She turned on her heel and left the room.

Grayson didn't watch her go. He turned away and fell back onto the chair again. Something inside of Greer had become twisted and warped. She was no longer his sister. She was a stranger who paraded around with his sister's face. A stranger who ruined his life for good.

Pushing those thoughts aside, Grayson ruffled his hair and began to pace. It should be easy—it would be *child's play*—to find Odette. Their amulets were always more active around one another.

Grayson pulled his jewel off of his neck and looked it over. The magic of locating someone was relatively simple. He had done it before, but he didn't want to think about those times, with those people. They didn't have an amulet; Odette did.

He took a step back, and something splintered beneath his shoe. It was the photo of Odette and her family he'd wrecked earlier. Truth be told, he wouldn't care if it was completely torn to shreds, and yet something stopped him. He picked it up, dumping all the broken glass from the frame, then tossed it onto her mattress. He considered this a mercy.

He kept his head down and trudged to his room, the darkness souring his mood. Thorn was already inside. Most of Grayson's personal items had been emptied in favor of candles and other mystic items (some fake, some real). Thorn stayed silent by the desk, with a large map spread out on it. In front was a picture of Odette on their wedding day and a lock of her hair.

"Y-Your hand sir—"

"Forget it," Grayson waved him off and settled in front of the desk, his eyes roaming the map. "This will be over soon enough."

He took the hair and tied it around the amulet. A ribbon was next. Grayson hooked it around the jewel and hung it on the pendulum stand which sat in the center of Africa. For a short while, it remained motionless. Then, slowly, the jewel began to sway back and forth, slowly turning to soft circles.

Thorn watched silently. He clasped his fidgeting hands behind his back. Wherever Odette was, he hoped she was safe.

Night fell. The only sources of light were the candles in the room. How many hours Grayson had been staring at the same piece of paper, he didn't care. It exhausted him, and yet he would not close his eyes for a moment. The only way he could find Odette was through concentration.

The amulet went from gently circling the map, to a blur of blue and brown as it spun around vigorously. It must have sensed his impatience. With the others, he didn't mind when it stretched out the game of cat and mouse, but this was no game. This was a matter of finding his lost property.

A soft knock came to the door, causing him to lose focus if only for a moment. Grayson ground his teeth together as the jewel stuttered, then lost its momentum.

"What?" he snapped.

Thorn peered inside; his head bowed in respect. "Dinner is ready."

Grayson would not look up; he could not allow his concentration to be broken. Gradually, the amulet began to rock again. "I'm not hungry."

"S-Sir ..."

"If you're so concerned, bring me a roll."

Grayson smoothed his hands out over the crinkled map and the pendulum picked up speed. Faster and faster it swung, he might have been hungry, but the deep, near-trance-like concentration he had on the amulet prevented him from noticing.

Softly, Thorn sighed. "Mistress says she will not eat without you."

"She can starve."

"Er ... No, sir. I-I'm afraid I can't allow that." He stepped closer, his feet clicking softly against the hardwood. "Please go down and join the others. I will look after the map. I promise it will be fine under my care."

From his periphery, Grayson could see Thorn's shadow edging closer. His sister's words rung in his head, the little seed of doubt blooming. "Thorn?"

"Yes?"

"You told me everything, right?"

He was at Grayson's side now, and a cold wind seemed to wash over him. "What do you mean, Master?"

"Odette," Grayson said simply. "You haven't withheld any ... *information*, have you?"

"No, sir. I checked every known place she could be. There is nothing more." Thorn folded his hands over one another. The pendulum swung faster. It seemed like it wouldn't stop.

Grayson nodded, the bloom of doubt withering. "I thought so."

Grayson settled into his seat, glowering at his sister from across the table. He wouldn't even be there if it weren't for her and her ridiculous insistence on this charade. However, Greer didn't seem to notice. Her attention was solely on their guest, the boy on all the Have-You-Seen-Me posters, the boy who captured national interest for nearly a month, *Skylar Fraser*. The boy incessantly shook like a leaf. He noticed Grayson's glare.

Grayson tried to not know Greer's pets. Skylar: however, was hard to ignore, especially with his face plastered all over television last month. Weepy friends and stone-face police all delivered more information than Grayson wanted, like his school and his hobbies and favorite color.

All the same, Grayson could honestly say he didn't know Skylar Fraser. The boy rarely—if ever—was allowed to join them for meals, not that he had any say in it. Grayson was almost certain Skylar would rather be anywhere else than the dining table with him and his sister. He also knew the boy was just too skittish and if he didn't change his ways, the likelihood of him surviving the month was slim to none. Grayson didn't care either way.

The one thing he did know about Skylar Fraser (well, the one thing he *cared* to know) was he spent too much time with Odette. The icing on the cake was Grayson couldn't do a thing to stop it. Odette roamed at her pleasure and her roaming often took her in the general direction of the dungeons. Grayson could only hope Skylar would be gone by March.

Briefly, Grayson thought of asking Skylar if Odette had mentioned any plans for leaving, but he decided against it. If she had, Skylar was under Greer's care, and he was an open book. His sister would be more than eager to share any information like that.

Grayson picked at his food, his mind wandering to his plan upstairs. Thorn was capable of overseeing things, it gave him some comfort, although he'd never admit it. He hated allowing that freak of nature to be involved in something like this. Thorn tainted his image of Odette because he was always around her. Why he cared so much for her, Grayson didn't know, but he didn't like it.

"Open up." Greer sang, holding a fork with some salmon on it. Skylar's lips quivered, his eyes watering, but he did as she requested. "Good boy!"

Disgusting. Grayson stabbed his fork in the fish, tearing it into smaller pieces. Wherever Odette was ... was she taking care of herself? Had she eaten? It wouldn't be good for her, or the baby, to continue on with an empty stomach.

He could imagine her shivering in the dark with grime on her face and hands. She was too thin. When he finds her, she'll be begging to come back with him, if only because she is scared and alone. He would take great care of her.

"Grays," Greer's voice cut into his thoughts, turning the pitiful image of Odette into smoke. "You need to eat. Don't make me come over there and feed you too." Her lips pouted playfully as she dabbed her napkin on Skylar's lips.

He continued to push the fish around, "I'll stab you."

All playfulness left her. Greer rolled her eyes and her lips peeled back in a sneer. "As if. Now eat, you're setting a bad example for Skylar."

The boy could starve for all he cared. Grayson pushed his plate away. "I'm not hungry. There are other things I can be doing."

He made the mistake of meeting her eye. In a flash, Greer's playfulness vanished. Her eyebrows knit together, and her mouth twisted up. She leaned forward, but Grayson had already turned away.

"Look at me," she demanded.

Grayson's shoulders tensed, but he was quick to relax them. "I'm too tired for this."

Before he could stand, the doors to the dining room swung closed with a deafening thud. Grayson swore. He was caught. It was pointless to demand she open the doors for him, it would only be a waste of breath.

"Your eyes, Grayson," she stressed.

There was no use in delaying; he knew she would take advantage of the situation. Eyes would be the tell all. A part of him cursed himself for not having Thorn do something to disguise his features, but it wouldn't have done him any good. Greer would see through it like the mirage it was. Slowly, Grayson met his twin's gaze. There was a notable pause in conversation, as she held his gaze long and hard, staring into his now brown eyes. An ugly snarl twisted onto her lips.

Greer slammed her palms against the table. "You *idiot*, you actually took it off so you could search for her?!"

"It's the easiest way—"

Greer rose out of her seat, leaning so far over Grayson questioned if she would try to throttle him. "NO! The easiest way is to go to that good-for-nothing angel and *demand* he search for her! You don't put yourself in a position where you are vulnerable! What if I had done something, hmmm? What if I tried to hurt you, it would have worked?!" The more she screamed, the higher water rose in Skylar's cup.

"Then I guess you might feel sorry for once in your life." Grayson stood up from his seat, clenching his hands into fists. His left hand stung, but he did his best to ignore it. It was true, without his amulet he was vulnerable, and he was beginning to feel it but he tried not to show it. He kept his chin high, not lowering it for a second, not even when he felt the table begin to rattle.

"Why does this girl even matter, Grays?! If any of the others ran, you wouldn't have hesitated to kill them?! Is it because she's pregnant?! I can fix that too. You know it doesn't matter. So, what is it?! What could you *possibly* love about this ... nobody?!"

It was the same argument every time. The only argument they'd had for the past several months and it was becoming tedious.

Grayson set his mouth in a grim smile. "Because she isn't *you* and that is good enough for me." He pushed away from the table without another word.

Remnants of the argument lingered in the room, crackling and waiting to erupt. Grayson stormed out of the dining room and didn't look back, not even as Skylar began to scream.

Thorn was crouched over the desk when he entered, his attention focused on the swirling pendulum. He didn't acknowledge Grayson, too caught up in his work.

"What has happened?" Grayson asked, "Anything?"

"I-I think ..." Thorn paused and straightened out the map once again. "I think I have found her."

His heart clenched painfully in his chest. It was a disgrace this beast found Odette first, but at the same time he didn't care. Grayson rushed to his side and knocked him away.

"Where?" His voice was scarcely above a whisper. "Where is she?"

Thorn's finger landed on the map, and the amulet followed like an arrow. It stuck straight out to the side, stiff and still, with no hesitation. "Ohio."

III

ODETTE

If Odette didn't know any better, she would have thought her eyes were still closed, and her body was seizing into a ball. She gasped loudly. Her hand flew to her chest. The thudding was loud and horrendous, like a drum. Her lungs felt like they were on fire and no amount of gasping would fill them as if she had run a marathon.

Inch by inch, she uncurled from her fetal position and felt around her surroundings blindly. The world was black, the kind of blackness where you couldn't see an inch in front of your nose. She blinked slowly, then faster.

It was cold—icy cold, her hands were so numb it almost didn't bother her. There was nothing to her immediate left, nor her right, but the ground was hard as concrete. Bits of rock dug uncomfortably into her skin.

Where? Odette's first thought made her stomach lurch, the chill making her mind conclude she was in the damp dungeons of the Mages' secret basement. Odette blinked again, slowly. This place was different ... *Where was she?*

The ground was rough. Wind. She had to be outside at night; but where. The last thing she could recall was the magic show. The trick? Was this part of it? No. Clearly, the trick had gone awry.

Odette couldn't simply sit there. She pushed against the rocky ground, pain blooming from sharp pebbles pierced her numb skin. She stood; her legs were wobbly from lack of blood flow. One shoe was gone, and a quick sweep with her foot couldn't detect it.

Just my luck, she sighed and rubbed her eyes, smearing the makeup even more. *Would it be too much to ask for something to go my way, just this once?*

How long had she slept? Hours? *Days?* She was hungry. Odette craned her neck and squinted up at the sky. There were stars, though not as many as you would see in the country. She had to be close to a town and she appeared to be on a road.

Odette wiped the rocks and mud off of her costume. She was cold and she knew the longer she stood there, the worse it would get. She needed to move so she started walking in the direction she was facing.

As she hobbled along the side of the road, Odette chewed on her lower lip, trying to figure out what happened at the show to make her end up here? It didn't make sense. The twins never messed up because of Thorn; he made even the most impossible tasks possible for the twins. He made their magic flawless because it was in their best interest, so why did the trick fail?

It had to have been her. That was the only logical answer.

Odette flexed her left hand, the heavy jewel sitting on her ring finger glinting in the dark. It was similar to the jewels the twins wore at all times, but hers was different. While Grayson and Greer could take their amulets off, Odette's ring was stuck. It had wound itself around her finger like an ever-tightening vine, and no amount of twisting or greasing could get it off. The only people who could remove it were Grayson and Thorn.

Another difference about her jewel and the twins': hers didn't work.

It only worked that one time. She was kidnapped by an insane man who thought, by holding her hostage, Grayson and Greer would be forced to give up their power. Odette had outsmarted him and the twins. The man ended up dead and she took away Greer and Grayson's powers. It didn't last, though.

The only way she could use those powers was by promising to marry Grayson. What could possibly be so bad about marrying him—the man of most teenagers' dreams? He killed her family. Odette thought she would have more time to get out of her promise; but Thorn, her closest friend and ally, said serving the twins came before their friendship, and the only way he could protect her was for her to marry Grayson.

Some protection. Soon after marrying him, the ring's powers began to diminish to nothing. Now look where she ended up.

And yet, Odette couldn't help but wonder. Grayson never made mistakes when it came to magic, and Greer would never sabotage her own show—she loved it too much. What stopped it? The only answer she could conclude was *her*.

The ring she believed to be powerless, might still work. Controlling it was another issue.

What if she could finally be free of the Magical Mages Twins?

That was a dangerous thought, but excitement thrummed inside of her, just imagining it. *What if ... What if ...?*

Grayson would be angry. She could see him now, in the aftermath of his rage. It frightened her to consider it, but here she was. If she could keep away, if that's even possible, then she'd never have to experience abuse by his hand ever again.

She'd be fine, she had to be. Sure it felt below freezing, she was wearing leotard and tights, and she was walking on the side of a road. But roadways meant cars, and cars meant a way to towns and cities. She would be fine.

"It's okay, everything is going to be okay." She whispered. She hugged her stomach tight. "I'm sure there's a nice warm place willing to help."

A lie. Even worse, she knew she was lying, but she kept doing it anyway. She was certain a restaurant would give her a free meal. The train station was probably giving away free tickets, too. If she looked over into the ditch, there might even be a fifty-dollar bill just lying there for her.

The lies piled up in her mouth. They tasted like acid.

Her skin stung from exposure to the February night. Odette wished she had agreed to a cape. Her magic was too unpredictable to make herself disappear again. Besides, Odette was still fighting off fatigue from the previous one.

And then, a pulse.

Odette's eyes snapped open. She stared down at the ring on her left hand. It was a gaudy piece of jewelry at the best of times, but now she could've kissed the thing. Deep blue rays of light emanated softly from it.

It hadn't lit up like that in months.

Perhaps, she wondered, *it was ready to work*. Or maybe, it sensed her desperation. Odette surmised it must be the latter as the former didn't make much sense. Her teeth chattered as she forced herself further off the road and flexed her fingers.

"Please, please, please."

Odette squeezed her eyes shut, small beads of tears falling, and rubbed her hands together. In her mind's eye she pictured what she needed: a backpack with clothes, and money. She could feel the texture and make out the color, similar to the one she used when she went to school. She could feel its weight.

Slowly, it wasn't her imagination anymore. There was a buzzing in her bones and sweat broke out on her forehead. A fabric loop hung itself on her finger, slowly weighing more and more as the rest of it materialized. When she opened her eyes, a small laugh left her. It wasn't a large pack, but she was hopeful it was just what she needed.

Odette tore the zipper open and found a pile of fabric within. It was far too dark to see, but she could feel it was packed to the brim. She was about to pull one of the items out when the sound of an approaching car nearly made her jump out of her skin with excitement. The girl whirled around and waved to the vehicle.

She squinted against the bright lights to make out the shape of the vehicle.

Oh, crap! Odette recoiled, nearly falling to the curb. It was a cop, and she was out in the evening looking like some kind of large, freaky, blue bird hooker.

The car slowly pulled up next to her and rolled down the window. "Hello, miss."

"Hi, officer."

A very serious, condescending look crossed the man's face. "Do you know what time it is?"

If it was any other time, Odette would have been perturbed. She hated it when adults looked at her like that. She shook her head 'no'.

"I'm kind of … stuck in a situation here, sir. Would you mind telling me where I am?"

The policeman narrowed his eyes, "Miss, have you been drinking tonight? Doing anything you shouldn't?"

"No, no!" She grabbed her temples, "Okay, this is going to sound really stupid, but … I'm an assistant at a magic show. The guy made me, you know, *disappear* and now I don't know where I am."

The lump in her throat didn't feel like it was vanishing any time soon. Surely, she could manage to get herself out of a simple situation like this. But the cop didn't seem to believe her. His steely, narrowed eyes made her clutch her backpack even tighter.

"Right ..." He inhaled sharply and glanced behind him, "Okay, um, I'm going to bring you with me because we have to get whatever is in you out of your system. Do you mind standing off to the side a little so I can just pull over?"

Odette *did* mind, since she was probably about to be arrested under suspicion of drug use or being a sex-worker, but she complied anyway.

He pulled to the curb and stepped out of the car. Her ears zeroed in on the sound of clanking metal and she froze. His face melted into the background; all she could focus on were the handcuffs dangling from his fingers.

Images flashed before her eyes. *The dungeon. Skylar. Blood. Thorn. Handcuffs.* Odette flinched, she hated handcuffs.

"Are those necessary?" Odette inched away. "P-Please, I haven't done anything!"

"Miss, I'm going to have to ask you to calm down," the man said.

It didn't make her feel any better. She covered her belly with one hand and extended the other to keep him at bay. Her breathing came fast and short, more tears gathering in the corners of her eyes; but this time, it wasn't due to the startling cold. Odette remembered how her poor friend looked, chained to the wall and bleeding. She didn't want this to be her. She wouldn't let them hurt her child.

He put both of his hands up, showing he meant her no harm. "Okay ... how about I put them away and you just come to me slowly?"

The cop put the restraints in his back pocket, but Odette still felt wary. She neared him, keeping her guard up the whole time.

"What's your name, miss?"

She chewed her lower lip. "Odette Mages," she replied honestly. "and I'm not 'Miss', I'm 'Mrs.'"

Saying those words. Had she really allowed Grayson to break her? She couldn't have. She was still her; it was just the circumstances changed.

While she was thinking, she didn't notice how the officer had paused. His posture loosened and he leaned in close. "Odette? ... Like, Odette *Sinclair*?"

The sound of her name—her real name—startled her out of her stupor. "Yeah, that's my maiden name. I was married in October. Do I know you?"

"Heath Thornton, Felix's dad. Wow, you look so different!"

Thornton? She hadn't heard that name in a long time, and no one in Sunwick Grove had it.

She cupped her hand over her mouth, but it didn't stop her cry of joy. "Oh, my God!" Odette rushed forward and embraced him. Officer Thornton gave her a one-armed hug and patted her on the back.

The amulet didn't just whisk her away from the Tent of Mystery, it took her away from Sunwick Grove *entirely*.

Officer Thornton decided not to take her to the station. Odette wasn't sure what to think of his act of mercy, but she was sure it afforded her more time before Grayson could find her.

"So, what happened," Officer Thornton asked. Odette could see him watching her from the corner of his eye as he drove.

"What do you mean?"

He shrugged. "Odette, you move away, and everything seems okay. Suddenly, there's no social media activity from your parents and they don't answer any messages. You show up in the middle of February, in a dance costume, raccoon eyes, claiming to be married, and you freaked out when I tried to cuff you."

"You forgot the pregnant part." she added.

The car swerved as Officer Thornton shouted in surprise and Odette grasped the door for support. "You're pregnant?! Odette, what is going on with you? What about your—your heart thing?"

She shut her eyes tight and swore in her mind. Of course, he knew about it. Officer Thornton had known her since she was small, and her condition wasn't one so easily fixable.

"I'm ... better now." The words tumbled out fast and twisted her tongue awkwardly. It was always hard lying to

Mr. Thornton. Something about it just seemed impossible, partially because he was a policeman. "Things have changed for me in the past several months. How have you and Felix been?"

He didn't answer right away, caught in between questioning her more and answering her out of politeness. "We're ... uh ... we're fine. He's missed you."

"I missed him."

"Anyway, back to the pregnant thing." Odette flinched, but tried to smooth out her expression before he looked at her again. Briefly, she wondered if she could use her power to make him forget like she'd seen Grayson and Greer do so many times before. She wasn't given a second to make up her mind on the subject before Officer Thornton spoke again. "You aren't running away, are you?"

"What?" She stiffened. "No. Why would you say that?"

"Well, I found you on the side of the road without a car and you haven't mentioned your parents once. I assume if you are in some kind of trouble, you'd tell me." He glanced at her from the corner of his eye. "You know I'll help in any way I can."

"Of course." A lie.

He tapped his fingers against the wheel, "What about the father?"

Odette felt like a large lump had settled in her throat. Yeah, she was in trouble with him, but ...

"Is this an interrogation?"

"No, I'm just—"

"Concerned," Odette finished. It wasn't like she could blame him. He was a second father to her. Odette sighed and rubbed the back of her neck, the feathers in her costume pricking her uncomfortably. "He loves me, if that's what you're worried about. He loves me so much he married me—before the baby, if you're wondering. His protective nature is ... wild. It stretches onto our child, too."

Odette repressed another shudder. He was protective for certain. Too protective.

Officer Thornton sighed, "Okay. I understand. You must be tired; you're on one of your medicines, right? That's why you were acting so weird earlier?"

Sure, she thought, *let's go with that.* "Yeah."

"You have to be careful with that stuff. Your body isn't just your own now. You need to be careful what you take when you're pregnant." He pulled the car down a street lined with houses—one very familiar to Odette. She spent a lot of time at Felix's house growing up, they were best friends.

Officer Thornton stepped out of the car and Odette followed suit, slinging her pack over her shoulder. The light outside of the Thornton's house was still on. She almost wanted to cry again, just being back in a place where she actually belonged.

"Felix might still be up, but I would think you would want to change first, right?" he asked quietly.

"I have some clothes in here," Odette whispered, lifting the strap of her bag.

Officer Thornton pointed her to the bathroom and waited until she was inside before he climbed the stairs. Odette found just what she needed in her bag, and she cleaned up and changed clothes. As she left the bathroom, she could hear the voices of the Thornton family.

"... I don't understand, why are you telling me not to freak out?"

"*Because*" Officer Thornton drew out, "there is a little bit of a surprise downstairs. Please, don't go over the top with your reaction. I don't really know why she's here yet."

"*She*?" asked the same, deep voice, "Who are you talking about; I just want to eat some cookies. Will you please let me through?"

The sound of loud footsteps on the stairs alerted Odette she wasn't going to be alone much longer. When she looked up, she was greeted with the sight of her old friend. The two of them stared at one another, not quite sure what to do. It was clear he didn't recognize her. Then, he narrowed his eyes and parted his lips as if to say her name, but still, he hesitated.

"Hey," she said, breaking the tension, "Are those new bigfoot pajamas?"

Felix's confusion turned to joy, "Oh, my God! Odette?!" He rushed forward and embraced her in a tight hug.

Odette struggled to stay standing but didn't push him away. Hugging him was intense, not only because of the strength at which he squeezed her, but because of the flood of emotion. This was home.

Even though Odette's powers stopped working in the traditional sense—Telekinesis, Pyrokinesis, Hydrokinesis, etcetera; there was one power that worked for her, and she decided it was the worst possible power anyone could have. *Mind reading*.

Mind reading sounds fun until you're the reader and you can't turn it off. It's a constant barrage of other's thoughts and feelings raining down on your mind with no reprieve, not even in sleep. Her head ached from it. Pain started in the eyes and ended at the base of the skull. No medication could wipe out Mind-Reader's Migraine, and it was constant.

Then there was the name, Odette took serious issue with it, 'mind *reading*'. You don't read them like a book, you hear them, and you feel their feelings like a random thought.

Since gaining powers, Odette was no longer her own person, but pieces of everyone else.

All of this came to Odette's attention the moment Felix came into the room. His thoughts were a jumbled, screaming mess—the worst kind to have to hear. He was confused, elated, and—for some reason—hurt. She might have learned why he felt this way, but he thought in half-sentences, words zipping through her brain at the speed of light. Tension formed in her eyes, and Odette winced.

She hugged him back.

Felix hadn't changed much since before. He was still a little too tall compared to Odette, forcing her to crane her neck when talking to him and his blond hair was an unfixable mess. His smile was as wily as ever, stretching his already rosy-with-acne cheeks.

At least his glasses weren't broken.

"How are you—why are you here? What happened? You look different." His words rushed together, questions bleeding into one another.

He released her from the hug. His eyes, magnified by his round frames, seemed to bug out of his skull like he really couldn't believe she was there. Felix pulled her onto the couch, not looking away from her for a second, thinking if he blinked, she would disappear.

"Things have changed for me. I guess I needed to come back here, but I can't stay long," she told him.

He frowned. "Really? You just got here."

Odette chewed on the inside of her cheek. He made a valid point. She would be a little upset if the roles were reversed, and he was like family. Where could she go in the middle of the night with no transportation?

Odette laid her head on her arm. "You're right. I don't have anywhere to go right now."

He gave her a crooked grin, his dirty blond hair flopping over. "Are your parents here? Are you alone? Are you ... wearing contacts?" He pushed his glasses up and squinted.

His curiosity pushed into her mind. The pain in her head grew. Odette squeezed her fists, pushing against his unconscious.

It was hard. Despite living with two people who also had amulets, they never taught her how to block on-coming thoughts, and she never asked. Besides, it wouldn't have helped her. She couldn't hear Grayson or Greer's thoughts, the amulet served as a kind of flood wall that kept stray thoughts in and wandering minds out. Thorn's mind was static, he had thoughts, but Odette could never read them.

Skyler was the only person in the mansion whose thoughts she had to hear, but she didn't mind his thoughts so much. His were quiet, much like his voice, lyrical even. He couldn't hurt her if he tried.

Sitting next to Felix, so curious and open, was a completely different experience.

Odette strained, building up an imaginary wall in her mind. She pictured it as building a wall, one brick at-a-time, to shield herself. After a few rows of 'bricks', Felix's thoughts weren't quite so loud. It wasn't a lot, but it was enough for the moment.

"Odette?"

She blinked, "Huh?"

Felix waved his hand in front of her eyes. "You, uh, kinda spaced out there."

"Sorry." She turned away, her cheeks burning with embarrassment. She scrambled to remember what he last said. "No, um, I'm by myself. Mom and Dad ... they didn't make it, the trip I mean."

He made a noncommittal noise, buying her fib. That made her feel worse.

Lying to Felix was hard. They rarely, if ever, kept things from each other and he was one of the few who knew when she was lying.

Why would he believe her now? Odette wanted to break down and tell him everything, but she knew she couldn't. Not when she knew Officer Thornton was lurking. A stray tear escaped her eye, but she was quick to wipe it away. She couldn't melt down here.

"Hey, what's wrong?" Felix quickly wrapped her shoulders with a blanket. When he spoke, his voice was low, barely reaching her ears. "Dad said he didn't know why you're here. I think he wanted me to figure it out so I could, well ... you know. But I'd never do that to you, Det. You can tell me. I can keep secrets."

Odette sniffled. *If only.*

"I—Really there's nothing to tell."

"Sure there is." Felix nudged her. "I mean, I haven't seen you since last year. There's a ton to talk about. And you know me; I don't go spreading stuff around. In fact, I'll probably forget this conversation in ten seconds. Were you even here? I don't know. I forgot. Pretty sure it's early Alzheimer's."

Odette couldn't help but laugh. It felt good too. She couldn't remember the last time she truly laughed at something.

"Shut up." She nudged him with her shoulder, shaking him off of her.

"Eh ..." Felix narrowed his eyes, "You know I can't. But seriously, if you're in trouble, you can talk to me."

Odette dabbed her cheek with the back of her shirt sleeve, soaking up the tears.

She could tell him about her summer. About how her sister-in-law tried to kill her for breaking up with her brother. About how she became an orphan when she watched her home go up in flames by a fire set by her husband. She could tell him she killed a man, using magical power she got from an angel.

Odette could, but she didn't. Instead, she forced a smile and realized how much she appreciated Felix's naivety to her situation.

"Yeah," she lied, "Thanks."

Felix reached out and ruffled her hair. "Of course."

HANNAH BOGGS

IV

GREER

G reer woke with a start, sitting upright in her bed. There was a strangeness in the air. With each hollow breath, Greer slowly placed the *feeling* in the house. It was emptiness - not like depression, Greer noted, but a legitimate vacancy in the home. It was as if a piece of the house had decided to break off and though she couldn't see it, she knew it, because everything seemed smaller.

Greer grabbed the long cord tethered to her amulet and adjusted it so it wasn't so tight around her neck. It was cold. There was no life in it, and for the first time in a long time, there was fear in her heart.

"Grayson."

She took flight. Her feet seemed to barely touch the floor as she tore from her room and down the hall. She reached Grayson's room, the door already wide open. It was dark, the candles on his desk had been burned to stubs and the scent of burnt wax hung heavy in the air. The bed was rumpled, and his closet was flung open with clothes strewn about.

"*No*," she gasped.

Next was Odette's room, but it was for naught. The room was still in shambles, inhabitable for anything but cockroaches.

"No!"

Greer ran the length of the house ten times over, checking the kitchen, the library, even grandfather's study, but he was not in the house. She pinched herself so many times, but all it did was mar her skin leaving a trail of bruises. Her once composed breath turned ragged as she tore towards the front door.

Greer fell against the front door, her fingers fumbling with the locks. She flung the door open, slamming harshly against the walls.

"Grayson!?" Greer staggered out into the cold night.

His car was gone. Tire tracks in the snow passed through the open gates left swinging in the wind.

She wasn't sure how long she stood there staring at the empty parking spot. The icy wind numbed her face and bare feet but she didn't move. The shock of it all struck her like a lightning bolt.

Grayson left.

He did it so easily, like the thought of being separated from Greer wasn't painful at all. If he could go just like that, then what stopped him from staying away?

Greer snapped back into focus, ran into the house and with a flick of her wrist the doors slammed shut. She took the stairs two by two, her vision clouded by anger, fear, and frustration. Who did Grayson think he was, stealing away in the middle of the night? Does he really think he can do this on his own, like some type of hero quest?

The temperature in the house changed the higher she went, going from chilly to arctic. The attic was a place the twins rarely visited—it wasn't necessary. The attic was Thorn's domain. When he wasn't in the dungeon, he was in there.

Greer climbed the last bit of stairs reaching the landing and the door. She beat on it, her palms stinging with every smack. If it were up to her, she would have blown the door away long ago, but it was barred from her magic.

Moments later, a rumpled Thorn opened the door. He was still in his day clothes, though his jacket and tie had been discarded in favor of comfort and his hair was slightly askew. He fixed his half-mask over his face, making sure it sat on him properly, before addressing her.

His one, good eye widened upon seeing her. "M-Mistress, what are you doing here? It is the middle of the night; you should be asleep."

Greer grabbed his shirt and yanked on him. "*Where is he*?!"

"Who?"

"You know!" Greer elbowed past him, forcing herself through the small door into the attic.

"Grayson's gone. Where is he?"

Thorn's mouth opened and closed, his eye darting about the room. "What— ... It's ... He went looking for Odette. I am not allowed to tell his location."

Greer fumed. Her arm reared back and slapped him hard. Thorn's head snapped to the side. The mask he wore flew from his face and shattered on the floor, revealing his grotesque features.

Thorn gasped, his hand shooting up to cover the mangled flesh; but Greer caught his wrist. "Ah! I didn't realize Grayson had more power than me."

"Mistress ...?"

"Well, obviously you think he's better than me. Otherwise I'd have equal access to your knowledge."

Thorn straightened his back, his bottom lip quivered. "That's not—"

Another slap. It held more force and came at him as more of a punch than a smack. Thorn clutched his cheek. In the dim light, Greer could see his dark hair start to fade. Good. She preferred him scared. It kept him subservient.

Greer threaded her fingers into his hair. "Does he have more ownership over you than I do?"

Thorn shook his head. "No!"

She pulled his head back harshly and he winced. "Then you have no right to keep something from me when I ask you for it! Tell me where he is!"

Greer released him and Thorn staggered back. He clutched his gnarled cheek, his eyes downcast.

"Your brother asked me to keep it a secret. He did not want you to follow. He wants to find Odette on his own, so he left in the middle of the night in hopes of eluding you." The angel walked over to one of his tinker tables.

Eluding her. Greer's lip curled. Had they grown so far apart he felt he needed to sneak off to do his *dirty* work?

"I believe he wanted you to continue with your tasks," Thorn added. "To ... To not worry about whatever he's doing."

"I have to worry about what he's doing, he's an idiot!" She relaxed her fist, tapping her fingers against her leg. "Where *is* he, Thorn?"

He barely looked over his shoulder as he fitted a new mask on his face. "Ohio. A town called Tadmor. That is where Odette appears to be hiding."

"Ohio?" Greer echoed. Her mind whirred a mile a minute. She pressed her fingers to her lips as she thought and paced. "It'll take him forever to find her. She'll have moved before he gets close. He should have brought me. That idiot!"

Greer knew the quickest way to bring Grayson home was to find Odette. What she could do was limited, but it didn't mean Greer couldn't help locate her. She had the name of the town and her victim.

But a more practical matter presented itself. They would have to postpone shows for an undetermined amount of time—a rarity for the Mages Twins, until this was resolved. With the show on pause, she might be able to wrap up this whole Odette issue in one fell swoop.

"I need you to call our manager."

"It—It's the middle of the night."

"You don't sleep, so I don't see the issue."

Thorn conceded. The man wouldn't be bothered in the slightest with a *business* call at any hour. He had been ensorcelled by the Mages' for so long, their magic had practically woven itself into his DNA.

As Greer left the attic, she called over her shoulder, "And take off that stupid mask! I never gave you permission to wear it."

The dungeons were frigid, but it didn't stop the putrid scent of death-and-decay oozing from the stone walls. In the last cell, Skylar rested peacefully. His eyelids seemed cemented shut, his lips parted as he let out soft snores.

Skylar was gifted with the talent of sleeping anywhere. And anymore, it seemed all he ever did was sleep. It astounded Greer, who was an insomniac and also rubbed her the wrong way.

As Greer approached the cell, the sound of her footsteps breaking the quiet, his snores stuttered. She hit the metal bars with a discarded chain, an obnoxiously loud *clang!* Echoed through the room.

Skylar awoke with a start. His hazel eyes were eclipsed by his pupils, his breathing erratic. Scrambling, he looked around the dimly lit room before his gaze landed on Greer. His mouth opened and closed like a fish. *What was she doing down there?*

"G-Greer ..."

"Hi, puppy." She released the chain, falling in a heap. "I need to ask you a couple of questions, m'kay?"

Still half-asleep, he nodded slowly and began to rub his eyes. "Sure."

Greer approached the bars, smiling fondly at him as one would a pet. "What do you know about Odette?"

Odette? The name banged around in Skylar's mind in an echo. Pictures flashed through his mind, the girl in question standing where Greer stood, smiling at him; looking at him sympathetically; even caressing his face after he'd been hurt.

"What do you want to know?" he asked.

"Where is she?"

"What ... do you mean?" Skylar came forward into the torch light. A frown marred his face, eyebrows pulling together tightly. "I haven't seen her."

Greer exhaled softly through her nose. He wasn't lying, Skylar hadn't seen Odette If he had she would have picked up on it. Regardless, Greer believed he knew something. He had to. He and Odette, being outsiders, had to share secrets. She believed he and Odette were closer than anyone in the house, despite what Grayson might think. She just had to get on his good side, maybe jog his memory.

"Are you cold, Skylar?" Greer knelt down, her silk pajamas brushing the grimy floor. "There's a blizzard coming and trust me when I say this house sucks at keeping out the weather. I can get you another blanket, if you'd like? Maybe ... hot chocolate?"

"I *am* cold," he admitted reluctantly. His only blanket was more like a sheet, and his clothes were threadbare, worn through completely in some places. "But—"

Greer didn't let him finish. With a snap of her fingers, a thick and fluffy blanket materialized in her open palms and she passed it through the bars.

Skylar crawled forward and grabbed the blanket, wrapping it around his frail shoulders. Faint, pink scars ran the length of his wrist. They were healing well, Greer noted, he hadn't tried to re-open them.

"Thank you," he murmured.

"Of course, puppy." Greer tilted her head, shrewdly observing him the way a hawk might look at a field mouse. "If you keep up the good behavior, I'll let you out of here. It's nice and warm in our guest bedrooms, warmer than this old place. And you want to be good, don't you?"

Skylar finally looked up from the blanket and, for the longest time, stared at her. She could hear him trying to figure out what was going on, his mind reeling; but he always came up blank.

"What do you want?"

"Information." Greer's soft, saccharine tone hardened. "Odette comes down to you all the time, right? You have to talk about something—your wants, your hopes, your dreams—I don't know. Tell me everywhere she's mentioned, even if you think it's insignificant, and you'll be rewarded."

"B-But—"

"I'm not asking. Either you tell me willingly and get something good out of it; or I force it out of you and leave you down here for a few days without food. Your choice, puppy."

Skylar was trembling, now; but it wasn't from the cold. His skeletal fingers gripped the blanket even tighter, hugging it around his frame. "Okay."

Greer smiled, patting the bars with a note of finality. "Good. It won't be too hard, I promise. You just have to try and remember; and I'll help you through it."

He pursed his cracked lips. The split she caused earlier spread and the tiniest bit of blood trailed out. *Where is Odette?*, rattled through his brain, *Where is Odette?*

Good. He was learning. Greer's smile threatened to grow, but she steadied herself. Now wasn't the time. She had a goal to complete, and an unofficial deadline to meet.

"Well, the, um ... the one place she mentioned the most was 'home'."

"Go on ..."

Before all of the others; before Odette; before Skylar; it was Greer. It was *only* Greer.

That's the thing when you're a twin. The two of you are always together. You are a built-in best friend, a worst enemy, a twin flame. Greer knew the two of them were destined for greatness from a young age, just as long as they were never separated.

At some point in her life she had been tasked with looking after her 'little' brother, and while some older siblings might have seen this as a chore, not Greer. Grayson was different. He needed assistance. He couldn't help it. It was like he attracted violence, and Greer wouldn't let any violence against him go unanswered.

She was very aware when she was younger. Greer was what her parents and teachers called 'gifted'. She liked being gifted, it garnered a lot of attention and she happened to thrive under attention but being gifted sometimes meant she had to be separated from her brother.

Grayson wasn't gifted. He didn't learn how to read at a normal age and progressed slower. Once, when she advanced a grade ahead in school, Grayson stayed in the normal class. He was alone. He was tortured by cruel kids who had nothing better to do with their time.

Then, somehow, Greer 'lost' her gifts and was moved back into her previous grade. She pretended to be average if it meant he wouldn't have to be lonely.

It was a thankless job being the older sister, but Greer loved it. Even if Grayson thought he had outgrown her, she knew the truth. She knew she was needed.

Sometimes, Greer wondered how much her brother told Odette about their childhood. They had so much history. It could take months to get it all out, to confess and purge their past until he felt like he was clean. Then again, Grayson was hell-bent on keeping her out of his 'new' life, so maybe this involved blocking out their past.

Nothing could be done to change it now anyway.

Greer could recall the events as if they took place yesterday. She liked to relive things from her past, it made her feel something. A kind of warmth before all goodness died.

It was a warm April afternoon, and Greer could remember the trees were just beginning to get their leaves back. Grayson had again gotten hurt in a fight at school.

"I ... I'm *not* weak!" Her little brother insisted while she patched him up. "That's all th-they kept *screaming*, but I-I'm *not* weak!"

"I'm almost done, don't squirm too much," she ordered.

There was a raging fire bubbling up inside of her. Greer was not a stranger to the feeling. She felt it when someone got too close to her Grayson, and when those bullies beat him up. She kept her face passive as she fixed him up so he wouldn't see how angry she really was. It was the fourth time that week.

When she poured alcohol on his wounds, he would squirm. It irritated her to no end, but she knew he had been yelled at enough for one day. Greer was more focused on the tears in his eyes. They made them sparkle like diamonds.

"They won't hurt you again," Greer assured him.

Grayson wiped his nose on his sleeve. "You don't know that."

Their mother burst in the door, a blaze of fury. She did not spare a glance at Grayson, who was tearful and in pain. Instead, she had those hellfire eyes trained on Greer.

"Come here!"

The woman hadn't given her a chance to move before she yanked her away. Her grip hurt, and Greer pleaded she had to help Grayson. It fell deaf on her mother's ears.

Greer sat uncomfortably on the couch as her mother sat beside her, too close for her liking.

"Your teacher called today. Do you know why?"

Greer shook her head 'no'. She genuinely didn't know. The teachers very rarely—if ever—called when Grayson was injured. They wouldn't admit it, but they picked on him too. They picked on their whole family.

Her mother's dark-as-coal eyes narrowed. "They said you hit a boy in your class."

Greer inhaled sharply. Bunch of snitches. "Yes, mother."

Her mother's eyebrows leapt high on her forehead, disappearing behind her bangs. "You hit a little boy?"

"After he hit Grayson. It was fair and square."

Rapidly, her mother shook her head. "No. *No*, if someone hits you, *or your brother*, you tell the teacher. You don't hit them back."

Greer narrowed her eyes. Clearly, her mother didn't understand the situation. "Teachers don't do anything. They know about the bullies. They sit there and let Grays get hurt. Someone had to stand up for him."

Her mother heard none of it. Greer was sent to bed that night without dinner and Grayson didn't bother to visit her either, which made matters worse.

Something dark came over her. Grayson wouldn't get beat up every day if their parents did a better job providing for them. He wouldn't be bullied if they actually talked to the principals and the teachers, and if they confronted those kids' parents.

This was the first strike.

There was a lot of yelling in the house that night. Greer and Grayson were grounded.

In the following days the school separated the two of them the best they could. Greer and Grayson weren't allowed to eat beside one another at lunch anymore. At home, they were placed on opposite ends of the table.

The shouts from their parents never relented but became more muffled as they learned to take it into different rooms where the twins wouldn't eavesdrop. The unease didn't let up for days.

Naivety was her fault back then. Greer hoped all the yelling would bring some good. All it did was create chaos.

Nothing changed. The separation was killing the twins, it made them wilt like flowers and wither under the scrutiny of their peers. Every new bruise and cut was seen, but not acted upon. Did they even care?

This was the second strike.

One day on the playground, Grayson was on the swing beside her, deep in thought. When he did speak, he kept his eyes on his ratty old shoes.

"Why did you do it?" he asked her quietly.

Greer didn't reply right away, mulling over his questions. There were a lot of things she'd done, so she picked one of the most recent involving him. "Why did I hit Eli? 'Cause he hit you."

He paused.

She frowned. "I thought you wanted me to help."

"W-Well I do, but ... I don't ... Greer, that's not what I mean." He scraped the ground with the toe of his worn sneakers. "No one wants to hang out with me."

"People are lame."

"They're scared of you ..."

Greer looked at him warily, "Are you scared of me?"

"No." He shook his head firmly. "It's just ... It's just you scare everyone when you always ... when you ..."

"When I ...?"

Grayson screwed up his face before finally spitting out the words. "Hit them."

"I only hit the ones who hurt you." Greer leaned back on the swing and kicked her feet up. "Don't tell me you want to start playing tag or soccer with the losers who bully you? That's not cool, Grays. That's pretty dumb."

Grayson shied away. Whatever he wanted to say, he didn't. Instead, he curled in on himself and fumbled with a plastic thumb—one she had seen before from a kid's magic box.

"Maybe they wouldn't be so bad if we *tried* to make friends." Grayson popped the thumb off and pocketed it. "That's what mom says."

She laughed. "Mom's dumb. We have each other."

He made a noise in the back of his throat and stormed off. Greer didn't follow. Something about his mood soured hers, so she stayed on the swing longer, pushing herself higher and higher until it felt like she was flying.

Grayson didn't speak to her the rest of the day. He distanced himself, his eyebrows drawn. It made her think he was trying to solve all the mysteries of the universe. When she tried to start a conversation, he shut her out and turned away.

It was like having sand slip through her fingers. The pain in her chest grew even more. She felt like she was losing her best friend.

On the bus ride home, Grayson sat in the back away from her but only because he was being picked on again. Greer felt great satisfaction when she kicked that boy between his legs. Grayson gave her a simple 'thanks', and it made her beam.

It was when they got home the elation in her died. If Grayson noticed it, he didn't show it. He seemed quite down already. He trudged past Greer with a small obligatory smile, headed straight for his room, and she didn't recall seeing him for the rest of the afternoon.

Greer's whole body was on edge. There was a storm brewing. It was far too quiet.

She left her backpack at the door and entered her bedroom, bracing herself. There, sitting on her bed, were her parents. They had her diaries strewn about them—the ones they could *find*. Greer bristled.

She remembered crying and screaming at them. How dare they invade her personal space, but they barely reacted. They only stared at her with wide, dark eyes, not really seeing her but looking through her. Just as soon as her fit came, she calmed and asked them to leave.

Surprisingly, they did.

Greer didn't know of many eleven-year-old girls who could order their parents about. She felt a swell of pride go through her and at the same time felt emotionally drained. She collapsed on her bed and leafed through the pages of her diaries, admiring the doodles and stories written inside.

She knew they would get mad at her again. They always did. This peace in the house wouldn't last for long. So, she picked up the books and put them back in their places and checked to make sure her hidden ones were still hidden. And then, she waited.

It was dark outside when Greer realized it had been much too long for them to wait to scold her. The house was too quiet for one usually filled with shouts. She narrowed her eyes and crept through the door.

Their room was on the opposite end of the hallway. Yellow light spilled out from underneath their door. They were awake. So, what were they doing?

Greer pressed her ear against the door and held her breath.

"We could send her to my father for a little while." She heard her father say. *"He might know how to deal with something like this."*

"'Something like this'?! Our daughter doesn't need time with her uncle, she needs to be in a professional facility! We can't help her, and with her being so close to Grays, day in and day out—"

"Are you seriously suggesting we send our daughter to a mental institution?!"

Her mother made a choked sound, *"Did you read what she wrote, Maxson? She wanted to* stab *another child with a fork multiple times, then cut him up and hang the pieces in the woods! Is that mentally stable?!"*

Greer narrowed her eyes. Her mother was crying, her breathing very shallow like she was terrified or something.

"I don't want to send her away," her mother sobbed, *"but she needs professional help. She needs to be away from Grayson."*

And this was the third strike.

Be taken away from Grayson? She could never allow this to happen. They were twin souls, mirrors of one another in almost every way. If she was separated from him ... No, Greer didn't even want to consider it. They had never been separated once in their life.

Rage normally reserved for her brother's bullies was suddenly brewing towards her parents. She never felt it like this before. It was raw and untamable and so strong; her mind went blank.

When she came to, she didn't feel like herself. She felt hazy, as if she had been dreaming only moments before. Instead of being in the hallway outside of her parents' room, she was in the living room. What happened she didn't know, but it all pieced itself together when her gaze landed on her parents.

They were sniveling and shaking on the floor, lying in a pool of their own blood. In her hand, a steak knife from the kitchen.

Greer released her white-knuckled grip on the knife into a more relaxed one and took in their injuries. Apparently, in her 'fit', it seemed she must have sliced their legs, as well as a few other cuts on her father.

She took a step forward, her sock touching something wet in the carpet. Her mother flinched and weakly threw her hands up as if to stop her.

"Greer, *stop it*, please!" her mother begged.

The girl cocked her head to the side. "Why did you want to send me away? I don't understand. Do you hate me?"

Her mother shook even worse. Her pale lips opened, forming the word 'NO' but before she could deny Greer's claims, a sob wracked her body.

"You don't have to do this," her father said in a low voice. "You can stop right now."

Greer shook her head. "I don't remember starting."

"P-please," her mother croaked, "Leave Grayson alone."

"Why?!" she snapped. "You don't care about him. I'm the only one who takes care of him. I'm the one who fights back when he gets picked on! You do nothing! Why are you trying to separate us?!"

"G-Greer?" came a small voice from behind her.

They screamed and cried even louder, their voices clamoring over one another as they begged him to run. Greer couldn't comprehend. Weren't they listening? She was the only one who took care of him, why would she hurt him?

"Hey, Grays."

Grayson stayed half-hidden behind the couch, and the color drained from his face slowly, turning to a pale greenish color.

"What'd you do?" He clutched his stomach, his eyes going so wide the pupils looked like tiny pinpricks. "You're killin' them ..."

"They want to send me away Grays," she said slowly. "If I'm gone, then the bullies will only get meaner and tougher. You know *they* don't do anything to help you. I'm the one who loves you." Grayson shook his head rapidly and she sighed.

"Why don't you believe me? The bad guys aren't just out there, Grays! They are everywhere!" She pointed her knife toward the adults on the floor. "They're in here! I'm trying to protect you. Do you want to be bullied all your life with no one to protect you? Do you want to be weak and vulnerable forever? Or do you want to be strong?!"

Her voice rose to a shrill level, until she was practically shrieking at her brother. Why couldn't he understand? Why was he still staring at her with those horrified eyes?

Grayson's bottom lip trembled, tears leaking from his eyes. "B-but, it's mom and dad!"

Greer's lips parted. The urge to scream at him again became overpowering, but she couldn't. Her head dropped low. Another piece of her heart cracked and crumbled into dust. He didn't believe her.

"So you hate me?" Greer said quietly. She lifted the knife and looked it over, eyeing its sharpness and its width. Then, she placed it over her beating heart. "I guess I'll kill myself, then."

It was a completely honest move, not a feint to make him feel guilty. However, she couldn't feel anything other than apathy as the tip scraped her chest through her shirt.

Grayson's eyes grew wider than she believed possible. His mouth dropped, but no words came out. Greer shut her eyes. It would be better this way. She moved her hand back, holding the knife aloft and prepared to plunge it into herself ...

But her head smacked against the floor before the knife made contact. Greer's eyes shot open to see Grayson struggling above her. They grappled for the knife, wrestling in the blood-soaked carpet. It stained their skin and their clothes, and the knife left shallow cuts if they grabbed at it wrong.

Grayson forced the knife out of her hands, tossing it off to the side. "You aren't going to *leave* me! You can't!" he screamed, "Are you stupid?!"

"It's them or me, Grayson," Greer said calmly. She wasn't afraid of death because she knew he wouldn't let her die. "Tell me, or I will kill myself. I know a bunch of different ways; it doesn't have to be a knife."

"Why does anyone have to die?!" he cried, his voice raw, "Why?!"

She looked over to where her parents were huddled together, their faces losing color and their eyes looking dull.

They weren't dead yet, but it was inevitable. Grayson was too hysterical to realize it.

Greer took his hand and made him look at her. "Do you think we will be in trouble even if they don't die? Do you?" she asked her twin quietly, "If they die, people will come to take me away. If they don't die, people will come to take me away. I would rather die than be separated."

Grayson shook his head, "B-but—"

"You have to choose."

"I can't."

"Choose."

He shook his head, horror crossing his face.

"Choose, Grays," she urged.

"I *can't!*"

"CHOOSE!"

He slammed his fist against the floor. "YOU!"

Though he didn't show it, Greer knew he was happy with his choice. Of course he would be. It was *her*; she would never ever leave him, and this act would be her vow to him.

Silently, Greer inhaled and stood from the floor. She picked up the discarded knife and approached her nearly dead parents. Really, she had thought, she was doing them a favor. They were almost there anyway; they just needed an extra push.

HANNAH BOGGS

V

GRAYSON

The car idled for a moment before Grayson killed the engine. He surveyed the area, eyeing the pale pink and orange early morning sky before opening his door.

Grayson had driven through the night and it wore on him. His eyes burned and his neck ached from being crouched over the wheel for hours; his fingers were stiff, and his leg was cramped. He needed something to keep him awake, to revive himself for the hours of driving to go.

Stretching one last time, Grayson studied the building before him; a local coffee shop and the cleanest place around.

Their sign boasted fresh pastries and thankfully, coffee. Further down, they listed thier hours. Grayson frowned, while there was a light on, they weren't technically open yet. Someone was moving around in the back and Grayson decided it must be one of the employees setting up for the day; maybe the owner himself.

He looked at his watch. Six-thirty, an hour and a half before their doors open.

What coffee shop doesn't open before 8? Grayson knew he couldn't wait; too much lost time would be lost.

He stuffed his hands in his pockets and stalked around the building to the loading area. The back door of the shop sat open, casting a yellow glow onto the cement ramp. Someone inside was clanging.

He entered the kitchen and across the room, towards the oven, was a man. He was older, possibly his grandfather's age, with a black apron slung over his shoulder. He had just finished popping a batch of frozen pastries the oven and was fumbling with his apron when Grayson approached.

Grayson's shoe scuffed the tile floor and the man looked up, startled.

"Sir, we're not open yet—"

Grayson tilted his head to the side and the man swallowed his words, paling ever so slightly. It was strange; he was already terrified and yet Grayson hadn't done anything. Maybe he recognized the look in his eyes—the malice and utter exhaustion. Or, maybe, the man recognized *him*.

"You … you can come back in about an hour, when we're open."

"You're going to serve me coffee."

The amulet on his shirt pulsed, electricity humming through his veins as his words turned into power. The man's shoulders slumped, and for a moment he seemed confused. It faded as quickly as it came; a pale blue sheen covered the whites of his eyes until they were fully glazed over.

"Of course."

It was too quiet in the cafe.

Grayson normally preferred silence, but now it was deafening. He didn't want to hear himself think. He especially didn't want to hear what the barista thought; his mind was a muddled mind field of incoherent sentences and images.

For the past several months he had gotten used to Odette. Though he couldn't hear her thoughts anymore, she had her own unique way of filling the silence. Her soft breathing; her soft footsteps; her voice when she would read aloud; all little reminders she was real and not a figment of his imagination. They were all reminders, she was his.

Now the world was back to being what it once was: one huge earache. The ticking of the clock rang loudly in his ears and grated on his nerves; a constant reminder of the time he was losing and the girl he missed.

If Odette were with him, he wouldn't have noticed.

Grayson scowled. *If Odette were with me, I wouldn't be here.*

Grayson had taken a seat by the window where he could watch the morning traffic. This coffee shop had a nice spot, just off the main road. It would generate a lot of attention here, locals and travelers alike. Grayson wasn't interested in the civilians though. He kept his eyes on the clock, his mind millions of miles away.

Without her, this warm room was oppressive. She wasn't there to stop the shadows from closing in. She was somewhere far from his grasp, probably scared to death.

Don't worry, Grayson assured her in his mind, *I'm coming to find you. I'll make everything right again.*

He and Odette were similar, but Grayson could not wrap his mind around it. Of all the places in the world, spectacular and amazing, Odette chose somewhere no one knew about.

Tadmor, Ohio. Tadmor, Ohio? Such an obscure place; he couldn't recall Odette mentioning it.

When they first met, it was easy to go through Odette's thoughts. Grayson knew almost everything there was to know about her. He could see memories of her old home, camping trips, and scenes from movies she'd seen stuck in her head. He knew all the places she dreamed of visiting. He knew all the places she hated.

Apparently, not all of them. His grip tightened around the paper cup. It seemed he missed this hole-in-the-wall place. Tadmor. No matter how hard he wracked his brain, he couldn't come up with a connection.

Was there a vacation he'd overlooked? Maybe a theme park?

No, there was no way it could be anything like that. Grayson knew all the places she'd been, the places she wanted to go. He was sure of it.

A growl birthed itself in his throat and he slid down in his seat. It was beginning to feel like he didn't know his wife at all! Something he could not put up with. They would not become strangers.

The place had to have some significance to her. Odette couldn't have just *teleported* to some place she didn't know. Their magic didn't work that way, there were limitations.

Grayson scrubbed at his eyes hard. Lack of sleep was something he was used to, but it could easily cloud his judgement. He needed to relax. Taking a heavy swig of his coffee, he grumbled and sat it back down.

His bones buzzed. The lack of sleep agitated him. His eyes burned, begging for rest, but his muscles thrummed with energy. He felt like he may explode at any moment.

The clock's ticking grew louder and louder, screaming in his ears. Grayson shut his eyes and held his breath. *One, two, three ...*

"Hey, you," he called the employee over. "Come here."

Tick-tock, tick-tock, tick-tock...

The barista's movements were unsure, jerky like a puppet being pulled by a string as he came forward. Grayson bared his teeth in a smile, breathing heavily through his nose.

... Tick-tock, tick-tock, tick- tock...

"Don't worry. This won't hurt."

Odette might not receive the message right away, but she would eventually. She'd see what she made him do. The feelings she made him feel.

The blue haze receded from the barista's eyes, his features melting from stone-cold to fearful. Grayson snapped his fingers and a small flame appeared between them. The man stuttered, backing away quickly but bumping into the table behind him. Grayson flung the flame at him, the ball of fire streaking through the air like a bullet and attached itself to his apron.

The fire instantly expanded and crawled up the barista's body as though it were alive, finger-like tendrils clawing up the man's clothes to his neck and pulled his head back. He opened his mouth to shout, but the flames invaded his mouth, crawling into his nose and ears, crawling all over him until he was completely engulfed.

There wasn't even a scream, only a gurgled cry.

It happened so fast, it was a blink-or-you'll-miss-it type of scene. He reached towards Grayson, but Grayson leaned away. The flames ate through him as if he dry dead wood, and in a matter of moments he was nothing but powdery ash on the wooden floor.

"I asked for no foam.

VI

ODETTE

Odette's eyes burned, like they'd been open for too long. She was slowly able to focus. For the life of her, she couldn't remember where she was or falling asleep

She pushed the heels of her hands into her eyes, but the burning did not stop. Her head bobbed against the back of her seat, her neck sore from hanging low. Wherever she was, it smelled of smoke. It burned her nostrils and clogged her throat.

Had there been a fire?

The white noise buzzing in her ears was deafening. She waited, allowing her eyes to become adjusted to the light. She winced and frowned.

She had no memory of how she got to this place.

The first thing she could identify was the dark leather interior of a car. Odette turned, realizing her head had been resting on the center console. A coffee cup sat inches from her nose.

Odette stretched her neck. There was a seatbelt. The red release button stood out against the dark background like a sore thumb. Her eyes trailed up the strap, studying cobalt blue fabric adorned by a body next to her. Up and up, she craned her neck until her gaze settled on the harsh profile of the last person she wanted to see.

Odette yelped, jerking backwards and pressed against the passenger's door. He had her! The grab must have been quick. She couldn't recall a thing. The last thing she remembered was being with Felix.

Oh, God. Felix. What did Grayson do to him?

"Grayson?" she whispered, licking her lips to hide their trembling.

The boy didn't respond; his eyes trained on the road. His knuckles were white against the steering wheel. Crescent-moon indentations had been pressed into the soft leather from his nails. She pressed her fingers to her lips. She would be strong.

Odette tried again, "Grayson, what's going on?"

Nothing.

Why was he ignoring her? Under normal circumstances, she'd kill to be ignored. But he was here and his silence was never good. Odette wasn't one to press her luck. It would be wise to leave well enough alone. She would get the worst of it when they got back to the mansion, she knew this, and yet ...

Odette swallowed harshly, a lump forming in her throat. It would be courteous of him to tell her if this was *the end*.

The thudding in her ears grew louder and louder. She shouldn't be scared; she didn't cause this, maybe. But she embraced it. She should embrace her fate. Fear would only make it worse.

Odette pressed her head back against the passenger's seat and closed her eyes. Moving to wipe her sweaty palms on her jeans, her hands connected with a piece of paper. Odette jumped, not expecting anything to be there.

Sitting in her lap was a map; an odd place to put it, unless this was some sort of scare tactic.

The words and roads all blurred together, like veins inside a body. No matter how hard she squinted, she couldn't make out the place he marked. Odette reached down to pick it up, but it wasn't real.

Though she was able to touch the map, actually holding it was another story. Her fingers seem to pass through the pages as though they were made of water.

A vision, she thought, this was a vision.

A small part of her was comforted that she wasn't *actually* in the car with him. She had not been discovered; yet a larger fear overshadowed this. If he hadn't found her yet, then he was certainly looking. Grayson was infallible, there was no way she could elude him for long.

Odette's gaze fell to the map again, but it was unfocused. The road lines turned into the contours of her face. There was a large, blood red circle around her eye. The location. Her location. Odette couldn't breathe. The red bled through the paper, macabre, a harbinger of *death*.

This was a warning.

Odette reached out to touch her husband's shoulder, but her hand passed right through him. She was a ghost. This wasn't happening.

As if he sensed her presence on the edges of his consciousness, Grayson turned his head. His gaze passed right through her, alight with fire. She knew the look. It wasn't a look he ever gave her, but one he reserved for those unfortunate souls who crossed him.

He was going to kill her.

Odette wanted to cry. This wasn't how she was supposed to go.

"This is a dream," she murmured, "and I'm going to wake up now."

Before she squeezed her eyes shut, something moved in the back seat. Odette barely caught a glimpse of it, a familiar face, then it was gone.

Everything around her stretched, warping into a nightmarish scene. She could feel herself being pulled apart, twisting into objects without meaning. Colors bled together until they drained away completely, leaving her in a striped, black-and-white funnel, spiraling down, down, down.

Until it stopped.

Odette jumped, disoriented and dizzy. She was no longer in a vehicle, and Grayson was nowhere in sight; however her discomfort didn't go away. She threw the scratchy, pink-knit blanket off and scrambled to gather the backpack she had conjured the night before.

Odette got two steps towards the door before the dizziness became too much of a hindrance. Her body sagged against the railing and she flung her hand over her mouth. This was not what she needed.

Staggering to the bathroom, Odette emptied her stomach in the toilet. Heat crept up her neck and sweat blossomed just under her hairline.

Was the nightmare Thorn's doing? If it was, he wasn't doing her ANY FAVORS with all the swirling. She would have words with him about that some other time.

Once she was certain she had finished, Odette stood on shaky feet and approached the sink. She took heaping handfuls of water, splashing her face and rinsing her mouth.

There was no time to waste. This was no ordinary dream; she knew it for a fact. Whether Thorn had a hand in it or not, it was a magical premonition. Grayson was coming and he was angry.

So angry he could kill me? Odette shivered. She didn't want to think about it. Giving herself one last splash of water, she deemed herself good enough to walk, possibly a little pale, but nothing out of the ordinary.

Slowly, she crept from the bathroom and back into the main room. There was no sound. Where was everyone?

Nausea twisted in her gut, but this time from fear.

On the wall was an old wooden clock. Odette's heart thumped, the two seemed to beat in time, pumping harder with each *tick*. It was almost three o'clock and the house seemed empty. Had slept half the day away?

Then ... it was possible Felix and his dad could just be out doing their everyday obligations. She would be able to slip away, and they would be none the wiser.

But she'd have to hurry. If Felix had gone to school, he'd be home any minute.

Odette threw on her shoes, grabbed her pack, and made a break for the door. She swung it open with force, thankful there was no one on the other side. The coast was clear. All she had to do was find a way out of town now.

As she rushed down the steps, a familiar car turned into the driveway. She could just barely make out the driver in the front seat, making her steps falter. Breaking out into a sprint now would seem conspicuous, but not running was just plain stupid. So, Odette ducked her head and continued walking a little faster, hopping over a low hedge onto the sidewalk, moving away from the vehicle

The car door opened and slammed shut. "Odette!" Felix called out. He sounded frantic and similar to the night before, his thoughts were a fast-paced, whirring machine. Curiosity. Fear. Anger. There was a lot of anger. "Where are you going?!"

She flinched, but kept walking, keeping her back to him. It was childish, but maybe he'd get the hint.

"I have to talk to you, Odette." Felix jogged to catch up with her and grabbed her shoulder, halting her in her path. He had always been persistent; she didn't know why she thought avoiding him would help. "I really have to—"

She heard the passenger side car door open and shut. Odette's head snapped upwards, looking at him with an accusatory gaze. True, she'd never explicitly said *don't tell anyone I'm here*, but she thought it was implied.

Felix frowned, his scattered emotions only growing the longer she looked at him, it was scary how much he looked like his dad when he did that. He nudged Odette back towards the house, towards the second person coming out of his car.

"Okay, I have all of my stuff!" Dark, cork-screw curly hair popped up from beneath the cabin of the car. The girl raised up on her tippy-toes, her doll-like eyes widening when they landed on Odette. "Oh, my God!"

The girl—Clara Niesenson—dropped everything in her arms and ran towards her. Odette could do nothing but brace herself as Clara collided with her, pulling her into a tight hug. She didn't let go for several moments, her smile never dimming.

Clara took a step back and lightly punched Felix's arm. "I thought this idiot was lying when he told me you were here! But you're here, really here! How have you been? I missed you so much."

"I just got here," Odette stammered. Clara shouldn't have come—but why wouldn't Felix tell her? After all, Clara was her best friend. They both were. "I'm not staying long. I was actually just about to go."

Clara shook her head. "Just a little longer? I mean, you don't have to go right now, right? After all, you just got here, and you missed Christmas break."

"I—uh ..." She shouldn't. Not after that dream, or premonition, or whatever. But seeing them in person felt good. Odette couldn't remember the last time she had spoken to them.

"It doesn't have to be long." Clara pressed. "A few more minutes while we work. We just want to catch up."

Odette pressed her lips together, exhaling softly. "Just a few minutes."

Felix's room had changed very little since they were children. Instead of throwing something out, he would cover it up. If you peeled away the layers of posters he had accumulated over the years, you might see what it looked like when it was his nursery; but Odette had a hard time imagining the room being anything other than what it had been since she'd known the boy.

The walls were plastered with Bigfoot memorabilia, UFO photos, and Mothman posters, as well as a map of all cryptids in the USA. Only a smidgen of green wallpaper could be seen near the ceiling.

Action figures all standing at attention lined his dresser and desk, which he never used to study. An old gaming system was wedged beneath his bookshelf, propped up at an odd angle and forcing the books inside to lean sideways.

It was strangely comforting to be back in a place frozen in time. Odette could pretend this was normal. Her lips pulled upwards, but she hid the smile behind her hair. The nostalgia turned bitter. Her chest ached and she inhaled deeply to calm the rapid growth of anxiety.

Odette eyed the old video camera on his dresser. At one point in time, they had gotten the thing to work. Now, it seemed to be just another ornament in the room collecting dust.

The door shut hard.

Peace broken; Odette whirled around. Instinctively she drew her arms out in front of her to block whatever flying object might have flown her way. She dropped them a moment later, seeing she was safe.

Clara and Felix stood side by side in front of the only reasonable exit, shoulder-to-shoulder, with twin expressions.

"Do you want to tell us something?" Clara started.

She regarded her friend warily. "Do you have something you want me to say?" Their thoughts didn't give too much away, but their faces did. No more games, they were serious.

"You disappear on us for months."

She fought the urge to roll her eyes. "I *moved*; I didn't disappear—"

But Clara held up her hand, silencing her. "It's been seven months." Odette bit her lip. "You blocked us. You wouldn't call us or text us. Now, you're here acting like everything is fine again?"

Now, Odette knew this was a blatant lie. She hadn't blocked them. The move was when she needed them most; however the more she thought about it, the stranger it seemed. Almost as soon as she arrived in Sunwick, Odette noticed her messages would drop. Eventually she left it alone, believing they had better things to do.

It could have been a coincidence, but the lengths of which Grayson would go to get her all to himself were great. Odette dug her nails in her hand and squeezed—she couldn't tell them about that. If she brought up Grayson, it would bring more uncomfortable questions. It would be better to let them think whatever they wanted than bring *him* into this.

Odette turned away and focused her attention on a giant photo print of a UFO on Felix's door. "I thought you had a project to work on?"

"That's not the point," Clara said, a little too fast. She rolled her shoulders back and forced the crease between her eyebrows to smooth. "The point is you disappeared to all of us, and we find out you *aren't* dead in an online article from the-middle-of-nowhere Maine. Not only that, but you managed to become one of America's top trending topics." Clara pulled out her phone and shoved it into Odette's hands.

On the screen was a news article, the title '*Mages in Matrimony?*'; the date was from October. The day after the wedding. She swore under her breath—there went her plan.

The picture made her stomach turn. Grayson, beaming from ear to ear, and she in his arms. He looked paler than usual in the photo, and she knew they'd edited the image to hide his dark circles. After all, he had only just been let out of the dungeons, and she had not been kind to him. In return, that day had not been kind to her.

Her hands trembled the longer she stared at the image— it was a lie shared for the world to see.

Only, Grayson wasn't the scariest threat looming over her anymore. No, what made her sick to her stomach was the look of betrayal on Clara and Felix's faces. They believed the lie and she felt no bigger than a speck of dirt. Her lips trembled, threatening to spill everything to them just to get them to stop looking at her like that, but she couldn't do it.

The Mages' were dangerous people. Odette had a feeling she'd only seen a fraction of what they could do, and she wouldn't wish that on anyone.

Clara's hurt transcended words pierced Odette's poorly constructed mental wall. "Were we not cool enough to talk to anymore?"

"No." Grayson's smiling eyes stared back at her through the phone, taunting her. He knew he could ruin whatever good thing she had left.

"Then what is it?"

Odette pushed the phone away from her. "You don't—" She cut herself off. *You don't understand*, she wanted to say. *Then help us*, they would reply. Odette cleared her throat and forced herself to look at them. "I didn't mean for this to happen."

"So it's true?" Felix paced back and forth, running his hand over his face. "This isn't some prank?"

I wish it was, Odette thought. "No. It's real."

"You could have told us." Clara shook her head, her curls bouncing. "I think we of all people would have been the happiest for you. Did you not want us there?"

Odette sat on the bed. "No! *No* ... It's complicated."

"What about getting married is complicated, Odette?" Felix snapped. His voice began to raise and a humorless smile formed on his lips. "Are you *pregnant* or something?" He spat it out like it was a dirty, four letter word.

Shame crept up inside of her, coloring her cheeks. Odette wrapped her arms around her middle, her eyes downcast. All too quickly, the atmosphere in the room shifted. Clara followed the movement, her mouth forming a small 'o'.

"Felix ..." Clara chastised softly.

Felix looked between the two girls before the realization dawned on him. His eyes bulged behind his glasses; his shock magnified. He opened and closed his mouth, gaping like a fish, but no sound came out.

Their thoughts were loud. They bled into one another, as if they were shouting in a different language altogether. It was an endless assault that pained her, adding insult to injury.

Odette couldn't stand it—the migraine, the shame, and her own regret for thinking she could hide something like this.

"I need to go," she said. A quiet, almost inaudible 'bye' left her lips as she tore out of the room, leaving them behind.

Their words fell deaf on her ears as she hurried down the stairs. It was foolish to think she could stay and play catch up when she had a real threat looming. She needed to think clearly if she were going to get ahead of Grayson.

That didn't stop the stray tears. She grabbed at her sweater sleeve and dabbed the corners. Crying wasn't going to solve anything.

Odette didn't stop once she hit the ground floor. She grabbed her backpack and left. The February air hit her full force, stinging her face and chilling her lungs. Grey clouds blotted out the sun, and snow was coming sometime this week. Odette would have to work hard to beat the weather.

Her steps on the sidewalk were light. She kept her head down so as not to draw attention. It was late afternoon, busses of children were still being dropped off to their parents, and people were getting off work. Not the ideal time to be outside and not be recognized. If she was going to disappear properly, Odette would have to do something about her appearance and fast.

She adjusted the neck of her sweater and kept her head low. Walking through town would be a nightmare. Not only was it bitterly cold, but people would be out. It's hard to hide when you grew up with these people.

Odette remembered when most of her friends lived on the same street. Her old dance studio wasn't far away, and in the warmer months she and Clara would walk from school. During the winter, most everyone was rehearsing for the year end recital, usually presented at the old theatre and rarely used for anything aside from dance and an occasional concert.

Everything about the town seemed like a distant memory, yet it hadn't been a year since she left. Funny,

Odette thought, how all she wanted back then was to get away. Now all she wanted was to be back.

Odette cut across the street and made a b-line through a cluster of buildings and into a darkened alley when the sound of a car caught her ears. She paused. She didn't even breathe.

Her eyes darted around wildly, and she backtracked towards the street. The engine sounded familiar. She pushed out of the alley quickly, her once leisure-like pace now turned into a jog.

She ducked into a larger alley but could hear the car turn into it. Odette fought her instincts to look over her shoulder. If she looked, it would be real.

The car was getting closer. It was no longer just a blur in her periphery, but she could actually see the car without having to turn her head. It jerked to a halt and idled.

She risked a glance back and felt her heart stutter. "Odette? Odette!"

Odette flinched. People were staring—this wasn't good. If he would just *shut up*...

"Odette, c'mon!"

"Go home, Felix." Her voice was weak, but he heard her.

The sound of feet smacking against pavement finally made her turn around. Felix's arm was outstretched, his fingers just grazing her wrist before she jerked it away. He had gotten what he wanted, which didn't bode well for her. She finally stopped and faced him, exasperated.

"I won't go home," he insisted, "I'm going to help you. You aren't getting rid of me again."

Clara popped her curly head out of the passenger side of the car, "Of *us*, moron!" she corrected.

"Why are you doing this?" she asked weakly. Warily, she watched as he reached for her hand. It took every bit of her willpower not to yank it away. The voices were wearing her down.

"Because we're your friends. You obviously came to town for a reason. Even if I'm pissed at you, I'm not going to let you walk through twenty-degree weather while pregnant. Let's go." He said softly.

Odette laid her hand in his, following him to his silver sedan. "Where are you going to take me?"

"Wherever you need to go."

He was eager—his thoughts were genuine, and this hurt her. Had he always been this way? So stubborn? It put her in a tough spot.

This was dangerous. Too dangerous, if she was going off the events from last summer. Involving anyone was placing a target on their back.

But, she thought, *this isn't like last summer. I'm not vulnerable.*

She wanted to believe in herself, but judging from her current track record, it seemed impossible.

Odette eyed her ring, and it winked at her in the sunlight, as if saying *I'll help you*. It might have been nothing, but it could have been something.

She sighed and looked up at him, her gaze hardened. "Fine. But, if you're going to do this, then you're going to do it my way, without question. Understood?"

HANNAH BOGGS

VII

GREER

The Tent of Mystery sat abandoned on a barren plot of land. The neon signage that pointed the way to the parking lot was shut off; the vendor's stalls abandoned. Purple velvet flaps fluttered in the harsh winter winds. If you were to drive by the scene, it might leave you with an eerie lingering feeling for miles.

Greer's mauve sports car pulled into the empty lot, sloshing mud on the vehicle and marring the lot with a new set of tracks. She exited the car with little grace, her boot sinking into the mud, forcing her to jerk it free. Coming to the Tent at odd hours like this always made Greer feel put off. Something about the air around her.

But she was a woman on a mission with no time for superstitions, and she set off for the Tent without another thought.

With Odette's disappearance and Grayson's quest to bring her back, everything (shows, television interviews, pre-agreed appearances for charities) had been put on hold. It was the only thing they could do—there was no "business as usual" without Grayson. Their show was the Magical Mages Twins, not Magical Greer Mages. Half of the reason people attended was, unfortunately, because of her brother.

This was bad for business. Not their magician shtick, though it was where much of the income came from. No, this put a severe wrench in Greer's itinerary. The show was her alibi, the people her witnesses; without it ...

Well, you know what they say? The show must go on.

Greer untied the Tent's flaps and stepped inside. Everything was the same as they left it—the props erect on stage; garbage still littered the floor.

She shrugged off her purse and left it on one of the aisle seats, approaching the stage. Her gaze was locked onto the large—now drained—tank, where everything went wrong. Greer used the stage left stairs and approached center stage. She shut her eyes.

Though it was cold and dark inside the Tent, she could see the bright white spotlights burning down on her. She could hear the audience, now holding their breath as Odette sunk into the water. She could smell the combination of sour water filtering through the pipes and hot popcorn in the audience.

Greer opened her eyes and the scene faded. What was she missing? Greer could replay the night over and over again with perfect clarity; but it didn't change the fact that there was a hole in it all. Somehow, Odette managed to master something that took Greer years to grasp on a basic level.

Thorn approached from behind her, his quick and light steps coming from somewhere in the wings.

"Have you found anything?" she asked.

"Only this," Thorn tossed something at her, and Greer reflexively caught it. "her shoe. It was in the dressing room."

"The dressing room ...?" Greer echoed. "So, she was in the Tent after teleporting from the tank?"

Thorn shrugged his shoulders. "Or, she came back once everyone had left."

"But it doesn't make any sense." Greer turned the shoe over in her hands. It was small, Odette's size. A blue suede character shoe, one both girls wore that night. "If she'd been in the area, we would have known."

"We should have."

"Then why...?"

Greer looked at the shoe again, sighed and pocketed it. She approached the dunk tank, her lip curling into a scowl. The answer seemed to be staring her right in the face, but she'd already gone there. If Thorn had any part to play in Odette's disappearance, she would have been able to tell. Thorn was a terrible liar.

"You were with her the first part of the night, yes?" Greer stopped in front of the tank, her distorted reflection staring back at her. She didn't wait for Thorn's reply. "How was she acting? Did she do anything ... *unusual*?"

"Nothing at all," he said, a little too nonchalant for Greer, but she let it slide. "She was reserved ... anxious ... nothing unusual. I remember she did not want to perform."

Greer clicked her tongue. "And *during* the show?"

"I made sure she behaved perfectly," said Thorn. "per your instructions, of course. 'Nothing can go wrong'." He quoted her, walking to observe the other side of the tank, just as she was.

"But it did."

Something went so very wrong, and just like always it would be up to her to pick up the pieces. Greer herself had done some crazy things with magic when she was afraid; but, for some reason, writing off this incident as a fluke didn't seem appropriate. Either Odette was much stronger than she let on, or someone was trying very hard to throw her off the scent.

Thorn looked at her quizzically through the glass. "Did you get anything from the boy?"

Greer exhaled sharply. "Skylar said she never gave him any kind of specifics. He knows about as much as I do."

"Are you under the impression she told the boy where she was headed?"

Greer shifted, the shoe tapping against her thigh rhythmically.

"I think," she said slowly, "she escaped someplace she feels safe. Wouldn't you?"

Thorn didn't answer, his Adam's apple bobbed.

They didn't talk to one another the rest of the investigation and arrived back home separately. Thorn vanished from the Tent the moment he wasn't necessary anymore; but Greer didn't mind. The drive home gave her time to think, time to plot.

Skylar received his reward as promised. He might not have divulged anything substantial, but he held up his end of the bargain. Greer freed him from the cell and sent him straight upstairs to wash up for dinner. He smelled rancid, and if it went on any longer, she might have to kill him just to put an end to it.

In the dining room, Thorn set out a plethora of hot food covering the center of the table. Beef stew, steak and lobster, broccoli, every one of the dishes steamed, filling the room with its delicious scent.

Thorn laid down the final dish, a large bowl of pasta, then stood back. He clasped his hands behind his back and bowed his head. "Will either of you need anything else?"

Skylar shook his head fervently, half diving across the table to pile everything onto his achingly empty plate. Greer, on the other hand, stayed completely stationary and made no move to touch the food. She stared at Thorn, and though he did not look her in the eyes, she knew he was aware of it. He was stock-still, pinned in his spot like a deer in headlights.

"Yes," she said. "An assistant."

Bemused, Thorn forgot himself for a moment and looked up. His head tilted. "Whatever for?"

Greer stood from the table and pulled Thorn away, leaving Skylar alone to enjoy his meal. He didn't even seem to see them leave, too engrossed in tearing apart his steak.

The two of them entered the foyer and Greer shut the doors tight behind them. Only the lamps were lit, which hung every-other-space on the wall, alternating with the windows.

"My little *disposal* project," Greer mused, "is put on hold while Odette is out there. It's not good, Thorn. People are getting antsy; I'm getting impatient myself. I don't think I can hold it off anymore. Grayson was supposed to help me; but he can't now can he?"

"I suppose he cannot." His voice betrayed his nerves. His eye darted anywhere but her. "How does this involve me?"

I've got him now. Greer smiled, her lips stretching thin across her face. Rightfully, he couldn't say no. And for what it was worth, Thorn would have been lending a hand in this endeavor any way—this was just a formal request.

"A trade, of sorts. Seeing as you won't tell me where she is—" Thorn stiffened, the tension nearly imperceivable. "then you're going to help me dispose of some bodies.

VIII

GREER

Once, she had pitied Thorn. Well, the truth was, Greer didn't *exactly* pity him, rather the man this almighty angel possessed. They were two separate beings joined in unfortunate circumstances; a case of wrong place, wrong time.

Grayson had evidently forgotten the event. He probably forgot their grandfather had a twin as well. If he remembered, he never spoke about it.

The first time she met Jeremiah Mages—who was Jeremiah Shelley back then—was the night she murdered her parents. It was also the only time Jeremiah ever had electric blue eyes.

The deed had been done; nothing could take it back. Grayson's screaming ceased, but he wouldn't stop shaking, he couldn't peel his eyes from the scene before him. Greer felt like a weight had been lifted.

Someone called the police to check on a disturbance at the Shelley household. When they arrived nearly an hour after; Greer answered the door still in her blood-soaked clothes. They stared at her in alarm and—instinctively, she guessed—one of the officers pulled her from the threshold, whispering encouraging words in her ear.

It's going to be okay.

Everything is going to be alright, now, I promise.

Funnily enough, Greer knew everything was going to be alright. She'd taken care of the problem, but all the same, she let the adults coo over her while they cleared the scene.

They stayed in their patchy front lawn for nearly two hours. An ambulance came, shock blankets were passed out. They examined her and her tearful brother to make sure whoever did this hadn't hurt them. Then, they were put in separate cars.

Grayson didn't put up a fight. He numbly allowed the pretty female officer to guide him into the backseat, his puppy-dog eyes not once leaving the ground. However, Greer wasn't about to be separated so quickly. She remembered biting a man's hand and drawing blood as they pulled her away from her brother.

It wasn't fair! She'd done all the work but was still split from Grayson. *It wasn't fair at all!*

When they arrived at the station, the separation didn't end. Greer was taken into the frigid interrogation room first. She couldn't see into the lobby, didn't know what they did with her brother, and it terrified her. Grayson was never alone. She had promised she would always be there for him, and not twenty minutes later she was breaking that promise.

She didn't answer their questions. Every time they asked *what happened*, and *we need you to tell us so we can help*, she refused to respond. *They* didn't understand. *They* were ordinary. *They* were people who claimed to protect those who they loved but wouldn't pay the ultimate sacrifice, unlike her.

Eventually, she was moved back to the lobby and sat uncomfortably in a plastic chair, her back stick straight. The shock blanket they gave her had been taken away, but when Grayson came out from the interrogation room, he was wrapped tight in his.

His crying hadn't ceased. It had been almost two hours.

The cops talked in hushed whispers. Things were brought in from outside in brown boxes, a fresh label tapped up on the side reading 'SHELLEY' in thick block letters.

Greer wasn't a fool. She knew she had limited time with Grayson.

Grayson refused to look at anyone or anything. For a moment, Greer worried. Had he talked? He seemed too emotional to do much confessing, but perhaps his guilty conscience got the better of him.

And yet his eyes showed no signs of betrayal. When their gazes met, he sniffed. His eyes were swollen and heavy, but he wouldn't close them. Greer was comforted by this. So long as Grayson was the same, life could go on. Yet, Grayson's sleepy expression turned sour the more he looked at her. He snarled; she had never witnessed him looking so angry. The hatred welled up in his eyes and he snapped his head away, burying it in his knees.

She whispered his name, but he didn't look at her again.

The front doors to the station lobby opened letting in the warm night breeze. A man came through. He didn't have a uniform or that stuck-up look the others wore. It only took a moment for recognition to click in her frazzled brain, though his sudden appearance did not comfort her.

Jethro Shelley. Grandfather.

Jethro Shelley was a man with a distinct look. Everything about him was square, rigid, and hard. His thick jaw squared off haircut, and wide shoulders made him appear to be some type of military man, a soldier. Though, in reality, Jethro was little more than a bookworm, wide plastic glasses magnifying his eyes and making them large and bug-like. He had been old since she knew him, and yet on this night he seemed to have aged more than ten years from the scruff on his chin and sloppy clothing choice.

This was *odd*. Very unlike the clean-cut grandfather she was used to.

Jethro was a moral man. He took almost every opportunity to explain right and wrong to the twins. If he learned she was the one who killed his son and daughter-in-law, well, there's no doubt he would toss her in the loony bin.

The man searched the station frantically, pushing through those who crowded him. Policemen rushed toward him, their voices carrying as they questioned who he was. Jethro wasn't interested in their questions. He was on a mission.

Finally, his eyes landed on the twins.

Greer shrunk away. She wished she could melt into her seat to hide. His gaze was piercing. *Inhuman.* She didn't recall him having such bright, electric blue eyes. They seemed to reflect light like a cat's would. For the first time that night, she was unsettled.

The policeman ushered him towards the front desk, their voices rising slightly but not enough to make out their words. Grayson finally looked up; catching the man's back side.

"Who is that?"

"Our grandfather."

But her tone let on that something was up. Grayson frowned.

Though she knew she recognized him, Greer questioned if she knew this man. Jethro Shelley was their grandfather, and it was his face, but he always dressed nicely everywhere he went. He never got out of bed unless he was half-way decent. The man standing there looked like he rolled out of a garbage can.

The twins watched him talk with the cops. His voice was gravely. If he wanted to enunciate, he would make a wild gesture with his hands. Every movement was over-the-top. Every sentence he spoke, a little louder.

The grandfather *they* remembered only spoke in soft tones. Not once had he ever raised his voice, not even when he was excited.

"Why are you questioning my grandkids?" The old man radiated a *power* that Greer felt resonating in her bones.

Both twins leaned forward, their elbows resting on their knees.

The cop looked like he didn't want to answer, but his words were suddenly forced out of his mouth, "They are the only suspects for the murder of Maxon and Eleanor Shelley."

Grayson sniffed.

Jethro leaned around the cop and looked the twins up and down. The moment their eyes connected, Greer felt different, as though the two of them had much in common. She couldn't put it into words, but something happened. A realization in his eyes, the way he seemed to know she was the one who did it. Maybe it was because, underneath all the false anger, there was someone as emotionally drained as she was.

"Those children aren't even ten years old, are you just that stupid to think they might have killed their own parents?!"

"I-I ... Well, sir ..."

"*They didn't do it!*"

His words rung throughout the room and pierced everyone. It felt like a sucker punch to Greer's brain. For a few seconds even she believed it. Yet, she slowly sewed the broken memories back together. How could she have blanked on something this memorable? It was her. She killed them to save her brother.

Like a flash bomb, all the cops seemed to pause their milling about as if stunned. A few seconds later they resumed their duties.

One of the female cops sitting away from all the activity approached Greer's side and rested a hand on her shoulder. "Your grandpa's here to pick you up, okay? Everything is going to be fine."

She nodded mutely and reached for Grayson's hand, but he didn't take it. He ran off to Jethro without her, leaving her feeling emptier than before.

That's when she realized this was not her grandfather Jethro Shelley, but his twin brother, the *grandfather* they had never met.

Jeremiah Shelley.

Jeremiah Shelley was more of a mythical figure than a grandfather, like the Easter Bunny and Santa Clause. The twins had heard of him, but never seen him. There was no falling out between their father and him, Jeremiah was simply a greedy recluse. He was busy chasing a fortune he could never attain.

He was a name on the occasional Christmas or Birthday card. He was discussed in whispers, and rarely caught in any pictures. Their parents didn't exactly approve of his gambling and drunkenness, but as far as Greer knew they never denied him into their home.

Just because they'd never seen Jeremiah in person, didn't mean they didn't know what he looked like. Jethro Shelley was his twin and he came to their pitiful Christmases and Thanksgivings. Jethro was the one they remembered coming to their house.

And yet, Jethro wasn't the one who came for them.

"Now you kids, I know it ain't much, but it'll have to do for tonight," Jeremiah said, unrolling two sleeping bags for them on the trailer floor.

Grayson quickly went to his designated bag and climbed in, not even saying goodnight. This didn't sit well with Greer, after all they went through that night, he ignored her. He *chose* her.

Jeremiah sighed and scratched his head. "Is he normally like that?"

"He's transitioning."

"Oh."

Greer looked up at him, staring curiously. "He doesn't think the way we do."

The old man blinked twice. Her words hit him hard. He fidgeted with an old piece of costume jewelry, rolling it between his fingers slowly.

"How do you mean?"

Greer looked at him, really looked, and crafted her words carefully. "You and I have a vision. We will do *anything* it takes to get there. I have someone I want to protect. I can't tell what you want, but I know you're like me. I can see it in your eyes."

Silence settled over the trailer. Jeremiah puffed his cheeks out and glanced down at Grayson, who appeared to have already gone to sleep. Soft snores left his lips, his chest rose and fell rhythmically.

"Why are you pretending to be Jethro?"

His unnaturally colored eyes snapped-to. He bit his cheek. Finally, he said, "Come with me." In a tone that left no room to question him.

There weren't many places to go in his trailer, but Greer followed anyway. She cast a look over her shoulder to Grayson, and took comfort in his deep breathing. Jeremiah led the way outside.

Greer had been given an old thin shirt to sleep in that night, but the night was hot and sweat gathered along her neck. The farther they walked, the stronger the idea grew that Jeremiah may be taking her to an early death.

And yet, she was calm. The idea of death did not frighten her. There was only one drawback—Grayson. Would he miss her?

Her thoughts washed away when Jeremiah stopped in front of a cellar. It was far from the trailer park with a good bit of tree coverage. She looked back but couldn't pick out his trailer in the dark.

"I know you have a lot of questions, but ..." he trailed off. Jeremiah clutched the costume jewelry and it glowed like a night light, soft and silver.

The cellar doors sprung open; a silver halo engulfed them. Greer's eyes widened. The old man motioned for her to follow him down into the inky blackness. Almost as soon as she put one foot on the cement stairs, she detected the rancid smell of death. The doors slammed shut behind her and it became even more dark than before.

"I wanted to show you this ... *thing* that I discovered. It was really all due to Jethro, but ..." Light flooded the underground room and there was Jeremiah, standing in the middle. He was preoccupied, seeming to forget about Greer for the moment, and walked deeper into the bunker.

Greer followed him with her eyes, until her gaze landed on a broken heap of a body. It didn't move, it didn't seem to be breathing. It was dead.

"You should get rid of that," she mumbled, "before the cops get onto you."

"The police can't touch me. Did you see what I did to get you and your brother out of there? Piece of cake." Jeremiah chuckled, but shook his head, focusing back on the subject at hand.

He motioned for her to come closer, and she did, curiosity taking over. The shock only lasted for a moment. Greer realized she was witnessing a much bloodier scene than earlier, so she curiously stepped closer to look.

It was a young man, possibly in his twenties. He looked normal aside from the stab wound in his chest and the large slash mark that cut through his eye. Greer didn't know him, and even though she hadn't known this grandfather for very long, he didn't seem like the type to kill at random.

"What did he do to you?"

Jeremiah sighed, rubbing the back of his neck. "That's the complicated bit, ain't it? I'm sure he—the real *he*—would be sad that you didn't recognize him, especially since he was the one who was around the most."

She shook her head, not understanding.

"It's Jethro, kid. Your grandpa. My brother. I killed him ..." His voice petered off, his nerves taking hold of him. He shook it off. "There's this deal I couldn't refuse. Jethro, he understood, ya know. I'd finally be in control of my own life." He sat himself down at the workbench behind him. It was cluttered with half-melted candles, pentagrams, and other symbols Greer had never seen before. "Maybe I should explain. Right now, that thing is no longer my brother, but an angel. My brother and I—while he was still alive—were just trying it out. He wanted to do it for discovery purposes, and I wanted to do it for the power you could have just by controlling it.

"We'd found this ... this 'instruction manual' on how to enslave an angel. It sounded fake. I mean, *an angel*? It still makes me laugh. But some of the incantations they had in there were for some pretty serious stuff apparently. Anyway, Jethro didn't want to do it because it involved killing someone, someone who shared your blood. I was fine with that until we actually got the thing to work." The old man's voice cracked, "He didn't ... he didn't understand the immense achievement that we were gonna make together. An angel? If that kinda thing got on television, or if the news caught wind of it, we'd be rich!"

His shoulders sagged and he ran a hand through his coarse grey hair. "Once we actually summoned it, the thing took possession of Jethro. I don't know... something inside of me told me not to let the chance slip by. Surely, Jethro would understand. I knew the only way to capture him was to do it. So I stabbed him and then cut his eye—the eye thing apparently is a symbol of ownership among the supernatural. Somehow, it seals the thing in the body. I finished the ritual and ... he's been 'de-ageing' ever since."

It was a lot to take in for a child. Greer frowned. Jethro was always a kind man, but ... if he had been the one to come to the police station instead of his brother, what would have happened? Would Greer have been sent away? Would he have accepted her reasoning?

No, she decided. Jethro was a strait-laced, ordinary fellow. He did not have the passion needed to protect someone with his last breath. If he had come for the twins, Greer would have been locked away and shunned.

"So ... at the police station?"

"Well, I know your dad has him as your emergency contact." Jeremiah shrugged his shoulders. "They wouldn't let 'Jeremiah Shelley' take you, but 'Jethro' on the other hand ..."

"I guess not."

Jeremiah was rubbing his chin wearily. "It's not like *he's* gonna mind ... He was always a better guy than me, anyway; had better stuff too."

"What are you gonna do about him?" she asked again. "People are going to question what happened to him, aren't they?"

"Yeah." He pursed his lips, the cogs within his mind began to whirl. "I guess I'll have to make sure no one knows *Jethro*'s dead."

A kind of thrill ran through her, the longer she mulled over what her grandfather said. If what he said was true—about angels and supernatural powers—and this wasn't one big hoax, then there could be some serious benefits to this.

They had control of a supernatural being.

She circled the body, watching color seep into his hair and elasticity return to his skin. Greer looked away from the unconscious angel and back to her grandfather.

"So, is he, like a pet now?"

"Yeah, sure thing, kid." Jeremiah let out a breathy chuckle, formulating a plan of his own.

HANNAH BOGGS

IX

GRAYSON

A bitter cold wind whipped around Grayson's body, blowing his hair, coat, and map in every direction. He clutched Odette's photo in his fist so hard it wrinkled. He leaned against the hood of the car, his forearm pinning the map into place.

Tadmor, Ohio prominently circled in bright red ink. It stood out like a neon sign on his map, and yet the same could not be said for what was physically before him.

The WELCOME sign, displaying the name of the next town over, stared him in the face. He had pulled off the road, parking across from it. The map must have a defect. There was no other explanation why he couldn't find it.

According to his map, he was on the outskirts of the town, and yet, he drove all through the area and found nothing but *forest*. Green trees and overgrown grass as far as the eye could see.

"Maybe I missed a turn ..." He grumbled.

Grayson pinched the bridge of his nose. No. There was no way he could have missed a turn. Not only had he studied the map religiously, the GPS said he was in the correct area. He was in Tadmor, no question about it.

Something was *off*.

If Odette were in the area, he should have felt it by now. There are only a handful of reasons why he wouldn't have felt her, but Grayson didn't even want to consider those.

No, he was in the right place and she had to be near. Frustrated, Grayson crumpled the map and tossed it into the car. He would have to find someone to help.

The diner was old. Not the charming type of old, either. The kind of old that made you feel uncomfortable.

Their sign had seen better days. Paint peeled off the side of the building, broken steps and splintered wood trim poking out in an unsightly manner. The windows were coated in dirt, grime making itself at home in the nooks and crannies.

Grayson noted the number of cars in the lot, which was surprising considering how dingy the place appeared. He repressed a shudder and dusted himself off, making sure he had his essentials: the map, the amulet, and a photo. He could get anywhere with those.

A bell dinged overhead as he entered. The door stuck to the floor. Grayson applied force to it, and it made a horrible noise as it scraped against the tiles. Few heads turned his way. Most of them belonged to old men with scruffy faces and pudgy bellies.

A waitress tottered over. She appeared to be somewhat young, and from the thoughts of the men Grayson picked up, what they mainly came for.

"Hi, sweetie. You can sit where you want." She motioned to the empty, sticky booths behind her. Their seats were ripped and discolored, the tables littered with crumbs and the last patrons' napkins.

He hid the sour twist of his mouth by faking a cough.

"Actually, I need directions." Grayson motioned towards the outside. "I'm looking for Tadmor. I have my map, but I think I'm missing the turn. Would you be able to point me in the correct direction?"

One of the old men snorted. In turn, it made the whole bunch chuckle lowly at his expense. The waitress blushed, bowing her head. She seemed to think there was nothing more she could do for him.

"Are you a tourist?" asked one of the men at the bar. He peered at Grayson over his white ceramic mug, his beady eyes gleaming with intrigue.

Grayson pursed his lips. "Of a kind."

The old man chortled, then went back to his coffee. It appeared he would say no more to Grayson; though, the smirk on his speckled lips said there was obviously more to tell.

Grayson raised an eyebrow. It irked him that such a ruddy old man found pleasure in his ignorance. If he knew something, he should speak up. But the miserable man shared a laugh with his buddies, saying something along the lines of *these dumb kids.*

He could always *make* him speak up. He quickly discarded the idea, there were too many witnesses.

Focusing on the group, Grayson pushed past the barriers of their simple mind. Their thoughts flooded over him instantly; but he waded through them, categorizing them and ignoring what he didn't need.

What motivated them ...? Some motivations were obvious, though Grayson was not the type to hand those out, others he could work with.

Simple minded. Simply motivated.

Grayson didn't take too kindly to some of the words they thought to describe him. Though, for the sake of time, he ignored it.

Greedy old men. Grayson's mouth twisted into a snarl.

Grayson was running on fumes, too tired to be able to control all of them. It would backfire before he got the information he needed. He rolled his eyes. It seemed there was only one option. Grayson stuffed his hand in his pocket and pulled out a wad of cash, brandishing it to the group.

"I'll pay you to take me there."

The man who seemed so *reluctant* before had a name. 'Skid'—a rather unfortunate name to have; but, in a way, it fit him. Whatever he'd done to earn the title, he certainly deserved it.

Skid jumped eagerly at the chance of money before any of the others had the chance. They were too busy gaping, their stupid faces frozen in perpetual shock. It wasn't everyday someone came in brandishing so much cash. Yet, it was Skid who leapt off of his stool and clasped Grayson's hand in his own meaty one.

"Why didn't ya just say so, kid. C'mon."

Skid lead—more like pushed—Grayson out to his vehicle, practically ripping the cash from his hands and pocketing it.

Both Skid and Grayson climbed into Skid's old truck. It hadn't been cleaned in years, and the inside smelled of sweat and garbage.

When he was younger, he spent many nights with no sleep, but he hadn't had a night like this in a long time. *A hunt.* Grayson forgot how draining it was. Nearly every time it was for naught, but Grayson was mature enough to know he gave up on those girls long before he found them.

They weren't his true match. They were only floozies who occupied his attention for a short amount of time. All the heartbreak and confusion lead him to Odette, and he was grateful for it.

Odette was different from the other girls. Every time she ran, she managed to come back to him. Grayson was married now, with a baby on the way. It was fate, he decided he had to go through all those bad relationships before finally getting it right. And that was why it was imperative to leave this instant. Grayson didn't know what kind of danger Odette could be in. No matter what it was, he would save her like always.

"So, what brings you to these parts, kid?" said Skid, breaking the silence.

Grayson noted they were driving the same direction he did before. It only relieved a small part of him, but he was mostly annoyed. If this had been the right way all along, he should have been able to find her.

"My wife."

Skid's eyebrows shot upward. "*Wife*? How old are you, kid?"

"Old enough."

He made a noise in the back of his throat. The thoughts in his head rung loud and clear. They questioned him, berated him. The word *kid* was spat repeatedly with mockery.

Grayson glowered at the man.

Suddenly, the car looped around, heading straight for the woods. Grayson almost spoke up, angry he was suddenly pulling off course, when he noticed a small path cutting through the trees. It was dense with dead trees that stretched in every which way towards the sky.

Then, he felt it. It was small, at first, a small tug which he felt in the center of his chest. Then, a growing pulse of warmth thrummed in his bones.

Odette.

He gasped silently. It was as if there was a tether which tied them together, urging him closer. She was calling out for him. His exhaustion vanished, replaced with adrenaline, his eyes wide. It took every ounce of self-control not to make the man accelerate the car. It was as if he wanted to keep them apart longer.

Grayson drummed his fingers on his pants. "How much further?"

"Oh, not too far."

Skid's tone of voice almost shattered his elation. His words mocked him, that tone of *I-know-more-than-you* dripped from every syllable. Grayson was never fond of cryptic people, even if he was known for being like that. Secrets meant harm. Skid's thoughts were as helpful as a rock. The harder Grayson looked into his mind, the more frustrated he became. Nothing but swirling images of his home and this was *the easiest cash he'd ever made.*

His greed uneasily reminded him of Jethro.

Grayson tucked his hands into his pockets. The crinkled photo of Odette was inside. His finger brushed the glossed side of it. It reeled him in from the darkness and brought him back to the task at hand—not dealing with the idiot pawn but finding his queen.

What would Odette be doing when he found her? She was not the type of girl to sit around and do nothing. She must have found some way to keep occupied in the dismal town. And then, Grayson's thoughts became darker. What if she hadn't found a way to keep occupied? What if she was in trouble? He swore silently. What if she had been denied *shelter*?

The thought physically pained him. How could anyone deny her anything? These people in Tadmor must be monsters. When he got his hands on them, he would tear them to pieces.

But ... this may have taught her a lesson, Grayson thought. After all, she now knew not to run away. He was the only one who would care for her. Everyone else would turn her away.

It occurred to Grayson, as he twisted around in his seat, that they had driven quite a distance away from the road, and the dirt path before them was only getting worse the further in they went.

They drove past a wide, wooden sign; but whatever words had been there in the past were rubbed off and covered by a weathered metal sign reading *no trespassing.*

"What are you doing?"

Skid rolled his eyes. The defiance made Grayson's jaw tick. *"Answer me."*

"Tadmor isn't technically open to the public, kid," he said pointedly.

Grayson blinked. Once. Twice. Then, the words settled in. He twisted around fully in his seat and stared him down, his eyes blazing with hellfire. "What do you mean?"

The old truck lurched, and then came to a complete stop. Grayson was almost too afraid to look and see where he had been taken, but he did.

Tadmor wasn't a town. At least, it hadn't been for a very long time.

Maybe at some point in the past, Tadmor had stood proud and its streets filled with the lively talk of people. Maybe it was a quaint place, a family-riddled town where everyone knew everyone. Maybe it had always been like *this*.

It was more rubble than building, rot infecting every surface of the place. Nature had come into its own, tree roots and moss growing over brick and splintered wood. Dead plants covered the skeletons of buildings and piles of rubble.

It was a ghost town, somewhere lost in time, forgotten even by the animals. It was uninhabitable to human life. And yet, Odette's presence was *strong*, calling out to him like it had in the car, urging him to go in deeper.

Come, he heard her voice whisper, *Find me*.

The amulet dimly glowed beneath his layers of clothes. Involuntarily, Grayson took a step forward, trending lightly on the ground. Wreckage littered the dirt, leaving no inch of space for a clear walking path. A branch snapped underfoot forcing him to shift his stance.

Find me, she whispered again. Or maybe it was the wind, which rustled the trees.

Grayson swallowed hard. "What happened here?"

Skid looked around with something like boredom and sighed. "No one really knows. Some say it was abandoned in the 1800s as new cities and towns were built. Others say it was a prototype town that never got to house people. Local legend says that some guy burned it all down because his sweetheart married another guy. He didn't want anyone to be happy if he couldn't be. They say their ghosts are still here today, restless and wandering."

Grayson stepped over a pile of brick, his steps staggered and his breathing ragged. He could feel her, but he couldn't see her. *Why couldn't he see her?* There was nowhere to hide.

"*Where are you?*" He picked up a frozen brick and tossed it to the side. Then another. Then another, until the pile was dwindled down to nothing but dirt and bugs. "Odette!"

His fingers became numb and scraped from the rough edges and hidden glass. He tore at dirt piles and stick piles that looked like they could have housed a human body. *Nothing.*

Adrenaline overtook him, his heart pumping a mile a minute, and he ran. He leapt over tree roots, over fallen logs and broken glass. The first structure he came to was tampered with, trash littering the gutted interior. Glass bottles, needles, a ripped sleeping bag that vermin had laid claim to.

The next structure was boarded up, to which he ripped away moss and tree roots from the door. Splinters embedded themselves in his palms, but he didn't care. The building was, like the first, empty. So was the next, and the one after that, and the one after that.

They were all *empty.*

Sure, some of them were littered with granola wrappers and crumpled water bottles, but they were too dirty and rotted to have been used in the recent past. This stuff was weeks—maybe months, or even years—old.

Nothing. Odette was nowhere.

Grayson staggered back, tripping over a wagon wheel. What was this? Was it the insanity he fought so hard to keep away? She was gone, but she was *everywhere.*

Her voice ran on the wind, like an all-too-distant echo. *Come find me, Grayson. Come find me.* The wind picked up and her words became louder and louder until his brain hurt. He clamped his hands over his ears.

Skid stood several yards away. He did not dare move, pinned to the spot as the boy he escorted went mad. Something about Grayson—the well-to-do, snobby kid— had come unhinged, and he had no desire to intervene.

Carefully, Skid backed away. His foot caught on a gnarled root, and he fell back. Something crunched loudly beneath him.

He rolled over, cradling his hip with one hand, and pulling the object from beneath him. It was a picture frame. Strange, he thought. Not once in his travels to this place had he ever uncovered a picture of one of the residents.

Candle wax dripped all around the frame, cementing hair to it. Bits of the photo were charred, but the people's faces could still be made out.

Grayson's head shot up.

He crossed the field in the blink of an eye and snatched the frame from the old man. His breath stuttered to a halt.

"I-interesting, ain't it?" Skid commented.

"Shut up!"

Grayson tightened his grip on the frame until it broke in half. Glass shattered and the picture ripped in two.

So, this was how she left him. The picture was of her and her family. The very one he had found in her room at home. Grayson's anger buzzed inside of him, rattling away all rational thought. Something inside of him snapped.

She had come back to the house.

Somehow, when they were searching for her, Odette had come back and grabbed this. Eluding him. Eluding Greer.

It seemed impossible, the girl who knew nothing of magic or the extent of her powers, had been able to do something so advanced. Not just teleportation—a feat in its own right—but an honest-to-god *spell*.

This kind of magic took time and planning. All this time, he had believed she was over what had happened last summer. He wrote her aversion to him off as nerves; but, no, she'd been plotting against him. Plotting to *leave* him.

Odette couldn't have done it on her own, Grayson knew it, she had to have had help. There was only one person he knew of with the strength to do this and the stupidity to help her. It all clicked into place.

Grayson's entire being shook with rage, staring down at the torn image of Odette's face. "No one is ever coming to Tadmor again."

He tossed the broken frame over his shoulder and it caught fire mid-air. It drifted through the air, a streak of blue, until it crashed into a scattered pile of bricks. The flames spread fast, crawling, consuming the entire rotted town.

Skid cried out in shock. His mind screamed, even when he could not. All the man could do was stammer, and his incoherent pleas fell on deaf ears.

He crawled as fast as he could on hands and knees to escape. Before he could get far, Grayson trapped him. His fingers caught the man's collar, yanking on it so hard he choked, fabric constricting his airway.

"It's no use," Grayson told him. "We all burn one way or another."

This place was only the beginning. He saw it now, in his mind's eye, a world on fire. There would be nowhere to hide, no place would be safe from his fury. He would start with the town, and not stop until everything was a pile of ash.

Grayson pushed him into the fire.

X

ODETTE

A sudden blazing heat enveloped Odette's entire body. She pulled at the collar of her sweater, but the warmth didn't relent. Her hot flashes during this pregnancy had become a common occurrence, however this wasn't a normal hot flash. It was as if she were being eaten alive by fire, from the inside out. Odette grabbed the car door to steady herself, an onslaught of dizziness accompanying the unnatural heat.

"Hey, do you need us to stop?" Felix asked cautiously, "You're looking a little green."

"No, I'm fine." Almost as soon as it came, the sensation passed. The only remaining sign was the warmth that clung to her skin. Odette cupped her head, nursing the dizziness. "Do you smell burning?"

Both Clara and Felix shook their heads. This didn't bring her much comfort. If it wasn't here, then it must be something else entirely. She looked at her ring, which appeared as dull as ever, and wondered.

Felix pulled into a parking spot of the local supermarket. Odette sunk down in her seat a little more. There were a lot more people milling about the parking lot than she expected. Didn't they have anything better to do with their weekdays?

In the front seat, Clara prattled off the shopping list they had compiled on the way then turned to Odette. "Did I leave anything off?"

"No. Just get in and get out. Don't talk to anyone."

She pressed her lips together, a look of determination crossing her face. "Got it. I won't be more than fifteen minutes."

"Try and make it ten," Odette said.

Odette pulled some cash from her bag and handed it to Clara. The magic backpack was full of surprises. Clara accepted the money and hopped out saying to text her if they think of anything else.

The two of them watched her go in silence, neither turning away from the window until Clara made it to the doors.

It didn't take long for the silence to become stifling. Felix was staring at her through the rear-view mirror, his golden eyes piercing. She pretended not to notice and occupied herself with something outside of the vehicle.

"She showed me that article during first period today." Felix said. "I don't know if she knew about it before or not—can't imagine she would keep it from me if she did."

It was meant to sting, and it did. Felix always knew where to strike when doling out insults. Still, Odette didn't flinch.

Felix exhaled softly and shifted in his seat so he could see her better. "Why did you hide it from us? I mean *us*, Odette. I could care less about how many other people you didn't tell. This is Clara and me."

Odette didn't peel her eyes from the window. Her mind swam with plausible answers—*we did it in secret; it was a small wedding; we had planned to elope; I didn't really want to marry him, but ...*

Felix shifted. His eyes became visible in the rearview mirror. "I'm worried about you. So is Clara, but she thinks by shutting up and playing along, you'll talk."

Odette realized she hadn't spoken for a while. Felix stared her down from the rearview mirror, his eyes not wavering. It was unnerving, but she didn't turn away, she met his gaze and held it, daring him to blink first.

"I'm doing what's best for me," Odette said simply. "That's all that matters, right?"

"When you say that, all I can think of is you've gotten yourself involved in something dangerous. Something you wouldn't do." Odette chuckled; he was right in a way. "Is it a gang? Is it drugs? Is it something worth going into witness protection for?"

Witness protection probably couldn't save her from Grayson, not when he had unholy power on his side. The gang, though, was comical enough to elicit a chuckle from her. As if she were the type. Felix didn't think it was funny.

"Did you kill someone?"

Her smile dropped.

A chill sunk into her bones. Her heart began to race. The car suddenly felt too small for just two people. Odette gave up on the staring contest and dropped her gaze to the floor.

Felix had a knack for catching onto her lies. When she'd ask him how he knew, he told her, 'it's all in the eyes'. But the boy she was staring at in the mirror didn't look too much like Felix anymore. For a split second, his honey blond hair reminded her a little too much of *him*. Claude.

To the rest of the world, the man once known as Claude was now a John Doe found in the remnants of the old lighthouse. After the night Claude died, Thorn demolished the lighthouse.

It was as much for Odette's benefit as it was for the Mages'. No one would ever know Odette was held hostage there—or Claude's brutality. No one would know she'd killed a man in order to live, or she'd taken revenge on the twins by doing what Claude couldn't, and ultimately fail again.

Yeah, no one would know, but Odette would remember.

Odette never learned the rest of his name, nor if he had any family. If she had, it wouldn't have made things any better. Claude was a sick, twisted man who only wanted power. She never asked why, but then again, who needs a reason to want power?

Felix blinked, "Still, you understand where I'm coming from, don't you? You show up out of the blue acting all strange. You're asking Clara for weird stuff from the store—

you also freaked out when you saw her this afternoon—and you haven't let that bag out of your sight since you got here. It looks to me like you're running."

Had he been talking the whole time? Odette swallowed thickly and gained the courage to look at him again. It wasn't Claude, it was Felix, her Felix. She sighed and relaxed her tense muscles against the car.

Maybe she was running, but God knows it wasn't planned. Odette never had more than fifteen minutes by herself when she was with the Mageses. Now she had almost unlimited freedom, and she knew better than to squander it. This escape was being played by ear. She had no way to predict Grayson's moves, but she knew he wouldn't relent. If Greer got involved, which seemed extremely doubtful, then it would be over for her. Odette had to be far away before either of them got to her, and she had to destroy the trail.

"Leave it alone, Felix, please."

"I don't want to lose you again; do you understand that?" Felix twisted around in his seat to look at her fully. "You didn't answer a single text, or phone call for forever. I thought I did something. I was so pissed off that I thought about *mailing* you an angry letter but decided you didn't deserve that kind of energy. If you're in trouble, I'm on board with helping you, but not if it's going to mean you're going to vanish again or end up dead."

Odette grimaced. "We all die eventually, just some of us earlier than others."

His eyes bugged, looking even larger in his rounded glasses.

She huffed, understanding how he misconstrued her words. "I'm not planning on killing myself, Felix. Don't worry."

He was worrying, though. Odette could hear it. His mind was loud, buzzing with thoughts, unasked questions and everything. There wasn't anything she could do or say to help the situation, though. Even if she explained it to him, he wouldn't believe her. Felix, despite believing in the Mothman and Loch Ness Monster, was a man of science. He'd probably think she was on crack.

"Fine," he said finally, "Just learn how to pick up a cell phone wherever you go. I'm kinda tired of being ignored." Behind his gruff facade, there was a hint of a grin.

Odette smiled softly at him, "I will."

Knocking violently on the passenger side window, Clara jerked the car door open. She fought with a couple of plastic bags before tossing them to the back.

"Start 'er up!" she shouted, flinging another bag into the back seat. Odette, narrowly avoiding being hit by it. Clara hopped in the passenger seat and slammed the door shut. "Seriously, go go go! You would make a terrible getaway driver."

Felix started the car and they sped out of the parking lot.

Clara's house was in the park. Once you crossed the street and broke through the tree line, there was a small pond and three fountains that worked during the warmer months. In the spring, Clara's side of the park was covered with tulips, and the pond was covered with lily pads.

Odette smiled inside. When they were younger, they believed the Loch Ness Monster lived in that pond.

It was winter now and there were no fountain sprinklers, no lily pads, and no tulips.

Everything was dead and muddy. It would be pretty again when it snowed, but until then it was depressing.

They pulled into Clara's up-hill driveway and exited the car fast, quickly moving to the front door without looking back. Odette slowly gathered the bags from the back seat, part of her not wanting to go inside. It was weird to be back. Just two blocks away was her old house with a new family living a perfectly normal life. They didn't know about magic—they probably wouldn't have to deal with death until one of them reached an old age.

"Odette, are you coming?" Clara called out.

She shut her eyes and shook away those depressing thoughts. It didn't matter. Odette forced herself out of the car and faced the house.

The house was just the same. It was still the only home with the most windows in town. They used it to their advantage during Christmas, setting up trees in almost every room and putting lights around the glass to make them really shine. It was always the prettiest house, hands down. Funny enough, they still hadn't taken their Christmas lights down. Odette knew they would be up until March.

Pushing her discomfort aside, Odette took a step forward. Nothing bad would happen by entering a house.

Clara turned back to her, dark curls falling out of the winter headband she wore.

"Grandma is at the beach, and Mom and dad are on a business trip. We shouldn't be disturbed." She unlocked the front door and ushered them inside.

Odette made a b-line for the kitchen table and began to dump all the shopping bags out one-by-one. The contents scattered, but it was Felix who organized them while Odette and Clara made sure they hadn't missed anything. So many colors to choose from.

"If we start now, it should be done by morning." Odette picked up the box of bleach and a shirt. She read over the instructions, pursing her lips. "I hope this works."

She headed for the bathroom.

Odette stared hard at her reflection in the mirror, her mouth set in a firm line. She had come too far to question her motives or want to go back. Sure, it started out as an accident, but it was also a chance. If she pulled this off, she wouldn't have to wake up afraid of what Grayson—or Greer—would do to her anymore.

She felt bad, if she were being honest, she didn't have the chance to go back and help Skylar. He had become a dear friend. Odette understood what it was like to be taken away from everything you've known, even though her situation was a bit different from his. Skylar wasn't *eased* into everything like she had been, if you considered what Grayson did 'easing'.

Greer had invited him over for a date. They went out a couple of times, but Odette wasn't sure of the exact number, and the next thing she knew there was a boy trapped in those awful dungeons. She didn't tell him what had occurred there a few weeks prior to his capture, but he eventually found out on his own.

Odette's guilt grew the more she thought about him. Skylar wasn't made for that kind of torture—then again, who was? He was a gentle guy, and she regretted not doing more to help him. Surely, Skylar would understand. If the situation were reversed, she'd want him to go and not look back.

She groaned and rubbed her face. Her guilt wouldn't subside; she'd simply have to live with it. Shakily, Odette inhaled and turned on the faucet. She splashed her face with water, soaking the t-shirt with it, but she didn't care. She needed to calm down if she was going to do this properly.

Odette picked up the scissors and brought her hair into three sloppily made ponytails before she began to cut. Her hair was thick, much too thick to just cut with one go. Odette hacked at it until the whole section came off. It was choppy and uneven in places, like a child hacked at it blindly instead of herself. It didn't matter. She just needed it gone.

Odette tossed the clump of hair into the trash can and started on the second ponytail, just as haphazardly; and then then third. When it all came off, she looked at her image in the mirror again. Her hair was a mess; varying lengths but most of them reaching the middle of her neck.

A knock came on the bathroom door, but Odette already knew who it was. "Come in."

It swung open to reveal Clara's tanned face. Whatever thought she was going to say was interrupted when she noticed Odette's hair. She gaped like a fish before finally managing to say, "What did you *do*?"

Odette ran her fingers through her hair. "Shorter hair means there's less of it to color."

"Your poor, pretty hair ..." She pursed her lips, stopping whatever comment might have come out. "Give me the scissors. I can't let you walk around like that. Just let me help you even it out."

Odette paused, the uneven look was growing on her, but she nodded and held the scissors out for her to take. "Thank you."

"Well, I can't let you go out, wherever it is you're going, with hair like this. Sit down." She pushed Odette to sit on the edge of the bathtub and took the scissors from her hand. "I'm just going to trim it a little, and then I'll be *out of your hair*."

Odette snorted. "Lame."

Clara shrugged; the corner of her mouth quirked upwards. The scissors snipped softly. Odette could feel the stray hairs falling down her back.

From the living room, the sound of the TV starting up caught her attention. She could see Felix on the couch and half of the TV. He appeared to be busy, looking down at something while the local channel played commercials.

The screen went bright yellow, and a cluster of people faded in wearing all white robes.

"*Tired of feeling out-of-touch with yourself and the universe?*" said a young, Asian woman on the screen. "*Longing for a sense of purpose in the world? We can help.*"

"*Come visit the Church of Cygnus today.*"

The church's name scrolled across the screen in large, turquoise letters, with a phone number at the bottom.

"That's new," Odette said.

"Hmph," Clara forced her head down a bit more. "Yeah, it came about a couple of weeks ago, but they claim to have been established longer than that. This channel's always playing their commercials. I don't think it's a real church, probably a scam or something."

Felix turned the channel, cutting off the acolyte mid-speech when the Church of Cygnus' commercial played anew.

"Do you remember the plan?" Clara said quietly.

"Hm?"

She made a noncommittal noise and shifted. "We were going to come and see you this summer. We wanted to do it as soon as you got there, but our parents wanted to give you guys time to settle in, remember?"

Slowly, it was coming back to her. "We were going to go boating."

"And make you try lobster." Clara laughed to herself. "I was looking at plane tickets, and Felix made a list of spots he wanted to hit. But ... we sort of stopped when we never heard back from you."

"I'm sorry."

Her friends and her old home felt so much more like a memory when she was with Grayson. She didn't miss this town when she left. Guilt crept in. How could she have been so selfish?

Clara turned her around to work on the front of her hair. "I won't ask why you're doing this. I know Felix has done enough of that already. But am I wrong to assume this has something to do with the Mages'?"

The sound of their name caused a shudder to rip through Odette. She was swatted, lightly, as a warning not to move.

"I don't ... Grayson is, um ... I'm sorry, Clara, I can't."

"It's okay." She was quiet for a moment as she measured another length of Odette's hair. "The celebrity life isn't for everyone. I'm sure you had to see a lot of things you didn't want to, like Grayson flirting with other girls. But I think you should really think this all through. Is running away, over whatever it was about, really worth it? Will you regret it? Because I think if you went back now and tried to make up, he'd be more forgiving than if you kept running."

Odette drummed her fingers on her knees. Clara didn't know how right she was. All the same, Odette couldn't. There was a fear surrounding her now. It had been too long. She was in too deep. When would she have another chance to escape? Besides, there were too many factors. It wasn't as simple as just asking—or begging—for forgiveness.

Grayson's obsession reached a new high. He became hysterical if she was out of his sight for too long; but this? This was something else entirely. Odette feared no amount of pleading would quell his murderous rage. Anyone standing between them would become collateral damage.

"I was never actually all that jealous of the girls he flirted with," she admitted.

"Oh?" Clara laughed, "Are you that confident he's that faithful?"

Yes. She glossed over the thought and tilted her head forward for Clara. "All that stuff's part of his job."

"With a guy like that, I would be concerned his words were genuine, you know? I'd want to know he wasn't just playing with my heart. I'd want him to prove it to me. But that's just me. I'm sure—"

The image of *that* night suddenly flashed in her mind. She could still smell the stench of rot hanging in the air and feel the blood between her toes. Jethro, Bonnie, and Nadia's mangled bodies would stay forever ingrained in her mind like *that*.

"Odette?"

"Yeah?"

"Are you okay?"

Odette cleared her throat and released the tension in her hands. Deep crescent moon marks were left in her flesh, red and ugly. "Yeah, I'm good. I was just lost in thought, sorry."

Clara just hummed but didn't press. "Can I ask you one thing about them?" When Odette nodded, she continued. "Is Greer as pretty in real life as she is in pictures?"

Odette frowned. It was difficult to think of Greer as anything short of horrifying.

She shrugged and said, "I guess" hoping Clara would leave it alone.

Clara laid the scissors down on the counter and brushed Odette's hair, getting all of the loose pieces free from her snarls. She pulled her up to stand and steadied her. With Odette's head between her hands, she moved it around, eyeing the length of her hair, and then released her with a nod.

"It's not perfect, but it's better than what it was. You're safe to color."

"Hey," Odette called out to her, "Thank you."

She nodded and shut the door behind her.

Odette gave herself one more hard look in the mirror. She already looked different from when she started; however, he would still be looking for a girl with brown hair and strange blue eyes.

Grayson wouldn't be looking for a blonde.

XI

GREER

Every Friday since the "disappearance" of Bonnie and Nadia was exactly the same. A set appointment that never wavered, the same place, the same time, the same people. Greer donned her all-black attire and gave herself a once over. Black, a sophisticated color, made her look subdued, important, and a bit too pale. Black was the color of mourning. It was a shame *they* didn't understand that.

It had been nearly eight months, now, since Grayson killed Bonnie and Nadia. Nearly eight months since they'd last been seen alive. A part of Greer felt wicked doing this, meeting with the mothers and playing the sympathetic best friend, all the while stifling her feelings of *I-know-more-than-you-do*.

It was a part to play. She was an actress and the world was her stage.

Thorn stood behind her, holding her coat out for her to shrug on. She addressed him casually.

"Is everything in place?"

He helped her into the coat. "I have all the *parts* you requested pulled from the cellar and bagged. There is supposed to be a storm this weekend. It would be an opportune moment."

"That sounds perfect."

Greer might have said more, but her thoughts were interrupted when her cell phone began to ring. Her heart leapt into her throat; and for a moment she didn't reach for her purse, fearing she'd misheard the noise. It continued to ring. She tore open her purse, dumping everything until at last her phone clattered to the floor. Thorn left her alone to collect the call.

She hoped—*prayed*—for this moment. Finally, Grayson.

To say she was relieved was an understatement. Greer's heart pounded in her chest like a drum going a mile a minute. Countless thoughts raced through her mind. Was he hurt? Had he found Odette? Did he kill her like the traitor she was?

Greer answered. "Grays! I've tried to call you about a hundred times. You had me so concerned. Thorn wouldn't tell me anything at all because he said you wanted to keep it a secret. Where are you?"

"*I'm coming home.*"

Something about the tone of his voice was different. It was ragged, she might even say broken. Greer had only heard him sound like this a few times in her life, and each time it meant one thing: betrayal. She bit her lip and chose her next words carefully. "What happened?"

"*She's not here. I was tricked.*"

"How?"

He sighed. "*A ritual of some kind. I didn't know she knew how to do this... It doesn't matter. I'm coming back. I need to regroup.*"

Greer tapped her fingers on her lips. First, Odette teleporting all on her own; now this. "It doesn't make sense. She shouldn't be able to do all of this."

"*I know.*"

"You were the one who tracked her, right?"

"*Yes ...*" He paused, "*... only me.*" Something in the background of the phone cracked. "*I should be at the house by the end of the day.*"

And he hung up.

☆☆☆

Greer's frequent appearance at the cafe had garnered some attention from the media. The owner had personally thanked her for it, but it was in poor taste if she was honest. Greer might have been a bad person, but she didn't lack social skills. A detail the cafe lacked was being respectful to the parents of missing children.

Mrs. Palit and Mrs. McBride waited patiently for her to show. They were pleasant women, if not a little emotional given the circumstances, who had been kind to Greer since she was a child. For this, she could truly say she was grateful.

A shame it all had to turn out like this.

"I'm sorry I'm late." Greer slid into their usual booth, bypassing the sun-bleached missing person bulletin of Skylar she pretended not to notice, and smiled at the two women. "I had a call from my brother I couldn't ignore."

"Don't worry." Mrs. McBride laid a gentle hand over her own, giving it a squeeze. "Thank you for meeting us again."

"It's the least I can do. Honest."

"You have done so much already," said Mrs. Palit.

"Have you heard anything at all?"

Their conversations almost always went like this, like they were all reading from the same script. Greer knew they hadn't heard anything—why should they, when she's the one supplying the information? Still, she asked.

Mrs. McBride sniffed. "No. The investigator is still looking. He says, given the amount of time that's passed, he doesn't know if ..." And the tears started.

Mrs. Palit clenched her fists and kept her face as schooled as possible. "They are giving up on us. If it were their daughters, they wouldn't be so quick to judge."

"I know." Greer dropped her head. "I wish there was something I could tell you to make this all better, but I never heard a word from Bonnie or Nadia about leaving, or ... anything else. They were always so cheerful."

Sometimes, Greer wondered how they would react if she came clean. If she told them she knew what happened to Bonnie and Nadia. That she knew their killer was her own baby brother and she helped hide it because she could never deal with the pain if he was the one locked up.

She wondered what their pain would be like knowing the truth. Would it be agonizing enough to end themselves, or would they be foolish enough to seek vengeance? There was nothing they could do to bring the girls back. Death was permanent. A gory death, life shattering.

Maybe, they would try to have them locked up forever. Greer almost snorted. It's futile, surely women as smart as Mrs. Palit and Mrs. McBride recognized this. The Mageses did a lot for this community. They owned the police. They were the law. It was out of the graciousness of Greer's heart that she put on this charade and danced around for her dear departed friends' families to feel there's hope.

The simple reality is, if the truth were known, everything would come crashing down, and Greer would be there for the fallout. She would have the very tedious job of picking up all the pieces. This *meeting* was the least she could do after Grayson murdered Bonnie and Nadia. He didn't even do it for a good reason, which made it all extra painful.

"We could never repay you for the debt we owe you."

No, they couldn't.

"Don't worry about it. What matters is we find Bonnie and Nadia, and we bring them home safely. I know they're out there somewhere, alive."

But they weren't. They were rotting in her home at that very moment.

The three of them finished up brunch, speaking of lighter subjects. Greer smiled and played along.

They weren't really friends, Greer reminded herself. *They were accessories.*

Greer knew she could have used girls who were more well to do, popular (but, no one was more popular or well liked than them), it was a fun project, turning the two of them into something like her.

Bonnie and Nadia knew their places. They were clever like that. So clever, they often played it down. She supposed that was what made them such good cronies. It was really a shame they weren't around anymore.

She remembered one of the first real conversations she had with the two of them was just after she transferred into the Sunwick Grove Middle School district. It was seventh grade and they were two of the few survivors of a blowout fight between both Grayson and Greer. It was all because of the amulets.

The news would later call it a "terrorist act" and they would eventually hunt down and falsely imprison a man, all because of the power of the amulets.

For her, it all started when Grayson confronted her.

He didn't want her to pick on the girls who liked him or wanted to be his friend anymore. And Grayson had seen her use the amulet to make Poppy Beck's lungs stop working, but it wasn't like she was going to kill her. She had just wanted to give the girl a good scare, to keep her away.

Greer remembered being furious, not because she was caught, but because Grayson was furious. He didn't understand she only did it to protect him! The show was new and Greer knew for a fact those snobby middle school girls only wanted her brother because he was cool, and she wouldn't allow him to be used that way. The two of them had a heated screaming match, shouting things Greer knew they both didn't mean. Students gathered around them to watch, but this was their mistake.

She felt sick. Not ill, but sick. She was terrified she'd made an enemy out of her brother, and she couldn't handle it. Her shoulders kept shaking and the back of her neck burned hot. It was his words that made her feel sick. His words started the fight.

An unbearable feeling built up inside of her. It was like the worst mix of emotions she could think of—anxiety, anger, fear, crushing sadness—and they all pressed down heavily on her. The amulet pulsed and throbbed, emitting a low buzzing noise an instant before a huge purple bubble exploded from her body and she burned like white hot fire.

Instinctively, Grayson threw his arms up to protect himself and a blue wall surrounded him. It didn't seem like enough, but it saved him. In fact, her magic bent around his own. She couldn't touch him.

Later, he would tell her he didn't do it. The amulet protected him. That was when they learned they could not hurt each other with their powers. It was also the first time they hurt people. Lots of people.

Greer could recall seeing those closest to her, getting blown back, slamming against the brick wall of the school. They just ... flew. It was strange, macabre, and yet serene all at once. No one made a sound because it all happened too fast for them to comprehend. Other students were thrown over the fence and wrapped around playground equipment.

Her magic shattered glass, bent metal, splintered wood and ripped clothes to shreds. In an instant, their schoolyard looked like a war zone. Everyone laid in haphazard, broken heaps; all motionless. They would later learn the 'terrorist attack' killed six kids and hospitalized dozens more.

Grayson stormed off, leaving her to stew in her thoughts and revel in her new powers.

She remembered staring at an old picnic bench. The thing was rarely used because it was rough to sit on, but as she let her eyes fall across it, she realized they had been complaining about nothing before. Now, it was just kindling, all because of a fight.

That's when she had felt the tap on her foot. At first, it startled her because in her thirteen-year-old mind, everyone was out cold. But not everyone. There were two girls at her feet, tattered and in shock.

Greer took them both in, with little interest. She still felt rather sick, but in her hazy mind, she could somewhat recognize their faces. They both were outcasts, unlike her. One was on the chubby side with a rat's nest of auburn hair, and the other wore a set of broken glasses.

"What do you want?" she had asked them.

"W-What are you?" The one with the glasses had asked in a raspy voice.

Greer felt both a little irked and prided by this. "I'm human, same as you, but better."

"Are you ... actually m-magic?" the other girl stammered.

Her Grandfather had warned against telling people. If they knew, they might try and take their angel, or they might try and bring harm to the family. So, instead, she shrugged. "Who are you two? You're in my class, yeah?"

"Y-Yeah. I'm Nadia. Palit." The little girl with glasses said, pushing herself up on her knees. Greer made a mental note of her name and injuries. A large gash that ran across her eyebrow and her glasses missing a lens.

"Bonnie McBride." said the other.

Greer watched Grayson out of the corner of her eye, swing open the boy's locker room door. His face was tearful. She could see those neon blue's—which seemed so odd on his face—flick between her and the two girls. She knew what was going on in his mind.

She tilted her head, shaking it out of her mind. Let him think that. "Do you two want to be my friends?" Greer had asked them.

It was an obvious choice.

The two of them still seemed to be shaking cobwebs from their minds otherwise they might have given a different answer. Only moments prior Greer proved to be a very serious threat to their safety. It didn't matter.

Greer needed allies; people she could always keep close. In return, they could think they were her friends. She'd throw them a bone every now and again—a sleepover, a mall trip, a girls day, etc.—but she knew their real purpose, and it was not someone to vent to or to have mani-pedi with.

When she arrived back home, she half-hoped Grayson would be there already; but he wasn't. Their driveway never looked emptier. She had just crossed through the door when her phone rang, the second time that morning. Greer's excitement got the best of her and she answered it fast. It had to have been Grayson calling.

She answered the phone. "Hey—!"

"*Greer, baby!*" The voice on the opposite end of the phone was loud and obnoxious. It was not Grayson's soft, deep voice that she expected to hear. "*What's this about you and your brother wanting a break? You know, we've talked about this before. Breaks are bad for business.*"

"Willy," Greer grit her teeth.

William Speck, big-shot manager who worked for many A-list movie stars and recording artists, just-so-happened to *discover* the twins when they were starting out. If *discover* meant their grandfather ensorcelled him over the phone and thus thrust them into fame.

"You know Grays and I work non-stop. We even do holidays for you. Now, what is so bad about taking off for a week or two?"

"*The people—they want more. You know how it is.*" Willy, their manager, huffed. "*I'll be straight with you, kid. Magic shows are on the out. We must keep this momentum going! Strike while the iron is hot, ya know?"* Greer snorted. Debatable. *"You two ain't kids anymore."*

It wasn't 'being straight'. This was the same speech Greer heard from Willy almost every time she got a call from him.

"And us as kid magicians was amazing, yes I know Willy, but here's the thing," Greer cocked her hip and rested against the wall. "We aren't trashing the show for the sake of making it more 'adult'."

"N-Now, I never said that did I?"

"Don't stutter," she demanded.

No, the man never explicitly said he wanted them to drop the family atmosphere, but it was in the papers he sent over. It was in his nudging. And, in person, it was in his thoughts. Willy was a sleazy man, but he was one of the best in the game. It was the only reason the twins still used him.

"All I'm sayin' is Vegas would be happy to house you and your brother for a while. I think it would really up your status instead of you all living out there in the middle of nowhere."

"Vegas is a no."

"Because of Grayson, I know, but if you could just talk to him—"

"He doesn't really listen to me right now." Greer tapped her foot against the floor. She was never truly opposed to Vegas. It seemed like a good next step. Magicians were a dime a dozen there, though. Grayson seemed to think it would cheapen them. And then, there was the issue with their grandfather. "Listen. Grays is on a honeymoon—"

"*Another?*"

"I *know*. Anyway, he needs to get this out of his system. We both need a break, just for a little while. During this time, we can work on some ... *rebranding*."

Willy clapped his hands. "*Oh baby, you just made me the happiest man in the world. I'll send some papers for you to look over.*"

"Yeah yeah. Do we have a deal or not, William?"

The man snorted. "*Of course, baby. You all take all the time you need. We'll need to work on your image and some new costumes. Just promise me you'll talk to your brother about Vegas again.*"

"I'll talk to him."

Willy hung up and Greer sighed. Grayson had better kiss the ground she walked on when he returned.

XII

ODETTE

Frantic knocking urged Odette and Clara out of their seats at the breakfast table. They exchanged looks. Odette's mouth pulled into a grim line, and she backed away towards the couch ducking down.

"I thought you said no one would be back today."

Clara shook her head, eyes wide. "They shouldn't be."

Odette's skepticism was not eased. Clara wasn't the type to trick her, but that didn't change the fact someone they didn't know was at the door. Clara motioned for her to get down; and Odette crouched behind the couch, watching her at the door.

The door exploded before she could touch the handle and Clara was blown back by the blast, landing mere feet away from where Odette hid.

Odette swore under her breath and sprung up to her friend's side. "Are you—?!"

Her speech was cut short, the wind knocked out of her as a second blast was set off. Odette was airborne and smashed into the opposite wall. She braced herself for the drop but it never came. Iridescent, blue chains shot out from the doorway and wrapped around her neck, arms, and feet. They kept her cemented to the wall, dangling her helplessly.

"Why'd you do it, Odette?" Grayson stepped through the threshold. "If you had stayed, I wouldn't have to kill these people."

Then she saw the fire. It consumed everything outside as far as the eye could see. Smoke filled the room. Odette tried to hold her breath but she couldn't. It had already gotten in her lungs. She coughed and wheezed, fighting against her bonds.

"It's useless. Now, because of your actions, we burn together."

Fire crawled along the ceiling, closing in on her at rapid speed.

"No, no, no! Grayson stop!"

His image flickered and vanished into a puff of dust. In his place was a tall, wiry man with ink black hair. A single stripe of his hair was silver.

"*Thorn?*"

Upon the sight of him, the chains and fire melted away into thin air. The nightmarish version of Clara's house was wiped away, returning to normal in the blink of an eye.

Thorn dusted off his vest and ash fell to the ground. "Apologies for the fright. I-I couldn't get away, this is the only safe way to t-talk to you."

Odette eyed him warily. Thorn had the powers of entering the mind, and often interacted with her via her dreams. She used to forget the dreams they shared, which was the product of the strong magic surrounding him. However, Thorn had done his best to help her retain the memories of their time together; whenever he visited, it was important, something she needed to remember.

"Why are you here?"

"I've come with a warning." He motioned to the home. "This place is no longer safe. I have tried my best to keep them at bay, but I fear my attempts were futile. He won't be fooled again."

From his vest, he produced a pocket watch. He stared at it for a good, long moment before tucking it back in his clothes.

"I don't understand."

"You need to relocate. I shall do my best to divert them."

Odette held up her hand to silence him. "Explain to me what is going on. I don't know what you mean." But before she could continue there was a nagging sensation at the back of her mind. She didn't want to believe it.

Thorn sighed; half of his face uncovered from the mask contorted. "Why are you here?"

"That's what I'm asking you—"

"No, Odette Sinclair. Why are you *here*?" The location shifted and the two of them were suddenly outside.

Welcome to Crabtree, Oregon, the sign read.

Why was she ... there?

Odette's lips parted. All this time, she believed she had done it on her own; that her ring sensed her extreme emotions and suddenly sparked to life. But this wasn't the case, was it. It was all him.

"You ..."

Thorn nodded slowly. "I have done my best up until now to keep you hidden from them."

"This is all your fault." Odette clutched her chest. Her heart was beating rapidly. It was painful, making her head spin. "Because of *you*, I could lose the only people I have left."

He set his jaw. "Everything I have done was for your best interest. To protect you, and your child."

"Screw you!" Odette grabbed her head. This couldn't be true. Thorn wouldn't be so reckless. But there he was, admitting it to her. "You know what he's capable of—this isn't protecting me; this is a set up! I thought you were my friend!"

"I have your best interest at heart," he assured her. "*Please* understand." Thorn laid a hand on her shoulder. "You have come so far. I know you can make it. Grayson hasn't discovered your location yet. You need to keep moving."

Odette chewed on her lip. She planned on skipping town as soon as possible.

"How is he tracking me?" she asked. Maybe there was something she could do to make things harder for Grayson, then maybe she'd have a chance.

Thorn remained silent.

"*How*, Thorn?"

He reached down and grasped her hand, bringing it up between them. Odette opened her mouth, about to ask again; but she knew what he meant. A knot formed in her stomach. *The ring.*

Unfortunately, there was no masking it. The ring was permanently fixed on her finger, no amount of twisting or pulling made it any looser. She learned months ago only Grayson and Thorn could remove it. Otherwise, if she wanted it off, she'd have to chop the finger off. She winced.

"Take it from me." she urged. "It belongs to you anyway, yeah? Well, I don't need it. It doesn't work."

Thorn pressed a finger against her lips, effectively silencing her.

"Don't say that," he warned. He removed his finger, cupping her cheek momentarily then dropped his hand. "No. That is just a rock. The powers you have are mine." Thorn pushed her hand back towards her. "I will not take it from you. Would if I could but it will be important to you on your journey. I can keep tabs on you this way."

Odette grit her teeth. It was truly hopeless. Despite what she was trying to do, what Thorn was trying to help her with, they both knew it was hopeless. Grayson would find her. She had a bad feeling the longer this chase went on, the worse his wrath would be.

"You're waking up." Thorn stated.

"Wait!" Odette grasped the cuff of his sleeve. "If Grayson gets me, and everything goes south, promise me something?"

He had a nervous look in his eye. All the same, he nodded.

"He can't hurt my friends. Please. They have to live, okay? Skylar, too. *They have to live.*" Thorn inhaled sharply. Before she heard his reply, her eyes opened and he was gone.

"Hey sleepyhead." Clara was leaning over her, her eyes large. "Wake up. I have breakfast on the table."

Odette rubbed her eyes. The dream with Thorn clung to her like a second skin. Grayson was onto her. Or he would be. It was confusing, but she wouldn't waste the tip.

The room smelled of sugary breakfast pastries. Clara had them laid out on the dining table on paper plates, smothered in a mountain of frosting. Odette's stomach rumbled at the sight.

She had just sat down when there was a frantic knocking on the door. Her heart practically stopped in her chest.

No!

It couldn't be him. Not so soon. Thorn said she would have more time.

Clara looked to Odette; confusion written all over her face. "I'm not expecting anyone today."

Odette rose with her. Her palms pricked with anticipation as Clara headed for the front door. "Wait, no. Maybe we shouldn't—"

But Clara didn't listen. She opened the door.

XIII

ODETTE

A gloved hand popped through first. Next came the bent
head, and the winter toboggan was pulled off to reveal
a cloud of blond hair.

"Finally! Did you want *Officer Dad* to catch me skipping
school?" Felix entered the home and shut the door hard
behind him. He tossed his hat and gloves onto a nearby
chair. He flexed his fingers repeatedly, then cracked the
stiff knuckles.

Odette sighed, her body sagging against the dining room
table. "Felix, thank God! You nearly gave me a heart attack.
How about calling or something next time?"

"Sorry, but—" He stopped, and his eyes bugged. "You're
blonde!"

Odette touched the ends of her hair. The bleach job had
taken forever last night. Now, her hair was a strange
yellow-reddish color, coarse between her fingertips. She

didn't even recognize herself when she looked in the mirror.

"How does it look?" she asked.

"... Yellow?"

Odette accepted that answer. The dye job wasn't the best, even with Clara's touch-ups, but it didn't have to look good. It had to be different. She didn't want to look remotely similar to her old self, anything to throw Grayson off, should it come to that.

"Why are you skipping?" Clara asked.

"What, you think you can and I can't?" Felix rolled his eyes. "I'm not missing out on this. Besides, I'm the one with the license. If we need to make a quick get-away, I'm the man. Shorty over here can't even reach the petals."

He rested his elbow on Clara's head. She punched him in the gut. Felix nursed his stomach, smiling through the pain.

Odette tapped her lips in thought. Thorn's warning ran clear in her mind. She did not know how much time she had left.

"Since you're offering, I need you to take me somewhere."

"Where?"

"Boardman Airport."

Felix's eyebrows jumped. "That's almost two hours away. We have an airport in Dayville that's—"

"I know what we have." she bristled.

Her head throbbed with frustration. Odette grit her teeth. It would be so much easier if they didn't question her motives. A dark thought crossed her mind. It may be easy to make them listen, but she stopped the thought there. Odette turned away from them, horrified with herself.

Taking away their will would be something Grayson would do. She wasn't him. If she needed to, Odette would have to convince them the old-fashioned way. The only way, in her book.

"Boardman is further away. I have less of a chance of being recognized up there. If we go anywhere else around here, there's no telling who we would run into."

Clara and Felix exchanged looks.

"Then we go there."

Felix nodded. He plopped down by the kitchen table and grabbed an uneaten pastry from the plate. "You two better go and get ready."

Odette nodded staunchly. The sooner they left, the better.

"Where are you planning on running off to?" Clara passed Odette a thick white sweater through the crack of the bathroom door. "And are you sure you want to do it like this?"

Odette slipped the sweater on over her head. "I don't know."

To be honest, Odette wasn't sure of anything. With every strategic move she came up with, she was pulled back to the same thought—*what would happen if ...?*

At this point, it was obvious what would happen if she was caught. Grayson's quick temper leads to him taking rash actions. The amulets kept the wearers from harming one another with magic and some physical violence, but there were grey areas. Grayson was aware of these. Odette guessed it was how he and his sister had gotten back at one another throughout the years.

The last time Odette caused him to become truly enraged, she had to deal with his wrath. He destroyed her room and put dead animals in her closet or bathroom. The scent of blood hadn't washed out of the room.

What would he do this time? Would her actions make him reach his breaking point with her? Odette learned not long ago; it didn't take much for Grayson to kill his past lovers. The most common occurrence was they all left him.

Odette realized she had stopped breathing. Her lungs ached. She inhaled deeply and clung to the sink counter.

Clara opened the door all the way. "You don't look so well."

She glanced side-long at her friend. Her eyebrows were pushed together, and her lips were pursed. Hot sweat trickled down her back.

"Italy," Odette blurted out. "I could get a tan there."

Clara's expression brightened. She leaned against the doorframe and nodded. "Imagine how the pizza would taste ..." The two girls sighed and shared a smile. "Do you think you can handle it as you are, though?"

She turned away. Her stare remained on the pair of fake glasses that rested in her hands. "My plan is to get the next flight out of here. I'll be fine wherever."

Even if she wasn't fine, she had to be. Odette slipped the glasses onto her face and stared into her reflection. She didn't look remotely like her old self. No one would give her a second glance.

"I'm on your side one-hundred-percent, you know." Clara came up behind her, her face scrunched. "But ... are you certain none of this could be solved by talking with Grayson Mages, or your parents?"

Odette ground her teeth together. It was still bitter to swallow. She wanted to smack Clara and cry to her at the same time. They were dead. But how could she tell her that without telling her everything?

"No. This is what I have to do." Odette grabbed the baseball cap from Clara's counter and fitted it on her head.

Not five minutes later they were outside. Clara locked up, tossing her keys in her bag. Odette took a step back, staring at the Niesenson's home for the last time. She didn't have a picture of it, all of them had burned in the fire, so she would have to do her best to ingrain it in her memory.

Or maybe not. Odette turned away from the home and stuffed her hands in her jacket pockets. Perhaps it would be best if she simply forgot everything about everyone, just like she wanted them to do with her. A clean slate for her fresh start.

Thick, grey clouds gathered in the sky. Snow was coming, Odette could smell it. Felix eyed the clouds skeptically before unlocking the car. The trio piled in, tossing their bags in the back, then set off on their destination.

"We shouldn't run into any snow yet," Felix said. "But there is a storm coming. It's supposed to be big."

Odette wondered if the storm might hide her from Grayson's tracking.

"It's a good thing we left when we did." Clara rummaged through her purse and pulled out her phone. "We'll have a head start." She thumbed through the weather app, looking at the forecast for the next several hours. Odette watched as animated flurries fell across the screen.

XIV

GRAYSON

A loud *thunk* drew Thorn away from his work. He looked up, his head brushing against the twinkle-lights, which hung from the attic rafters.

He abandoned the little model house he was painting and went to the small circular window that sat above his desk. It was dark out, dawn on the horizon. The air was thick with the promise of snow. Thorn peered down into the driveway; his paintbrush held aloft.

Grayson was home.

Thorn's cat-like eye spied through the darkness, down in the driveway. Grayson's car had materialized, the boy laying in a heap on the hood.

Hmm, he teleported here all on his own. That could have killed him, but Thorn was not concerned. It wasn't his time yet.

Thorn sighed and abandoned the brush on his desk. In a matter of seconds, he materialized outside on the steps. Thorn stuck to the shadows, lest he be discovered by a nosy outsider. It was cold out, the bitter wind brushing across his face. He reached up and chastised himself, realizing he'd left his mask up in the attic. Oh well, what did it matter? If Grayson was conscious, (Which he wasn't, thankfully.) he would've preferred Thorn without it, wanting to enjoy the misery of his face.

Grayson hadn't moved an inch from the hood. Now that he was closer, Thorn could hear the boy wheezing. His chest rose and fell in short, staccato breathes. No, he wouldn't wake, Thorn determined as he inched closer. The boy was out cold.

His pallor was severe, taking on a greenish hue; and his eyes had a purplish ring surrounding them, appearing sunken in and bruised. Ash covered his coat, his hair, and the tips of his fingers, blackening them and possibly hiding burns that needed care.

Thorn tutted, already imagining the pain he would soon experience. "Greer will not like this."

Grayson awoke in his bed. A disgusting stale taste lingered in his mouth and his limbs felt like they had been reduced to jelly. One of his old black-and-white movies played on TV, the volume low but buzzing in his ears.

For a moment, Grayson couldn't remember anything. A fog settled over his mind, glossing over the events of the hours prior. How had he gotten home? The last thing he remembered was a town—that god-awful town—and fire. But even that was fuzzy.

Grayson ground his teeth. He was not a fan of being left in the dark, especially by his own mind. What he could piece together was it had something to do with magic. It always boiled down to that. Magic was the root of all his issues and yet he needed it.

Shakily, he pushed himself upright. The simple movement exhausted him. Black dots swam through his vision, dancing over his head in swirling, blobbing patterns. He squeezed his eyes shut, and when he opened them again.

His gaze circled the room lazily, hoping to pick up on something to help him remember before. Over his desk chair sat a heavy wool coat, bits of the fabric discolored and singed. He could smell the smoke from where he sat.

Grayson pushed the covers off and placed his feet on the floor. They pricked with numbness, the static climbing all the way up his calves and digging in deep. He walked anyway.

Each step was a challenge making him knock into random objects and have them scrape against the floor. If his sister didn't know he was awake, she did now.

Grayson dropped into the chair, the coat to his back. He ignored how short of breath he became after doing something as simple as walking and pushed his hand into the coat pockets. It had obviously been worn recently.

A piece of paper brushed against his fingers. He grasped it hard and pulled it out. It was folded crudely, much too large for the pocket, and caught on the edges. He had to yank on it a few times before it gave out.

It wasn't a piece of paper, Grayson realized. The more he unfolded it, the more the crinkled image became clear. It was Odette. Memories rushed forth like a rush of air. The photo dropped to the ground and landed face down.

"Thorn!"

Greer was the first to his door. She seemed to be just as disheveled as he, in her pajamas and wild hair. She looked around first, not seeing Grayson where he was sitting in the chair.

"Grays—Oh, there you are." She stepped back and clutched her heart. "You scared me! How are you? What happened? Thorn scared me when he said you were back, but you looked like ..."

'crap.' He finished silently. That was fair, he certainly felt like crap. Grayson rubbed the heel of his palm against his eyes. "Where is Thorn?"

"I'm sure he's on his way."

Greer looked around the room once again before inching inside slowly. She perched herself on the far edge of his bed and didn't say a word. He expected her to gloat, she'd been right after all, but Greer stayed quiet. Grayson scrutinized her, waiting for the moment when she snapped and taunted him for his failure. It didn't happen. She only sat there and stared at her hands, apparently deep in thought.

Thorn entered and brought the shadows with him. His posture was reminiscent of a wilted flower. His hands fidgeted with his gloves every few seconds, and he did not look at Grayson.

"You called?"

"Odette wasn't there." Grayson ran a hand over his face, then added, "Obviously."

Greer leaned forward; her eyebrows furrowed. "How could she trick you?"

"I knew something was off the moment I arrived, but what I found solidified my earlier thoughts. There was a spell, I had no idea she was aware of how to do something like that. It was advanced, well beyond her, and good enough to trick me into going to this location."

"How is that possible?" asked Greer. "She shouldn't know how to do anything."

Grayson shrugged his shoulders and moved on. "I'll have to start from scratch. I don't think she knows I've found her spell, but it won't matter. She has a whole day on me now."

Greer sniffed, her face hardening. "She won't stop. Who knows where she's gone to, now."

"That's why I need to get started immediately."

There's no time to lose.

Thorn nodded solemnly.

"If she diverted you once, what makes you think she won't do it again?"

"A hunch." He peered at the angel from the side of his eye. "That kind of magic would exhaust her even if she's mastered it. She couldn't have gotten far."

Greer slammed her hand against the mattress, so suddenly it startled him. "Why are you even bothering with her? This is so stupid—you've never allowed a girl to walk all over you like this before! Why now?"

"She has my son, Greer."

"Oh, please!" She rolled her eyes. "Like you won't have another chance to be a father. We're *young*, Grayson. There are plenty of devoted fans out there who would willingly have your baby. You don't need Odette. She's trouble and you know it."

"Don't talk about her like that," he warned.

"Or *what*?" She raised her eyebrows, challenging him. "What are you gonna do? You know I'm right, you're just too stubborn to admit it!"

The air crackled around Grayson. Anger flared within his chest burning him from the inside out. Objects around him lifted off the ground.

"Do you really think that's going to scare me?"

A lamp flung towards her. It would have flown into her head had the transparent purple barrier not formed at the last moment. Instead it smashed into bits, some parts hovering in the air stuck in the shield. It vanished, and the pieces crumpled to the ground.

"Someone has to tell you how to run your life, Grays, or else you do stupid things like chase after a girl who wants nothing to do with you."

Greer's words were razors, tearing at the edges of the pit and making it larger one chip at a time. He clenched his fists hard.

He didn't want to listen to her, but there was the smallest bit of him that considered her words. What if what Greer said was true? Was he clinging to Odette too hard? Was she just another lost cause, like all the others?

No, she had to be different. Her feelings were genuine at first. Grayson had seen those same feelings resurface time after time, even if she tried to hide it. Odette was scared. He could understand that because he was scared too. Together, they could learn to love again.

The objects dropped, landing in their rightful places.

"She gets one more chance." His voice sounded raw in his own ears. "I will not hurt her unless she forces my hand."

Greer's lips twisted, but she did not shout again. She nodded stiffly, but Grayson could see it in her eyes—she expected death.

"Please leave," he grumbled. Greer exited the room with grace, a little bounce in her step, and did not look back again. Thorn, too, turned to leave; but Grayson held up his hand to stop him. "Not you."

Once the door shut, Grayson turned his glare to Thorn.

Neither of them spoke for several moments. Grayson sized him up, eyeing the nasty scars on his face. It had been a while since he'd gotten a new one, all his old lashes fully healed. Grayson hadn't laid a hand on this ... *vermin*, since Odette had taken his amulet. She asked one thing of him, a troublesome promise, but up until now he'd honored it: *don't hurt Thorn.*

But Odette wasn't here now. From his point of view, she'd broken the only promise he asked of her: don't leave me. Simple, right? Much simpler than hers.

It would only be fair to break his promise, too. You know, an eye for an eye and all that.

The longer the quiet held, the more discomfort showed on Thorn's face. He knew what was going to happen.

Rage boiled in Grayson's blood. Thorn couldn't hide his guilt; it was written all over his face. His mouth pulled into a deep frown and he shied away from Grayson, shrinking back towards the door.

"It was you."

"I-I don't know what you mean—"

"Are you really denying it?" Grayson shook his head. "All you're doing is making this harder on Odette."

Still, Thorn didn't confess. His thin lips remained sealed; his nostrils flared.

Grayson lowered his voice. "Does she know?"

It would be just as bad if she did know. Having Thorn be so close to his wife on an everyday basis made his skin crawl but imagining they had been scheming for her to leave in secret made it so much worse. How much was he not aware of?

"She doesn't," Thorn muttered.

The words brought no relief to Grayson, strangely. "What did you *think* would happen when I found your little spell in Tadmor?"

Thorn swallowed and clasped his hands together. "I wanted to give her more time."

"*Why?*" His carefully constructed facade was cracking. "You know she is mine!"

"I swore to protect her," Thorn answered honestly.

Grayson sputtered. He threw himself from the chair, unable to sit still any longer. "What do you think I have been doing since she arrived?!" Chains wound around Thorn's neck at their own accord and brought him to his knees. "She is mine to protect, Thorn! You—you have—"

Grayson shouted and tugged on the magic chains. They burned white-hot, singing Thorn's skin. He screamed, but the sound wasn't human; it was animal, a howl that sent chills down the spine and made the hairs on the back of your neck raise.

Thorn tried to claw at his chains, but his hands passed right through them. His fingernails left deep, red marks down his throat. Any harder and he would draw blood.

"You are nothing but scum!" Grayson spat. "Ever since she arrived, you've tried to tear her away from me! *Why?!*"

More chains. They wrapped around Thorn's torso and bound his legs. Spikes protruded, piercing and ripping the creature's skin causing it to bleed, filling the room with the scent of blood. It spilled onto the floor, but it wasn't red like a humans. It was silver at first, then black when it touched the floor as it withered and died. The blood was as much a living thing as Thorn.

"Am I not allowed to be loved?!" Grayson screamed, his shouts rattling the walls around them.

Thorn's gargled cries became worse. Blood dribbled past his lips, one of the spikes piercing his cheek and wedged between his teeth. Grayson did not give him the option to speak, even if he wanted to.

"I won't be refused any more. No one is going to stand in my way—not you, or Greer, or any of your little tricks! Understand?!"

Thorn nodded rapidly, whimpering. He didn't care about how the spikes dug deeper, or that moving made it worse, he needed Grayson to know he was sincere. He needed the pain to stop.

But Grayson wasn't done yet, he needed the monster to suffer. Grayson knelt beside Thorn, his voice barely above a whisper. "Then I want you to take me to where my Odette really is."

XV

ODETTE

They didn't beat the storm. Twenty minutes into the drive, flurries descended from the sky. Odette pressed her face against the window and stared up at the clouds. They were an angry grey as they swirled and twisted. The wind howled like a dying beast outside, blowing the flurries rapidly.

Ten more minutes passed and not much changed, but Odette could feel it in her bones. There was more to this storm.

"I hope this is as much as we're going to get," Felix commented. He craned his neck upwards once they stopped at a light, watching the way the snow fell.

Clara scrolled through her phone absentmindedly. "The weather app says there was only a forty percent chance, but ... They're already talking about cancelling flights."

Two pairs of eyes stared back at her through the rearview mirror. They both looked at her expectantly, waiting for her to add her two cents.

"It'll get worse." Odette turned back towards the window. "Can't you tell? Look at the sky."

Felix snorted. "The appearance of the sky doesn't really mean anything. I'm sure we'll be fine."

Not an hour later the roads were blanketed, and snow was falling so bad they could barely see. They needed to pull off the road. Felix commented they were small flakes too, implying it wouldn't stop any time soon.

Odette felt frustrated. Though she didn't want them to be injured by the storm, and the airport had no doubt closed down due to weather, they were losing time. The longer they lingered in one place, the more dangerous everything became. Though, without another visit from Thorn, Odette could only be so sure.

Odette reminded herself, Thorn wouldn't lie. He wasn't the type. If he said there was danger, she could not afford to doubt him.

"Look!" Clara pointed off to the left. "I think it's a motel. We can probably wait this out there."

It was hard to see, anything beyond ten feet was a white sheet of nothing. And yet, as they drove toward it, Odette could see the lit up yellow-and-red neon signs. None of them complained. Felix parked haphazardly in the lot. The snow had covered so much, no one could tell where the lines began or ended.

The sign flickered in red neon, Hollywood Motel. It certainly wasn't the best place to camp out in but judging from the outside it was much cleaner than the others they had driven past. At the very least recently remodeled.

Odette adjusted her jacket and hat in the rearview mirror, then spoke. "I'll deal with the person inside. You guys stay here and work on getting our stuff."

If my powers decide to work at all, Odette thought, *there's no way I want them anywhere near me.*

Thankfully, neither of them complained. Odette shouldered her backpack and headed for the main office, a cheesy '*Hey, we're open!*' sign hung from the door. She had to force her weight against the door, as the hinges were frozen solid and made no effort to move on her first attempt. The door squeaked as it opened, resisting her every step of the way, until she had it open wide enough that she could step inside. Odette fell back against the dingy door, and it slammed shut, startling the manager.

The inside wasn't much better than outdoors. The room was practically an ice box. There was an electric heater in the corner, but it appeared to be nothing more than an ornament now, collecting dust rather than heating the space. Odette watched her breath puff out in small clouds as she exhaled.

Behind the desk was the manager, who might have been sleeping up until she entered, as his thoughts didn't make much of an impression on her. Those types of people—the ones with dull minds—were the easiest to use magic on, according to Greer.

He was a middle-aged man, bundled up with so many layers that the only part of his face readily visible was a pair of bloodshot, beady eyes.

Odette stopped right in front of him and smiled. He might have smiled back, but his dull eyes gave away nothing. With every ounce of energy she had left, she focused her intention on her voice. "I need a room for a night."

There was a long pause before the eyes finally blinked. The man sighed, his voice muffled by his many scarves, and said, "ID."

Odette quickly patted her pant pockets, then moved to her bag. She withdrew her ID. It was old, probably expired, but it was one of the things to appear in her backpack when she conjured supplies. The manager's eyes only glossed over it.

"That'll be ninety-nine dollars."

Odette's smile wavered. "N-No. *I need one room for a night.*"

Again, she forced every ounce of power she had in her voice. She could hear it, echoing in the room. It bounced around, whispering like the wind.

The man rolled his eyes and unclasped his hands. He pointed to a sign on the wall, with pricings for rooms. "That'll be *ninety-nine dollars.*"

It was useless.

She huffed, her nostrils flaring. Odette jammed her hand in her pocket and pulled out her dwindling wad of cash. At this rate, she wouldn't be able to afford a plane ticket—or food. It just didn't make sense. Earlier, she had been able to do magic, why couldn't she now? Was it need based? She needed that money.

Reluctantly, Odette passed over the money to the manager. He shuffled around behind the desk for a moment, then returned with a key, the number worn and scratched on the plastic piece.

"Thanks ..." *For nothing.*

She couldn't really blame him, she guessed. It was all her. Maybe Greer had said that people like him were the *hardest* to use magic on. Whatever. It didn't matter now. She just needed to get out of town. If Grayson were to show up at this moment, Odette wouldn't be able to defend herself.

The trio hurried inside; a blast of warmth hit them as the door opened. Odette's fake glasses fogged up instantly, but she didn't mind. The warmth spread to her fingers and toes, and her discomfort from before nearly vanished.

The room was much warmer compared to the main office she had been in minutes before, but no less dingy. Still, it was a room.

She dumped her bag onto the floor, Felix following suit. Clara perched herself on a near-by chair, her phone out and her eyebrows furrowed.

"The airport is grounding all flights for a few hours. Possibly the whole day," Clara read aloud. "Unless all this clears up, you may need a backup plan."

Odette swore under her breath. *Of course they were.* She flopped onto the bed; her mood soured. There had to be *something* she could do, she wasn't entirely helpless, and she had gotten this far.

Maybe she could do the teleporting thing again ... but, Thorn had admitted to doing that, not her. If he was the power behind the ring, then maybe she had no control of it at all. He could have been the one making clothing and money appear, not her. If this was true, then Odette really didn't know the extent of her powers—for all she knew, it could all be a sham.

But Thorn was her friend. If he had been the one to pull-the-strings before, who was to say he couldn't do it again? All this time, he'd been promising he would keep her protected, and he finally made good.

If I could just speak to him again. Odette chewed on her lower lip. It wouldn't be too suspicious to take a nap, especially if all they could do was wait; but that didn't mean Thorn would come to her. He'd have to want to.

"So ... are we just waiting now?" asked Felix.

Odette nodded. "Yeah."

"Cool." He situated himself at the head of the bed and grabbed the remote, turning the TV on. He flipped through the channels, mindlessly at first, before tossing the remote with a groan. "There's nothing good on. I mean, it's daytime, what can you expect, but still."

His phone buzzed and he groaned. Felix nodded to Odette, "You pick something"

"What's wrong?" Odette laid the remote down beside her.

"It's just my dad." Felix shook his head, like the idea of his father calling was so bad. "This is sort of like a field trip, right?" Felix asked the room. Neither girl answered. "That's what I'm going to tell him. I can't *lie* ... but ... ya know."

Clara looked up from her own phone. "You could lie, you're just bad at it."

"Shut up."

Odette picked up the remote and played around with the channels. A particular image caught her attention and she paused on the station and turned the volume up a couple of notches.

"There are now three confirmed arson attacks along the Eastern coast, and possibly more, though authorities are reluctant to share."

The screen switched over to a burning building. Its fire raged red hot, the flames reaching out the broken windows. The image changed to one of rubble. It took Odette a moment to realize it was the same building as before, now reduced to nothing. Her hair stood on end as the icy tendrils of dread spread throughout her veins; she couldn't tear her eyes from the screen.

"Police have informed us there were at least two casualties in these incidents. One in Amity, New York; another in Tadmor, Ohio. A few people in the third incident were taken to the hospital. Law enforcement say there are no casualties to report, but at least one man is in critical condition."

Images of the destruction were thrown up on the screen, fast and uncaring. They flickered past, like the fire, and showed places that were affected were all now nothing but ash. Odette clutched the bedspread so hard her knuckles turned white.

This couldn't be coincidence. Her heart pounded hard in her chest, the flames flickering on screen dancing across her eyes. She could feel their heat and smell the smoke. These couldn't be random acts of arson, Odette stopped believing in coincidence a long time ago.

"He's sending a message."

"What?" Clara's voice was small; it barely registered in Odette's ears at all. "Who?"

Odette's head spun. She grasped her temples, but nothing would stop it. Those images were burned into her brain, a world on fire. It was like images she'd only seen in a nightmare, and Grayson knew it. He was bringing them to life. This had to be her punishment for running.

The newscaster showed a map of where the fires were. It all seemed to follow a pretty direct line, but the only oddity Odette could pick out, why was the last fire in Ohio? Where was he now? Eventually, Odette stopped herself. There wasn't a point in deciphering Grayson's madness. His only purpose in life was to create fear. If he hadn't found her already, he was about to.

Odette stood up fast, the muscles in her legs screaming for her to run. She didn't care where she went, she just had to go somewhere—anywhere—away from this room. She grabbed the ice bucket and dashed to the door.

"I'm going for a walk."

It's cliché to think of freshly fallen snow as a clean slate, because it isn't. It gives the illusion of a clean slate—a fresh start, but let the day warm up enough and you'll see the ugliness the snow was hiding.

Odette pressed herself up against her motel door and took deep breaths, inhaling the frosty air. Snow fell in heavy sheets, blanketing the parking lot and the cars in it. This might have been the first time in her life Odette wanted the snow to stop. She needed to get out, and it served as an icy barrier, keeping her from completing her goal.

Deep breaths.

Finally, her panic began to die down, and Odette rolled her shoulders. Her fingers tapped against the metal bucket—frigid against her thin fingers and looked down the open hall. Both ways seemed dismal, so she picked the left and began to walk. Though she grabbed the ice bucket, she didn't have a particular destination in mind, she'd only hoped it would give her a reasonable excuse to be out.

Somewhere behind her, the sound of a door opening caught her attention. Odette tensed, praying it wasn't Clara or Felix, but it didn't *sound* like either of them. The sound of footsteps approaching grew louder, until finally a small woman appeared in Odette's periphery.

Odette didn't want to look—she by no means wanted to engage in any unnecessary social interaction, but something about the woman's profile was familiar. Odette did a double take, but she couldn't remember ever meeting her in her life.

The woman caught her staring and gave her a polite-but-confused smile. "Sorry, but do you know where the ice machine is?"

"No, I'm trying to find it myself."

"Oh!" The woman perked up, and matched Odette's pace. Did she think she wanted to help her? "My friend brought soda and they are surprisingly warm for being exposed to this weather."

"I'm ... anemic." Inwardly, Odette chastised herself. There was no reason to keep talking to her. Something about the woman made her uncomfortable, but Odette couldn't put her finger on it. Perhaps she was just being paranoid.

They walked in silence the rest of the way, spotting the neon ICE signs overhead not long after.

Odette contemplated turning back, but if she didn't come back with ice Clara and Felix would question her about her outburst, and she felt strangely obligated to sell her anemia story. On the other hand, the woman stared a lot. It started out as normal, considering they had been talking to one another, but she just kept doing it.

Where have I seen her before? It was going to drive Odette nuts.

Finally, the wall dipped and inside were a couple of vending machines and the ice machine. A thin layer of dirty frost covered each of the machines, their lights flickering.

Obviously, no one had cleaned them in years. Odette was reluctant to touch the thing but approached it anyway.

Odette went first. She put her bucket under the dispenser, but before she could fill it, her hand was snatched away. Odette's bucket clattered to the ground with a loud bang, rolling away into a dark corner. The pain jarred Odette out of her sense of peace, the woman digging her nails into her wrist so hard they might as well be a permanent anchor.

"Hey—!" Odette tried to jerk away, but it only hurt worse.

"What a lovely ring ..." The woman's words, unlike before, were soft and dreamy. A dopey smile took up most of her face. "It matches your eyes."

Odette stiffened, pressing herself as far against the vending machine as she could. There was something wrong with her, and Odette felt if she even touched her clothes, she might die.

Once again, she tried to rip her hand away, but it didn't work. Her skin stung from where the woman's nails were digging in, hard enough to draw blood.

"Please ..." Odette ran her free hand slowly along the vending machine, reaching for anything she could use as a weapon. The bucket would have been perfect, but it had fallen too far from her. "You're hurting me."

"You're one of them," the woman whispered, nodding her head. "I'm certain of it. I can feel it in my bones."

"Just let me go."

"To think, plain old Camille Chen, would run into *you*." She laughed, as if it were the most amazing thing in the world and pulled on Odette's arm. "My prayers have been heard. They always say have patience and good things will come, well ...!"

What Odette would give to have her friends come and find her now. Shouldn't they suspect something was up? Surely, she'd been gone for at least ten minutes. Or did time only feel that way because of this fear?

Shakily, Odette took a deep breath—she had to remain calm. "I think you have the wrong person. I don't know you."

"I don't expect you to, but you can get to know me now. You know, so many people would kill to have this moment? They would be so jealous to think I was the one. Now, I don't expect you to make time for them all, but there are a few very good friends of mine I would love to introduce you to."

It was positively insane. The look on the woman's face was unlike anything Odette had ever seen before. It was pure adoration. There were actual tears in Camille's eyes the longer she looked at her.

That was when it hit her. *The TV*, Odette realized, *That's where I've seen her. That fake church ad.*

There was no way this was random. This had to be a trap. *He* had found her. He was using some sick girl and her beliefs to get to her.

Odette forced herself to lean in, her voice no louder than a whisper. "Is Grayson controlling you?"

At the mention of his name, Camille's eyes lit up in awe. No one, not even his most devoted fans, had ever looked that way when he was mentioned.

"You have no idea! There are always naysayers who tell us Higher Power has abandoned us, but I know that's not true. Have faith and be patient. Good things will come to you, and they have!" She took to stroking the ring, her fingers dancing along the metallic finishes.

Though she seemed convinced, Odette was not so sure. There were no tell-tale signs of Grayson's handy work. Her eyes were not glazed over, and they had no blue shine to them. While she couldn't make out all of her thoughts, Odette could hear enough to know she was not a mindless slave. Camille was as lucid as ever. That frightened Odette, because if she was not controlled by Grayson, then why would she act in such a way?

"What do you want from me?"

It was obvious Camille wasn't interested in money. The thing that caught her attention was the ring. This woman's attraction to the ring eerily reminded her of Claude, how he seemed to fixate on it when they spoke, even if he did know it held no power at the time. She would willingly give it away, now, if she could take the stupid thing off.

The girl shook her head. "I can't ask for anything. It is you who must give it to me."

"Please, let me go. I don't know who you are, or what it is you think I can give you; but whatever it is you're wrong."

"N-No—"

"Just leave me alone. Please."

As a last resort, Odette kicked Camille, hard. Her foot connected with the woman's shin and Camille released her with a howl. For good measure, she kneed her in the gut and broke into a sprint.

Camille started after her, shouting at the top of her lungs. "You can't go. We need you! *I* need you!" She was gaining on her. "Come back! Please!"

"You're crazy!"

A firm grasp wrapped around Odette's wrist and she was jerked around. Camille towered over her with crazed eyes, her bottom lip trembling as she tried to smile. Warning bells rang in Odette's mind. She should scream, call out for help, do something ...!

"I get it." Camille insisted. "You can't just give me your power. You need me to prove myself."

"I don't need you to do anything!"

From within her hoodie, Camille pulled out a switchblade. With a flick of her wrist, the blade was out. Fear clogged up Odette's throat. Suddenly, her tongue felt thick. Her body went completely slack, and she held her hand up. There was nothing she could do but tremble as the woman brandished the knife.

"Please." It was the only thing that made sense to say. The only thing she could. "I'm pregnant. D-Don't ..."

Camille's smile broadened unnaturally. There was too much teeth and gum for it to be considered friendly or beautiful. "And he will be more powerful than any of the others before." Tears flowed down her cheeks. Before Odette could stop her, Camille brought the knife down on herself and made a single, broad slash across her neck. The wound gapped at her, like a second mouth, but Camille didn't seem frightened. In fact, she smiled at Odette. It was brief, light still in her eyes and her hands reaching out to hold her.

Then the blood came. It spurted out of the wound, splattering Odette's face and clothes, landing on her tongue. The light in Camille's eyes dulled, but the smile was frozen in place.

Odette screamed.

People ducked their heads out of their motel rooms, curious as to what the commotion was about. When they saw her, many did not react for several seconds. It was as if time was standing still, and though Odette was paralyzed, she felt those seconds stretch on for an eternity.

The rawness in Odette's throat suggested she was screaming, but she had gone deaf to the sound. No one came to help them. No one moved from their rooms. She was left alone, in that open hallway.

Camille was on the frozen floor, her blood trickling out from the wound on her neck and spreading across the ice. She wasn't dead, but God did Odette wish she was. The woman kept gasping and wheezing, and with every labored breath more blood spilled. Odette was certain she was going to lose all of it, but she never did. It seemed more kept flowing, like some divine force was keeping her alive in that misery.

It had been a while since she'd seen so much blood. The sight haunted her, spilling over into the blank corners of her mind and dying them the same bloody red. Memories, she had repressed came flooding back. Memories of those who had been butchered before Camille. No, Odette hadn't forgotten them, but she had tried to forget what they looked like.

And yet, with the girl bleeding out before her, she couldn't help but see the rest of them. They were hanging on the edges of her vision, their rotting hands reaching for her.

Come with us, they all screamed. *Join us. It's where you belong.*

Hands laid on her and voices clamored, filling her head with more pain. They were knives, jabbing her brain and scrambling any bit of sense she had left. She screamed and screamed, begging for help, and yet it seemed like none came. It was just her and the ghosts.

Eventually, the pain became too great. Odette passed out, and she was thankful. At least in the darkness, she didn't have to deal with the dead.

When she came to, she found herself sitting in a chair in her motel room. Clara and Felix sat in front of her, staring, their faces paler and hollower than they had been before.

Everything was warped, like a worn-out tape. Time seemed to skip, slow down, or speed up around her without any warning. Odette couldn't make any sense of it anymore, and she wasn't even certain she was awake.

Odette wanted to tell Clara about Camille Chen—how she was the woman from the commercial, but words required effort, and she had no energy to spare. Odette would simply have to tell her about the woman some other time.

One moment she had been sitting up, and the next she was laying. Clara was at her side, when only moments before she had been on the bed. Words were spoken, but they didn't register in Odette's mind. They were far away, as if spoken underwater. Odette blinked slowly and made eye contact with Felix, who hadn't stopped staring at her. His mouth was hanging open and it moved, but she heard nothing.

Everything was dulled. A thought registered in a far-off part of Odette's brain that it didn't take the twins to ruin her. Anyone could do it, and she was defenseless towards it.

"The woman cut herself right in front of me." The words sounded foreign, like they came from someone else's mouth, and yet Odette knew it was her lips that were moving. "She was crazy. She cornered me and I got away. If I had stayed, maybe she wouldn't have ..."

Odette hiccupped. A harsh sob wracked her body and she crumpled to the floor.

"This isn't your fault." Clara said.

Hands pat along her back, rubbing circles on her sweater, but it was irritating. Everything irritated her. All Odette wanted to do was shed her skin and start anew.

"I don't know what I did." Odette sobbed. "I don't know what is happening around me anymore. I want it all to stop!"

XVI

GREER

G reer pressed. "You shouldn't go alone. You know things work out smoother when we do them as a team. You need me."

Grayson bristled.

He dodged once again, ducking into his bedroom and attempted to slam the door. Greer stopped it easily and followed him inside. He wasn't going to allude her this time. She would force him to hear her out if it was the last thing she did.

"You *know* I'm right."

"Leave me alone."

Greer picked up the nearest object she could grab, but ultimately decided against throwing something. "Because she has a stupid amulet, she's going to be tricky to catch," she pointed out. "You lost her once before because she shares our powers, what's going to stop her from using it again!"

He said nothing.

"*If* you find her—" She emphasized *if*, because with Grayson going alone it was looking doubtful, he'd bring her back at all. "—you have to take that ring away. It's too dangerous. What if something like this happens again?"

He wouldn't listen to reason. Grayson's face twisted up and he glared at her. "That amulet keeps her from being sick *and* serves as protection from you."

It almost hurt. Not the glare, but the conviction in his voice. He believed what he said. It was painful to realize, but he lied to himself so much she wasn't surprised he had begun to believe it.

Greer sighed and leaned against the wall. "You killed her family, remember? She might be afraid of me, but she hates you."

Grayson's eyes flashed. A pain she hadn't seen in a long time covered his face, but it was masked by anger a moment later. Her words hit a sore spot. Deep down, she enjoyed it. Greer couldn't say why, but it made her feel good. Watching him shatter was devastating, and yet she loved to push him over the edge. Maybe it was so she could prove to herself she could still do it. What made her feel even better was picking up the pieces.

"*Shut up!*" Grayson roared. "You're the one who tried to kill her! Remember that, *hmm*? I would never do something as heinous as that. You're the villain here!"

Grayson turned away, his body stiff. She watched as his shoulders shook. Barely visible, but she was used to it. He was still that little boy who needed protection.

Greer went to his side and laid a hand on his shoulder. He jerked away, but she persisted. "If that's what you want to believe ... Listen to me. You need to take the amulet from her, Grays. As long as your pet still has wings, she will try and fly away. Clip them."

Slowly, he shook his head. It hung low like a kicked puppy. Greer couldn't bring herself to feel sorry, not when he was acting like a petulant child.

Her voice hardened. "I'm only trying to help you."

"I don't care." He snapped, his bottom lip jutting out childishly. "Odette is mine—you have your own little toy to worry about. Back off!"

Greer stepped back. Expecting him to kick her out, like he normally did, but for the longest time he just stood there and stared at the wall. His jaw shifted from side to side, clearly mulling something over. He might not act like it, but she knew he considered her words.

Greer stalked the length of the room until she came upon his desk. Candles were practically cemented to the wood, their wax spread far out and melting into one another. A pendulum swing sat in the center of the map. There were several scribbles along it, but the largest and most prominent was a circle around the state of Oregon.

Notes in the margin of the map were barely legible but seemed to be theories of Odette's location. At least, her first location. Tadmor, Ohio—a hoax, a ghost town.

Greer still couldn't wrap her mind around it, but at this point she was certain the girl hadn't gotten out on her own. Odette was not advanced in any way. She was a novice in life and would be a novice in death. It could be possible Greer underestimated her, but she doubted it. In the brief period of their friendship, Odette had trouble doing most things by herself.

There was only one person—with magic—who would be idiotic enough to assist such a low life.

Greer took a closer look at the map and sniffed. "*Crabtree, Oregon*? That's all the way across the country, you can't go on your own. I'm coming with you."

Her brother snapped to attention, indignation flashing across his face. "No, you aren't. I don't want you there with me."

Greer scoffed, her finger tracing the little circle he made around Odette's location. "You don't know what you want. Besides, with that brat, you'll need all the help you can get."

"I can do this without you. You always make things worse." He crossed the room and snatched the map off the dresser and stuffed it in his backpack.

That time, his insult hit its mark. *Ouch.*

"Grayson, I ..."

He glared at his sister, waiting for whatever vile thing it was to come out of her mouth. It was like he slapped her, her mouth slightly agape and her eyes wide. Good, at least she took him seriously.

"This won't take long," he muttered. "Two days, *tops*."

"You said that the last time. How do you know this isn't another trick? She did it before, I'm sure she won't hesitate to do it again."

"Because I know." He paused, adjusting his hold on his pack. The back of his hand brushed against his amulet. "I made sure there would be no mistake this time."

Greer bit her tongue. *Doubt it.* Grayson got sloppy when he was emotionally involved. He couldn't see past the fantasy in his head.

Her brother paused, her silence speaking volumes. "You think I'm stupid."

"I never said that."

"You don't have to." Grayson rolled his eyes. "I know what she's doing. I know she doesn't love it here, or love me as much as she once did, but you can't get rid of feelings. She cares for me. She has to, or else she wouldn't have stayed. This is all a mistake. I will rectify it. Everything will go back to the way it was."

"And if it doesn't?"

Something on his face shifted. Grayson parted his lips, but hesitated. "I won't be so forgiving, but that doesn't mean she has to die. We've come too far."

Grayson left it at that, and exited the room. Greer followed at his heels, keeping her eyes to the floor. It was good to know he wasn't as ignorant to the situation as he sometimes pretended to be.

Though it was day, the hall was dark. Curtains had been drawn to obscure the windows. Even at this time of year, fans of the show would stalk their home and try to get a peek inside. It was unnerving. Not that Greer liked the sun very much. She preferred it dark, but she would like to have the option of opening her own windows should she choose.

Greer stopped short at the corner. There, at the top of the stairs stood Thorn. Grayson's coat slung over his arm, and that God-awful mask and eyepatch combination Odette had given to him. It made him look like a living Picasso painting, misshapen and jarring to take in.

"I have your coat, Master," Thorn said. Slowly he lifted the item up and Grayson turned to slide his arms inside.

Grayson began to speak, but his voice was no more than a hushed whisper. Even though she was only seven feet from him, she couldn't make out the words. They seemed to be somewhat angry though, as Thorn turned pale and the silver streak in his hair grew brighter.

The angel recoiled, "No, sir. There was never e-even an inkling she would ..."

This is about Odette.

Greer's lips parted as she strained to hear more, but there was no more to hear. She hated feeling like a spy in her own home, but, when she was left out of the loop, then something had to be done.

Though she couldn't hear what they said, she *knew*. Grayson's earlier attitude, all the advanced magic Odette couldn't know. It was obvious from the start, but Greer didn't believe Thorn had the gall to do it.

That little rat!

The men moved down the steps and stood before the front door. Thorn placed his hand upon Grayson's head, and in a brilliant flash of light her brother was gone. He didn't even say goodbye.

Not like he had the first time either.

Thorn sighed. When he opened his eyes again, they landed on Greer, and he straightened up instantly. "M-Mi—"

"So," she began as she descended the staircase, "The jig is up, isn't it?"

"What?"

Greer was by no means stupid. She knew it from day one, the way Thorn seemed all-too at ease with Odette's disappearance. There was never any evidence until now—with the way Grayson was acting and Thorn's secrecy.

She reached the bottom of the stairs and approached him. Thorn hastily backed away, but he wouldn't escape her.

She reached up and Thorn winced in anticipation of the slap, but it never came. Greer took hold of his cheek and squeezed. Her thumb pressed on what appeared to be a fresh wound he hadn't been able to heal all the way. Hidden within the fear and pain, defiance glittered in his eyes.

"You helped Odette, didn't you?" Her thumb caressed his cheekbone, ghosting over a nasty looking bruise.

His Adam's apple bobbed guiltily.

The corner of her smile tightened. Her fingernails dug into the wafer-thin flesh of his cheek. "You filthy little liar. You've really done it now."

XVII

GRAYSON

It was snowing. Grayson wasn't totally opposed to snow. He liked it better than the oppressive heat of summer, if he was honest. What he didn't like was standing out in the snow. To someone else, it may seem Grayson had been caught in a storm, the way the snow clung to his coat and his hair. This wasn't the case.

How long he had been outside, he wasn't sure, but he was positive it wasn't too long. Grayson wasn't some novice with this teleportation business. His body was used to it; however, it was weak. Grayson felt the exhaustion. His eyes watered, aching for them to close, but he forced himself to stay awake.

There was no time for sleep, Grayson reminded himself. Sleep would come in time, now he had to finish what he started. He had made it so far.

Crabtree, Oregon. Or, at least, a very small part of it. Grayson blinked once. Twice. His eyes cleared and he could now clearly see the scene that lay before him: police station. He grimaced. The last thing Grayson wanted was to involve the police, and yet, it seemed this was his best option, at least for now.

All he needed were spies. It was nearly impossible for Grayson to be in more than one place at once without physically exhausting himself. If he rested like Thorn and Greer encouraged him to, he might have had the strength to do this all himself, but knowing where Odette was and not doing anything about it was torture. Grayson could rely on foot soldiers to do much of his work.

Grayson's feet wouldn't move. Police stations did not bring back the happiest memories for him. It would be childish to say he feared them, but they made him uncomfortable. They wouldn't trust him no matter what face he put on, it was in their nature to question everything. Even under his control he was doubtful they would do anything to help.

Stop it, he chided. Inserting doubt would weaken him. They will do what he said. They would believe him. Grayson had nothing to worry about because he would make them do their jobs.

He turned his glare to the giant, brick building that taunted him. Cop cars were parked out front in various spaces as well as a few officers walking out taking a smoke break.

It's just another performance, he reminded himself, and he walked.

Heads turned the closer he got to the station. Grayson ignored them, even though their stares were like an itch he couldn't scratch. It was the amulet's fault. It made him seem magnetic. They could sense the air of power that surrounded him. It was annoying at the best of times.

Grayson pushed the thick glass doors open. The building was spacious and warmth enveloped him as soon as he was free of the doors. Discomfort settled in his chest. There were more cops inside, but it was a police station. Grayson inhaled deeply and forced himself to walk towards the front desk.

"Excuse me," he started. "I need to file a missing person report."

The officer at the desk, a woman with olive toned skin and long black hair, looked at him bewildered. "Missing person?"

Her voice caught the attention of a group of nearby officers. They stared unabashedly, as if they wanted to distract him from what he was doing.

The woman's head was a barrage of thoughts she wanted to ask. They shot at him like arrows, her eyes wide though she tried to mask it with professionalism.

"May I have your name, sir?"

"Grayson Mages." He swallowed hard, fumbling with the edges of his coat. He might as well give her some of her answers before she asks. "I am not actually from here, but my wife is. This is the last place that I am certain she was before she went missing."

Skeptically, the woman looked him up and down, then nodded discreetly to one of the officers in the group. "Have you already filed one in your city?"

He clenched his jaw. Of course it would turn uncooperative, "Yes." Before the woman could think of sending him away, he leaned against the desk and looked into her eyes. *"Please help me."*

Grayson's fingers just barely touched the amulet. Her eyes widened, and her lips parted, stopping mid word. He watched as almost all apprehensions melted away and a light blue sheen covered her eyes.

"When did you last see her?"

It was almost too easy to get into the part now. Grayson knew he was gaining an audience. That was all he needed. Watchers. He willed tears to gather in his eyes. "It's been days. Please. I'm so worried. She's pregnant."

She swallowed and reached for some papers in the file cubbies. "What is her name, Mr. Mages?"

Grayson sniffled then cleared his throat, "Odette Sinclair Mages."

The officer scribbled down the name. She continued to fill out other parts of the form, areas Grayson assumed he had no authority to write on, her pen twirling on the paper in quick strokes. Before she could pass it to him, another person interrupted.

"Excuse me," said someone behind the pair. "Did you say that you were looking for Odette?"

Grayson had to keep his expression schooled as he turned around. It was the officer the woman had motioned to earlier. He must have been eavesdropping the whole time. The man didn't have much thought pollution, so it made sense how Grayson hadn't been able to pick up on him. Either this officer was very dull, or very guarded.

He was an older man, probably in his fifties, with a potbelly and grey hair. He had worn lines on his face and wore a deep frown as he studied Grayson. The man's eyes lingered a bit too long on his amulet, before he looked away.

Maybe this officer was one of those cultists? Grayson believed they were all destroyed, but more could have popped up in the time he and Greer had been there.

Grayson stepped away from the desk and approached the man. "Yes, I did. Odette Mages, she's my wife. Have you seen her?"

The man scrutinized Grayson from head to toe. He didn't appreciate it one bit. Once again, his eyes lingered on the jewel adorning Grayson's lapel, and his lips pursed.

Grayson pushed forward into the man's head. *So... this is who she was talking about*, the man's thoughts whispered. Hm. Not a cultist, but the officer had been in contact with Odette. Grayson narrowed his eyes, but he played it off by wiping away the tears that had collected.

"I've been so worried ... She got in a fight with my sister. I think some things were said to hurt Odette's feelings, and I wasn't there to comfort her." Slowly, Grayson reached up and touched his amulet. "I think she believes I've abandoned her. If only I could talk to her ..."

The amulet pulsed once between his fingers. A tendril of blue smoke, unseen by anyone but him, snaked around the officer's leg and climbed up him like a vine. His eyes turned blue—only for a moment—before turning brown once again. The officer's back straightened and his face went blank.

"I've known Odette since she was little. I found her walking on the side of the road around eleven-thirty a couple nights ago, and I decided to take her over to my house. She and my son are best friends, and they've known one another since preschool. I think of her as my own child." The officer tilted his head, his eyes completely blank, "I left the house yesterday morning with her asleep on my couch."

"Is she still there now?" Grayson asked.

"No." The officer took a breath and continued. "She was gone by the time I arrived home. Felix wouldn't tell me where she went. Today, I received a call from my son's school that he wasn't in attendance. He wasn't home, either. I suspect he went after her."

The woman at the desk stood up, the spell Grayson had over her broken, utterly confused by his sudden confession. "Heath?"

She glanced between Grayson and the man dubbed 'Heath' and grew quiet. He could hear what she was so reluctant to say in front of him.

Search party ... Look ... Send out ...

Grayson was distracted and allowed his spell to drop off Heath. So, Odette had run off with another man? His lips twisted into a sneer, his eyes burning with rage. He hadn't thought her quite like that. It had to be a misunderstanding, right? ... *Right?*

Heath clapped a hand on Grayson's shoulder, startling him out of his murderous thoughts. "Are you okay, son?"

"No." He could no longer find it in his heart to be saddened. This was anger. She was doing this on purpose now. "My wife has run off and I don't know where she is! She's not only putting herself in danger, but our child!"

Grayson saw nothing but red. If he had it his way, he would burn this town to the ground here and now, Odette be damned.

But that was exactly what Greer wanted. She wanted him to break, like all the times before when she made him break. Grayson had to get himself under control. She did not define him. His past did not define him. He wasn't weak.

"It will all be okay," the man comforted, "We'll find her. She couldn't have gone very far."

Grayson kept his jaw clenched shut. It was so tight that it hurt, but he wouldn't allow himself to snap. He was the master of his own fate.

Taking a hold of his amulet, Grayson met Heath's eyes. "Yes. *You all* will *find her.*"

It worked fast. The mystical force within him took the men and women before he could snap his fingers. They went slack, their eyes glazed over and their minds blank.

They were all nothing but zombies. Grayson could already feel the weight of it all pressing down on him, but it didn't matter. He would keep every one of them under his hold until the very end if he had to.

"Except for you, Officer." Grayson's command pulled Heath out of his stupefied state. He staggered forward like he was sleepwalking. "You're going to help me personally."

One by one, the officers marched. All of them, searching. All of them, under his control. They were like ants: mindless. They shared one singular thought and goal.

That is, all but one. Heath Thornton had been given a very special task upon considering his close connection with Odette.

Grayson watched it all from the safety of the Chief's office. The door stayed firmly shut, but the blinds were open wide so he could watch every single movement they made. Being in control of such a large group of people was strenuous, he couldn't slip up. If he did, the consequences would be severe. Even so, he had to give himself props for the impressive work.

Heath sat in an uncomfortable chair, crammed in the corner with his phone in his hand. A boy's contact information, name: Felix Thornton, was pulled up. Every few minutes, he'd press the *call* button, or shoot him a text.

He didn't speak, his eyes blinking at a lethargic pace. Out of all his troops, this man might be the most valuable by far. He was a direct link to Odette and this *boy* she was supposedly traveling with.

On the desk, the police radio crackled. Voices carried over the channels, each reporting their findings. So far, nothing.

"South Street is all clear," said a voice. Grayson's jaw tightened, and he scratched off another street on the great map that laid before him.

"Nothing on 5th Avenue."

Another scratch.

"The girl isn't on 17th—"

Grayson picked up the police radio and hurled it against the wall. Metal and plastic flew in different directions, the frame smashed to the floor. He was done playing cat-and-mouse.

Storming towards the door, Grayson flung it open. He gnashed his teeth at the officers, his hatred boiling over.

"You're all useless!" He roared.

None of them looked up. They were too deep under his spell to react. It should have made him overjoyed, but he wasn't. He wanted a reaction and yet all he got was blankness.

"Widen your parameters! You aren't to let anyone go anywhere without checking them first!"

The loudest reaction he received was the bat of an eye. Then, the officers went off and did as he ordered, their faces as blank as ever.

Grayson slammed the office door closed a little too rough. "You." He jerked his head at Heath sharply. "It's been a while since you talked to your son, right? How about you check in, *again*."

Slowly, Heath turned to his cellphone, which laid loosely in his palm. There were no new messages on his home screen. The boy was beginning to grate on Grayson's nerves more than usual.

All afternoon, he'd had Officer Thornton message his son. In that time, only one message had been received, something about the boy being on a field trip. Obviously, it was a lie; but the punk didn't answer *anything* after that. He'd called him, texted him—even attempted to track his phone! Still, nothing. It was as if the boy didn't care about his father at all.

Heath dialed his son's number, but the phone would just ring. By the eighth ring, Grayson knew it would be much of the same. He clenched his jaw so tight that his teeth began to hurt.

He could feel Odette slipping further and further away. What he thought would be his Ace turned out to be another dead end. His bottom lip trembled, and he bit down on it hard.

"And here I thought you would be the *useful* one."

Grayson reacted before he realized. His fist closed around a silver letter opener, perched conspicuously on the edge of the desk. Then, he drove it forward into the man's gut. *Once. Twice.*

Heath wheezed.

Grayson slashed at the man's gut, his boiling rage dissipating with every stab. Crimson stained his hands, spilling violently from Heath's wounds until it seemed there was more on Grayson than inside the man.

The letter opener dropped from his hand, blood making his hand slick. His thumb cramped uncomfortably. He stared down at the man, chest rising and falling rapidly. Heath didn't move. His last breath had already come and gone, but Grayson had been too preoccupied to notice.

"*Useless* ..."

He stepped back and crushed something underfoot. The phone. It had dropped from Heath's hold, but it didn't matter anymore, did it? Grayson was back to square one—he didn't need some dead man's phone.

Grayson cleaned his hands in the bathroom. The ends of his sleeves were stained, but that was easily covered up when Grayson rolled them up to his elbows.

Everything was falling to pieces. Why couldn't anything go the way it was *supposed to*?

Grayson found himself in the cold, the flurries turning thick and fluffy, swirling about his head in the frosty wind. He pulled his phone out of his back pocket and dialed a number. It didn't take more than two rings before she picked up.

"I need your help." The words tasted acidic on his tongue. He knew he wouldn't do it unless it wasn't imperative to his mission.

"*Mmm.*" Grayson could hear her smiling from the other side of the phone. "*I like the sound of that. Talk to me.*"

Hannah Boggs

XVIII

GREER

Greer leaned against the far wall, watching silently as Thorn moved around her room, clearing off shelves and replacing nick-knacks with fat wax candles. Reluctance rolled off him in waves. He didn't want to be there, he didn't want to do this, but he would. He had no choice, the filthy traitor.

"You know, if everything works out, she'll come back," Greer said. Though he didn't turn around, his hands stilled. "We do this to help Grayson, and he'll bring her home."

"Do you really think so?"

Unfortunately. Greer rolled her eyes, pushing off the wall. Grayson was always too sentimental for his own good. "I do. Though she might be in a body bag."

Thorn turned. He might have snapped at her, but after their little chat earlier, he remembered his place. The fire in his eyes dimmed and he lowered his head. "If you think that is what your brother will do …"

Greer hummed. Honestly, she had no idea what Grayson would do, not anymore. He had broken so many of his own rules for this girl. If she were anyone else, she'd be dead already. It didn't make sense to Greer. Odette hadn't changed her brother in any way, behavioral wise. The girl had been just as dumb and naive as all the rest, so what was it that made her so special?

"You know who I wish he would have kept alive?" Greer remarked. Thorn didn't reply but resumed setting up as she asked. "Georgia. She was fun."

"I thought you killed her?"

"Oh!" She tapped her lips, thinking back. "Who was after the hippie girl?"

"Georgia."

Greer shrugged her shoulders. "Must have been why I killed her. I liked her too much. I'm starting to regret that now." In her pocket, her phone beeped. In the back of her mind she hoped it was Grayson, but she was not so lucky. "I have to take this. I'll be right back."

She stepped into the hallway and examined the caller ID. It was the private investigator. She took the call, pressing the phone to her ear. "What's this about?"

Across the line, the investigator sighed. "*I've caught wind of some unsavory gossip concerning Grayson connecting him with those two girls' disappearances.*"

"Who?"

"*I'll send over the names.*"

Odd that he was calling her—most of their conversations consisted of Greer doing a little misdirection or gaining a peek into a police investigation. Rarely was he ever used for looking into missing persons.

"I'll take care of it," she said without hesitation.

Like the P.I., the Mages' had the local police in their pocket, and it wouldn't be anything to convince them to drop what they had on Grayson. Greer could be very persuasive. When he didn't hang up Greer grew suspicious. "Is there something else?"

"*Not on your investigation. Local P.D. is thinking of finally allowing the trail to go cold. Gossip is the only thing keeping it open.*"

Greer made a noncommittal noise. The case would be closed soon enough, but, like always, Odette had gotten in the way. Her disposal project had taken a backseat. Though she shared none of this with the man. He might have been under her control, but one could never be too cautious.

"*Do you know a boy named Skylar Fraser?*"

"Why?"

He sighed. "*Questions are being raised about his disappearance. There's been a lot of death around you and your brother. People are starting to talk.*"

Greer grit her teeth. Again, she replied, "I'll take care of it."

Already, she could feel the strain. Ensorcelling a small group of people was nothing, but a large population was a completely different story. She would have to do it one at a time. Greer hated this; Skylar—despite his flaws—was one of her favorites. It would be a shame to have to get rid of him so soon. She would have to wait until the rumors died down.

"Is that it?" she asked.

"I'll call you if I hear anything more."

Greer hung up and fell into a well-placed decorative chair. A knot of tension formed in between her shoulders. There was so much to do and so little time. If she were going to be helping her brother, she couldn't be so tense.

Greer moved everything in her room to the side, leaving the center of the room open for what she needed. Thorn already set up a table with a large glass orb sitting dead center. Candles lined every inch of her room, but only five sat on the table with her scrying materials.

Greer's shoulders dragged, finally she allowed herself to be exhausted. Just looking at the crystal ball gave her a headache, but it was a necessary evil.

Greer took a deep breath, tossed her hair over her shoulder, and approached her crystal ball. She thought she would be a little calmer about all of this. Turned out, it didn't work.

Guess I'll have to pretend, she thought. Withdrawing her phone, she dialed her brother's number and put it on speaker. It didn't take him long to pick up. There was no hello on his end, no acknowledgement of any kind. In fact, she wouldn't have known he was on the line at all if she hadn't heard the background noise.

"Are you ready?" she asked.

"Are you?"

Greer chose to ignore his comment. She settled herself over the equipment, running through the list of required items before moving on.

Her face reflected in the crystal upside down and warped so it no longer appeared like her. She centered her energy and stared at the reflection, her blue eyes the focal point. Almost instantly, the five flames on the table shot up higher. There was no point in being afraid, this always happened when she focused her own energy.

The crystal was murky aside from her eyes. She pursed her lips, leaning in closer. The fog seemed to move, only visible to her eyes. It swirled ever so slowly until the outline of a face formed.

"What are you doing, Odette?" she muttered to herself.

Greer was leaning in so close now, her nose centimeters from the orb. No matter how close she got, the image didn't become any clearer. Side effects of long-distance scrying, Greer had learned. It worked best when the target was close.

The girl in the orb was barely visible and was looking severely uncomfortable. She kept looking off to the side, like there was another person over there. Greer wanted to scream in frustration. This wasn't Odette; and yet …

The vision went in and out of focus like a camera lens. Greer frowned; her magic was never wrong. She scanned the girl's face, placing Odette's eyes, her nose, and the freckle just below her eye. It was her, but it wasn't. So, what was throwing her off?

It clicked, and the image cleared as if she put on a pair of glasses.

Odette changed her once long, ratty mass of dark hair for short, pale hair. Greer couldn't tell the color, as the vision was only in shades of grey, but it must have been in the blonde range. Maybe light brown.

"She's done something to her appearance." Greer muttered to the phone.

"*What?*"

She couldn't answer. Scrying was difficult, requiring full attention; but here she was trying to split it between her brother and her vision. He would have to be content with what she found.

As powerful as the crystal was, Greer could only see people who she knew or knew of. Even amazing power has limitations.

Odette wasn't alone. Greer knew this from what she'd seen and from how Odette continued to look off in the distance.

"You sneaky little ..."

Greer bit her lip and allowed her eyes to go unfocused as her intention changed. She might just be able to find a way around those pesky rules. The image in the orb swirled again. This time, there was a building. Greer could see a set of doors. The crystal focused on a number, fifty-six, before piercing the door and going into the room.

"They're in some kind of lodging," Greer said. "A hotel or motel, or an inn."

The line crackled. "*Well, which is it?*"

"I don't know!" The image wavered and Greer shut her mouth.

There was nothing on the inside of the room to reveal where this was happening, only Odette who sat in a chair. She slumped down and covered her face with her hands. Her shoulders shook, softly at first, then with more vigor. She was crying. Two shadow-like figures loomed over Odette, their words lost.

Greer swore. If only she had gotten in the vision sooner, she might have discovered more information. Maybe she would have seen Odette driving to wherever she was now.

The world around her was growing dim. She was really running out of time now. Dark spots danced in her vision. Greer pierced her flesh with her nails desperate to regain her footing in the shadow world. She hadn't seen enough yet. There had to be *more*. She forced herself to focus, her body tensed, and her muscles hurt.

Odette looked up, only for a moment, and seemed to look directly at Greer. Her face was speckled with something dark. It covered her clothes, too. Before she was able to discern what it was, the connection snapped. The flames of all candles extinguished instantly and it felt like the room sighed with relief.

Greer shouted and ripped at her hair. It was too soon! She was starting to discover something, but she needed more time to know for sure. Briefly, Greer thought about throwing herself back into the vision, but doing that would surely kill her. She didn't have the stamina for it.

"*What? What is it?*" Grayson shouted.

"Give me a minute," she snapped.

Even though it was dark, Greer knew exactly where everything was. She pulled herself upright and flopped onto her bed, phone in hand. Her muscles burned and her limbs trembled, like she had just run a marathon. Advanced magic had this effect on people, even advanced magicians. She wasn't so weak though that she couldn't finish the job.

"She's with two others," Greer informed him. "I only saw their silhouettes, but there were definitely two and they were talking with her. She might be in trouble."

"With who? The people with her?" He asked.

"I don't know. I didn't hear anything, but they didn't seem threatening."

"What did you see?"

Greer shut her eyes and recalled the room. "Well, she always has that weepy look about her, but there was something else going on. She was crying hard. There were people around her—just the two—and they might have been comforting her. They didn't give off a violent vibe, so I don't think they were dangerous. And there was something on her. It might have been blood. I didn't have time to take a closer look before I was thrown out of my vision."

Grayson's breath hitched. *"Blood?"*

"Or paint. You never know." Though the likelihood of Odette being splashed by paint seemed very small. Greer had a hunch. "Isn't that cult up in Oregon?"

"There used to be a branch of it, but I thought Thorn handled it." Grayson paused. *"Why?"*

"I think wearing our ring makes her a massive target for crazies, whether we 'handled' it or not." Greer picked the fuzzies on her duvet. "You know these things spring up more frequently than weeds. Not that I particularly care about what happens to her, but I'd rather you *take care of her* than have her torn to pieces by a power-hungry mob."

"*That's not funny.*"

Greer bit her nail to keep from smiling. The image was, in fact, very funny; but laughing would be laughing at Grayson's expense, and she decided against it.

Grayson sighed, "*I'll look into the cult thing.*"

"Smart."

"*I think one of the two is a boy named Felix Thornton. His father was a policeman. I tried to follow the lead, but it was a dead end.*"

"What did you do about him?" Without her, his magic would be less powerful. It was dangerous to keep around loose cannons like this Thornton fellow.

"*He's dead. I made sure of it.*"

"Good."

"*I wasn't aware there was a third.*" He paused. "*Is there anything else I need to know.*"

"She obviously isn't in Crabtree. If you give me a little more time, I may be able to locate her."

"*No need. I'm still at the police station. If there is something odd going on around us, I'll know before you.*"

"She changed her hair. It's shorter and blonde, I think. You may need to update your description of her." Greer inhaled deeply and shook her head. "I think it's safe to say she's officially on the run."

"*I think I'll decide that.*" And the line went dead.

What a heartbreaking revelation. Greer was right all this time. It wouldn't help anyone but her ego to gloat. Greer scoffed. She stared at her phone's screen for a while before it faded to black. "I help you, and this is how you help me?"

It was much later when Greer recovered. She could now move on her own; though, every step made her joints creek and muscles tighten in protest. No amount of rest would fix the ache in her bones. That was something only time could take away.

Greer laced up a pair of winter boots, her nerves raw from scrying earlier. She couldn't afford to lay around all day—there were things to be taken care of. The people the investigator mentioned, the ones stirring up gossip about Grayson, it needed to be nipped in the bud.

Talk was fine if it was just that, talk. Though from the sounds of it, the gossip was one of the few things keeping this an open case and putting scrutiny on their family.

Greer observed the names written down on her list. A couple of the names were average, everyday people. It was the ones with influence that concerned Greer. There was a senator's assistant, a therapist, and another was a tabloid journalist. The therapist was low on her list, but the journalist might cause some issues.

After that ... Greer pursed her lips, casting a glance over her shoulder, out into the hall. The hallway was normal—

for now—but with a simple wave of her hand, it would change. Like a snake shedding its skin, the facade would fall away and reveal a long and dark corridor leading down into the dungeons.

A clever trick, Greer had to admit. It kept all their secrets hidden from prying eyes, and it prevented their *secrets* from escaping, as well.

She finished lacing her boot and prepared to leave. Before she could exit, though, Thorn appeared out of thin air, blocking the door. His good eye was wide with worry. Blood speckled his crisp dress shirt.

Greer stopped short. "What's going on?"

"It's Skylar," he said.

Nothing more needed said. She swallowed thickly, anxiety twisting in her gut. Unconsciously, the slip of paper she'd been clenching fell from her hands and onto the rug, forgotten.

Greer sprinted down the hall to the guest bedroom that became Skylar's when he wasn't in the cell. The lights were off, Skylar's pathetic sobs trailing out into the hall. Unceremoniously, Greer flipped on the light causing Skylar to howl in protest.

"Oh, Puppy."

He laid in a heap on the floor, his new shirt soiled. His mouth was coated in crimson, blood dribbling from his lower lip. Thorn had evidently bandaged him before coming to get her, as the grisly aftermath of Skylar's self-harm was covered with bloodied gauze.

"It was bad, this time," said Thorn. "You might reconsider the hospital."

"No!" she hissed. Skylar began to writhe on the floor, blubbering incoherent words. "With everything I'm having to deal with right now, you really think the best solution is a hospital?"

Thorn shook his head.

A hospital? Greer scoffed, pinching the bridge of her nose. *This is just what I needed* ... What else can you do for him?"

"I've taken care of the worst of it. But magic isn't a suitable substitute for medical attention—"

But his words fell on deaf ears. What sort of all-mighty being couldn't fix a flesh wound? Greer went to Skylar's side, brushing his too-long hair out of his face. He was pale, his normally golden skin taking on a greenish hue; his lips, bloodless.

He flinched under her touch; teeth bared like a wild animal. Greer continued to smooth his hair back, checking him over for unseen injuries. He had to have done this while she slept—she wouldn't have heard anything, and he knew it.

"Puppy, you'll get better", though Skylar didn't seem to be listening. He continued to babble, his crocodile tears falling freely. "... *Gone! She's gone! ... Ah! ... Odette* ..."

Greer's eyes flashed, her jaw tightening. Something within her snapped. *Odette*. Always, *always* Odette.

She glanced back at Thorn, but he was at a loss for words.

XIX

ODETTE

When the Sherriff approached, the woman known as Camille Chen, pale as death, had been wheeled off to the ambulance. Police were taking pictures of the blood-stained exterior corridor. One of the medics bandaged up Odette's arm, though it wasn't necessary since her wounds were nothing compared to Camille's.

Someone '*up there*' must be looking out for the crazy woman. Apparently, the wound only went so deep, missing a major artery, and she was still alive despite losing a lot of blood. Camille would live if they got her to the hospital in time.

This left Odette scrutinizing her very being. She couldn't bring herself to meet his eyes, her bottom lip trembled as he stared her down.

"And you say she was harassing you?" the man reiterated.

"Yes."

She followed me down the hall and grabbed me. Despite my repeated pleas for her to stop, she wouldn't. She had a grip on my arm. When I finally got free, I ran.

"And then she pulled out the knife?"

"Yes."

I thought she might use it on me. It never crossed my mind she might use it on herself.

The sheriff nodded, "So you used the knife in self-defense?"

She looked up, meeting his cold stare. Though he tried to look neutral, it was clear he didn't believe her story. His doubt echoed faintly in her mind. Odette wanted nothing more than to curl up and die. If no one believed her now, who would believe her if something truly terrible happened to her?

"No." Odette said firmly, but her voice sounded hollow. "She did it to herself. She said she had to ... prove herself or something. It didn't make any sense. I-I really don't remember, I'm sorry. It all went so fast."

The officer frowned. He began to write again, then tapped his pen to the notepad. "Do you know if you've had any previous interactions with this woman? Maybe you met her on the street or at a restaurant?"

Odette was about to deny him but paused. Though she didn't know her personally, she had seen her before on that commercial, and Camille seemed to know who Odette and Grayson were as well. It seemed counterproductive to tell him all that, but a woman almost killed herself over it.

"Um ..." Odette sniffed and wiped her eyes on the back of her sleeve. "She might be a fan of these ... these magicians in Maine. When I mentioned a name she reacted strongly towards it."

"Are you one of them?"

"No." She shook her head. If they had their way, she would be. "I'm married to one of them."

More notes. The pen scratched on the paper irritatingly slow. "What are you doing in Oregon?"

"I'm here visiting friends. It's been a while since I last saw them."

The officer stood and turned toward the door, "You should probably stay in the area in case we need to bring you in for more questions. Just a precaution."

A lump of protest formed in her throat. She did not plan to do that. In fact, Odette planned to get out of the area as soon as possible. He wouldn't understand and she didn't have the time to explain something so unbelievable to him.

For the officer she nodded, more tears spilling over. "Of course."

He left with a curt nod. Once he was out of the room, both Clara and Felix came back inside, bundled up in their coats. Odette didn't acknowledge them, she only sat still in the chair and flexed her fingers, her ear trained on the officer's footsteps. She waited until she couldn't hear him anymore, stood, and closed the door.

"When does the airport open?" she asked Clara. The girl frowned. "Uh—I don't know, but I don't think it matters right now. Didn't they just say—"

"I know!" Odette shouted. Clara recoiled, bumping into the bed. Inhaling shakily, Odette continued. "I know what he said. It doesn't matter."

Felix stepped up, scoffing. "It kinda does matter. It makes you look all the more guilty by skipping town."

"It doesn't matter!" A ball of anxiety had formed in her chest ever since Thorn's visit. It only grew larger with every moment they weren't on the move. "The airport?"

"It probably doesn't open for another hour or so," Clara stated stiffly. "There's no point being in a rush. Besides, they might need to question you again."

Odette buried her head in her hands with a soft swear. They didn't understand. How was it they could be so calm at a time like this? If only they knew all the bad stuff that went on while they bickered. Every precious second wasted was another Grayson was closer to finding them. They didn't have an hour, they were lucky they lasted this long with the snow storm and the attack of the crazy woman.

"They shouldn't need to question me again. When they get to the hospital, they'll see the wound was self-inflicted, and I had nothing to do with it." She couldn't keep the bitterness out of her tone. If they weren't going to listen, she didn't have to be nice about it.

Odette trudged over to where her backpack was and began to pack the items strewn about the room.

"Actually, I think this *is* beneficial to us," said Felix. "You know, we're basically following you blind. It doesn't take much to guess you're running from Grayson. I get it, he's a bad dude, but you're acting so desperate right now that you're actually talking about skipping town. What did he do? What did he really do?"

Odette bit down on her lip hard. "If you don't trust me, you can leave. I'm not keeping you here by any means." She glanced at Clara. "Either of you."

"You're my best friend. I'm here right now because I want to help," Clara insisted, "but ..."

"But you're making it hard." Felix finished. "I just want answers!" Felix flung his arm towards Clara, who remained uncharacteristically silent. "We both do, because you're worrying us."

Odette pressed her lips tightly together. "I've told you what you need to know. You don't need to know anything else. Okay?"

She couldn't keep her voice even. Despite her protests, there was no way she could fend the two of them off for much longer.

Felix screwed up his face, his cheeks bright red with frustration. His words tumbled out of his mouth as fast as he thought, barely giving Odette any time to think up a lie. "Is he cheating on you?"

"No!" she snapped.

"Is he beating you?"

"No!"

"Did he rape you?"

"... No."

Felix's expression softened. "Odette."

"I said *no*." She crossed her arms over her stomach, rubbing the bump that protruded ever so slightly. The words did nothing though. All conviction had been drained out of her, what was left was exhaustion.

The wall she built up between her and the two of them was crumbling. Odette didn't know how much more she could keep in.

"Why aren't you getting help from your parents?" Clara asked softly. "Why run?"

"Because they're dead," she spat. Odette expected to feel dread or shame, like she did when she first admitted she was pregnant, but she didn't feel anything. Instead, she felt … lighter, like a weight had lifted from her shoulders. So, she let the words fall without consequence. "They died. They can't help me. The one person I thought could help me turned out to be a complete psycho, and I hate him!"

Odette's knees gave away beneath her and she collapsed onto the bed, crumpling on contact. "You two are the only family I have left and that scares me, okay?! I can't even tell you everything because … because I don't want you to get hurt. I just want my life back!" She hiccupped, dry sobs wracking her body. She sat there for several minutes and shook.

Though it wasn't the whole truth, it made her feel a weight had lifted. Odette clutched her stomach, feeling nauseous from the tears.

A pair of arms wrapped around her. Then another. They didn't say anything, only held her tightly. They only wanted to let her know they were there. She hadn't been hugged in so long, something as simple as this made her heart ache and tears fall.

Maybe they didn't have to know the whole truth just yet. Maybe just this once, everything would work out the way it was supposed to. Odette wrapped her arms around the two of them and held them close.

Thorn. If anyone could guarantee safety, it would be him. He wanted her safe, and if he wanted her to stay safe then he would protect them.

When Odette's sobs subsided, they stopped squeezing her so tightly. Clara was the first to pull away, discreetly dabbing her eyes with her sleeve.

"We'll get you to the airport," Felix said softly. "But first, I think you should clean up. You look like *Carrie*."

Clara smacked him on the back of the head.

HANNAH BOGGS

XX

GRAYSON

A bell tinkled above Grayson's head as he entered the quaint diner. The scent was something akin to stale grease and coffee. He wasn't impressed. This was the closest restaurant to the police station—an old mom and pop diner with kitschy ornaments lining the walls. Grayson debated on turning back but returning to the station sounded like a far worse alternative.

Everyone—*everything*—was getting on his nerves today; even his sister, who gave him barely any useful information. So what, Odette wasn't in Crabtree? He figured as much already. She was in some hotel or motel? There were at least ten from here to the next town over.

The only bit of information he found helpful was the hair. Grayson's heart lurched every time he passed a blonde girl on the way to the diner, but none of them were her.

He had scrubbed off as much of Thornton's blood as he could before he left the station, but there was no salvaging his shirt. He burned it, trading it in for the one he packed in his duffle. Better safe than sorry.

The doorbell alerted a portly waitress, and she turned away from the customer she was chatting with and shot him a kindly smile. "I'll be right with you, honey," she told him, holding up a single wrinkled finger, "Just sit wherever you'd like."

The woman gestured to the many empty tables, and Grayson nodded politely. He spotted what appeared to be the cleanest out of all of them and sat down. A large, dirty window to his right, with a view of the town. Little flurries mingled with the dirt, turning muddy the moment they touched the ground. Cars drove past at a lazy speed, pedestrians jogged across the street to avoid the cold, and everyone seemed to be going on with their lives like nothing was wrong.

Odette was out there somewhere, and she was afraid. Or, she was about an hour ago. Greer could have made half those things up just to get a rise out of him, but she wouldn't mislead him at a time like this. For once, she wasn't half as creative as she let herself believe.

It was the blood that worried him. If someone hurt her, there would be hell to pay. However, he couldn't rule out the possibility of Odette harming someone else. She was capable of more than she allowed herself to believe, murder included. He witnessed it firsthand during the summer.

Grayson's stomach growled in an undignified manner. When was the last time he had eaten a proper meal? Meals were meaningless lately; all they did was consume time he didn't have. But here he was, in Crabtree; Odette had been here and she was close. This brought the smallest portion of his appetite back.

A small commotion drew him away from his thoughts. There, in the corner of the diner, was a group of old men. They all appeared to be discussing something important because they held stern expressions on their faces and gruff tones. Grayson eyed them, and a couple heads turned. They were bad at hiding their spying. Even if he hadn't been given the ability to read thoughts, they weren't subtle about staring.

Grayson ignored them all in favor of looking at the menu. He'd only glanced at the first item when the waitress arrived at his table, still waving goodbye to her previous customer. "Sorry 'bout that, honey. What would you like?"

"Coffee. Just coffee, please," he said, though his stomach cramped in protest. He didn't trust anything coming from the kitchen.

The woman nodded, her pen scratching the pad of paper rhythmically as she wrote. She finally looked at him, really looked, and gave him another smile. "I hope it makes you feel better. You look like you're having a rough time."

Grayson spread his lips into something like a grimace but said nothing. People prying in his business was a pet peeve.

"Just let me know if you want anything else, hon." The waitress tucked her notepad in her apron and started for the counter.

But then, Grayson thought. "Wait, just a moment, please. I … I do need something else, but it isn't food," Grayson admitted. He reached into the inside of his coat, feeling the pocket for what he needed.

Out of his periphery, Grayson could see as the gathering of geezers leaned closer toward his table to hear what he would say.

The woman's eyebrows shot up. "Uh-huh, and what's that?"

His fingers caught the edge of the photograph and he pulled it free. Slowly, he unfolded it until the full image was revealed. "My wife, she ran off. We had a fight, and we both said some things we didn't mean. She left before I knew it. I know she's here, but I don't know where. Have you seen her at all? Maybe she came through here?"

The woman leaned over to take a better look. It was their wedding picture. Grayson was glad he brought it, until now it was just a painful reminder of something he didn't have. Grayson knew how to read people, and if the woman knew anything about Odette, she would tell him anything. All he had to do was put on a sad face and use that precious photo. However, as the woman looked it over, he could feel her apprehension. A swirl of thoughts ran through her mind, starting with the fact that she was doubting Grayson's story. He didn't like it.

Grayson took a deep breath and felt tears prick his eyes. Power dripped from his voice as he spoke, "Please, she's pregnant."

As he spoke, a strand of translucent blue light traveled towards the waitress. It slithered into her yellowed eyes, and they glazed over for a moment. She touched her hand to her lips. "Oh my. Have you gone to the police?"

Grayson nodded his head somberly. "Yes ma'am. They're working on it, but ..."

Playing the part of a grieving husband was sickening. Especially as the woman made a pitying 'aww' sound and rested her hand on his shoulder. It took everything in him not to shrug it off and demand to know everything the woman knew.

"But there's only so much they can do and tell you." She shook her head, her lips tugging downwards, "I'm afraid I ... Well, now, hang on a second. What did you say her name was?" She bent down closer and inspected the photograph with more vigor.

Finally. A grin tugged his lips, but he forced himself to keep a straight face. "It's Odette Sinclair-Mages. She grew up here."

Before he could finish his sentence, recognition flashed across the woman's face. "Yes! Lil' Det Sinclair, I knew her, yes I did. Such a sweet girl. She used to dance at my sister-in-law's studio. A beautiful girl, really. Beautiful dancer too. She started so young and really made herself into something fun to watch. She had these really distinctive eyes—" the woman trailed off as she looked at the photo again, frowning.

Grayson quickly spoke up, "Trick of the light. But, yes, I know what you mean. She's beautiful. I love her with all of my heart. I would do anything for her."

"That's so sweet. It's a shame about what happened to her." The woman grasped the little cross she wore around her neck and shook her neck.

Grayson shook his head, repeating her words slowly. "What happened to her ...?"

"Yes, yes, her medical condition. It seemed her health was in such a decline she'd never be able to get well again. Fought it her whole life, apparently. I only learned of it when she had that bad collapse on stage. The family kept it quiet. Haven't a clue why. Tragic. Some of us even wondered if she'd ... Well, I guess it doesn't matter. But you say she's all better?"

Grayson furrowed his eyebrows. Following this woman's train of thought was more difficult than he thought. It jumped around faster than she could speak.

"Much," he forced out. "I'm just worried about her and the baby. I haven't had any contact with her."

"Oh, right, right. That's just terrible. Marital spats happen all the time, though. She'll come back; don't you worry. I can't even count the number of times I've fought with mine. It's just something you go through, it helps you grow as a couple, especially if you're young as you are. Don't let something like this slip by, young man. Divorces are a silly thing. If you marry, you make sure it sticks. But I'm afraid, I haven't seen her in town at all. Not in such a long time."

Grayson nodded, having tuned out half of the woman's speech, and drummed his fingers against the table. That ugly feeling bloomed in his chest. This ordeal was a bust. He shouldn't have tried to ask such a chatty waitress.

"I see ..."

But, it seemed the woman wasn't finished. "Odette was a real sweet girl. Before her issues were—erm—*too hard to handle*, she was a lively girl. Went to the dance school for as long as I can remember. Always nice any time I saw her and yet she never seemed to have many friends. But there was this one girl she danced with. They were thick as thieves. What is her name ..." The waitress tapped her chin and grumbled under her breath.

His eyebrows rose. Could this possibly be the third that was with Odette?

"Carrie ... Cara ... Clara! Yes! That's her name!" the woman cheered. "Clara Niesenson. Best dancer in the ballet company. I would be surprised if she didn't go pro. I'd bet anything, if Odette were back in town she'd be with Clara."

Grayson's lips parted in a satisfied smile. Finally, he was getting somewhere. "Really? That's a relief. You know, I believe she mentioned her name once or twice when she talked about home." A lie. Odette never talked about her past. Just trying to learn about it was like torturing her all over again. Grayson eventually stopped trying.

"Oh, they were the best of friends. Met in a ballet class when they were real young, if I'm not mistaken. Those girls were inseparable." The waitress tilted her head and nodded. "When she had to leave, Clara was devastated."

"I know," Grayson nodded solemnly. "Odette couldn't bear to be away from here." The old woman was practically melting in his hand. "If only I could contact Miss Niesenson."

"They live in the same house as always. Big and modern, only one like it, right off main street near the park. You could try there."

A flash of the house went through the waitress' mind. Only for a moment, but it was enough. Grayson's heart leapt. Whether it would pan out or not, he'd have to try. "Thank you. You've helped me more than anyone else."

The woman blushed, the red reaching all the way up to her ears. "It was no problem, honey. I hope everything works out with you and Odette. Oh! Would you like that coffee in a to-go cup?"

Grayson really didn't. It took all his strength not to run out of the diner and seek out Clara Niesenson's home. But, he couldn't. Grayson had a part to play. He cemented himself in place and clenched his teeth together in a grimace-like-smile.

"Yes, please."

Grayson sipped on his coffee and trudged down Main Street. His phone was plastered to his ear. The call didn't connect twice already. He didn't know what Greer was doing that was more important than this.

Finally, on the start of the third call, Greer answered. *"What? What?"*

"What were you doing? It took you long enough."

"*I've been dealing with real life, brother,*" she purred, taking the tone she used with him when they performed on stage. "*Apparently, the Mages Twins taking a break is some kind of crime. This is all your fault.*"

"Yes, well, I couldn't care less at the moment."

"*Oh?*"

"I think I know who the people with Odette are. The boy, you already know, is Felix. There's a girl with them. Apparently, she's another one of Odette's best friends." Grayson skimmed his finger over the plastic lid of his cup, eyes racing as each car passed.

"*Name.*"

"Clara Niesenson. I'm looking for her house now. I know you said they weren't in Crabtree, but they might have been in the home. If they were, there's probably evidence as to where they went."

"*Why not check the boy's home?*"

Grayson paused at the crosswalk. "I already have. Didn't find anything."

Not a trace of her anywhere. If that cop hadn't admitted to harboring her, Grayson wouldn't have believed him. "This is my last stop before I burn this place. It's completely useless."

Greer hummed. "*I'll see what I can do. Perhaps do a little digging myself.*"

"How?"

"*While you can interview people in person, I have the internet. Odette might not be active on social media anymore, but her profile remains. If I have a face, I can find the other two. Maybe they're going somewhere they used to hang out. We don't know until we check."*

As he turned the corner, he spotted it. A giant house with large windows and fairly modern construction. The woman in the diner was correct, there wasn't another house like it in the area.

"Just be fast about it." Grayson hung up and stuffed his phone in his back pocket.

Before he could approach the house, a sleek red car sped past him, pulling into the driveway. Grayson hung back; watching from a distance as a couple slowly emerged from the car. They laughed, their voices echoing down the street, and then disappeared inside as soon as they had appeared.

Grayson shifted on his feet. He hated unexpected arrivals, they complicated things. Grayson stood for several minutes, weighing his options, and checking the street for any more unwanted cars. No one else came for several minutes. Nothing would stop him from getting into that house, so he would either have to wait for those people to leave, or conduct his search whether they liked it or not.

Waiting could mean the end of everything. He hated to even think of Odette in such a bad way, but he couldn't ignore the truth: she was running. The longer he stood there on the street, the further away she got.

I've come too far to wait things out now, Grayson resolved.

A light came on in one of the upstairs windows. No, those people weren't leaving anytime soon. Grayson tossed the plastic coffee cup to the group and shoved his hands in his pockets. He was going to pay a visit to the Niesensons.

XXI

Skylar's fit calmed down to the point where he only sniffled every-so-often. His normally vivid eyes were void of life and light, staring at the television blankly. He might as well have been a ghost, for nothing Greer did drew any sort of reaction from him and he passed lifelessly throughout the room if he dared to stand.

Greer sat beside his bed stroking his hair affectionately. He remained unresponsive, the only sign he was even alive being the tremble of his lower lip.

"I have to go," Greer said gently, as if speaking to a child. "I have something I have to do, but I promise I'll return soon."

She stood and gave him a hug—which he couldn't have reciprocated if he wanted to. A strong chain tethered his arms to the bedpost, and a piece of rope around his torso kept him flush against the mattress. It made it virtually

253

impossible to move, but Greer didn't mind. She didn't want to risk him biting himself again.

"Is it true?"

Greer paused, pulling away from him. This was the first time he'd spoken in hours, he had shut up after his outburst, calling out for Odette like she could save him.

"Is what true?"

"Odette," he rasped. "Is she really gone?"

She frowned. *Why did it matter so much to him?* Greer wanted to interrogate him. *Was she the reason you tried to take your life?* But the words seemed to catch on her tongue, and she couldn't make herself. She didn't want to know the answer.

"Odette ran away," Greer said simply.

He didn't seem perturbed by that. He nodded slowly, resignedly. Skylar already knew that much, he'd known since Greer first interrogated him, but that wasn't what he was asking.

"Is she alive?"

Now, her nose wrinkled. *Is she alive*—what type of question is that?! Odette was a cockroach, no matter how many times you squashed her, she somehow always came out unscathed. It made her blood boil.

Skylar looked up at her with his sorrowful puppy dog eyes, unshed tears gathered in the corner. "Earlier, I heard you say … well, I overheard you saying that Odette would be coming home in a body bag."

So he'd been eavesdropping. If he wasn't already so weak, Greer would have been forced to kick him around a little. Eavesdropping is a big no-no, but apparently he refused to follow the rules.

"I just ... I need to know," he finished.

Skylar continued to stare at her like he was trying to read her. Despite his drastic actions, there was still hope in his chest. It fluttered, like a small heartbeat, it radiated warmth and he clung to it like a vice.

Her eye twitched.

Why should he rely on Odette—who was she to him? *Nothing!* Greer wasn't as oblivious to Skylar's secret thoughts as much as she pretended to be. He thought her wicked, like some kind of villain in his fairytale. And Odette—(Greer clenched her fists so hard they shook)— Odette he saw as some kind of golden, shining heroine. Didn't he understand that Greer was the one who did everything for him—not Odette. She was the selfish one, she caused Skylar to try and kill himself!

Greer would bet everything she had that Odette hadn't so much as given him a thought, not when she left and not when she was doing ... whatever it was she was doing, now. But still, he hoped Odette might come back and save him. It infuriated her more than she wanted to admit.

"No," Greer said finally. Skylar lowered his gaze, the hope he held so close diminished. "I didn't want to have to tell you like this, puppy. I wanted to wait for the right time. I'm sorry; I know you were close with her."

Empty words, though they seemed to hit their mark with astounding accuracy.

"A-Are you sure?"

"I'm positive," she said.

His face fell and it was glorious. Greer leaned over again and planted a kiss on his forehead, then exited the room. At least he waited until she was out of the room before he started to cry again.

Dusk had turned the sky a cool purple, and in the distance thick snow clouds hung, watching and waiting. Greer's mind was far off like those snow clouds. Grayson should have called again, he should have texted her at least. She couldn't help but worry even though it had only been hours since they last spoke. When would he be home—he'd gotten all the information he needed to find Odette, so why didn't he just go to her?

Go to her and kill her, her mind hissed. *One person already believes she's dead ... Why not make it true?*

"Here?" Thorn laid a large sack on the frozen ground.

Greer came back to the present and unclenched her jaw. She took a moment and surveyed the area. It was deep in the woods, off the beaten path where wild animals tended to prowl. No one liked to come out this far. Not since The Bacheller Family Incident.

Several large strides to the left would take you to a hidden wolf's cave. Ten yards straight ahead, you'd drop off a cliff into the sea. It was the perfect place to dispose of evidence.

Greer nodded staunchly, pointing towards the cliff. "Here."

(Greer could see her now, skittish as a doe, backed into a corner. She could feel her hands wrap around her neck, watching as the light left Odette's eyes.)

Together, they tore open the sack. The scent was strong through the bag, but opening it up was a completely different story. Greer held her breath, the scent hitting her full force. Rotting flesh and decay. It was more horrific than she would let on.

(Killing Odette would get rid of so many problems. That child, for one.)

Bonnie's skin, or what was left of it, had gone grey-ish green. There were black lines where blood once pulsed through her veins. Greer picked the girl's head up by the sparse strands of hair and tossed it out into the darkness. She didn't need those dull, milky eyes staring at her while she worked.

(Grayson would get over it—he'd even thank her one day. It wouldn't take much for him to forget Odette, like he had so many countless times before. He could start another family, someday, when he was older and ready for the responsibilities it brought.)

Thorn began to toss parts over the cliff's edge one-by-one from his own sack. Greer, however, stood silent along the precipice. Her thoughts consumed her, leaving her immobile.

"The snow will take care of the tracks," said Thorn. He paused, only for a moment, to peer at her through his lashes. His eyebrows creased, as if he was curious what was occupying her thoughts.

"You know I don't care about tracks," she said unconsciously.

Her eyes were trained on the rotting head in her hands—Nadia's, she was sure of—imagining it as Odette's.

It would be simple, she thought, *I already know where she is.* And Skylar, poor Skylar, he wouldn't be tormented by Odette anymore. He only needed to depend upon Greer, anyway. *How would he react if I died?*

Thorn eyed her curiously from the edge of the cliff. "Are you feeling well?"

Greer snapped to attention, dropping the head onto the forest floor. She felt like a woman possessed, her blood boiling with rage. Why should she wait on the inevitable? Odette had been a thorn in her family's side for long enough!

"Thorn, you good for nothing traitor," she began. "Your days as my assistant have only just begun. You will send me to Crabtree, Oregon. Now."

Thorn's eyebrows shot upwards, "B-But the bodies—!"

"Leave it, the wolves will get to them soon enough." Greer stepped over a half-decomposed arm. "You have a chance to redeem yourself, here. Don't let it go to waste."

Even if he denied her—a stupid choice, really—it wasn't going to stop her. Greer had a better grasp of teleportation than Grayson did, Grayson who nearly killed himself just to get home. She appreciated his urgency, but he really could be an idiot.

The angel swallowed thickly, then nodded. "Yes, mistress."

He ungloved his left hand, the cloth soiled from the corpses, and grasped her shoulder firmly. For a second, she felt nothing at all, only the cold evening air and the uneven earth beneath her feet. Then, it was as if the earth split open beneath her and she was swallowed whole, enveloped in darkness.

The sensation stopped rather abruptly, leaving her woozy and disoriented. When she opened her eyes, Thorn pulled his hand away, the wrinkle between his eyebrows deeper than before. She wasn't in the forest anymore.

Snow poured down from the sky, covering the surrounding area in white. She was in a parking lot, nearly empty save for a couple of police cruisers and civilian cars. It was a police station.

Thorn tucked his hands into his coat pockets. "What are you planning?"

They shared a look. Something passed between them, better left unsaid. Thorn knew what she was going to do, from the way his lips tugged pathetically downwards, he knew even better than she did herself.

"I'm going to help Grayson."

The station was practically deserted, all except for a woman who wrung her hands obsessively. She was scared. She jumped to her feet the instant the station door opened, not caring that the girl and her companion were strangers. Not caring about the warning bells blaring in her mind.

"I don't know what's going on," she said. "There's nobody here—the officers on the street are acting so strange, I—" She stopped before Greer, clasping her hands together. "Do you have any idea what's happening?"

Greer scrutinized her, and within moments determined she would be nothing but a hindrance. She waved the woman off flippantly, *"Don't worry about it."*

The woman's lips sealed together, her back straightened. She stepped aside, moving back towards the public seats, her gaze straight ahead. Greer eyed her, she might just need her to get the job done.

Greer continued on, heading deeper into the abandoned station. Foam coffee cups laid abandoned on the floor, paperwork went unfinished on individual desks. Every now and then the phone at the desk ring, the sound shrill and unwelcome in such a quiet place.

"He wasn't kidding," Greer said aloud. "He really did a number on this place."

In her periphery, something caught her eye. Greer glanced at Thorn, who seemed all together uninterested in being there with her, and started off towards the office doors. The metallic scent of blood filled her nose the closer she got. She pushed the door open.

Inside, slouched over in a chair, laid a cop. His shirt was all but ripped off, blood crusting around the torn edges of the fabric. It wasn't yet dry, not even close, but the kill was not fresh. Possibly hours old.

"This must be the one Grayson talked about." Greer knelt down in front of the body, inspecting it. Aside from the shredded stomach, the man wasn't in horrible condition. Dead, but the body was not in bad shape. "I have to thank you, you're extremely convenient."

Behind her, Thorn spoke again. "Your brother has not been here for several hours. This is a dead end."

"That's okay," said Greer. "I'll meet up with him after."

"After...?" Thorn took a step back. "I thought ... I thought you wanted to help him?"

"There are many ways I can help my brother."

It seemed, then, Thorn caught on. "I won't have a hand in hurting her." He stood his ground firmly. "It goes against my mandate. You'll have to go on without me."

"You don't have a choice."

He was quiet for a moment. "Odette is now bound to this family by blood. You can't touch her, and it's my duty to protect every member of this family so long as I am able.

Greer bit her tongue, the urge to shout at him and force him back into his place was strong. But, she needed his help, and he was more likely to do that when he wasn't injured.

"If I promise not to lay a hand on her myself, will you shut up and do your job?" On the floor was a blood splattered letter opener. Greer picked it up and weighed it in her hands.

Thorn stayed silent for several moments, weighing all his options. She glanced back at him and quirked an eyebrow. Reluctantly, he nodded, as if to say *Well, if you promise not to lay a hand on her...*

"Good." Greer laid her hand over where the man's once beating heart sat. "I'll need you if this goes awry."

With a swift, supernatural strength that you wouldn't have known she possessed, Greer slammed the point of the letter opener through her hand and into his chest all at once, hard. She screamed, the pain blinding as her hand was forced apart by the dull blade. It made a sick *thunk*, the dull blade sinking into the hilt.

Thorn rushed forward, as if he just then understood what he'd agreed to and wanted to put a stop to it, but a sharp *NO!* from Greer forced him to stay back.

"This is ... *madness*! You aren't strong enough—this could kill you."

His words were lost on her, though, as her own cries of agony drowned out anything else. Her amulet came to life, glowing a bright vibrant blue. It pulsated with her pain, the glow becoming brighter and brighter until it nearly engulfed the room.

Maybe he's right, thought Greer. Already, she felt weaker, never mind the stab wound pain. This was the kind of weakness only brought about by magic. It was as if her magic was siphoning out every bit of life force it could pull from her.

Maybe, I should stop. Her head was spinning, her muscles spasming. This wasn't like before, when she had been scrying, this was tenfold the pain. She tasted iron. If she stopped now, Thorn could heal her, no harm no foul. She would find another way ...

No, I won't! She pushed aside her doubts. This would work because it had to, because she needed to show Thorn and Grayson and Odette that she had the most power.

And, slowly ... *slowly* ... did the magic begin to work.

The weaker she felt, the more alive the corpse-man before her appeared. Greer's blood seeped into the wound, into his heart. He twitched.

She shut her eyes, splitting pain spreading from one temple to the other. Her eyeballs felt as though they were being burned right out of her skull.

When she opened her eyes again, she recognized that she was not looking through her own eyes. She was instead looking through the eyes of the dead man, straight at herself. Her eyes had taken on a strange blue hue, completely glazed over, and she smiled.

"Perfect." She jerked her head—forcing the dead man to follow suit. Their gaze now rested on Thorn, who watched them in horror. "I promised you, *I* wouldn't lay a hand on her."

HANNAH BOGGS

XXII

ODETTE

Felix stood. "Toss me the keys?"

Odette grabbed his keyring off the table and tossed them over Clara, who had bent over to pack the bloody mess of clothes Odette wore not twenty minutes before.

Felix caught the keyring and nodded to her. "I'll be downstairs."

"We'll be there in a minute," she assured him. Despite how desperately she wanted to be calm, Odette couldn't keep her voice from wobbling. It had been twenty minutes, but apparently she was unable to rein in her emotions.

Felix hesitated by the door and watched her carefully. His eyes reflected his thoughts. *I'm here for you. Everything's going to be okay. If you need to talk I'm always going to be here for you.* Odette waved him off and grabbed the nearest bag. Emotions had no place in her life at the moment. She had more pressing matters to attend to. She grabbed a couple, strewn about items, and stuffed them in her bag. Everything packed, all she needed was transportation.

"Did we leave anything in the bathroom?"

"Nope."

Clara nodded, clapping her hands together. "I think that's every—"

Before she could finish her thought, the phone on the bedside table began to buzz. It was Clara's phone, which she had tossed aside as soon as they determined they were leaving. They shared a look; Clara's face morphing into worry. She reached over and picked it up.

"It's my mom," she said.

First Felix's dad, Odette thought, *and now this*. If they were lucky, this was just an angry parent call about Clara skipping school. "Answer it."

Clara put the phone up to her ear, "Momma! Hey, I— What?"

Color drained from her face. Odette watched carefully, her packing stalled. The nagging became a dull throb. Her gut twisted, anxiety eating her up inside.

"Slow down, momma. What are you saying?" Clara pressed her finger in her free ear. "I-I can't ... What? ... *What?*"

"Clara, hang up," Odette ordered. The feeling grew stronger, this wasn't good.

She waved the girl off, her eyes lit with panic. "I-I don't know. Tell me what to do, please! Where are you? ... Momma? Mom? *Mom!*"

Odette grabbed their bags and stormed out of the motel room. "Felix!"

He ducked out of the car, confusion written all over his face. Odette tossed both bags over the edge. They landed on the concrete, inches from where he stood. Felix jumped and a slew of swears leaving his mouth.

"Put those in the car!"

As she turned back around, Clara stood in the doorway. Silent tears streamed down her cheeks and she trembled as she turned the phone flat on her palm. She selected the speaker button.

There was something happening ... in the background. Odette might have thought it was simple feedback from the phone, but the sound wasn't consistent. Then, the sound of something cracking came across the line; something smashing followed by a sickening thud.

"Is she there?!"

Odette's blood ran cold. He wasn't supposed to know Clara's cell number, he wasn't supposed to even know about her. Of all the ways Odette imagined this going down; him calling her like this, wasn't one of them.

Grayson's voice was venomous. Odette could feel the hatred from where she stood. The look on Clara's face was too much—she had never seen her appear so betrayed, so hurt. She seemed to be daring Odette to speak; however both of them remained silent and still. Only static from the phone's speaker echoed between them.

"I'll take that as a yes. Odette, princess, it's time to come home. I think you've caused enough damage here."

Odette flinched. His voice was grating on her ears. It made the throbbing pain in her head agonizing. Was he trying to pry his way inside her mind? She pressed herself against the railing, as if distancing herself from the phone would somehow make it all go away.

"Don't play hard to get. We've passed that stage. Just tell me where you are, and I can fix everything." He sniffed. *"It'll all go back to normal."*

Clara looked up at her, pleadingly, but Odette just shook her head. It wouldn't go back to normal. He didn't have that kind of power. There was too much damage already done. But, Clara didn't believe it. Odette could see it in her eyes, the spark of belief.

She extended her hand to silence her, to stop her before she did something she would truly regret. *Don't*, Odette mouthed.

"You'll really put things back to normal?" Clara's voice trembled as she spoke.

"*Stop!*" Odette commanded, and yet it did nothing. Clara's eyes glistened with Grayson's false promises.

"Of course. I keep my word. Just give me your location."

Their location was the only thing they had over him. If Clara gave it up, she and Odette and Felix wouldn't live to see another day.

Crocodile tears spilled over her cheeks. Her thoughts were too unpredictable, Odette couldn't read them. Frantically, Odette pleaded under her breath, she wished if there were ever a moment for her magic to be a sure thing, it was this moment. She would crush the phone, forget her friend's sanity.

"*Come on,*" Grayson goaded, "*it's a simple thing to give up, an address for mom and dad. Or are you okay with your parents being pulverized?*"

Clara inhaled sharply. "You're sick!"

Before she could say anymore, Odette smacked the phone away. Clara shrieked, lunging for her, and Grayson's voice crackled over the line before Odette smashed her heel on the screen, breaking the phone in half.

"Oh, my God!" Clara collapsed, but Odette caught her. "What have you done? You've killed them."

Odette held onto her tightly, "I saved us."

"No! He's done something to my parents," she cried. "He made me listen. I don't know if they're hurt or … or—" Clara cried harder. "I have to go and help them. I have to call the police!"

"There's nothing you can do," Odette said grimly.

"W-What?"

"They won't be able to stop him." Odette knew what she should do. The right thing would be to go back and help, but she was a coward. Going back was death. "The best thing to do, right now, is hide out."

Dumbstruck, the girl merely stared. It seemed her words wouldn't go through. Slowly, she began to shake her head until it was fierce and shook her whole body. "No. *No!* This can't be." Clara pushed away from her. "He's just a man, Odette. He can be stopped."

"You would die trying."

Clara wiped her eyes with her sleeve. "Look, I get you're afraid of him and everything, but he isn't some kind of unstoppable monster."

"If he's just a man, then why were you so willing to believe he could bring your parents back?" That shut her up. Clara clenched her jaw, her bottom lip quivering. "By all means, call the police." Odette paused, "Just don't be surprised when the worst happens."

Clara shot her a dirty look then stepped back into the room, picked up the motel phone, and Odette watched as she dialed the number. Odette wanted to scream—why wouldn't Clara just *listen* to her? But Odette stayed back and watched her babble into the phone, a small part of her wished she had been strong enough to do that months ago.

Odette turned away and pushed herself against the partial wall overlooking the parking lot. Clara's voice carried from the room but not the words, only the sad, pathetic sobs. There was no movement in the parking lot at the moment; Felix wasn't down there, but he was right beside her in a matter of seconds, nearly out of breath from jogging up the steps and his cheeks ruddy from the cold. "Are you ready yet?" He paused, wiping his nose on his sleeve. "Where's Clara?"

"Inside."

Odette turned around and the two of them peered inside. Clara was hanging up the phone, her eyes more puffy than before and her breathing uneven.

"Nothing," she said. "I got *nothing*."

"What do you mean?" asked Felix, "What happened."

Clara's attention seemed to be solely on Odette, though. "They—they didn't make any sense. They were telling me to calm down ... to breathe ... don't they understand that they have to help them?"

"Help who?"

"But did you tell the operator?" Odette pressed.

"I hung up." Clara pressed her hands to her cheeks and vigorously scrubbed at her eyes. "If he's hurt them, what good can an ambulance do? *Nothing.* They're all useless— telling me to calm down. I have to go home. I have to help them myself."

Felix, frustrated from being ignored, inserted himself between us. "Can one of you tell me what happened?!"

Odette stared at Clara, and Clara stared back, both of them waiting for the other to speak. Clara narrowed her eyes, her gaze glistening with unshed tears. *This is your fault.*

Odette reluctantly sighed, her heart aching with every word. "It's Grayson. He's in Crabtree, and he's done something to Clara's parents."

It's all your fault.

"What? How?"

"I don't know." A lie. It formed a bitter knot in her throat, but she forced herself to continue. "But he called us while you were downstairs."

"And now we have to go back," Clara finished. Fat, crocodile tears spilled down her cheeks and she clapped her hand over her mouth to silence the sobs. "We have to, Felix. *Please.*"

Felix set his mouth in a grim line. "I agree." And just like that, freedom was but a distant dream, too good to be true. "But, it's going to be difficult, possibly impossible. On the radio, the news channel, Crabtree has some kind of ... road block going on. The police just set it up. No one is getting in or out."

"What?" Clara practically collapsed against the wall. "Why?! I need to get back there. I need to help them!"

"They're claiming it's because of the snow. I'm sorry."

Clara's face crumpled, a small mantra of *no* falling from her lips. Odette knew exactly how she felt. She might have extended her condolences, but the look she had given her, the look of complete disdain—*this is your fault*—made her stop.

Of course this was her fault. If Odette hadn't been so bull headed, believing she could protect her friends and they protect her in return, she would have seen the danger having them around presented. She had effectively signed their death warrants, and everyone around them. This was her fault; she might as well have killed the Niesenson's with her own hands.

Realization washed over Odette. Of course there was no such thing as a coincidence. She fell back against the railing, "He's already gotten to the police ..."

"Huh?"

It all clicked into place. If Grayson had arrived in Crabtree, he would try and choke her out by commandeering the strongest army in his power—the police. From there, he would send them out to the town and have them scour the area. When they found out that Odette was nowhere near Crabtree anymore, Grayson would demand they block it off and try to draw her back in.

Somehow he figured out she was with her friends, and somehow he had located the parents. It wouldn't be too hard to find Officer Thornton—that might explain all of Felix's texts—but Clara's parents weren't due home for another couple of days. He had to have faked it.

"The phone call had to be a ruse," Odette stated. "You said so yourself, Clara, they don't come home early. Grayson faked it all. He didn't need us to tell him our location; he was going to find that out for himself."

The two of them stared back at her, confused.

"He knew faking the phone call would get you to call the police. He probably had them on standby all day. He knew by scaring you, you would want to call the police, and then they would track us from that call."

Felix shook his head, "No. This guy couldn't have bought off the police like that. I mean, I can't speak for every single person on there, but I know my dad wouldn't go along with this."

"You'd be surprised."

Odette started to go, but Clara caught her by the sleeve. "How are you so certain he hasn't hurt them? That sounded just like my mom on the phone. That was my home phone number."

The fact Grayson was in her house, Odette couldn't deny. It sounded very like him to break into someone's home—she had first-hand experience with that, however, to give Clara peace of mind, she didn't bring it up.

"Grayson's a magician. He's talented. If he didn't fake the voices, he probably engineered them from some of the old videos." She stopped and pressed her lips together. "I'm sorry. I know this is confusing, and probably doesn't seem believable, but you've gotta trust me."

Clara hesitated, but nodded. "You know him better. We promised to get you to the airport, and that's what we'll do. Afterwards ..."

"Afterwards, I can't stop you from doing whatever it is you want to do." Odette looked to both of them. "But if you're going back to Crabtree, you better be safe."

They nodded.

Odette twisted her fingers in her sweater, rubbing her thumbs along her belly. Her eyes constantly darted towards the clock. Sunset was upon them, the sky turning a hazy purplish gold color, but soon it would be completely dark.

"How much longer until we get to the airport?" Odette asked.

Clara checked her phone again. "Six more minutes, maybe."

Six minutes was an eternity. It seemed to Odette they'd been in the car longer than an hour, when in all actuality it had been a matter of minutes. Butterflies tickled her stomach; the trio had nothing and *everything* to worry about. Grayson was in Crabtree—and though Odette felt a tug of empathy towards Clara, the circumstances didn't change her mind.

On her hand, the ring winked at her, a buzz of electricity jolting through her skin. The hair on her arms began to raise, the butterflies in her stomach kicking up a tornado. Odette glanced behind them through the dirty windshield. There was nothing but a stretch of snowy road behind them, tall fir trees towering over the lane on either side creating a tunnel as far as the eye could see.

No one should be following them, Odette knew that; yet, she couldn't shake the feeling of invisible eyes peering at her from somewhere behind. The feeling had come and gone since they had checked into the motel, but now, it was stronger than ever. Every time she turned, she expected someone or something to be there, but there was only fog.

"Relax," Felix said, looking at her through the rearview mirror. "We aren't being tailed."

"I know." It didn't change what she felt though, something she couldn't fully explain. It was almost like anticipation; someone was coming, but she couldn't tell *when*.

No, she was paranoid. If she was right and Grayson had taken control of the police, this meant they weren't safe anywhere. How long had he been in control? Obviously, not too long since she had been fine when she had seen Officer Thornton last, otherwise she would have been taken in for sure. It's possible Officer Thornton might not have been in the station when Grayson arrived, but that just seemed like wishful thinking.

No, it was more likely that Thornton was under Grayson's control; or worse, dead.

And, if Grayson had control of the police, he had probably already set up a search. It was possible they were being followed right at that very moment.

As if sensing her thoughts, Felix began to speak. "There's no way they could have gotten here this fast, anyway. We're, like, forty-five minutes away. They'd have to already be out here, ya know, lying in wait and all that."

"That's what I'm worried about."

Felix gulped hard. "Right."

Then, she heard it—the low, rumbling of a car's engine. Her ears perked up and she turned around again, watching a black sedan seemingly come out of the fog. It was a distance away, barely a speck on the road, but it was gradually gaining on them until it was little more than a mile away.

The ring on her hand pulsed.

"Felix," Odette said, "Speed up."

"I'm already going ten over—"

"Do what she says!" Clara shouted.

Felix tightened his hold on the steering wheel and hit the gas. The car lurched forward; however, the new car behind them seemed to anticipate this and sped up, red and blue lights lit up from the grill. Odette swore under her breath, it was an undercover car.

The subtle electric jolts emitted by her ring finger turned white hot, burning her. Odette bit her tongue to repress a cry. She had endured a lot from the ring, but never before had it burned her.

Felix slowed the car but Odette kicked his seat. "Don't pull over."

"Are you insane?" He shot her a look in the mirror. "I'm not going to jail for you, sorry."

He pulled off to the side of the road, ignoring her as she kicked him again. The cop car passed, but slowed and pulled off the road ahead of them. Odette clenched her hands, the white hot heat radiating up her arm. Now would be a great time to be able to control someone.

"I recognize those plates," said Felix. "I think that's my dad's car."

"Your dad's car?" Clara echoed. "What would your dad be doing out here?"

He swore under his breath, mumbling about GPS in the car. Sweat beaded up on Odette's forehead. All of her thoughts were muddled, her head swimming through a thick heated fog; but she was conscious enough to understand the two of them.

"When was the last you heard from him, again?"

"A couple of hours ago." Felix glanced at his phone, resting on the center console.

The cruiser's door opened and out stepped Officer Thornton. His steps were heavy, his figure more imposing than usual.

Felix swore again, ducking low on the seat. "This is just *great ...*"

The closer he came, the louder the warning bells rang in her brain. *Danger*, whispered her subconscious, *Get out, now.*

Despite everything, nothing about their surroundings—not even Officer Thornton—appeared outwardly threatening. Odette trusted her instincts more often than not, but there was truly nothing wrong. Officer Thornton had no blue sheen to his eyes; no dull, lifeless look about his face. If it weren't for the warning bells, Odette could have believed he'd simply tracked them via car GPS.

And yet, there would always be a bigger force at work, pulling the strings. She'd learned the hard way to never trust appearances. Odette shrunk back, pressing herself as close to the backseat as humanly possible.

Felix rolled down his window, gaining a bit of confidence back, and yelled to his father. "Dad! What's going on?"

Officer Thornton didn't answer, limping slowly towards the car.

Limping?

Odette pressed her face against the cool glass, scrutinizing him. The limp was heavy, his left foot beveled inwards. Odette knew the limp was new. Then—as if someone had changed the radio station—her mind was overcome with a roaring wave of static.

Get out!

The sound was deafening, and yet she knew she was the only one of them who could hear it. Officer Thornton's mind was blank. There was no other way to describe it, just

... *blank.* Something powerful was causing this mental block and it kept Odette from getting into his mind, from reading even the simplest of thoughts.

The only other time, Odette thought, she had experienced such a block was when she was near the twins.

The fever-heat induced by the ring made her feel like she was boiling alive. Odette swallowed hard, "I don't feel good about this."

Clara shook her head, "Odette, *not now.*"

Officer Thornton stopped right in front of Felix's window, his eyes dead ahead at the trees. A strange smell clung to his skin and wafted through the open window, like a heavy perfume. It was strangely sweet with an underlying stench Odette could place anywhere. Rot and decay.

Felix tried again, his voice much softer. "Dad?"

Officer Thornton's eyes were unfocused and a little cloudy, as if he was seeing some far off horizon. He didn't even blink when his son spoke, almost like he couldn't hear him. Odette shifted away from the window, and the officer's head suddenly snapped in her direction.

Odette had no time to react as Officer Thornton smashed his hands through the backseat window, grasping wildly around for her. Glass sprayed everywhere, cutting her cheek and scattering about the seats. Odette made a mad dash to the opposite side of the car. Officer Thornton wedged himself further and further inside, grabbing anything and everything that came between him and his prey.

"*Dad?!*"

Officer Thornton pushed himself halfway through the window, with no regard for the glass shredding his iniform and skin. The stench of death so heavy it invaded the car. One of his hands grabbed her foot and began to drag her out, her back scraping against the glass. Using her free leg, Odette kicked him, nailing him in the face hard several times with no effect.

"Let go!"

Odette reached to the floor, hoping to find a weapon. There was nothing there but an old atlas, everything else was in the trunk. Odette grabbed the Atlas and smacked him with it, but she might as well have been swatting a tree with tissue paper.

Officer Thornton improved his grip around her around her calf and had her half way out of the vehicle before Clara caught her by the wrist and Felix by the shoulder, the two of them having a tug-o'-war to get her back in. Glass tore against her back.

Odette maneuvered both her feet against his chest and kicked hard. Officer Thornton fell back, landing on the pavement a couple of feet away from the car, his head slamming to the ground making an awful crack. It didn't faze him. Hell, Odette was positive it didn't hurt him.

Odette pulled herself back in.

"Go!"

Felix slammed on the gas pedal and the car lurched forward. He twisted around in his seat, watching as his father tried to run to catch up with the car.

"Felix, watch out!"

He looked and swerved hard, scraping against the parked police car. Their car sped forward, but before he could straighten the wheel, they ran straight into the ditch. Felix's head smacked hard against the wheel. Odette was slammed against the front seats, hitting the headrests hard enough to leave her dazed.

Odette blinked, pushing away from the seat. She felt sick and her wrist throbbed, from her poor attempt to stop her from hitting the seat. It was—at best—sprained. She cupped her head, wincing.

Reaching out, she shook Felix by the shoulder. He didn't budge. His face was cushioned against the airbags, which had deployed too late. Clara's head rested against the passenger window. She made a small groan, but like Felix, didn't budge, her eyes sealed shut.

Out, she needed out of the car! But the passenger-side door wouldn't budge, Odette couldn't tell if it was her own strength failing her or if the door had truly jammed.

A hand reached through the already broken window, latched onto her and dragged her out onto the harsh, snow laden pavement. Bits of stone and glass scraped her skin and dug into her knees as she landed.

Officer Thornton half-held her in the air, dangling by her arm. He smiled a strange, bloodless smile that seemed far too mechanical and cold.

"You're not dead. Good. How stupid would it be to die like that? With all the effort I went through?"

The words he spoke weren't his. They were, but different. A little different tone but the cadence was familiar. It reminded her of another that made her shiver.

"*Greer*?"

"Surprised?"

It all made sense—the supernatural strength; the empty thoughts; no glowing eyes—this man wasn't under Grayson's control, he was *possessed*. Odette hadn't witnessed the twins possess a person before; it was only ever talked about quietly like it was some *arcane* thing. But, at least the smell made sense now. Thorn had been benevolent enough to explain possession to her and how—among other things—it required a corpse.

Officer Thornton was dead.

The smug smile on his face was most definitely Greer's. Nasty and full of unspoken cruelty. She'd killed an innocent man just for ... what? Revenge? It didn't matter why she did it, Greer's mind was so twisted she had no hopes of figuring it out.

Odette braced herself with her good arm and fell free from his (Or was it *her*?) grip. She should have been thinking of how to get away, but all her thoughts could focus on was Felix. God, how was she going to explain this to him?

"Greer, what have you done?"

Greer-Thornton shook his head. "Oh, no, I haven't done anything. Don't put this on me; give credit where credit is due. This is all you. Do you really think any of this would be happening if it wasn't for *you*?"

The slap came out of nowhere. There was enough restraint behind it to not snap her neck; but, if Greer wanted to, she most certainly had that kind of power in this form. This was about toying with Odette, prolonging the kill.

Greer-Thornton grabbed ahold of her neck and squeezed, the skin cold and bits of flesh cracked or missing. "Unfortunately possession speeds up the decomposition process." He (*She? They?* Yes, Odette settled on *They.*) forced her to look up into the man's dead eyes. It seemed, with each second that passed, the eyes grew cloudier, and their hands squeezed harder. "But, I don't need long to kill you."

Greer-Thornton pulled her upright and threw her at the car. Odette flipped in the air before landing hard on the hood, the metal dipping beneath her weight. Pain and heat radiated throughout her body.

Odette rolled onto her side, wheezing. Through the windshield she could see Clara and Felix, who still appeared unconscious. This could only go on for so long before Greer shifted her attention to them.

Fast, heavy footsteps on the pavement alerted her that her enemy was approaching. Odette scrambled further up the hood of the car. Officer Thornton, his dead eyes focused on her, arms outstretched was upon her.

And then, the feverish heat which had overtaken her, skyrocketed. White hot, her anxiety and fear and anger all seemed to explode, breaching a new level. It was a supernatural heat, and she no longer felt like herself, but something *stronger*. With a sharp jerk of her fist, Odette punched the air. Like a ricochet, an explosive puff of air sent the possessed man flying. His body made a high arc before slamming onto the pavement with a sickening crunch.

Odette winced, covering her eyes. No one could survive that.

When she peeled her fingers away, she was horrified. Greer-Thornton's body jerked as it attempted to peel itself off the ground, arms rising in awkward angles. His hand was shredded, but there was no blood. Only the gruesome flaps of flesh, which peeled back to reveal muscle and bone.

"Did you think it would be that easy?" Greer-Thornton hissed. "You can't kill something that's already dead."

Horrified, Odette watched as the bones began to snap back into place, the body creaking and spasming with every grisly crack. Then, Greer-Thornton smiled a mouthful of yellowed teeth. They charged at her, much faster than one would expect.

Odette slipped off the back of the car, landing in the snow bank. Greer-Thornton leapt over the car, landing inches away from her. Their fist reared back and Odette dodged at the last second, their hand connected with the car.

Odette made her move to run, but they grabbed her legs, pulling her down.

"You can't win, Odette," Greer-Thornton said. They spat at her, displaying those decaying yellow teeth. "The only reason you've lived this long is because of Grayson, but his judgement can't be trusted. I know what's best for him."

Odette dug her fingers into the pavement, rock burying itself deep within her nails. Greer-Thornton was crushing her with their weight and she could only grit her teeth and bare it. The shadow of a fist loomed above her and she rolled to the side just as it came crashing down, creating a small crater in the road where her head had been.

Greer-Thornton roared with anger, the fist rearing back once again. Odette shut her eyes, bracing for impact. Pebbles dug painfully into her hands. Her mind flashed quickly imagining her head smashed so deep into the pavement nothing but bloody pulp would remained.

Odette winced.

The car door swung open with a sickening thunk. Greer-Thornton was knocked off of her with a yelp, dropping into the snowbank.

Odette wiggled onto her side and locked eyes with Clara, her eyes darting around like a skittish animal.

"Wh ... What was that?"

Odette swallowed hard, pushing herself upright. There wasn't a way to answer her—none she would understand— so she ignored her. Her gaze settled on Greer-Thornton, whose movements were shaky as they tried to regain their footing. Their movements were jerky and inhuman, almost like someone pulling on a broken puppet's strings only to find it didn't work the way it used to.

They popped upright, snarling. Officer Thornton's face was concave from the hit it took by the car door, his nose smashed inwards, his cheek and forehead sloping awkwardly.

"You can try and keep fighting," they said, "But you and I both know it's only a matter of time ..."

The bones seemed to no longer be able to mend themselves, the flesh unable to sew itself together.

Greer-Thornton lunged, arms outstretched to pull Odette in. She thrust her arms out instinctually. Her ring pulsed once and the energy rippling through her body like an electric current. It reached her finger tips and *something happened.*

Greer-Thornton's eyes widened, turning a milky-yellow color before crusting over. Behind them, the Douglas firs had stretched out their limbs before her very eyes. The limbs pierced the possessed man, drilling through his chest and ribs, halting him midair.

They hung there for a moment, dangling a mere foot away from where Odette stood with her out-stretched arms. And then, the trees curled the tips of their branches around the body. Odette clenched her fists. They squeezed the body tightly. Something crunched.

Odette scrambled back, cowering by the car's tire. Bile tinged the back of her tongue and she cupped her mouth. *The trees ... how had the trees ... done that?*

She stared at her trembling hands. Fear paralyzed her tongue, and though she could hear Clara screaming behind her, the sound was quiet compared to the loud roar of blood rushed through her ears.

It wasn't the trees, said a knowing voice. Strange, how her subconscious sounded like Thorn. *It was you.*

There was no blood, Officer Thornton was already dead wasn't he? So why did he look afraid of the protruding roots and branches, how could he seem so alive? Why did he twitch like that?

His body twitched, like some perverse puppet on a string. "You ... think you're so ... clever don't you?" The words were pained, his voice mixing with Greer's into an unearthly growl. "Little *cheat.*"

Odette shook her head, her eyes welling up. "I didn't ..."

"You did this." Officer Thornton grimaced, his dead skin cracking with the wind. "I guess you win ... for now."

Officer Thornton, finally, went limp. The skin on his body slowly began to flake off, fluttering through the wind like tiny snowflakes, until nothing but his insides remained. Odette shielded her eyes, but it couldn't remove the image now burned into her mind.

You did this.

No, she couldn't have. Odette didn't have any powers; she couldn't ensorcel a motel manager, let alone control trees. This wasn't her, but it didn't change the fact that she could feel the magic pulsing through her, emitting from her ring. She had used magic whether she realized it or not.

She turned around to the car. Clara sat there, her expression mirroring Odette's own. Wide, glassy eyes; mouth agape. She was trembling.

"It's okay, now," Odette sniffed. "It's all over." She took a step forward, but Clara flinched away.

"*What the hell!*" she cried, pointing towards the tree where Officer Thornton's corpse hung.

The wind rustled within the trees. Snow flurries fell, faster and faster. Odette gaped, her mouth opening and shutting mechanically. She needed to say something, but her tongue refused to work.

Clara continued, "You ... you saw that, right?! The trees—! What was that? *What was it?!*"

She didn't want to look back, knowing what was behind her was horrific. "I don't know—"

"But you saw it," Clara interjected. "You had to. You had to! He was talking to you and then the tree." She couldn't wrap her mind around it. "I'm not crazy ... It was right there. They reached out and ... and."

Odette knelt down beside her friend. She touched Clara's forehead, noting a cut along her hairline. "I think you hit your head."

Clara touched her forehead unconsciously, wincing as she made contact with her injury. "Ah. I didn't even notice ..." She frowned, curling her hand into a fist. "It all happened so fast."

"It'll be okay," Odette assured her. "How is Felix?"

Clara looked at Felix's slumped-over body. "He's breathing; but I don't think he's going to be getting up anytime soon." She looked back to Odette. "Are you sure you didn't see anything?"

Odette didn't answer. "Neither of you are fit to drive. Do you think you can move?" Clara nodded. "Okay, I need you to help me move Felix to the back seat. I can't do it by myself, my hand ..."

The two girls hobbled to the other side of the car and pulled Felix out. His glasses had shattered, cutting him along his eyes. They fit him in the back seat, brushing away as much glass as they could find before laying him down.

Clara shut the door and leaned against the car. Her fear was still palpable, but it wasn't as prevalent as before. She looked up, something in the distance catching her eye.

"Who's that?"

Too preoccupied with her injured arm, Odette didn't look up. "Hm?"

"Hey!" Clara called out, waving her hands like crazy. "Maybe they can help us—*hey!* Over here!"

Odette turned away and her gaze landed on the new pair on the road.

Oh no.

Not five yards away, in the middle of the street, stood Grayson and Thorn. They were stagnant staring at the car and the two battered girls before them. Icy tendrils of dread crept down Odette's skin. She wished she could just disappear; but, there was Clara, flagging them down like her life depended on it.

Oh, if only she knew.

"Odette," Grayson called out, "What's going on here?"

XXIII

ODETTE

He didn't wait for Odette's reply, stalking closer to their car. "You must be Clara Niesenson." The way Grayson said it, it ought to be pleasant, but something in his eyes and the way he held his mouth made it sinister. "I've heard a lot about you."

Clara hesitated, lowering her arms. "Do I know you?"

Grayson's eyes flicked towards Odette, as if to say *you really haven't told her about me?* "Forgive me; I thought it would be obvious. Grayson Mages. I'm going to have to cut your road trip short, I'm here for Odette."

"*You're* Grayson?" Now, it was Clara who glanced at Odette, shooting her a *why-did-you-not-warn-me-sooner* look. "You're so different from your photos."

Grayson pressed his lips into a thin line, taking it as an insult. Odette had shifted her focus to Thorn.

Thorn, the man (or angel, if you wanted to get technical) who had promised he would protect her but was now at her greatest enemy's side. How could he stand behind that man, looking so stoic, like he hadn't been trying to help her all along? Had he been playing her all along?

Sensing her inner turmoil, Thorn lowered his head dejectedly.

Grayson continued to speak, warily eyeing the wreckage around him. "Is Felix Thornton in there? It's nice to put a face to a name." He bent down and waved to the window. "I met his father as well. Not very helpful, though. Your parents, on the other hand ..." He stopped and inhaled deeply, setting his gaze on Odette. "Their hospitality is unmatched."

"What did you do to them?" asked Odette.

Grayson didn't answer her, but the corners of his lips twitched ever so slightly. "It's time to come home, princess. I think you've done enough damage to these people."

An unspoken threat lingered in the air. He wasn't going to hurt them if she complied. After everyone he had harmed, he might actually allow Clara and Felix to live. They were the only two people in the world who mattered to her and Grayson knew it. He was counting on it.

"Get in the car," Odette said quietly.

Clara made a face. "I don't know—"

"*Just*, get in the car."

Reluctantly, Clara nodded and climbed into the front seat, locking the car behind her. That was merely for her own peace of mind, as several windows were shattered, allowing anyone to climb in if they wanted to.

With Clara out of the way, Grayson crossed the remaining distance between them and embraced Odette, his arms wrapping around her like two bands of iron.

"You're freezing," Grayson whispered, "How long have you been out here? This isn't healthy, not for you or for the baby. Do you ever think?"

Odette stayed rooted in her spot, her arms limp at her side. "How did you find me?"

"Thorn. He's been helping me this *whole* time." He smoothed his hand over her hair, petting her like a dog. "Anything for you."

Those words alone knocked the wind from her. She could just barely see the angel over Grayson's shoulder, who was still staring at the pavement in shame.

Grayson pulled back and petted her head. "I'm not sure how I feel about this hair, to tell you the truth; but we can fix that. Right now, you need to get warm. I've got a place for us to stay."

His hand hovered above her lower back, and he urged her forward, the two of them slowly leaving the car with Clara and Felix behind. Odette hardly registered that she was walking; her mind whirling, unable to accept she'd lost.

Blood rushed in her ears, silencing everything. No matter what she did, it wasn't enough—even Thorn was always, ultimately, on their side. She could never win.

Grayson's voice floated into her consciousness. "Where did you get these bruises?"

"You should know. Your sister was *just* here." She pulled her injured hand from his. "Was that your plan all along, leave Greer with the distraction and you come in when my defenses are low?"

"I didn't know Greer was here. I told her to stay away." He frowned to himself, "I thought she would've listened … never mind, if everything goes as planned, you and I will never have to see her ever again."

Alarm bells sounded in her head. Gently, Grayson reached out to cup her cheek. The pads of his fingers barely brushed against her skin when she sprung away, smacking his hand away.

"No!"

He blinked. "No?"

"No," Odette repeated. She took a step back, "Don't touch me! I'm not going back to that… that *cage*. I'm not going back with *you*."

Though she'd gone numb in the fingers, she felt the ring pulse. It was begging to be used, and it would probably get its wish, whether she wanted to or not.

"Odette," he said slowly, like he was speaking to a wild animal, "I think you should choose your next words carefully."

"I said what I said." She swallowed thickly, but her throat was too dry and too tight. The trees that sat on either side of the road swayed to an unfelt wind, bending and bowing inwards.

"No, you don't."

Odette put more distance between the two of them, but for every one step she took, he took two. "I don't want to be with you anymore!"

"You don't mean that."

The surrounding woods seemed to shake with a ferocious wind, but no air blew through the branches. The bark crackled and groaned and the trees bent inwards at unnatural angles, surely ready to snap.

"*Shut up!*" Odette clenched her hands into fists, a white-hot heat pricking her arm like needles. Then, she swung at him. The air whistled loudly, and there was an ear-piercing shatter.

Pain bloomed across her knuckles; but, her fist hadn't connected with Grayson's jaw. There was a ghostly, silver light surrounding her left arm; cracks sprung forth from the point where it had met an iridescent blue wall.

Like glass, shards of the wall fell off into the ground, melting away into wispy puffs of smoke. Even more strange was that above Odette's fist, hovering in perfect alignment with her arm, was a pointed tree root. It had attempted to pierce the wall, which surrounded Grayson, only to stop short because her fist couldn't penetrate the wall itself.

Grayson's eyes were wide, his lips parted in shock. Had he not expected her to lash out? Or, had he not expected the tree? If it was the latter, Odette had to agree, that was accidental but not unwelcome.

"*Thorn!*" Grayson roared. He whipped his head around to where the angel had been standing, but Thorn was gone. Grayson huffed, and turned his attention back to her.

Odette reeled her hand back and moved to slap him. The root slashed out, like a whip, and smashed against the wall surrounding Grayson. He ducked, instinctually, and more pain flared through her arm.

But, then he was gone.

Odette couldn't move, as a hand landed on her shoulder a second later, and another encircled her wrist. She tried to rip her hand away, the tree root mimicking the movement.

"Let me go!"

Grayson's face morphed into something less friendly and more frustrated. "I don't want to hurt you, Odette, not when you're carrying my child, but you are making it very difficult."

His hand tightened on her wrist. His nails tore at her bandages, irritating her already raw wounds inflicted by that maniac Camille Chen. She flexed her fingers and silvery light filled her vision. Grayson grunted as the root smashed against the shield once again.

"You can't hurt me with your magic, Odette."

No magic? Odette set her jaw and reared her knee back, nailing Grayson in the shin with her foot. He shouted and let go, allowing her freedom. She elbowed him in the stomach for good measure, and took off.

What she needed was distance, so she headed for the woods, leaping over the snow bank and ducking under low hanging branches. Grayson said she couldn't use magic to *hurt* him; but that left a lot of things open that magic could do. Odette just hoped the amulet would continue working.

In the distance, Grayson's heavy footsteps pounded against the snow as he ran after her. He'd caught up fast, but it didn't surprise her. After all, he wasn't the one carrying a small human inside of him.

Odette clenched her hand into a fist and the woods groaned. With her ring sparked to life, it was like she could see every part of nature surrounding her, and every root beneath the earth. She was in nature and it was within her. They fed into one another, an endless cycle, and it was equal parts exhilarating and overwhelming.

From the corner of her eye, she thought she saw Thorn standing in between the trees, but it was a trick of the light.

Trust me, she recalled him saying.

That was probably the last thing she ever wanted to do, especially now that she knew he had been leading Grayson towards her the whole time.

Warmth expanded from her ring, like it had before when she fought Greer, only this time it wasn't so oppressive. It was welcome and comforting.

Odette cast her arms in the air, the tips of her fingers streaking silver light as she went. Tree limbs, roots, and other broken bits of bark rose up into the air by her command. They stayed suspended, swirling above her head like a darkened tornado cloud before they fell. The precision at which they landed was sharp, building and stacking into the damp earth. Odette might have been afraid they would impale her if she weren't in control of it all.

Odette stole a glance behind her as she ran and found the trees and branches had formed a wall between the two of them. It stretched as far as her eye could see and nearly two stories tall. Grayson was no longer visible. Only the harsh, blue glow of his amulet shining through cracks in the wooden wall showed he was still on the other side.

"Odette!" Grayson shouted, his voice muffled by distance and the barrier between them, "Come back here, *now*!"

She ran harder. There was no way of telling where, exactly, she was going but she would put as much distance between the two of them as she possibly could.

"I don't want to hurt you!"

All she needed to do now was find where the trees broke—

Behind her, something cracked loudly. The sound echoed loudly throughout the empty forest, like a gunshot. She wanted to stop, for fear of whatever it was, but she couldn't. The scent of smoke caught her nose, and a blue blurred light whizzed past her. It was only when it hit the tree directly in front of her and set it ablaze that she understood it was fire. *Grayson's* fire.

Odette dug her heels into the dirt, her arms swinging wildly to pull her away stopping inches away from the flame. She fell on her back, scrambling as far away from the burning tree as she could, a scream lodged in her throat.

Not fire, anything but fire.

The heat hit her face full force, thawing the cold that froze her skin with one hot puff. It reached out to her, ready to eat and feed on anything it possibly could. It wanted to destroy.

She trembled, the blazing heat taking her back to that horrendous night all those months ago. Odette didn't have a night go by where she wished she could run into the house to save them. She should have tried. Even if she hadn't been successful and she died, she wouldn't have to live with this guilt inside of her, and she wouldn't be in a situation like this.

Behind her, she could hear the sound of shoes scuffing the frozen ground and crunching dead leaves. How she wanted to curl up into a little ball and hide away from him, but it was too late. He had cornered her.

"You can't run from me," said Grayson.

Odette clenched her jaw. "I can try."

He clicked his tongue, obviously unimpressed. "You know I hate fighting with you. I hate seeing you so upset with me. Why can't you just … forgive and forget?"

The swell of pain in her chest was too much. The heat made her lungs burn and her skin blister. She craved the cold, fresh air. How long would she be expected to live through this torture until he let her go?

Odette peeled her face away from her knees and searched for an out. The flames in front of her laughed as they crackled, whispering there was no escape. They were right. Everywhere she looked, blue fire touched. Grayson had created his arena and he would either kill her or capture her.

The fear of dying crept up inside of her. No amount of self-inflicted pain would take it away. Had he really won? It seemed like no matter what she thought up; Odette knew

Grayson would be two steps ahead of her. He was intelligent, and even though he seemed to care for her, she was his adversary at the moment. There wasn't a doubt in her mind he wouldn't hold back, so she couldn't either.

This wouldn't be the end. There had to be a way. Odette stood up on shaky legs and faced him, her gaze hard. She wouldn't allow him to kill her—her body or her spirit.

Grayson met her harsh gaze with his own, just as cold, just as evil. Odette could admit she was afraid of him when he got like this, he was too unpredictable, but she wouldn't let her fear dictate her.

"Do you understand all this fighting is pointless?" Grayson asked in an authoritative manner. "It doesn't only hurt you, but it hurts me, too. Give up, come to me, and we can forget all about this."

"Don't you understand?" More sweat gathered on her skin, sitting on her brow. "I don't *want* to come with you. I don't *care* about who gets hurt, and I will *never* forgive you." She thrust her arm towards him and a burning limb fell from the tree beside her, streaking through the night sky in hot white.

Much to her dismay, he expected it. Grayson had lunged towards her, missing her attack, and the thick tree branch collapsed onto the ground into a pile of ash. Their bodies connected hard, and Odette's head smashed against something hard on the dirt floor.

XXIV

ODETTE

Sunshine shone down on the little yard. It warmed Odette's skin comfortably. A soft breeze rustled the tall grass and ruffled her long, brown hair.

"You haven't finished your food," said Pamela. She pushed forward a bowl filled to the brim with fat strawberries. "You need your strength."

"Sorry mom." Odette grabbed one of the strawberries, but didn't eat it. "Do you want one?"

"No. Those are for you."

Returning from the house with a refreshed basket, her father sat down in the spot reserved for him. From a giant wicker picnic basket, he withdrew their household sugar bowl and laid it out on the blanket.

"Do you want some sugar with those, pumpkin?" asked Jonah.

Odette sprinkled some of the sugar over her bowl of fruit and leaned back against the tree behind her. Their lawn had gotten overgrown, which was strange to her considering her dad mowed every weekend it wasn't raining. Little wildflowers grew erratically around them; dandelions, violets, morning glories—all of them decorated the green lawn, adding dots of vibrant color.

Odette bit down on her strawberry, but it was bland. She looked up at her parents again, and she noticed a third guest who she hadn't seen originally.

"Thorn."

"H-Hello."

She frowned and dropped the strawberry, the ground swallowing it up like quicksand.

"Of course ..." Odette stood and brushed off the front of her dress, cleaning it of dream dust. "I have nothing to say to you."

Odette started for the forest, her feet leading her through the familiar path with ease. Surprisingly, Thorn let her go. She wondered how elaborate this dream world was—if it truly stretched out towards the Mages' property, or if it dropped off into nothing.

She soon got her answer when she stumbled onto what she thought was a clearing—but it was her own backyard again. Thorn had made her go in a circle.

"I apologize," he said.

"And that fixes *everything*?" Odette crossed her arms over her chest, glaring down at him. "It was just a game of cat-and-mouse for you, wasn't it? You said you cared, that you wanted to keep me safe, but you bring him right to me? I thought you were a friend ..."

"I-I held them off," Thorn said lamely. "I tried to redirect Grayson's attention, but he caught onto me."

He stood; with trembling hands, Thorn lifted the edges of his mask and peeled it away from his skin gingerly, as though it pained him to remove it. Odette had gotten used to the sight of his face; one half of it was covered in the Mages' abuse, burns, and cuts that left numerous scars.

However, she was not prepared for him this time. Thorn healed relatively fast, given his otherworldly abilities, but he was trapped in a human body and it could only handle so much apparently.

The remaining skin was paper thin, the bone beneath his flesh poking and stretching it abnormally. Flesh was dead in many places, blackened and or yellowed, purplish lines running along his hollow cheek. His nose was all but gone, and half of his mouth ripped. His good eye seemed to bulge out of the marred skin.

"Thorn ..."

"I endured it as long as I could to give you more time, but Greer got in the way." He slipped the mask back over his face.

Odette paused in thought.

"What happened to Greer?" she asked uneasily. Though the fight had been brutal, Greer had given in a little too easily.

"She has been using her powers excessively over the past few days, so she was weak to begin with. I warned her that possession would be too much on her, but she didn't listen to me."

Odette's heart thudded loudly in her chest. "Is she dead?"

"No." Thorn smiled wryly. "She fell unconscious after you struck the final blow on Thornton. She felt everything you did, on a much smaller scale, but coupled with the strain of magic exhausted her. She passed out and I took her back to Maine to rest."

"Oh ..." part of Odette was a little relieved. While she hated Greer, the thought of killing her made her feel even worse. "What about me?"

"What about you?"

"I remember there was a fight. I don't know what came after." Odette looked around her; at the overgrown backyard; at her parents, still snacking, blissfully unaware of the conversation going on behind them. "This looks like Heaven to me. And ... you are an angel."

Thorn smiled softly at her, but there was pity in his eye. "You think you're dead?"

"It seems right."

"Would you be upset if you were?"

Odette shrugged her shoulders. "I don't feel upset. I think being in here is better than being out there." She exhaled softly, glaring at a blue butterfly near her feet. "But, I have a feeling this is just a dream, right?"

"It's not your time, Odette Sinclair." Thorn laid his hand on her shoulder. "That's why I saved you in the first place."

"… Do you think that matters to me? … Go to bed, Greer. I know it's three in the morning in Maine … I'll—*we'll*—be back when Odette gets better … She's sick … Yes, I said sick … Haha, very funny … It's a cold, or something. She looks rough … *Take that back* … I don't want to hear this. Gree— … I'm done talking, Greer!" Grayson aggressively shut off his phone and slammed it down on the dashboard.

Upon waking, Odette was overcome with an immense amount of pain. It seemed worse than it was before. She felt raw and vulnerable, and her heart clenched painfully in her chest.

Odette remained still, hoping to not attract attention; the events from the forest fresh in her mind. Fighting was a futile now that she thought on it; Grayson had the upper hand.

What about Clara and Felix? Odette swallowed hard, but no matter how hard she pushed, she couldn't recall anything about what happened to them. The last time she saw them they were in the car. Grayson may have forgotten all about them, but he wasn't the type to leave loose ends.

If she could just get a look behind her into the back seat
…

Grayson leaned over her, his silhouette blotted out the oppressive dashboard security lights. His arm slid across her, reaching for the seat buckle. Odette watched him from beneath her eyelashes; his eyes boring holes in her, they were unfeeling and far away, yet curious. It was almost like she was some organism under a microscope and he was the scientist.

"I didn't mean to wake you," he murmured. His voice was much softer now, like he hadn't just been shouting at his sister.

Their eyes locked and he smiled. He reached out gingerly, brushing his thumb across her cheekbone in a swift stroke. Whatever he touched stung and she flinched; there had to have been a cut there. He frowned, put a little more pressure on the wound, and then removed his hand.

"We're here." The way he said it, assumed she knew where *here* was. "I'll carry you inside then I'll need to unload some things."

The thought of him putting his hands on her after everything sent a shudder down her spine. Odette shied away; and in the corner of her eye, she caught two dark, people-like shapes propped up in the back seat.

"I think I can walk."

But Grayson continued talking as if he hadn't heard her. "You hurt yourself pretty bad in the woods, princess." He shook his head, his knuckles brushing against her stomach. "I don't want you under any more unnecessary strain. Understand?"

She bit the inside of her cheek, refraining from saying anything stupid. In the back seat, one of the shadow people moved.

"Where did you get the car?" Odette asked.

"It doesn't matter. *He* won't be missing it." Grayson shot her a pointed look and got out of the car.

Odette watched as he went around the car, her eyes darting to the rear view mirror. "*Clara?*"

306

There was a whimper, but it was cut short when the passenger side door opened. Odette wasn't able to put a foot out of the car before he wormed his arms underneath her arms and legs, pulling her too close.

"Hold on to me," he ordered softly.

"I'm serious, I can walk—"

The grip he had on her became too hard, pinching her skin. "*Just*, hold on to me, Odette. Listen, for once in your life." His voice was coarse, but he kept his temper in check and refrained from yelling.

Odette chewed on her lower lip to keep from showing fear. Slowly, she slid her arms around his neck and clasped them together. Grayson jostled her once before pulling her out of the car.

He bumped the door, it shut hard, and he headed up the walk towards the front door. Odette had to squint, but even in the dark she knew where she was.

"Grayson ... Why are we here?"

"I don't understand why you sound so scared, princess." And yet, his tone of voice suggested he did. Without releasing her from his hold, Grayson twitched his fingers and the door unlocked, opening up all on its own. "The Niesenson's have been very accommodating—I told you we had a place for us to stay, didn't I? And your friend Clara was so nice helping me get back here; I don't know why you didn't mention her before."

Something pungent tickled her nose the further they went into the home. "What do you mean accommodating?"

"I thought this could be a fun little get away. You know, since it turns out I don't know a lot about my wife anymore. I thought we could use this time to ... reconnect."

The way he said the word *wife* made it sound like it was a vulgar four letter word. Odette never felt smaller than that very moment. This was the untouchable Grayson everyone idolized in his natural state.

Grayson paid her shivering little attention and dumped her onto the sofa unceremoniously, then retreated towards the kitchen. With each step, her anxiety increased. This had to be her punishment for not coming back—and now, because of her stupidity, she was going to be forced to watch her friends die.

The stench was worse where she sat, and Odette squeezed her eyes shut. She was afraid of what she might see.

Light flooded the room, and she opened her eyes. Grayson stood near the switch, no emotion on his face. To him, she was a stranger. Then she noticed he wasn't looking *at* her. No, Grayson's gaze fell just beyond where Odette sat on the beige couch, his lips pursed.

She knew she shouldn't look, but her eyes betrayed her before she could force herself to stop. Her stomach rolled, nausea bubbling up. "Grayson, what have you done?!"

Smears of blood were splashed across the wooden floor, as if someone had dumped a large can of viscus, red paint on the floor. It stained the wood, stained the walls, and soaked into the ivory rug turning it a rusted brown. In the corner, piled haphazardly on top of one another were Mr.

and Mrs. Niesenson. Deep slashes stretched all along the length of their bodies, staining their dark skin with red.

"I think you know," he said. "You were on the other end of the line, after all."

Odette didn't know how long she stared, but all she could hear on repeat was Clara's words. *This is all your fault!* That phone call was real, he wasn't bluffing. She had killed them.

"Heath Thornton was a dead end, and fortunately for me the Niesenson's came home early. Calm down Odette, stress isn't good for the baby." Grayson shrugged off his coat and tossed it onto the nearby sectional. "I meant to have this cleaned up before you got here, but I was a little distracted with your tantrum."

This is all your fault.

Grayson was beside her, the couch sinking with his weight. "Quiet, now? Where was this attitude when I came to rescue you?"

Odette clenched her jaw, biting back a harsh slew of swears. She curled her hand into a fist, readying herself for a rematch. If she could do it in the woods, what was stopping her from doing it again?

She leapt towards him blindly, prepared to smash his smug face in. But she never came close. Grayson raised his hand and Odette was thrown back, colliding with the couch. Odette winced; her head throbbed even worse, now.

Propping herself up, she glared at him. "I thought it was impossible for you to use your powers on me?"

"I was," Grayson confirmed. "But, after your little stunt, I took matters into my own hands." From his pocket, he withdrew a very familiar ring.

Odette's stomach dropped. She should've been elated. For months, she had done all she could to get rid of the thing. But now, without it, Odette felt naked. She was acutely aware of her vulnerabilities against him.

"We'll discuss this more, tomorrow," he said, a note of finality in his voice. A touch of pity colored his face. "You should go freshen up."

There was no fighting him; not now, and if she ever got another chance would she be able to take it?

Her dread grew the farther away Grayson got from her. She knew what was going to happen—if the evidence before her wasn't enough, then the memories of what he had done to his grandfather, Zeke, and Greer's best friends would suffice. If she had any hope of saving the two people she still cared for, she had to act.

He was halfway across the living room when Odette found her voice again. "Please, don't hurt my friends."

Grayson stopped short and inhaled sharply. He turned his head ever so slightly, his jaw set. "Let me be frank, Odette. You have annoyed me to the point where I'm angry. I don't want to lash out at you—I love you, but something has to be done."

"No—"

"If you want something, princess; you've got to prove to me you deserve it. Given your performance earlier, you're on thin ice. Now, I want you to listen to me; go upstairs and clean yourself up. I'm done talking about this."

A lump formed in her throat, effectively silencing her. She rose slowly from the couch, staring only at her feet as they dragged across the carpet.

"Oh, and Odette?" he called out, "Fix your hair while you're at it."

The mirror had fogged up upon Odette leaving the shower; a towel wrapped uncomfortably tight around her chest. She made a quick swipe at it with her hand and looked her into her reflection, cringing. Her face was a mess, all bruised up and scraped from recent events. Whatever she smashed into at the end of their fight, probably a rock, left a nasty looking gash on her temple.

Odette dug through the medicine cabinet and found a bandage to stick over it. It was pathetic, barely covering a third of the injury, but she didn't have the energy to fix it.

Her newly darkened hair dripped fat water droplets onto the tiled floors. Even though Clara must have purchased nearly twenty boxes before, none of them matched her original color.

It was strange: while she'd showered, she thought she heard screaming. Odette had to force herself to stay where she was. No matter how badly she wanted to help, she couldn't just rush in, vulnerable and unprepared. She needed to wait for the right time.

Odette pushed away from the mirror and looked at the clothes that had been laid out for her. Grayson must have been in the Niesenson's home for quite some time, as the bathroom had been fully stocked with everything. It made her sick to know she'd have to wear something of Clara's, especially after seeing her parents mangled bodies, knowing it could've been prevented. Odette tried to think about something else.

The clothes were a bit snug, (Clara was much smaller than Odette), but she found a way to make the sweatpants more comfortable. They ended just above her ankles and no amount of tugging would make them lower.

Odette sniffled and looked herself over. It was as good as it was going to get, and any longer, Grayson would track her down.

Odette turned to the dark hallway, overreaching shadows clinging to either side of the wall. Grayson left no light on and no instructions as to where he'd be; but, there was a faint flickering of color on the far wall that drew her attention.

She forced herself to move and crept up the stairs slowly. The further up she went, the more she could detect the sound of voices.

She frowned and pushed onwards. Clara's parents' bedroom door was shut, and so was her grandmother's. As she rounded the corner to her friend's bedroom she found Grayson, standing by her dresser and flipping through a photo album. On the TV, a movie played.

No, it wasn't a movie. Odette stared at the screen for several seconds before a small smile formed on her lips.

"*Why did we have to go out today of all days!*" a younger Odette complained off screen. The camera shakily pointed towards her as she swatted at mosquitoes with a look of discomfort plastered all over her face. "*It's supposed to rain.*"

"*Bigfoot doesn't care about rain,*" said a young Felix. He was noticeably smaller in the video and loaded down with a bunch of supplies.

"*Bigfoot doesn't care about your face,*" young Odette shot back.

The footage turned black, then resumed playing with the three of them standing all together, a sign in hand, which happened to be a collection of papers taped together to form one large poster.

Clara counted down to three under her breath before speaking, "*This is our thirteenth monster expedition in the Crabtree forest. We are still on our hunt for the elusive Gumberoo.*"

Once again, the camera blacked out again before cutting to the next scene.

"Why are you just standing there?" Grayson asked. His eyes flickered off of the page he was looking at for a moment and motioned at her to come in with his head. "It's late. You need sleep."

Odette didn't want to. She felt if she took one step into the room, she might cry. Grayson being in here was a reminder nothing was safe.

"Why are you watching these?" She gestured towards the TV, where the three young versions of herself and her friends were now running through the woods. "They're just ..." *silly, unimportant, painful to look at, unwanted memories*. All of them fit, but she couldn't finish her thought.

"Because, I want to know what my wife was like." Grayson shut the photo album and took Odette by the wrist, jerking her into the room.

"*Watch it, moron!*" young Odette screeched on the recording.

Grayson frowned but soon released her. "I never would have thought you were interested in things like this."

Like this being the giant BigFoot she happened to be next to in a photo. Grayson picked it up and examined it, his expression unreadable.

Odette pinched her mouth together tight. It was painful to divulge any information to him, not because she didn't want to, but because she didn't want to remember those times. It wasn't all because of him, either.

"Yeah, well you never asked."

Grayson moved across the room and settled himself on Clara's plush red chair. "I never had to ask before, you know. It was always just ... clear to me, what was going on in your head."

The younger version of herself collapsed onto a rock on the screen, out of breath. Her face was red, her eyes bleary and unfocused. Off screen, both Clara and Felix were practically screaming. It wasn't anything bad. It was just her heart.

Odette turned away and focused on the bed spread. "But you can't really get to know someone that way."

"It's easy." He shrugged his shoulders, smiling at her like the fight they'd had just hours before hadn't happened. "Besides, sometimes it's painless to learn about things from someone's head rather than their mouth. They can't lie that way."

"But that's like cheating."

"Why did you leave me that night?" Grayson's words cut through the air like a knife. "I want to believe this was all a mistake; but everything I've witnessed tonight suggests otherwise."

Odette dug her nails into her palms. "You wouldn't believe me if I told you."

Grayson leaned forward on his elbows, bits of hair falling forward to obscure his eyes. "I would. That is, unless I knew you were lying to me."

There were so many things she could say to him, she *wanted* to say to him. Most of them were only to save her skin, though. Grayson's piercing blue eyes made anyone want to tell the truth because they knew he was capable of anything. And the way he acted earlier in the night? Odette could not be certain he wouldn't try and harm her. He said it himself, she had angered him.

What would he do to someone he claimed to love if he was angry? Odette began to tremble, thousands of starters coming to mind but none of them making their way to her tongue.

Grayson sighed and ran his hand over his face. For the first time that night, Odette noticed how truly tired he looked, with shadows beneath his eyes and his face looking pale.

"I've decided we need a vacation."

Apprehension took hold of her, "'We?'"

He nodded staunchly, "Yes, you and I. Until I know you're well enough, we won't go back home."

"What ... are you talking about?"

"You need to be away from Greer. You never said it explicitly, but I know her. She was a part of the reason why this happened. And she can be ... fiercely protective. Possessive. I worry about your safety, and the baby's."

In theory, it sounded perfect. As far as Odette was concerned Greer couldn't be trusted. Staying away from the mansion, a place filled with deceit and death, was one thing Odette could agree to. But, it came with an obvious price: Grayson, for the rest of her life.

"You've already made up your mind, haven't you?" she asked.

Grayson shrugged, "It's what's best. You know it, too."

Seconds stretched on like hours in the dark, Grayson's soft snores reminding Odette he was very much alive and in *Clara's* room.

It was some kind of cruel joke that they were resting in a room covered in happy childhood memories, while Mr. and Mrs. Niesenson's bodies rotted downstairs and Clara and

Felix were stowed away, hopefully still alive. Grayson hadn't mentioned a thing about them, aside from a couple of questions about her childhood; but nothing about their whereabouts. Then, he grabbed some blankets and nearly all the pillows and built himself a nest on the floor, leaving the bed to Odette.

While she was glad he hadn't forced himself in the small twin bed with her, the fact that he was mere feet away still made her tense, putting a stop to any hope of sleep.

Silently, she sat up and rubbed her eyes. Grayson made a noise in his sleep and she paused, not moving again until he had rolled over on his side.

Odette pushed off the bed, sparing one last glance at the boy on the floor, before quietly padding out of the room. There was no way she could sleep; her mind was too wired and alert from everything that had transpired within the last twenty-four hours.

Every creak of the floor grated on her already raw nerves; the shadows played tricks on her mind. Though Odette knew, rationally, she was safe, Grayson was asleep upstairs, and Greer away in Maine; she had witnessed far too many preternatural events to be sure of anything anymore.

Odette hovered by the banister only a moment. *You can go now,* said her mind. *It'll be easy. There's no one here to stop you. Grayson's asleep.*

She eyed the door, barely visible in the moonlight. It stood there, taunting her, freedom just on the other side.

Her muscles screamed for her to move, tense beneath her skin; but, Odette didn't go.

She squeezed the banister firmly, solidifying her resolve. Odette had already abandoned one innocent soul, leaving him at the mercy of Greer Mages; she would not abandon the people who stuck by her side for years growing up.

Instead, she skirted through the living room, (not looking at where Mr. and Mrs. Niesenson had been), and tiptoed around the rug that laid just inside the door, not daring to even step on it; knowing if she did, she would go without a second thought.

The kitchen was dimly lit by the moonlight from the large windows in the living room. The curtains had been drawn just enough to keep anyone who might pass by from thinking anything was wrong. Odette carefully opened a cabinet and grabbed a glass when she heard a noise.

Her stomach dropped, and she stayed still for a moment, straining her ears. The house groaned. Someone drove by on the street. Something in the basement rustled.

Odette abandoned her glass, and crept towards the basement door. It sat beside a half-wall, not visible to the living room or the front door when you first walk in. The Niesensons' used it as a pantry and to store gardening supplies in the off-season.

It was also the only place Grayson could've hidden Clara and Felix, if he hadn't already disposed of them.

Red stained the once white door. She gingerly laid her head against the wood, listening for the noise again. There was a soft shuffling of movement.

Odette reached down and jiggled the handle. Locked. She swore under her breath. Of course it was.

She rocked back onto her heels and chewed on her bottom lip. The Niesenson's had a ring of keys somewhere, and Grayson might not know about them. If he did this on a whim, it was likely he just sealed the door with magic—he wouldn't have time to search for a key. So, she still had a chance.

Odette laid her hand on the door, an unspoken promise resonating between her and the universe.

Something scuffed on the other side of the door and Odette stood straight, prepared to run or fight. The door muffled a good bit of the person's words, but she could hear them with relative clarity.

"Is someone there?"

Startled at first, the voice soon registered with her. She pressed up against the crack of the door, putting her lips to the wall. "It's me—it's Odette. Clara?"

"Odette?" the muffled voice repeated. *"Is that really you?"*

"Yeah, it is. Are you guys okay? What happened?"

Between the pauses, Odette's heartbeat thundered in her ears, drowning out all else. If she spoke louder than a whisper, Grayson would almost certainly hear, and she didn't want to imagine what he'd do if he found her down there.

Clara sniffed and the sound of something scraping the wood echoed through the room. *"Get us out. Please. It's horrible down here! Felix is hurt, like really hurt, and my—my parents are ...*" She choked on a sob and slammed her fist against the door. Odette leapt back. "*You said it was a bluff! You said he wouldn't hurt them!*"

Odette whipped her head around in alarm. The slam was loud, they would be lucky if it didn't draw Grayson's attention. He was a light sleeper.

She stared down at the golden handle dismally. "I-I'm sorry. I didn't think he would do it."

"*You thought wrong!*" Clara choked on a sob. "*Because of you, my parents are dead. Because of you Felix can't see anymore. If we'd only come straight here ... If you hadn't brought us along this wouldn't have happened!*"

The sad truth of it, she was right. If they had never come with her at all, their parents would be alive. It was all her fault.

"I know." Odette pierced her palm with her nails, willing her voice to stay strong. "I'm going to get you out. I promise."

There was no response. Odette backed away, her jaw set. Clara had no idea how much she *did* understand.

A pair of hands grasped Odette firmly by the shoulders and shook her out of her fitful sleep. Her eyes burst open, pushing away the intruder; however, Grayson caught her wrists with ease and gently worked her down from her fit.

"Why are you down here?" he asked.

Odette glanced around the living room; evidently she had fallen asleep on the couch.

She spent half the night, after her talk with Clara, scouring the kitchen for the key ring. She found it in one of the junk drawers, underneath rubber bands and ticket stubs, and spent the rest of the time trying to fit the keys into the lock.

It was dawn when she'd finally given up, binding the 'dud' keys with a rubber band, leaving a little less than half to go. She just needed an opportunity to try them in the door.

Odette rubbed the burn from her eyes, glaring at the wall clock that read seven o' five in the morning.

XXV

GREER

Greer's head had been pounding non-stop for hours. Her body ached, her temperature fluctuated between dangerously hot to freakishly low, and she had already expelled any and all food from her body. If she didn't know any better she might have thought she had the flu, but, she did know better.

She also knew Thorn, gluttonous for teaching opportunities, was eating this up despite the worried frown on his hideous face.

"I warned you what would happen," he said. Thorn replaced the cool cloth on her head with another.

"I was so close. She was going to die." Thorn said nothing. He dried his hands on a towel and moved to fuss over the tray of food he had brought. "I could have made her bleed."

Thorn laid the tray down on Greer's lap, a little too hard for her liking. "Of course."

Greer scoffed at his skepticism. *What did he know, anyway?* "I'll get my chance. I just have to wait. What about Grayson?"

"He is well."

She snorted. *He is well*—of course Grayson was *well*, Grayson was an impenetrable fortress. Her brother was invincible; Greer helped make sure of it.

"You know that's not what I meant." Though, a small part of her might admit it was. If, by some chance, Grayson had been hurt, she would want to be the first one to know about it. "When is he coming home, Thorn?"

Thorn opened his mouth, but before he could respond the doorbell chimed Beethoven's Fifth. The tune, overly loud and obnoxious to Greer's sensitive ears, made her wilt and cover her head with a pillow.

"In a moment, mistress." Thorn gave a curt bow. "I will return." In the blink of an eye, he vanished from his spot, leaving no trace he had been there.

Greer exhaled hard, shoving the food away. There was no way she could eat anything Thorn brought her, not because it didn't look appealing, but because her stomach churned at the sight.

Mere seconds later Thorn reappeared, his lips spread in a grim smile. "It is Mrs. Palit. She says it's urgent."

She sat up fast, "Where is she now?" Greer didn't wait for him to speak, she was out of bed and gathering her robe around her waist.

324

She didn't call—Mrs. Palit always called if she was stopping by. She was the more courteous of the mother-duo. Could Thorn have gotten it wrong? No, he'd never confuse the two. A surprise visit like this was so out of character it increased her unease. What could she want?

The bodies ...?

No, it was too soon for them to be discovered. Although they were interrupted in the middle of their dumping, it wasn't nearly as thorough as Greer would have liked. It had to be something else, she resolved.

"She is in the sun room," said Thorn.

Greer left the room, shutting the door behind her. She was in front of the sun room before she had anticipated, the winter sun just barely casting a glow through the frosted glass. Greer observed Mrs. Palit alone, standing then sitting and then standing again from one of the jade couches in the room. Her face was pale and drawn, like she hadn't been sleeping, and she continually twisted the straps of her purse between her hands.

Out of the corner of her eye, Mrs. Palit spotted Greer and the space between her brows creased.

"Greer—I'm sorry I came without calling, but I had to talk to you." She opened her arms to usher Greer into the room.

The two of them hugged, awkward and stiff, before Greer pulled back and looked Mrs. Palit over. She wasn't injured, maybe a little pale, but otherwise fine.

She knows, her mind hissed.

"What's happened?"

The air between the two of them turned tense. Mrs. Palit wouldn't look her directly in the eye; instead, staring at a spot on the floor, her lips pursed so hard they trembled. She made the first move to sit, perching herself on the very edge of the large settee. It seemed to Greer the woman might bolt at any moment, but for the time she stayed stock still and clenched her fists around her knees.

Greer sat, too, eyeing the woman. She made no move to pry, but the longer they sat in the silence the more uncomfortable Greer became. Her leg bounced anxiously off the floor, the movement unperceivable beneath her robe.

Mrs. Palit cleared her throat, her black eyes shining with unshed tears. "I got a call from Laurie McBride yesterday. The police found ... *pieces*. Body parts."

Greer inhaled sharply, her leg pausing mid-bounce. "Oh?"

"Nothing has been confirmed yet, and I haven't received any calls to go in to identify anything, but who else could it be?" Her hands clenched so hard her knuckles bulged from her wafer-thin skin, trembling. "This sort of stuff ... it doesn't happen every day. I mean, what is the coincidence that body *pieces* turn up after my Nadia goes missing?"

Greer could hardly focus on Mrs. Palit, her presence melted into the background of the room.

How could this have happened? She was careful—she never left any tracks to show what she'd been up to. But, maybe she hadn't been as careful this time. Greer bit her tongue hard; no, she had been distracted. She left quickly to handle Odette.

Once more, Mrs. Palit's voice filtered into her consciousness, "... There are mentally ill among us, Greer, living in our town beneath our very noses. Who could ... could do this to an eighteen year old girl? *Why*?"

"I understand your fears." Greer held up a hand, quieting her. She needed to nip this in the bud, and quickly. "But, like you said, nothing's been confirmed. This could be some prank. Until you know I think it's best you try not to fret."

Mrs. Palit was not dissuaded, in fact, it seemed she became even more fired up. "But it makes sense, doesn't it, Greer? This isn't the first time someone was discovered in pieces like that. In those woods no less. This can't be an accident, it was deliberate."

The girl, of whom she spoke, Romy Bacheller, was indeed an accident. She and her brother were young then, they hadn't learned they needed to cover their tracks better.

It took all of Greer's willpower not to sneer. Instead, she turned away and pretended to inspect something at the far wall. "Where did Mrs. McBride hear this?"

Mrs. Palit blinked rapidly, stammering to accommodate the change in conversation. "Sheriff Landry's mother was talking about it at church, apparently—"

"You know you can't trust anything a senile old woman says. She probably overheard the sheriff talking about some animal they discovered and her mind concocted some elaborate story." Greer smiled at her, patting her hands sympathetically. "I'll get my P.I. on it, okay? You have a real source—a direct source. *If* what Ms. Landry says is true, then we'll have our confirmation from a professional."

The grin was beginning to hurt her cheeks, but she couldn't stop; not until she knew Mrs. Palit was sold. The woman surveyed her face, looking for an ounce of insincerity or something to back her doubts. Greer wouldn't let her find it.

"You're right," she allowed. "I'm sorry to have bothered you ..."

"Don't be!" Greer interjected, rising to her feet. "You have every reason to be upset over hearing something like this. And you can tell Mrs. McBride everything I said, too. Better yet, tell her to come and visit me; it'll probably make her feel better."

They walked towards the door together; the only noise was the soft patter of their shoes on the marble floors. For a brief moment, Greer contemplated killing the woman then and there. It would be easy, with no witnesses around, and it would take care of one problem. On the other hand, it would make things difficult in the long run. The police were already investigating the disappearance of her daughter. If she died now, it could be too obvious; all signs would point to Grayson and herself.

Mrs. Palit said quiet goodbyes, not quite meeting Greer's gaze when she finally exited. Greer watched and waited until her car was gone from the driveway, passed through the gates, and off the private road before she closed the door and locked it.

She laid her head against the wood. "Did you know?"

Behind her, Thorn shifted uncomfortably. "I wasn't aware the news had spread so fast."

"But, you knew." Greer glared at him over her shoulder. "You didn't think that this was something important to let me know about?"

"An error I won't make again."

She clenched her jaw and said nothing. Thorn was lying, though calling him out would be a waste of energy. For whatever reason, he seemed to be hell bent on inconveniencing her as of late. Greer blamed it on Odette giving him confidence.

"I'm going to my room. Don't bother me."

☆☆☆

Overnight, it snowed non-stop. The weatherman said Crabtree had accumulated a little over two feet of snow, record snowfall for this time of year, being so close to spring; but, not as much as the surrounding counties. School called, announcing their closure.

Things couldn't have worked out better for Grayson than if he'd burned down the town like he first planned.

Grayson nudged a bowl of cereal across the table until it was centered with Odette's crossed arms. "You're quiet this morning."

She glanced at the bowl, then back at him, pouting. "I don't have anything to say."

"You have to eat. It's not healthy to skip meals."

"Not hungry."

However, as he said this, he picked over his own food and swallowed the sugary breakfast tart in one bite, more or less, and repressed a gag.

Odette pushed the bowl away, leaning back in her chair. She didn't look at him, but instead focused on the television and whatever new story they were running now.

It was strange. There she was, in front of him, and yet she felt so far away. Anger twitched within Grayson's chest. It wasn't supposed to happen like this. They were together now, they were in the same space, no longer separated; and yet the issues Odette held onto made him feel like they were miles apart.

Grayson was frustrated. It made no sense. He had done everything—eliminated every obstacle—and yet her love might as well be unattainable.

He shoved away from the table roughly, finally catching her attention. "Fine. If you want to destroy yourself, do that."

"Where are you going?" she called out.

It didn't matter where, all he knew was he needed space. Strange, right? Space from the one person he wanted to be close to, from the one person he actually loved. But he couldn't take any more of it, and he knew if he spent another second near her he would snap.

"Away."

Alone in Clara's room, Grayson paced back and forth until the floor felt as though it might give out beneath him. He tugged at his hair and rubbed his eyes, frustrated, but nothing afforded him clarity. Had he really made a mistake in choosing Odette?

It wouldn't be the first time; there had been so many girls before her, equal in sweetness and naive. They all had that same ... spark; but, in the end, it always fizzled out. Odette seemed different—but ever since the wedding she had been different. Distant.

Grayson groaned, falling back on the bed. He didn't want to get rid of Odette; that would be admitting defeat to himself, and to his sister. Marriage wasn't supposed to be difficult, was it?

Across the room, in the breast pocket of his coat, Grayson was startled by a sudden vibration. He snatched the coat off of the chair and withdrew the phone. Greer.

Of course she would call, even from thousands of miles away she could sense his wavering faith. It was her superpower; infecting doubt and making it fester. He had half a mind to ignore it, she wouldn't say anything he needed to hear; but, he picked up on the last ring, reluctantly.

"Hey."

"*We might have a problem,*" said Greer. "*I just had a visit from Mrs. Palit.*"

"Who?"

"*Remember Nadia, the girl that you killed for no reason last year?*" Her words were clipped, each syllable packing a punch. "*Her mother.*"

Grayson frowned—to be honest, that entire period of time was a blur of passion and rage; the only figures that stood out with any prominence were Mr. and Mrs. Sinclair, but even they were distorted by his memory. He forced himself to remember, the name was familiar, and a vague image of a girl came to mind. Small, tan skin, dark hair, glasses.

"Oh. Her. You've been visiting those mothers for a while now, haven't you?" Greer made a noncommittal noise of agreement. "Then what makes this any different?"

Greer sighed, her voice weaker than before. "*I disposed of the bodies during the snowstorm, but I got ... distracted.*"

"Distracted?" he echoed.

"*It doesn't matter now—what matters is that they were found.*" She paused and then added. "*Mrs. Palit is already suspicious because of the location. She didn't explicitly say it, but I know that some part of her doubts me. I know we can fix this, but I can't do it alone.*"

Grayson began clenching and unclenching his fist. There were many things he'd like to say—no, not say—shout. *How could she be so stupid?* They were barely able to throw suspicion off the first time with the death of the Bacheller family, and that was with Jethro at their side.

But, they're stronger now, and that was years ago when he barely had a grip on his powers. He exhaled slowly and loosened his fist. This was just a bump in the road—nothing major. "Of course; but, I'm not done here."

"*Grays ...*"

"I know, but I need to tie up some loose ends. I can't come home just yet." Grayson sighed, pressing his finger to his lips. "Odette will need to be prepared, as well."

"Then I'm coming to you."

XXVI

ODETTE

Odette waited until she heard the slam of the upstairs bedroom door before she made a move. She bolted from the kitchen chair, her heart thudded in her chest as she tore open the junk drawer.

Last night had been dangerous enough, sneaking down and trying not to make noise; but this moment was even more nerve wracking. Now, Grayson was awake, and at any moment he could decide to come back.

Odette pushed the thought to the back of her mind and began the task at hand: the keys. Most of them had been taped off, a little more than half. It could be any one of them on the ring ... or, none of them at all, a bleak thought Odette didn't want to consider.

The smell coming from the basement was more pungent than just a few hours before. The cold didn't mask it like she expected. Odette cupped her hand over her nose and mouth to keep the stench out, but it didn't help.

Each key she tried took a good minute, trying it each way twice, before giving up and tying it off. She may have gone faster if she wasn't so concerned about Grayson on the floor above, so each of her movements were slow and methodical avoiding any noise that might alert him.

Odette pushed another key aside and fumbled with the next. Had it been an hour or more? It was getting difficult holding back all the 'dud' keys, there had to be forty or more.

Odette chucked another key and grabbed another. She could practically hear his footsteps already. She could feel him breathing down her neck. She was already dead—

The key fit.

Yanking her hand back, as if the key burned her, Odette stared in awe. It fit? *It fit* ... The fact didn't seem to register. She wasn't sure how long she stared at the key, hope filling her. *This was it*!

A laugh bloomed in her chest. Odette clasped her hands over her mouth to keep it from escaping her. Quickly, she pulled the basement key off of its ring and returned the other keys to the junk drawer.

Once more, she fit the key in the lock and it turned effortlessly. The large wooden door squeaked ominously; the hinges trying to resist the pull. Odette paused, surveying the room in case she was about to be caught, then swung it open with a harsh jerk.

The stench hit her full force; death and decay, ten times stronger in the basement than above. Odette gripped the doorframe so hard her fingernails tore into the wood. She squeezed her eyes shut tight and regained her balance. No matter what, she was going down there.

Odette slipped the key into her jean pocket and stepped over the threshold. The light from above only illuminated a few steps, the rest dropping off into darkness. Hastily, she gripped the lumber railing and quickly descended the steps. All she could think about was getting them out.

The stairs creaked with age; despite looking well maintained, they always frightened Odette because of the way they shook and swayed when more than one person climbed on them. One of her worst fears was that one day the steep stairs would break and she would fall.

Odette's eyes slowly adjusted to the dark. At the base of the stairs was Clara. Even in the darkness, it was easy to see that she'd gotten paler and scraped up since being locked up in the basement.

"Odette?" Clara croaked.

She hopped off the last step and helped her friend stand. "I came as soon as I could," Odette said. "Where's Felix?"

Clara pressed her lips into a thin line. "Did you bring us something? Food? Blankets?"

"No. I'm getting you both out of here." She glanced back up at the top of the stairs. The door was still cracked open, freedom just beyond it. "I'll help you as much as I can, but you have to go now. You have to hurry."

Clara nodded rapidly, trying to keep up with the sudden influx of information. "Okay. How are we getting out?"

I haven't gotten that far yet, but Odette didn't say it. Grayson kept the car keys on the coffee table in the living room, taunting her. She could grab them on the way out. As for the front door ...

"What about Felix?" Clara asked. She bit her lip, looking back behind her. "It's bad."

"Can he make it out of here?"

She turned her head towards a far corner of the room. There was a human-ish shape propped up against the wall. "I ... I don't know."

The hair on her arm stood on end. "What did Grayson do?"

Clara bent down and picked up a flashlight from the floor. She switched it on, and a yellow light shone on the water heater in the corner where the bottom of Felix's shoes could be seen. Clara walked forward a couple of steps, motioning for Odette to follow. Each step slowly revealed more of Felix's limp body.

They stopped about a foot away from where he laid. Clara lifted the light to fully illuminate him.

The sight was horrendous. Felix was sprawled out like a rag doll, arms and legs thrown haphazardly around him. His shirt had been practically ripped from his body, held together by the threads, revealing his burnt and bruised torso. His left arm was twisted in an unnatural angle and had turned an ugly shade of purple.

Then she noticed his eyes. Blackened pits replaced where his pretty golden brown eyes had once been. His eyes had been removed. They weren't bloody, and Odette couldn't say it was an act of mercy, but they were cauterized. There were burn marks on his nose and cheeks, from where the flames had gotten a little out of hand.

Odette clasped her hand over her mouth. "Is he ... dead?"

He might as well have been. The longer she stared at him, the more he looked it. Odette found no visible signs of breathing. He was so ragged and pale it uneasily reminded her of Officer Thornton and his mangled, undead corpse.

Felix couldn't be dead. She had just spoken with him the other day! He was just alive! He couldn't be dead. He wasn't ... No ... If he was ...

Odette's breaths came in short, fast pants and tears blurred her vision. Felix couldn't be dead. He was one of her oldest friends. Her stomach lurched.

"T-Tell me he ... he isn't dead," Odette begged.

Clara laid a hand on her arm. "He still has a pulse. It's just ... we need to get him to a hospital."

It was hard to hear her over the sound of the rushing blood in her ears. *Felix.*

"He's asleep, I think. He doesn't spend too much time awake and I don't know if it's because awake means he feels pain, or if it's because the pain is too much and it makes him sleep. I just let him, what else can I do?"

Odette suddenly felt weak, clutched her chest and fell to the ground. He wasn't dead. A small amount of sickness, perverted mercy from Grayson, but better than the alternative.

"I can't lose you both, too," Odette cried. She shoved her hands in her hair and tugged. "I don't care what it takes.

I'm going to get you out. I swear to you. I will get you out of here!"

Clara stared at her oddly, "We're ... We're surviving, Odette."

"No, no! You both have to *live*." She wiped her face with the back of her hand and stared back at her friend, "It's bad enough he's done *this*. I won't let him ... kill you, too. If he does, I won't have anyone left."

Clara stared at her with wide eyes.

No, she might not have her ring anymore; but she wasn't powerless.

"Come on. I'm going to need your help getting him up those stairs." Odette gingerly stepped over Felix. He smelled like death; it clung to his clothes and was woven into his skin. Touching his shoulder once, he didn't move. She did it again, this time with more force.

Felix jerked, his head swiveling about like a chicken's. "Wh ... what ...?"

"It's me," she said. "I'm here to get you out."

He turned to her, blindly looking up. Those eye-less pits stared back at her. "Odette?"

"Yeah. Can you give me your hand?" She took his good hand and gave it a squeeze. "We don't have much time—"

"What's the point?" He grit his teeth, his words slow and painful. "I'm dead either way. Just leave me."

"No." Odette squeezed his shoulders. "Once you get out, you and Clara will find help and you'll be just fine."

"I don't have any *eyes*, Odette. That doesn't count as *just fine*."

Clara joined her at his side, kneeling down beside him. "Please, Felix. I can't go without you."

Felix flinched; then nodded reluctantly. He raised one hand, then another. Clara appeared at Odette's side and helped pull him up, slowly, settling him around their shoulders. Felix tried to stifle his cries of pain.

The three of them slowly shuffled towards the staircase and Odette's anxiety skyrocketed. It was hard enough to make it down the steep stairs in the dark as one person; but, to do it as three people ...?

"Those stairs are narrow." Clara voiced Odette's very concern. "We can't fit like this."

"No," said Odette. "We'll go sideways. We can make it."

"Just leave me behind," said Felix.

"We're not leaving anyone," said Clara, "So shut up. We'll try sideways. Odette, you go first."

Together, the girls hoisted Felix onto the stairs. Odette took the lead, feeling out the step above her before she stepped onto it. It was more difficult than she imagined. They were like dead weight clinging to one another as they shuffled through the dark, narrow space. Odette used her free arm to hug the railing, using the extra leverage to pull them up the stairs.

"We're almost there," Odette whispered. Her heart thumped so loud, she was positive everyone could hear it. "After I get you out, you're on your own. Clara, drive as far as you can and find a hospital."

Clara knit her eyebrows together. "You aren't coming? I thought we were getting out of this together?"

"You're better off if I don't." She glanced back to Clara, hoping she would understand.

Odette reached the top and kicked the door open wider with her foot. Harsh daylight shone through the windows with no regard for the darkness they were use to. However, something blocked the sun's harsh rays. Two somethings, standing in front of the basement door.

Odette froze in place causing Felix and Clara to trip over one another. Instinct told her to back away, but there was nothing to back into except the pit which she'd just come from.

"I was coming to see you, actually, but it's so sweet of you to come to me instead. And you brought your friends. I'd love to meet them," said Greer.

Grayson stared blankly at the wall behind Odette's head. There was nothing on his face, no perceivable emotion, and for some reason that scared her more than anything. She wished he would frown or plead or even look at her. But, he kept staring at the wall, like she was nothing.

"That's Greer Mages," Clara said.

"Unfortunately," added Odette.

Greer looked exhausted. Odette was used to seeing her perfect—never dressed in anything but the best and complexion so good it glowed. The Greer in front of her might as well have been a whole other person.

"Let's just get this over with," said Grayson.

Greer pouted playfully, but it was gone in an instant. She thrust her hands outwards towards the trio and they were flung back into the basement by an invisible force.

Odette was airborne. She couldn't scream, though her open mouth did try. She grasped wildly at the air around her, but nothing was there to catch her. She watched as the hollow expression on Grayson's face morphed into something else. Her eyes squeezed shut, bracing for impact.

What would she hit first? Would it be the stairs; or the cement floor; or the shelves on the wall?

Pain bloomed instantly from an area in her body, but before she could pinpoint it she was enveloped into darkness.

☆☆☆

Odette sat upright, panting hard; her breath came out short and fast leaving her light headed. She clutched her chest; her heart was beating far too fast to be considered healthy. Odette squeezed the area over her heart, her nails biting into her skin through the thin fabric of her sleep shirt. She needed to *breathe*; in, one two ... out, one two ...

Ever so slowly, her heart rate decreased into a more manageable level. The spottiness of her vision receded, and she was left with only the darkness of the room. Silhouettes of familiar belongings (her chair, the desk, boxes still unpacked) gave her comfort. Odette was safe in her bed ... everything was fine.

Briefly, she debated on calling out to her mother; but decided against it. Her mom wouldn't understand. She'd probably make her share the whole nightmare and ... well, Odette didn't want to have to fess up to all of that.

She turned to her bedside table but didn't see her phone, nor her alarm clock. *If the alarm clock wasn't lit up then the power must be out.*

Going back to sleep wasn't an option. Odette wrapped the sheets around her tightly and hugged her knees. She'd sit there all night if she had to.

Out of the corner of her eye, something moved. She stiffened, her breath stuttering to a near-halt.

"Runt ...?"

But it wasn't the kitten. Runt would have acknowledged her name, and Runt wasn't as big as ... as *that*!

It moved through the shadows, crawling and slithering like a monster. All she could hear was the whisper of feet against the floor. Odette could only whimper, even her voice was paralyzed. She was truly trapped in her body.

The thing took shape at the foot of the bed, a shifting and swirling black mass. It garbled and hissed at her, as if it were trying to speak in another language. Blood dripped from its many heads and limbs.

The longer she stared at the beast, she recognized pieces of it. Zeke, the kindly caretaker from the Mages' home; Jethro, the twins' grandfather; Bonnie and Nadia; the boy from the forest; Officer Thornton; Mr. and Mrs. Niesenson; her parents.

But none were as she had remembered them. They were grey; no color touched their skin, except for dull yellows and vibrant or rusted red specks.

They were corpses, a horrible agglomeration of flesh. A moving abomination.

Their faces—were mangled and marred—stared at her with their dull eyes, unseeing and yet all-knowing. The monster's many appalling limbs grasped the sheets, tearing at the fabric with ragged nails and clawing her bare legs. The stomach was nothing but a gaping wound, entrails dangling just above her exposed feet.

Odette might have screamed, but her voice lodged in her throat and she couldn't do anything but kick and push the beast away.

Who would do something like this, Odette thought. *How could something so terrible exist?*

And when she thought the monster—obviously malicious—was about to strike a killer blow, a gentle hand landed on her shoulder. The touch sent a jolt through her system and she shrieked, scrambling back to the head of the bed.

"It will be alright."

The monster melted into the shadows. Odette might have thought she made the whole thing up if she couldn't still feel their hands on her.

Thorn. Shadows covered the lower part of his face, leaving his eyes exposed in the moonlight. He looked alarmingly human in moments like this; not beastly and not strange. Odette assumed he frowned, as his eyebrows dipped downwards and his eyes slanted.

"This is not real," Thorn reminded her gently, his voice soothing. "It is all in your mind."

Suddenly, the room seemed too artificial. Odette blinked, finding that the intimate details she had mooned over were now softening into misshapen blobs. The room didn't quite seem like her bedroom anymore; but a blackened room upon which she had projected furnishings and toys.

It wasn't real.

She pressed her hands hard to her eyes, hoping to make it all clear again, but there was no pain. Her hand might as well have passed right through her. Then it came to her, this was just a dream.

"They were real," Odette murmured as reassurance.

One by one, she tried to recollect their faces happy and natural, not scarred and evil, but how they had been before. It was difficult to do, as some faces were already a little fuzzy in her memory.

More of the room faded into nothingness, leaving only Thorn's solid shape and herself sitting in the abyss.

"You ... you are right," he conceded, "I apologize."

The calm atmosphere had vanished and Odette was left with this cold, hard reality. This place wasn't her home and Thorn wasn't her friend. Maybe he'd never been one; and Odette, naive and stupid, thought they had common ground.

She narrowed her eyes at Thorn, drawing her knees up to her chest. "What do you want from me?"

"I want you to be safe."

He said it as he always had: earnest and soft. The words seemed to pass easily from his lips, but Odette doubted them. Maybe they passed a little too easily, a little too practiced.

She sized him up, "This whole time, you've done nothing but contradict yourself. What do you want? Honestly."

Thorn's gentle expression melted into exasperation. "Why can you not believe me?"

"You've made it extremely hard."

Thorn sighed, as if he was mulling over his options. She could practically hear the cogs turning in his mind as he debated, *how should I play this?* A part of Odette wanted to believe him, but after everything in the past few days she couldn't trust him anymore.

Finally, he spoke. "I care for you, Odette. You're special, I have seen it."

Odette frowned; this was the same speech she'd heard from him before. That he cared, that he wanted to protect her, that she had to trust him. Still, she let him speak.

"I have watched many humans die prematurely because of these twins. All of those lives cut short ... Under normal circumstances, and please do not judge me too harshly, I would not care. It is not my design to care about mortals. I was not created with human emotions in mind; but being in this mortal vessel for as long as I have has softened me.

"I am tethered to these particular mortals because of events in my past; they have a great source of unnatural power flowing through their veins because I am in them. It is their belief that in order to have power, they need to *take* it. From everything.

"They are stupid and reckless and ... and they do not understand they could be more; they could do more, if they did not take. But, the Mages' are takers; it is their way of life. They are parasites."

It was the most unforgiving speech Odette had ever heard Thorn make. He didn't look, or sound, like himself anymore. The weak, fragile butler was gone; replaced by something much older and wiser, something much more dangerous.

Thorn's gaze was far off, hard, and yet exhausted at the same time. He carried a great burden, something Odette had never noticed before. Then, his great gleaming eye focused, snapping towards her fast.

"And then, there is *you* ... I saw it the first time we met, the possible routes your life might take. Grayson could have killed you that night, and he almost did; but luck saved you that time. Luck saved you so many times and you have not even realized it. The longer you survived; I realized that it must be you."

"What do you mean?" Odette asked uneasily.

Thorn's icy cold hand grasped hers. "You are the end of their reign. You are the key to my emancipation."

"Me?"

He nodded, shadows curling along his cheeks, almost like a smile. "It is because of you; you are their story's end. So far, everything is going according to plan."

"You're crazy. I don't want to kill anybody!" Odette jerked her hand back, the skin burning from his cold.

Thorn shook his head, his salt-and-pepper hair falling askew. "I never said you had to."

But it frightened Odette. She couldn't tell what scared her more: the fact Thorn knew all this before and hadn't told her, or he had the power to know it. He was using her. In a way, Odette could understand and she didn't blame him; yet, that didn't stop the hurt in her chest.

The darkness of the room rippled, like someone had thrown a pebble to disturb a lake, and light filtered in. Her surroundings shifted, like sinking sand, and she was slipping into a new place all together. Shapes began to form and harden, until Odette was sitting in the middle of a room. Not just any old room, she realized, but the upstairs office in the Niesenson's home.

She found herself sitting on top of the mahogany desk, Thorn perched on the edge unmasked and unashamed. He appeared to be preoccupied, no longer interested in her.

"What are you doing?" she asked.

"Checking in. Don't you want to see?"

Odette followed his gaze and noticed for the first time the trio in the corner of the room. Greer, who leaned against the floor-to-ceiling bookshelf, arms crossed. Grayson was near the couch, kneeling on the floor over the third body. Odette blinked and realized the third, unconscious person in the room was her.

She pushed off of the desk, nearing herself. "How is this possible?"

"Have you ever heard the old wives tale that the soul leaves the body when you sleep?" Thorn asked. She nodded slowly, still trying to wrap her mind around it all. "You humans come up with some funny things, but occasionally you get one right."

Odette turned to Thorn. "Can they see us?"

"*She's not dead,*" said Greer, her voice muffled, as though she was underwater. "*You can stop.*"

"*I'm not going to stop,*" Grayson hissed. "*This is your fault. What if she doesn't wake up?*"

"*Problem solved.*"

"*No.*"

"If someone is particularly sensitive to the astral plane, or if they travel there often, they may catch glimpses." He walked towards Greer and waved his hand in front of her face. She didn't so much as flinch, but her hair did flutter ever so slightly. "You won't have to worry about Grayson; Greer is a little more susceptible, but ultimately harmless."

"*How was I supposed to know you took her ring?! You haven't exactly kept me in the loop.*" Greer pushed forward, walking through Thorn. She paused for a moment, as if she sensed something, but the moment passed. "*You said, 'take care of it', and I took care of it. It's not my fault she wasn't protected.*"

"*It's always your fault.*"

Odette unconsciously touched her hand, noting the absence of the ring. On the couch, her body slept on peacefully. Something about knowing the two of them were in the room there, with Odette unconscious and defenseless, put her on edge.

Thorn put a hand on her shoulder. "They won't hurt you. Not right now."

"You can't be sure." He might have awe inspiring powers, but Odette knew what they were capable of. There was a look of pure hatred on Grayson's face, and he was all that stood between life and death.

"They won't because of me."

Odette snorted bitterly, "Because of your 'influence' over them?"

"Precisely."

He had told her this before, that his influence was all he had to stop the twins from acting on their despicable urges; however, Odette had never seen any proof. If he could influence, then he could influence the twins and keep them away from her. He could influence them to stop this insanity.

Greer lifted her head, her lips quirked. "*How can you be so naive?*" She rolled her shoulders back and turned her eyes to the ceiling. "*What will you do about the others?*"

"*Dispose of them,*" said Grayson with an air of superiority.

"*When?*"

Grayson didn't answer this time, focused solely on holding Odette's hand. His thumb stroked the back of it. Faintly, she could feel it.

"*The answer is* now. *You've dragged this on for too long, Grays. You need to pack this up. We have bigger things to deal with back home, remember?*"

"*You think I don't know that?*"

Their bickering rose in volume, until they were both shouting indiscernible words at the other. It was hard to tell who was saying what.

The others they mentioned ... Clara and Felix. Where were they? Stashed away somewhere, probably the basement, and probably in a worse state than she was in. There wasn't much she could do for them like this, and knowing she was powerless significantly diminished their odds.

"How about you use this influence of yours to take their powers," said Odette. "That would be fair, right?"

"I am not permitted to influence them like I can you," Thorn said. "I was reprimanded for doing so years ago. They have put great limitations on what I can do to them. But you ... I have the ability to help you as long as you permit me to."

"What?"

He tapped his fingers together. "I'm sorry if things haven't gone the way you wanted them. I have tried to work in your best interest. When it conflicts with the twins though ..." Thorn shuddered. "Keeping your powers on lock was the best thing I could do."

Keeping her powers ... locked?

"You did not think this was a coincidence, did you?"

Odette's heart thundered in her ears. "What did you do?"

"I did what I promised. I have been protecting you the best way I know how."

It then dawned on her, all the times she tried her magic, it only worked in uncontrollable spurts. Every time she felt like she was not her own person, she believed it to be the amulet. But then she recalled he had told her the amulet was an extension of him. Everything tied back to Thorn.

"You haven't been influencing me." Odette's trembling hand covered her lips, then slid down to her throat. "You've been *controlling* me?"

"I did it to keep you safe."

Odette's mouth ran dry. "Thorn, how could you?"

"It was the only way you could possibly survive them. Understand, I do not use this on you unless you are in total peril. And, very rarely, has that been the case."

But ... Odette desperately grasped at the times she knew she had used magic on her own; there was on the side of the road, the first time she had arrived in Crabtree, and then at Felix's. After that ...

"You're just like him," she whimpered.

"No."

"He's trying to control me. What if he finds out you already have and—and he makes you do it for him? You said so yourself, you can't deny him."

"Odette, stop." Thorn laid a hand on her shoulder. "I only ever used magic through you. I never controlled your thoughts. I never wanted to. Everything you have ever done was up to you. I simply ... gave you a push."

It didn't keep the tears from burning at the back of her eyes. "You are a monster."

"I'm sorry." His nearly black hair slowly faded from the roots as the despair took over, turning more and more silver. "Everything I did was only to help you. It may be too late for your friends, but—"

"What about my friends?"

"A-ah. Well, um ..."

There was no time to wait on him. Odette made a mad dash for the door, passing through it like a spectre. However, just as soon as her body went through the wood, her movements slowed dramatically, as though she was running through thick syrup. Odette strained against the invisible force but didn't gain any ground.

"This is still a dream, Odette." Thorn passed through the door, walking beside her with ease, "They will not be down there."

"Then wake me up!"

He sighed. "It is not a good idea."

"Wake me up now, Thorn!" Odette fought against the slowness encompassing her. "I can't let them die! You promised me you would protect them!"

Thorn set his mouth. "I can't do anything against my master's wishes. What I can do is keep you from further trauma."

What he said made sense. She wanted to believe, on some level, he was looking out for her, but there were too many things going against him. He could have been spouting out a script the Mageses gave him. He could be lying.

Felix and Clara's lives were at stake, and Thorn was standing in her way.

"Wake. Me. Up."

XXVII

ODETTE

The room was empty and cold by the time she woke. There was no sign of Grayson or Greer, or that they had been in the home office at all.

Odette sat up fast; her heart thundered in her chest. It had been awhile since her old illness affected her, the ring protected her from symptoms that made her weak. It seemed to be back in full force, making her woozy and short of breath in a matter of seconds.

She couldn't wait for it to pass though. Forcing herself off the lumpy couch, Odette catapulted into the wall, swaying side to side as she felt her way to the door. The floor seemed to sway with every step like the ocean in the midst of a storm.

She smacked into the door face first, felt for the handle, and then pushed. She was met with resistance, something heavy blocking the other side of the door. Odette slammed herself against the door several times before it moved just enough and she was able to slip through. One of the heavy dining room chairs had been forced up against the backside of the door.

Odette held onto the walls for support and crept down the halls as slowly as possible. The house was unnaturally quiet, not even a creak or a cry to give away where the twins might be.

You know where they are. Odette swallowed hard. She *did* know; she'd just hoped she wouldn't be right.

Tip-toeing down the stairs, Odette hugged the wall and peered around the corner. Nothing. It was almost like they'd left the home completely, trusting the chair would've kept her locked away.

The air had a strong and earthy scent, like dirt after rain. Down and around the corner to the kitchen was a hazy blue glow that flickered and danced with the shadows.

Odette rushed from her hiding spot down to the basement door. Her heart pounded painfully in her chest, leaving her short of breath and lightheaded, but she ignored it and pushed on. Clara and Felix were down there, scared to death. They probably thought she abandoned them.

The basement door was now blackened around the edges and smoldering. Little tendrils of fire poked through, having already burned so long the wood was all but ash. Odette kicked near the bottom, her foot crashing through the wood. On the other side, the fire licked greedily at her exposed leg.

Odette withheld a shout of pain. Never before had the flames touched her—Grayson hadn't allowed it, but Grayson wasn't here now and she was powerless. She kicked again, harder and harder until the door was riddled with holes and crumbled. A great wave of fire rolled towards her with nothing there to hold it back. The flames leapt out at her, reaching for her, pulling her in.

She leapt through the wall of fire, though it was a foolish move. The stairs weren't wide enough to hold her, and her foot slipped off the edge. Odette grabbed a hold of the railing, but it crumbled into cinders under her touch. Odette fell into the pit below.

Water splashed up all around her, coming up to the middle of her calf. It stung her burns, but the warm water was a thousand times better compared to the burning stairs. Odette pushed up, wary of the burning metal shelf beside her as she leaned against the wall to catch her breath. The ache in her chest worsened.

When the stars cleared from her eyes, she spied a large shovel, seemingly untouched by the fire, on a shelf. Odette snatched it up. Better safe than sorry.

In the center of the basement stood Greer, her back to Odette, amulet glowing a bright blue. Her hands aloft in the air, as though she were orchestrating a set of invisible strings. Floating in the air, under the command of Greer, were gardening tools. They danced about, encircling Clara and Felix, threatening to drop at any moment and tear their flesh to shreds.

Grayson was nowhere to be found, but he'd obviously been there. The flames were his calling card. A way for him to say, *Your time is up. There's no escape.*

Greer lowered her left hand—her right keeping the objects afloat—and formed a fist. Above, a metal pipe splitting open, spraying harshly on Clara.

"*Stop!*" Clara shrieked. She gasped for air, but it did no good. The more she inhaled, the more water filled her nose and mouth. "*I can't breathe!*"

Odette clenched her jaw and crept slowly behind Greer. The water sloshed around her, rippling towards the girl. One false move and it would all be over; the element of surprise was the only upper hand he had.

She stopped just short of Greer, and swung the shovel with all her might. The *crunch* echoed loud throughout the room, slamming down hard on her target's head. Greer cried out, crumpling to her knees like a broken marionette.

The gardening tools fell, hard and fast, into the water. Clara jerked her knees closer to her chest, narrowly avoiding a spade.

She looked up, bewildered. "Odette?"

"Can you stand?" Odette jogged through the water. She knelt beside Felix, dropping her shovel to the ground. He was unresponsive. "You need to get up those stairs, now, they're already unstable. They won't be standing for much longer."

She shook Felix by his arm vigorously. Finally he groaned, but it was weak, like he was still sleeping.

Clara nodded, unblinkingly. She stood shakily and jerked her head behind her. "What about him?"

"You're going to have to get him out on your own." Someone had to stay behind and distract the twins.

Clara pressed her lips together, not thrilled at the prospect of having to do it alone, but she didn't dare contradict her, resigning herself to the fact Odette wouldn't be coming with them.

Suddenly, her eyes went wide. "Look out—!"

Before she could finish, Odette was wrenched around and facing Greer. The girl was livid, her nails tearing through her clothes, scoring her skin. The punch came out of nowhere, slamming into the side of Odette's jaw.

"Odette."

In this lighting, her eyes were dark and took on a strange lilac hue. Greer hit her again hard enough Odette's ears began to ring. Greer released her and Odette collapsed. "That was pretty unfair, you know? If you want it to be a fair fight, come at me like a real woman."

The shovel, where was the shovel? It was getting harder to breathe, though Odette couldn't tell if it was due to the smoke or her heart. Odette slid her hand along the gritty cement floor and her hand bumped into a handle. She curled her fingers around it.

"I hoped you'd show up." Another smack and blood invaded her mouth. The amulet atop Greer's head began to glow, and the spade levitated threateningly behind her. "Grayson was all, *No, leave her be*; but, I wanted some retribution after our last fight."

Odette lunged. She swung the weapon in hand, a mattock, in a wide arc, aiming for her side. Greer's eyes widened. Her hand shot out and the mattock sunk into her forearm. The levitating spade shot forward like an arrow, only grazing Odette's bicep.

"You missed."

Greer smiled through the pain, "No, I didn't."

Wrenching the mattock from her arm, Greer tossed it away. It splashed somewhere in the distance, too far out of reach now. Odette frowned. Yes she missed, or else she would be dead. Greer's smile broadened with sadistic satisfaction.

Odette glanced over her shoulder and her blood ran cold.

Felix.

The spade was lodged in his neck, nearly separating his head from his shoulders. Blood poured forth, like a waterfall, drenching his shirt and staining the water.

Oh God, Felix!

Clara sat beside him, face frozen with terror. She couldn't blink, she couldn't scream; she only sat there, mouth agape and trembling. A single, solitary tear slid down her cheek.

Not Felix.

He didn't move, there was no twitching or unnatural gasping for breath. He just sat there, the same way he had when she'd first came down, like a ragdoll. If it wasn't for the spade lodged in his throat, Odette could have believed he was sleeping.

Greer leaned forward, her chin resting on Odette's shoulder. "*Oops.*" Her words dripped with sarcasm and no hint of humanity.

All at once, Odette whirled around and tackled Greer, pulling her down into the water. She crushed her against the hard cement floor. She was a woman possessed, no longer in control of herself, consumed by an arcane fury. The splash sent up a wave of dirty water, invading Odette's nostrils and mouth.

They thrashed about in the water, clawing at one another. Odette didn't feel any pain; she had long since gone numb. There was only rage. She slashed at Greer's face, wringing her neck with as much force as she could manage. Greer caught her with her nails, biting and scratching with ferocity. They were no longer human, but animals, consumed with the intent to kill.

It's her or me.

Greer gained the upper hand and thrust Odette back with a surprising amount of force. She landed on her back, the water engulfing her, wrapping its slimy hands around her and anchoring her to the bottom. Greer clamored on top of her, her icy hands wrapping around her neck.

She knew she should have been more afraid. The water was a prison; there was no escape from it, or from how it invaded her nose. She had been in a similar situation before and she was terrified, but all she could think of was Felix.

Like so many others before, she'd failed him. Hopefully, in some cosmic way, he understood she hadn't meant it. If she could've, she would have taken his place. Would he be with his dad, now? Or, was he stuck in some dark and endless void, alone and afraid?

Greer's hands tightened her grip like iron. Odette coughed, violent bubbles floating upwards to the surface. Water filled her nose and mouth, though she tried to push it out. Her lungs craved air.

She was certain she was about to black out. Her heart thundered wildly in her ears, her chest burning for oxygen. No matter how hard she thrashed, it did no good. She was too weak, her arms slithering back into the water in defeat.

Greer pulled her up, gnashing her teeth. "You think you're clever? *Ha!*" And she was pushed back under.

Greer tightened her hands around Odette's throat, controlling the exhale of air she took underwater, before dragging her back up again. Her hands loosened, only a little to allow a slip of air in Odette's lungs, before tightening once more.

"You're worthless. The only reason you're still alive is because of—" Odette didn't hear the last bit, as she was shoved into the water once again.

No, she couldn't let her win. She wouldn't let Greer, of all people, be the one to take her life. She owed Felix that much. Odette sunk her fingernails deep into Greer's wrists, but the girl wasn't moved by pain. It only made her grip all the more terrible.

When she was brought up again, Greer was still talking. There was madness in her eyes. And … what looked like a figure moving just beyond her vision.

"—with you gone, he'll see that it'll be like old times. He'll get over this family fantasy of his."

Odette was prepared to be dunked again, but it didn't come. Greer screamed. It was a sound so ragged and animalistic it shouldn't have escaped a human. Her grip went lax on Odette's throat and she withered, shouting profanities.

Odette blinked to try to clear her cloudy vision. Clara was there—*really there*—behind Greer. Her lips were bloodless, her eyes wide with disbelief at her own actions. She jerked her arm back and scurried away. In her hands was a set of bloodied pruning shears.

Greer screamed again, twisting and turning, grasping at her back. "You—!" she fell forward and Odette scrambled back, avoiding her. Greer caught herself with one hand, pushing back to an upright position. "You *stabbed* me!"

She was more surprised than hurt. Greer pushed herself upright with one hand, murder in her eyes. She glanced in Clara's direction; the jewel on her headband burned bright with her agitation, and ripped the pruning shears from her hands.

Clara recoiled, putting as much distance between the two of them as she could. The shears flew to Greer's side, hovering right beside her head, the sharp end pointed towards Odette.

"Do you think you're clever getting your friends to do your dirty work, *coward*?" Greer spat. "You're so pathetic! All I have to do is kill your friend and you'll beg to be next."

The pruning shears were in motion before Odette could blink. They zipped around the room, too fast for her eye to follow, and Odette heard the sick squelch of flesh ripping. Clara fell to the ground with a cry, cupping her arm.

The shears were speeding up. They ripped through everything in the basement, sending shelves crashing down and slashing through water pipes in seconds. Finally, they came back around, barreling towards Odette.

They came close, but dropped suddenly, inches from her nose. Odette's reaction was delayed, jumping back as the shears splashed at her feet. Confused, she looked around. Greer wouldn't just stop when she was about to drill a hole in her head.

Grayson stood behind his sister, eyes alight with rage. He had a hand on the back of her neck, and threw her to the ground.

"You were told who you could kill," he snarled. He jerked his head towards Odette, accusatory. "*She* was not one of them."

"I was doing you a favor!"

Odette waded through the water, careful not to catch their attention, to Clara. She reached down, helping her up. The cut on Clara's arm was ugly, but not horrible. She jerked her head towards the smoldering staircase. It looked even worse than before, almost completely blackened, burning from the inside out. There was every possibility it would break under their weight, but it was the only way out.

Greer tore at the ends of her hair. "*No*! No! I will not let you do this to yourself over and over again, Grayson. You're delusional if you believe keeping her will solve any of your problems! It's *me* or *her*!"

The two girls held onto one another, limping toward the staircase. Clara went first, gingerly placing her weight on the first step. The wood groaned, blue flames popping out of the knots. Odette gestured for her to go on.

"Make your choice, Grayson!" Her words rung throughout the room with a note of finality.

Grayson stiffened. The fire in his eyes burned brighter. "I *hate* you. I have always hated you, and I always will. I will never in my life choose you over anyone else again!"

Odette started up the stairs, swaying slightly. The heat was nearly unbearable under her feet. The burn on her leg screamed in protest, aching from being near the heat. She pushed on, stepping a little too hard on the second stair. The wood cracked audibly and her foot fell through the step. Clara whipped around, terror written across her face.

Go on, Odette silently urged her. She tried to pull her foot free, the splintered wood catching her skin roughly. *Go.*

But Clara didn't, pinned in place by fear. Odette continued to wave her on, but it suddenly occurred to her the room was a little too quiet. The twins' screaming match had silenced. Odette didn't have to turn to know; they'd spotted them.

"Move," Odette ordered quietly. Clara swallowed hard, her gaze flitting between Odette (who was still stuck) and the twins (who were ready to pounce). "*Move.*"

Clara turned and ran up the stairs.

Greer crouched like an animal in the corner, a predator spotting its prey. Odette grit her teeth and ripped her foot free of the hole, the wood raking her flesh harshly. The pain was severe, but she sprinted up after her friend, hoping for a miracle.

Greer leapt after her, pushing past Grayson who tried to grab her, catching her by the edge of her shirt. They grappled with one another, before Grayson forced her to the side. Greer smacked into the railing, the wood giving away behind her. She swung her arms wildly, trying to regain her balance as she teetered on the edge. Grayson, however, had already pushed past her, headed for Odette.

"Why are you protecting her?!" Greer screamed. "She's done nothing but hurt you from the beginning. You know she'll continue to do so! She has no loyalty to you or to this family!"

"You're the traitor here!" Grayson snapped, "You've always been—you don't know how to be anything else!"

Odette was near the top, breathing hard, her lungs burning for oxygen. The smoke was making her sluggish, but she couldn't stop. She couldn't rest. Odette blinked rapidly, the smoke made her eyes hurt. *If only she could close them ...*

Greer shrieked in anger. The entire staircase shook from the weight of her sprint, clashing with Grayson for a moment before gaining the upper hand and tossing him to the side. She'd gained on Odette and grabbed her hair. With no hesitation, Greer ripped her hair back and pushed her off the side.

The world tilted, gravity laying claim to her. She flailed pathetically, reaching for anything, but there was only air. She'd been so close, the doorway right there, but not close enough.

Without expectation, an arm thrust itself through the wall of fire and grasped Odette's wrist, catching her fast. She stared up at the mysterious hand, startled, and was met with Thorn's gaze. He was gone just as soon as he appeared, as if he'd been a mirage. In his place was Clara.

Tightening her grip, Clara propelled Odette up the final stair, pulling her to safety. Greer too staggered forward, because of how strong a hold she had on Odette. Clara curled her hand into a fist and, when Greer was only a step away, punched her hard in the nose.

Shock colored Greer's face, barely visible through the blue flames. The fall was instantaneous. Not even Grayson could have stopped it.

Greer's head snapped back, her hands flailing as she tumbled back, taking the fall that was supposed to be Odette's.

It's her or me.

Neither Grayson nor Odette reached out to her. They had the same unspoken but known thought: that Greer would pull another back-bending stunt to save herself. There was no way she had been bested—no, not Greer—

who had no weaknesses and an unnatural liveliness which possessed her.

Maybe if they had reached, if they'd shown the slightest bit of desire to help her, it wouldn't have happened.

Greer slammed back-first into the railing, and it gave way. Though, by some strange stroke of fate, she didn't hit the cement. No, it was much worse. She stopped fast, the broken railing catching her, impaling her. She lay there, arched over the thick blackened piece of wood in an unnatural way, a post poking through her stomach, ripping it wide open.

She made a strange, strangled sound. Her legs twitched helplessly, her toes just brushing the top of the stairs. Then, it stopped. She stared lifelessly at the fiery ceiling, her glassy eyes reflecting the flames.

Open mouthed, Odette couldn't tear her gaze away from the sight before her. A wound like that doesn't happen without blood. Where was the blood? Did the burning wood cauterize it like Felix's eyes? There was only the plank, jutting obscenely from her gut.

She should have felt relieved, but she didn't. Slowly, she faced Grayson, her legs shaking so hard she was sure they would give out.

But he didn't look at Odette. For once, it wouldn't have mattered if she were there or not, because she was nothing but a figure in the background. If she'd ran then, he surely wouldn't have noticed—not even cared—but she didn't (though it would have been the smart thing to do).

Grayson did not tremble. He did not frown, nor did he smile. He was blank, staring down at his sister's twitching body. He watched until she finally stopped moving, dangling awkwardly across the burnt railing.

Odette couldn't read him. He had once said the two of them wished they weren't family; not ten minutes ago he proclaimed he hated her. And yet, there he stood, his bottom lip jutted out ever so slightly, his fists clenched. In a way, it was almost remorseful, but that could have been Odette projecting onto him.

Like a crack of thunder, the railing snapped free. Greer's body fell to the side, finally smashing into the watery pit below. The whole structure was collapsing. The stairs shook under Grayson's feet, the wood bowing dangerously.

The smoke was starting to go to Odette's head. She swayed dangerously close to the flames, coughing. Clara tugged on Odette's sweater sleeve, pulling her away from the basement. She said something, but Odette couldn't hear her.

Another crack, this one shook the whole room like an earthquake. Grayson broke out of his trance, steading himself on the wood. He looked up, his eyes meeting Odette's briefly before she was pulled away.

Odette was faint. She staggered through the kitchen, the smoky haze growing thicker by the second, choking her. She needed air, but she also needed rest. God, did she need rest ...

Clara pulled away, a little too harshly, and disappeared. With all the thick smoke, it was impossible to tell which way she'd gone. Clara had been right behind her—or, had she even been with her? Had she been a figment of her imagination?

Odette's knees bowed, her eyes fluttering shut. Before she hit the ground, a set of strong arms caught her, pulling her to stand. It was Thorn, she could tell from the cold. Was he imaginary as well? More often than not, Odette saw him in her dreams. She had a hard time deciphering imaginary from reality when he was around.

Thorn laid his cold hand on her cheek, patting it lightly. "Open your eyes for me, Odette. No ... stop closing them. Look at me."

She pried her eyelids open, staring up at him with annoyance. "What?"

"You hurt yourself," he commented. He moved his hand to her forehead, and then her heart. "I warned you. You should have listened to me."

"But you were wrong," said Odette. She stood a little straighter, but leaned on Thorn for support. "I ... I made a difference. Clara's alive." Was she, though? Odette still couldn't see her—where had she gone? *I made a difference.*

Thorn pressed his lips together. He said nothing, his gaze settling on something behind her. "We need to get her out of here."

"Yeah ..." They needed to get Clara out, she needed to go and get help. Where was Clara? She tried to turn, but Thorn guided her face back to him.

"In a minute," said another voice.

Odette turned her head again. This time, Thorn didn't try to stop her, allowing her to sate her curiosity. Oh, the other voice had been Grayson. She hadn't heard him come out of the basement; he was quiet on his feet.

And, there, cowering behind him, was Clara. Thank goodness she found her, Odette had begun to think she'd vanished forever.

"It's not safe for her," said Thorn. Grayson must not have reacted in the way he hoped because the angel's frown deepened. "Or the baby."

"I said," Grayson began, his voice hard, "*In a minute.*"

Thorn made a noncommittal noise and looked back at Odette, the harsh frown-lines softening. His once pristine mask was now sooty, ash smeared along his cheek. He pressed a cool hand to Odette's protruding stomach.

"Things are not going according to plan." He *tsked*, feeling around her stomach like he was trying to locate something. "Not at all ... Not at all ..." Thorn pressed his lips in a firm line.

"What plan?" Odette asked airily.

Thorn ignored her, so Odette turned back around to see Clara. She was barely silhouetted in the smoke, which seemed to flow more rapidly now. Odette wanted to call out for her, but all she could do when she opened her mouth was cough.

Clara said something, her sentences frantic and jumbling together in unintelligible words. Odette frowned, taking a step towards her, but Thorn tightened his grip on her.

"It's not your time," he hissed in her ear.

Something about his words seemed familiar, like words from a dream; but Odette was far too sluggish to fully comprehend it.

Grayson had gotten closer to Clara, keeping her pinned to the counter. "You have caused more than enough damage, don't you think?"

"Leave me alone...!" With a sudden swiftness, Clara grabbed a hold of something on the counter—a knife, laid carelessly away from its block—and took a swipe at Grayson.

It barely grazed his clothes. He dodged, the blade catching the outer part of his shirt and tearing it. Before she could try again, Grayson smacked the knife from her shaking hands and caught it by the blade.

Blood dripped from his palm, onto the clean tiled floor, as he clutched it hard. Maybe he didn't know he was doing it—maybe he didn't care. Clara's eyes widely sought out something—anything—she could use to defend herself, but there was nothing.

"No." It came out no louder than a whisper. Odette tried again, louder. *"No!"*

Odette struggled against Thorn, knowing she needed to break free, knowing she needed to help, but his grip was relentless.

"You promised me," she babbled. "You promised me! You said they'd be fine—that they'd *live!*"

Her words meant for Thorn.

She should have done better; she should have helped them sooner. She shouldn't have gotten them involved at all.

Grayson turned his head for a single second, his emotionless state far more terrifying than any emotion he could've shown at that moment. Her words agitated him, rubbing away the last bit of sanity he possessed.

Thorn pulled her away completely, back into the living room, like he thought being in a different room would somehow save her from what she knew was about to happen. As a last ditch-attempt to shield her from the horrors at hand, he covered her eyes.

Despite his efforts, Thorn's fingers were partially spread which allowed a small view of the room, and she watched as Grayson sunk the knife into Clara. She watched as life left her friend's eyes.

The stabbing continued for what felt like hours. Every time the blade made contact, Odette felt it. Every whimper made the pain in her heart worsen. It wasn't until the thick puddle of blood collected on the floor, trickling towards Odette, that it ended.

Clara fell to the floor, nothing more than a dull thunk.

Grayson's shoulders were tensed, his arms spread wide, the knife held loftily in one hand. He huffed, kicking Clara's body once to assure she was, in fact, dead. The knife slipped from his grasp and fell to the floor, sloshing in the blood.

When he turned around, Grayson was covered in blood from head to toe. Her friend's blood. Thorn finally dropped his hand, yet Odette wished he kept it up. Out of everything, this was the one thing she didn't want to look at. This *monster*.

So, Odette refused to give Grayson the satisfaction. She stared at the small trail of blood gathering at her feet, unshed tears stinging her eyes. If she only looked at her feet, (And, ignored how warm the blood was.), she wouldn't have to admit this was real.

Grayson's shoes came into her vision, stepping carelessly through the blood (No, don't think of it as blood.), stopping in front of her. He reached out and cupped her chin, his hand ragged from the cut he had inflicted on himself, and coerced her into looking at him.

Odette thought she would be sick. The agitation he'd held towards her since they were reunited was gone. He almost seemed *affectionate*.

Grayson brushed his thumb over her cheekbone, smearing blood across her skin. "We can go home now," he said.

Home. That mansion of horrors. Somehow, even though Greer was gone, the place seemed more dangerous than before.

And yet, all the fight was gone. Behind her and before her were the two most important people who had been left in her life, and they were dead. Everyone was dead.

Finally, her body supposing she would no longer need it, her strength left her. Odette's eyes shut, blocking out the horrors and the burning smoke. Her knees went weak and she collapsed. Before she could hit the floor, a pair of arms wrapped around her, nestling her against their chest.

Voices floated above her, one frantic, the other calm. They weaved themselves in and out of her consciousness, fading in and out with the blackness. She wished they would just *shut up*—all she wanted was to sleep. Why wouldn't they let her sleep?

As they exited the Niesonson's home, Odette became aware of how bright it was, like the sun was shining against her eyelids. Strange, she thought, because it should have been night. How could the sun be out at this hour.

Odette opened her eyes—just a crack—and saw the world around her was on fire.

Hannah Boggs

XXVIII

GRAYSON

All hospitals had a very distinct smell—it was clinical, clean, and leaned heavily on bleach. Bleach mixed with the sharp scent of blood and vomit. It was easy to pick it up if you'd been exposed to it many times before. It was enough to make Grayson sick.

On the small, flat screen television, stuck up in the corner of the room, national news played quietly.

Crabtree, Oregon was the topic of interest. The smoldering remains of buildings, blackened brick, and broken windows all scrolled past his line of vision. The devastation reached as far as the eye could see.

"Authorities are still puzzled about what exactly occurred last night that sent this entire town ablaze. So far, firefighters have searched the area but have found no survivors. One person who escaped this disaster was taken into the hospital, but pronounced D.O.A."

Odette pretended to sleep, feigning unconsciousness for the past couple of hours; but her shivering gave her away.

The newscaster switched stories, reporting on some woman in the hospital who survived a slit throat. *"My faith saved me,"* said the woman, who smiled despite the bandages around her neck. *"It's a miracle I'm alive, but I'm not surprised. I saw the light, but my God told me it wasn't time yet."*

Grayson got up and searched the room, finally finding a cabinet with extra blankets. He took one and laid it over Odette. She winced, and curled away from him awkwardly. Though her IV tugged painfully on her arm, she didn't make a peep.

She was in pain and he hated it, but she couldn't see that he was hurting, too? Grayson squeezed the bridge of his nose in an attempt to rub away fatigue. The events of the past several days were catching up with him, leaving him weary.

Greer was dead.

It was beginning to seem real to him; even though he'd said those three, horrid words over and over since it happened, it hadn't sunk in. Greer was *dead.*

Grayson couldn't lie—originally, the idea of having his sister out of his life was enticing. She'd caused him pain, and was the root of most of his problems. Strangely though, he wasn't happy. He should have felt happy—at the very least relieved—instead, he felt empty.

A soft knock alerted Grayson; he dropped his hand and pushed upright. Doctor Rojas poked his head through the door, a courteous half-smile on his lips.

Grayson got up, his limbs heavy. He leaned against the glass door, positioning himself so he could just make out Odette from the edge of the privacy curtains.

"The burns she sustained can be easily fixed with a skin graft, but the baby ..." Dr. Rojas' soft voice petered off. He cleared his throat and started anew. "She's sustained some severe trauma. She's very lucky to have not lost the fetus"

Luck? Luck had nothing to do with it. As if he would allow Odette to lose his baby after everything she put him through. Thorn had done as much as he could to heal her after they left Crabtree, but her injuries still warranted a hospital.

He continued. "I'm concerned for the wellness of the child. She's in a very dangerous place, one more slip-up and ..." The doctor didn't finish his sentence, he didn't need to.

Grayson crossed his arms over his chest. "What can I do?"

Dr. Rojas tapped his clipboard, eyebrows furrowed. "The best option—and only option, in my professional opinion—would be to keep her here for the night, at the very least. You can stay here and support her. She's going to need as much comfort as she can get right now. We need to watch in case it makes a turn for the worse."

As much as he hated it, he agreed with the man. A part of him would love to take Odette and hide her away in the mansion. At least there, he knew the environment; there, he had control and power to keep the world out.

The reality of the situation was he didn't have the time or patience to care for her. So many things had been left undone by Greer's death, issues he now had to deal with. A smaller part of it (one he didn't want to admit, even to himself) was he wanted space. That seed of doubt had begun to bloom. What if Odette ... really wasn't the one?

Beyond the glass door, Thorn stood in front of the nurses' station. He nodded at Grayson, urging him to wrap things up.

"Alright." Grayson dropped his arms. "I trust you'll take care of her."

"Of course, Mr. Mages."

Grayson quietly excused himself, leaving the doctor to go check on Odette. Thorn came to meet him halfway. The nurses and patients all passed around them, all focused on their own tasks as the two men conversed.

"You decided to leave her here," Thorn stated. He had heard everything that transpired between Grayson and the doctor. "Are you certain that's a good idea?"

"She won't talk. Even if she did, no one would believe her." All the same, Grayson couldn't help but check over his shoulder. Odette was 'awake', now, nodding slowly to whatever the doctor was saying. "It's better this way."

Thorn said nothing more on the subject, but that didn't stop his eye from wandering in her direction. "Your manager has been calling all evening. He has been asking for your sister."

"Did you tell him anything?"

"No, sir. I thought it best for you to handle this ... delicate situation."

Grayson clenched his fist. No one knew about Greer yet, save the three of them. He had to do something. It would look suspicious the longer he waited.

"Is that all?"

Thorn withdrew something from his pocket. It was a small, crinkled piece of paper, no bigger than his palm. He passed it over for Grayson to read.

"I found this. I don't know much about the situation, but I believe your sister had planned to *take care* of these loose ends."

Grayson recognized the tall, slanted writing instantly as Greer's. There were no more than six names on the list, the ink smudged like she hadn't waited for it to dry before touching it. He studied the names, but none of them rang a bell.

"What connects them?"

"Rumors of a kind." Thorn shrugged nonchalantly. "I was never informed of what, but it seemed important."

Grayson hummed, "I see."

Dr. Rojas slipped out of Odette's room, leaving the privacy curtain fully open. She was upright, now. They met eyes for a moment. Odette looked terribly lonely and small in that hospital room; all bandaged up and tubes coming out of her like she was a science experiment. Grayson's heart tugged at the sight of her.

Odette looked away suddenly, turning to the nurse who came to replace her gauze.

That seed of doubt within him withered just a little. They would make it work—he would make it work; because, unlike Greer, he had faith in Odette.

I promise, Grayson thought, *everything will go back to the way it was before.*

The sound of the doorbell broke Grayson away from his work. He stood from the couch, pausing only a moment to hide his work (on the off chance the person came this far into the house) before leaving the study. The doorbell rang again, and then one more time, Beethoven's fifth restarting abruptly. Whoever it was, they were in a hurry.

He wrenched the door open just as the bell rang for the fourth time, and came face-to-face with a short South Asian woman staring up at him. She seemed startled to see him, stepping back abruptly.

"I—"

"Yes? Can I help you?"

She bit her lip, pulling her coat tight against her body. "Is Greer here?"

Grayson's jaw tightened. "*No.*"

"O-oh." She peered around him, glancing around the foyer like she thought he was lying. "When will she be back?"

He didn't answer her. "Who are you?"

"Alisha Palit," she said.

Grayson studied her. She seemed familiar, and it only took a moment to figure out why. "You're one of the mothers."

Greer had mentioned her just before coming after him. Grayson shifted his jaw. *Why was she here ...?*

Mrs. Palit nodded slowly, astonished he didn't recognize her. "When you see Greer, can you tell her to call me?"

"I can't, I'm sorry."

Her eyebrows raised, her lips parting in astonishment, either by his answer or the tone he took. "Why?"

Grayson leaned against the door frame, pulling the door closed even more. "Greer's gone."

"Well, when will she be back?"

"I don't know," he said through a clenched jaw. Mrs. Palit stammered as she tried to find her words, but Grayson had enough of this. There were more important matters that needed attention. "Now, if you'll excuse me."

"B-but—!"

He shut the door and headed back to the study. His shoulders tense, an ache forming in his neck. He didn't know why he hadn't outright told the woman; something held him back. *It's none of her business*, Grayson decided as he settled back into his chair and resumed his work.

Thorn appeared in the study somewhere around three in the morning, bringing food Grayson had no plans to eat.

"What are you going to do about the boy?" asked Thorn.

Grayson didn't look up, enthralled in his research. The names on the paper turned out to be influential people who had been drumming up conspiracy theories about him. Whatever vague thing Thorn was talking about had no significance to him.

"What boy?"

"Skylar Fraser."

Oh, him. Grayson froze mid key-stroke, looking over the screen at the angel. "I certainly don't need him. Get rid of him."

"You're going to let him walk?" Thorn tapped his fingers together.

"Of course not," he snorted and resumed his work, typing one of the names in the search engine. "Take care of him. Dump him in the Gulf."

He focused his attention on *Noel Short*, a freelance therapist, and the third name on the list. It was only when he realized Thorn hadn't moved that he broke from the computer once again.

"*What?*"

"I don't think that's such a good idea," he said. Then he added, for clarification, "killing the boy so soon."

"And why not?" Grayson slammed the laptop closed, eyes blazing.

"Having another person turn up dead so soon after those girls were found will only make you look more suspicious."

"They haven't connected me to either of those murders," said Grayson. "It's all rumors. Besides, they have no reason to suspect that boy has anything to do with me."

"That isn't quite right." Thorn stepped forward, biting his cheek. "Those rumors are being investigated. It didn't help that you were absent when the bodies were discovered."

Grayson frowned. For a couple of days now, he'd felt sure of himself. He'd crossed off two of those names, horrid people who were stirring up trouble and throwing suspicion on his name. But, at that moment, he could feel his confidence slipping. He had no reason to doubt Thorn's claims; though he was a pain, he had never truly lied to him before Odette's disappearance.

"How bad is it?"

"Someone leaked to the press that you were a person of interest." Thorn gestured vaguely to the laptop. "It has been all across the news."

His eye twitched. More and more issues, all piling atop one another. Grayson felt he would drown in it all. *No,* Grayson assured himself, *no. I've dealt with this before, I can do it again.*

Only before, when he and his family had been the prime suspects in the Bachallor case, he had his sister and grandfather on his side. It was difficult then, with the three of them, to erase all doubt from the public's mind. Now, he was alone.

"So what," he said, sounding far more confident than he felt. "I only need a few more days."

On the fifth day of Odette's stay at the hospital, Grayson arrived to pick her up. As the days passed, his visits few and far between, she'd become a hollow shell of herself. Despite all the care she'd received, somehow she appeared even smaller, her injuries even uglier, than when she'd first come. She hadn't been sleeping; dark circles, prominent on her sickly pale skin, made her eyes seem sunken in and small.

"You're all set, Mr. Mages." Dr. Rojas' tone was congenial, but Grayson could see the suspicion in his eyes.

Ever since the talking heads had caught wind of him being a potential suspect, hardly anything else was reported. Everywhere he'd go, nearly everyone he encountered had the same look of *could it be?* written across their faces.

"Thank you," said Grayson. The doctor bowed out of the room, leaving the two of them alone.

Grayson turned to Odette, who sat placidly, her hands folded over one another. The nurse had already come to withdraw her IV, and helped her dress in clothes Grayson had brought two days prior.

"Are you ready to go home?"

Odette blinked slowly, then spoke. "The nurses have been acting strange. They kept watching me, they wouldn't let me watch the TV. I didn't understand at first. But, then I heard a couple of them talking when they thought I was asleep." She looked up at him and her eyebrows twitched towards each other. "The media thinks you're a murderer."

"I know."

Odette continued to stare at him, her gaze like an X-Ray, crawling under his skin and dissecting his soul. He couldn't help but be nervous, though he hid it well. Odette could easily unravel this whole thing. He didn't think she was the vindictive type; but, one could never be sure.

As if sensing his thoughts, she shook her head. "Some of them weren't sneaky at all about prying. They asked about your past, what you were like and all that. Then, they started asking if this was really an accident."

Grayson swallowed hard, his Adam's apple bobbing.

"I didn't say anything to them. I don't know why." The shadow of a smile crossed her lips. "If I had the chance again, I think I would."

For a brief moment, Grayson was grateful. She protected him—them—because a small part of her still cared. He could feel a comforting warmth radiate off of her. But, like he said, it was brief. Odette smiled spitefully up at him, that warmth diminishing into nothing. He flexed his jaw, holding off his anger.

He matched her venom, "I'm sure you would. Now, sit up, will you? I need to put on your coat."

They moved in silence. Grayson tended to Odette, making sure all of her belongings were in the hospital bag before helping her into the wheelchair. She was no help, moving stiffly any time he touched her. At least she didn't shy away.

Just as he was about to wheel her out the door, she spoke again, softly. "What've you done to Skylar?"

Grayson paused, the two of them coming to a halt. Outside the glass doors, a small group of nurses had gathered, whispering and glancing at the two of them.

"I haven't decided yet," he said.

"So he's still there?"

He didn't like how bright her voice became when talking about the boy. "Yes. But not for long."

Odette's breath caught in her throat. "You can't."

"I *can*." He didn't want to tell her it was more likely he'd drop the boy in the middle of the desert rather than kill him. His stubbornness prevented him. "And anyway, it doesn't concern you."

He began to push her again, but Odette slammed her feet on the floor, pushing back.

"Wha—Odette!"

"You're not killing him." Her voice was low so as to not catch the attention of anyone. "I won't let you."

"Oh, really?" he mused. "And how do you plan to do that?"

Her bottom lip jutted out ever-so-slightly, quivering with emotion. She said nothing, her frail hands gripping the armrest with all her might. She was holding back. *Figures*, Grayson *thought, She knows the truth but she's too willful to accept it.*

"I thought so. Cheer up, princess, misery's bad for the baby." Grayson touched her chin sweetly. She turned her head.

"I'll leave," she said.

His hand curled around her shoulder, squeezing. She was really starting to get on his nerves. "You won't get far."

Odette turned around and met his gaze. "Then, I'll die."

At first, he couldn't help but chuckle, "What?"

It was only when he noticed her face, and the tone she took, did he stop. His throat constricted painfully, like the air was being manually sucked from his lungs, wanting to hollow him from the inside out.

"No." Grayson forced a laugh, shaking his head. "No, that's not possible. Understand? I won't let you."

"I mean it." She was shivering despite the thick coat she wore. Though, he couldn't be sure it was caused by the cold. "I'm done, with you, with this place, with this life. You've taken *everything* from me. I don't want to be a part of this, not when I've seen what you've done."

His control was slipping. "You don't know what you're saying."

Odette continued, ignoring him. "This isn't normal—it's not healthy. You and me ..." She cut herself off with a sigh. "Skylar has done nothing to you, or *Greer*, or me. He's normal. Why should he die?"

Grayson stepped back, abandoning the wheelchair. *Was he losing his grip on reality?* He could hear her talking, and that was her voice, but her words went in one ear and out the other. No, no this wasn't real, he decided. This was a hallucination, a dream. The Odette he knew, the purest being in existence, couldn't possibly be contemplating suicide. Not over a boy. (More importantly, a boy that wasn't *him*.)

"Stop talking," he demanded.

"Why?" The hallucination wasn't wavering, wasn't disappearing like they usually did. "You don't like hearing the truth?"

"Shut up, you don't mean any of that." Grayson squeezed his eyes shut in a vain attempt at pushing this false reality from his mind. It didn't, and that made his stomach squirm. No more denying it, this was real.

His ire reared its ugly head. Grayson pushed back his hair, pacing back and forth on the linoleum floor. "Are you even hearing yourself right now? It's nonsense, Odette. We're fine—we're *normal*. This is just a stupid fight, *normal* couples fight all the time."

She shook her head and started to speak again, but Grayson cut her off. "This ... this boy is the root of our problems. No one on Earth should make you act like this. He's obviously toxic; you have no business being around someone like that."

"No, he isn't," she insisted. "He's good and kind and—"

"He'll talk if he lives." Grayson chose to ignore the way her voice broke. "He'll be a danger to us and our family. The police will get involved; they will drag you to prison and isolate you for months. They'll take your son. If I let this boy live, he'll sell us down the river and damn us both."

Odette was crying now. A stream of tears rolled across her bloodless cheeks and dribbled down her chin. In between his words, she had tried to interject with *no's* and *you're wrong's*; but he wouldn't stop. A part of him relished her tears. He was getting through to her, but she was in denial. It didn't matter, he would show her the truth.

He leaned down, a mere hairsbreadth away from her nose. "Does that sound like something someone *good and kind* would do?"

She glared at him with glassy eyes. For a long time, she was silent, letting his words hang in the air, leaving only an oppressive and all-encompassing quiet. Then, she sniffed and looked down at her lap. "You don't know him."

"No, I don't." He straightened up and took hold of her wheelchair, pushing firmly. "You shouldn't either."

They said nothing more on the subject all the way out of the hospital or the entire trip home. Thorn met them at the door with an old, rickety wheelchair his grandfather left behind. He helped Odette into it, exchanging a look with Grayson, before he pulled her away in the direction of the sun room. Grayson waited in the foyer, silently seething, until Thorn returned.

"You need to keep an eye on her at all times," Grayson grumbled. Thorn nodded, but he continued anyway. "If you see anything—and I mean *anything*—suspicious about her behavior or emotions spike, I want you to alert me."

"Of course, sir."

"And the boy—I want him gone. I don't care how, I don't care if he leaves in a bag, I want him out of my house."

Thorn furrowed his eyebrows, possibly peering into his mind to see what provoked this. "Of course."

"I'm going to be out. You know what you need to do if someone comes snooping?" Thorn answered yes, and Grayson went on. "Good."

Grayson took the stairs two-by-two, headed to the study. If he couldn't hurt Skylar, (though he really wanted to) he could at least take care of some problems of his own.

Ms. Emmy Ansel—a politician's assistant with some rather harsh opinions—sat a couple of tables away from him. She sipped her coffee slowly, her focus solely on the laptop in front of her. She hadn't looked up from it since Grayson sat down. That was probably a good thing, considering how vocal she'd been about Grayson's involvement in the murders. She might've confronted him, or, even worse, run.

This woman, however mousy she might've appeared, was number one on Greer's list. Grayson read the thread of tweets she'd posted. All of them were nasty and vindictive—all of them true. Somewhat.

He had to give her credit. Ms. Ansel had done her research. If he didn't know better, he'd say she was a super fan. It seemed she knew a whole lot about him, about the girls, though that could all be chalked up to internet presence. A couple of things she had got wrong, that was only natural, but for the most part ... Well, she knew too much, and that's all there is to it.

After a few more minutes of watching her, she moved to close her laptop. Grayson sank lower in his seat, watching the woman from the corner of his eye. She did a quick sweep of the room, her eyes glancing off of Grayson with no hint of recognition, and headed out the door. Grayson waited until she was out the door that he pushed out from the table and followed.

Ms. Ansel was about a yard ahead, her steps quick and light as she headed for the parking garage. She held her head high, not bothered with looking at the others who she passed. She had an agenda, a pile of duties to attend to.

This was her downfall. If she had taken a moment to turn her head, she might've seen him. She might've had a chance. It wasn't like he was really hiding.

The parking garage was all but deserted. Grayson stuck close to the columns, pausing a moment to allow a car to pass. It was only them, now.

He didn't try to sneak up on her—sneaking would only make things worse. No, he walked calmly up to her car, where Ms. Ansel was fumbling with her purse.

"Can I have a word with you?"

The woman jumped, her keys soaring into the air. She screamed, short and sweet, and pressed her hand to heart. Ms. Ansel peeked at him with one eye then swallowed hard. "Grayson Mages."

"Yes."

"What do you want?" The fear had drained from her voice, replaced with disdain. "And why did you think here was the place to do it?"

Grayson shrugged, flashing a charming smile. "I saw you come in when I was at my car."

Ms. Ansel glanced about the garage level, looking to see if she could match him with any of the cars. "Okay ... So what do you want?"

"To talk."

"About the investigation, right?"

"Precisely." He didn't let his smile slip. "I think we should work out whatever ... issues, there are between us. Your accusation was pretty harsh, you know?"

"I only said what others are thinking." She studied him carefully. Though she did a good job at hiding it, she was beginning to feel afraid. "Besides, I didn't think you were the kind to be swayed by public opinion."

"Public opinion is what keeps me employed. You should understand that." Grayson slid closer to her, boxing her in. "Besides, all a man has is his reputation."

Ms. Ansel sneered and bent down to retrieve her keys. "I'm not interested in whatever back alley deal you're trying to make."

"Hm. That's a shame. I rather hoped we could do this the easy way ..."

Grayson came closer still. Ms. Ansel tried to back away again, but she'd run out of room. The only way she could have escaped him was either by jumping over the hood of her car. (Which was rather ineffective, he could grab her without a struggle) Or charging him. (Again, easily caught).

Reaching up, Grayson gripped the blue stone which he'd fastened to his collar. It flared to life, blue rays shining through the space between his fingers.

"*You are going to forget about me and whatever connection you think I have to those murders.*" Ms. Ansel's eyes grew wide. "*You'll never speak about me or the case again.*"

Ms. Ansel stood paralyzed, unable to tear her gaze away from him. But then, she blinked, frowning. "What are you trying to do?"

"What?"

"Is this how you intimidate people? Well, it isn't going to work on me. If you don't leave right now, I'm calling the police."

Dumbfounded, he stepped back. His hand dropped from the amulet, hanging limp at his side. *It didn't work. Why didn't it work?!*

No, no. He must have not done it right. He straightened his back and tried again, with more force. *"There's no need to involve the police."*

"If you don't get out of my face—"

Fear chilled his veins. Grayson grabbed his forehead, his head swimming, overwhelmed by it all. It wasn't working. *How? Why?* His heart raced faster, beating so loud he was positive she could hear it.

Ms. Ansel put herself together again, brushing a stray lock of hair from her forehead. "I don't know how you thought this would make you seem innocent Mr. Mages. All this is proof of a guilty man." She spared him one last nasty glare before getting in the car.

If she leaves, she'll talk. His fingers twitched. *You'll be ruined.*

Grayson reached out quicker than the woman could blink, and wrapped his hand around her throat. Ms. Ansel gasped, reaching up to claw at his arm, to pry his hand off her windpipe, but Grayson squeezed harder. Something about the way her throat flexed—trying to scream or breathe or something—under his palm made him feel powerful. Control had been restored in his world. His grip tightened.

She was really struggling, now; fighting with everything she had left. It wasn't enough, though. He could feel the life draining out of her, her fingernails slowly un-anchoring themselves from his forearm. Grayson reached through the window with his other hand and squeezed. Her eyes bulged, the veins bursting, spreading red through the glassy whites.

Grayson only released her when he was positive she'd stopped moving. He shook his hands out to encourage blood flow. They'd gone a tiny bit numb.

Ms. Ansel slumped over in her seat, head lolling out the window. Her eyes stared unblinkingly at the cement wall in front of her.

Somewhere on the level above, a car engine turned over. Grayson's head snapped in the direction, overcome with a sudden wave of fear once more. Looking back at the corpse, then at the ceiling, Grayson swore under his breath.

This was not good—no, that was the understatement of the century. This was horrible. It would be even worse if he didn't get out of that parking garage, though. Grayson broke into a jog, keeping his head low and his collar flipped up.

Losing control like that was exactly what Thorn warned him about. If this wasn't damning evidence, he didn't know what was.

As Grayson exited the garage, he pressed himself into a cut-out in the stone, slowing his breathing. The car from the upper level exited not a moment later. He watched it go then buried his head in his hands. This was bad.

But, he could handle it. Grayson inhaled deeply and straightened his jacket. Yes, he could handle it. He's survived much worse. As he straightened himself out, he noticed a long jagged scrape along his forearm. Ms. Ansel must have nicked him with her nails. How annoying.

Deeming himself calm enough, Grayson exited his little cove of safety and *walked*—not sprinted or ran, those would draw attention—to his parked car.

Everything would be fine.

XXIX

GRAYSON

Grayson watched the reporter on the screen, silently seething.

"Greer Mages is missing! That's right, according to our sources the famed magician has not been seen since last week. This on the heels of an abrupt ending to their last show and the recent discovery of two dismembered bodies thought to be that of two young girls who went missing several months ago, and were known to be close friends of Greer Mages. A source close to the investigation told us on the condition of anonymity that all this has the police looking into the timeline and known whereabouts of Grayson Mages. Even saying that he claims his sister is dead. Now, sources close to the Mageses say that Greer had no planned vacations and they were not aware of any out of town appointments. Her brother, Grayson Mages, has not given any statement on the matter and no official charges have been filed. For now he has also been staying

out of the spotlight. However, it has been confirmed that he is still in Sunwick Grove, having been seen frequently visiting the hospital to visit his wife, Odette Mages. No confirmation from her either."

"It looks like they're onto you," Odette commented.

He glared at her from the side of his eye. "It's fine. It's nothing but hearsay."

She snorted—which was the first real emotion she'd shown since arriving back home. "*Okay.*"

"If you need to get up, call for me." He lingered in her doorway a moment longer than necessary, then left and closed the door behind him.

The study sat on the opposite end of the hall, far from the bedrooms but close enough to be in earshot.

Thorn was inside already; leaning against the mahogany desk, his attention on the morning's newspaper.

"'*Murder in Downtown*' is the topic of interest today." Despite himself, Thorn's voice held an edge to it. Grayson couldn't help but feel like a scorned child.

"It wasn't intentional." He sat behind the desk on the overstuffed leather chair he claimed from Jethro's room. "My persuasion had no effect on her. I was powerless."

He missed the way Thorn's eyes glinted. "Interesting ..." He folded his hands together, twiddling his thumbs. "However, I do not believe that argument would hold up in a court of law."

"It won't get that far," he snapped. Thorn raised his eyebrows, but said nothing to this. Grayson exhaled slowly, his fingers dancing across the leather of the chair. "I've got this under control. Everything will be fine."

He said mainly to reassure himself and possibly to restore Thorn's faith in him.

"Have you decided what you'll do with the boy?"

Grayson bristled. "Let him rot in that cell for all I care. He tried to kill himself once already, right?"

"Twice," the angel amended.

Grayson shrugged his shoulders indifferently. "Then we'll throw him a bone. He can do all the dirty work. We'll deal with the remains when it happens."

This was certainly the easiest, but not the most satisfying solution. Letting the boy go without a couple of bruises was his least favored option. Even if he planted him in the most remote area on the planet, he wouldn't suffer enough for Grayson. He needed retribution. Odette needed retribution.

But as Thorn pointed out, no matter how they disposed of the boy, the police could find a way to trace it back to him. There were too many deaths, too many loose ends, which all linked to him as the culprit (and a few crack-pot theories stated Odette was in on it too; the slander would never cease).

No, it would be wise to head Thorn's suggestion. There was too much speculation, too many theories that linked to him. He'd have to leave the boy alone for now.

Thorn's attention broke from their conversation. "Uh ... Sir—?"

"*What?*" Grayson slammed his hands down on the armrest. "What's wrong with my plan, now, huh? Go on—tell me. As a matter of fact, just deal with it yourself since you seem to know best!"

"N-no, it's not that ..."

Grayson pinched the bridge of his nose. He could feel a migraine forming, and Thorn certainly didn't help matters. "*I thought you finally fixed that stutter ...*"

The study door creaked; a round, white face peered through the crack. Grayson's annoyance melted away as soon as he saw her. He should've been angry—Odette was on bedrest, and he took that seriously—but all that was overshadowed by concern.

He sat up; rising halfway out of his chair, but Thorn beat him to Odette's side. "Is something wrong? What are you doing out of your room?"

Thorn took her by the arm and led her towards the daybed. She wouldn't budge, choosing to stand in the middle of the room instead. "I want to see him."

"You were listening ..." Grayson huffed and fell back in his chair. It didn't matter how long she was there, she must've heard enough to concern her. He shut his eyes and rubbed them tiredly. "Princess—"

"It won't matter if I go," she said. "You've got it all planned out, don't you? You're going to kill him no matter what I say. One visit won't hurt anything."

"It's—it's the principle of the thing, Odette."

Her eyes narrowed. "Will you at least let me say goodbye?" Thorn opened his mouth, but quickly shut it after deciding better. "I should be able to say goodbye, for once, before you kill him."

Maybe it would have been humane to tell her he didn't intend to kill Skylar, but Grayson kept that information to himself. Her seeing that boy was the last thing he wanted and part of the whole reason he wanted to get rid of the punk.

He and Thorn exchanged glances.

"I can supervise them," said Thorn. "Nothing will happen under my watch."

Odette made a face, like Thorn watching over them was the last thing she wanted, but she didn't protest.

"You would visit him, anyway, if I said no, correct?"

"I'd find a way," she confirmed coldly.

"Fine." The word left a sour taste in his mouth. He nodded to Thorn. "Take her now."

Thorn bowed and pulled Odette from the room. Grayson watched as they left, silent and contemplative. It wasn't until he was sure they were far enough away, he got up and followed. Thorn could 'supervise' all he wanted, but Grayson had reason to not trust him. He might have changed his tune and helped recapture Odette, but the angel had caused her to leave in the first place.

The pair teleported down to the dungeon, Thorn deeming the steep stairs too dangerous for Odette in her delicate state. The room was just as dim and musty as Odette had remembered the scent of earth and blood was heavy in the air.

"There is something I should probably tell you before you go to him," said Thorn. However, Odette was already walking.

Blood rushed in her ears, drowning out all sounds. Her focus stayed on the last cell in the row, barely lit and far removed. Her steps quickened until she was running towards the cell.

The sound of footsteps made Skylar aware, though he stayed curled up in the corner of the cell, resting his head against the grimy stones.

Odette's heart beat painfully in her chest. She grabbed the bars to steady herself, her breathing ragged. It had been a long time since her heart affected her like this.

Skylar peeled one eye open and at first glance mistook her for Greer, but then he realized.

"Odette?" His voice was hoarse, his eyes wide with awe. "You're … You're …"

"I'm back," she supplemented, kneeling to the ground so she was eye level and smiled at him.

"*Dead*," he finished. "You're supposed to be dead."

Slowly, Skylar gained the courage to inch toward her. She certainly seemed real. Neither of them noticed a fourth person joined the dungeon, watching them interact.

"Who told you that?"

"Greer," said Skylar. "She said that Grayson would be bringing you home in a body bag. That you ran away and he killed you."

"I'm alive." Odette smiled, but it didn't match her eyes. "I promise I'm okay."

He rubbed his eyes, but Odette remained. She was no figment of his imagination. Skylar laughed, though it sounded more like a sob. He reached through the bars to take her hand, but hesitated just before he made contact. Odette, seeing his hesitation, met him halfway and enveloped his hands in her own.

"You're freezing," she said. Odette took one of his hands between her two and attempted to warm it up. It was only when she noticed the bandages on his wrists she stopped. Her face fell. "Skylar?"

"It's been real bad," he admitted, pulling away to hide the ugly, discolored bandages.

Odette didn't chastise him—how could she?—but her expression hardened. "Have they been treated?"

At this, she looked at Thorn. He nodded, leaning against the cell bars. "I did what I could. Magic is not a substitute for medical help, and I am no doctor."

"Well, it would help if he wasn't in this dirty *cell*," she snapped. "Show some real compassion for once, Thorn."

Skylar butt in, "It doesn't matter anymore. It's over and done with." Both Odette and Thorn stayed quiet but they weren't ready to quit their argument. They would have it out when they were alone. Skylar, wanting to change the subject, spoke again. "Where's Greer?"

Fear struck Odette like lightning. Again, she turned to Thorn, and in a low voice she asked, "He doesn't know?"

Thorn crossed his arms over his chest, "It isn't my place."

"What?" Skylar looked between the two of them. "*What?*"

"Skylar, Greer is ..." Her voice gave out, so she cleared her throat and tried again. "Greer's dead. There was an accident."

"An accident," he echoed. He had a far off look in his eyes as he tried to wrap his head around the concept. *Greer. Dead.* Those two words together were an oxymoron. "Are you sure?"

Odette nodded solemnly. The event played over and over in her head, burned into her mind at that point. "I saw it happen."

Skylar sat back on his haunches. The news floored him; this whole time he had been grieving over the wrong girl. Though, he didn't actually feel grief over Greer's death. It was like a weight had been lifted off of his shoulders and yet, anxiety kept him tethered.

"What's going to happen to me?"

"What?" Odette reached through the bars and laid her hand on his knee. "Nothing's going to happen. You're going to be fine."

He didn't believe it. "Greer's gone. Grayson isn't going to keep me around."

Odette pressed her lips together tightly, choking down the words threatening to come up. "Please don't talk like that."

Skylar patted her hand reassuringly and gave it a gentle squeeze. They understood each other in that moment, without having to speak. When Odette laced their fingers together, it was an *I'm sorry, please understand*. When Skylar stroked the back of her hand with his thumb, it was an *It's okay, this isn't your fault.*

"Time's up." Grayson came around the corner, stoic as ever. "Come here, Odette. Thorn." He gave the angel a pointed look.

Thorn dragged Odette to her feet, but she didn't let go of Skylar's hand. They stayed connected, him reaching through the bars as far as he could until their fingertips finally separated. Tears welling up in her eyes, but maybe if she cooperated, Grayson wouldn't do it.

She stumbled back, Grayson laying his hands on her shoulders protectively, but tight enough to send a message. *Stay put.* And she did.

Thorn laid his hand on the bars, and a mechanical click echoed through the room as he unlocked the door with his powers. Almost as soon as he pulled Skylar from the cell, the two of them vanished.

"You got what you wanted," said Grayson. "Are you happy?"

"Elated."

Grayson flicked her nose disapprovingly. "Don't be sarcastic, it doesn't work for you, princess. Now, *smile*."

Odette smiled on command. He frowned, having seen the smile she gave the boy and how bright she'd become; but, this one was watery and scornful. It was her pregnancy, he decided, that was making her so disagreeable. All the books he'd read said mood swings came with the territory.

He laid his hand on the small of her back and guided her up the stairs, the two of them moving gingerly.

When they reached the grand staircase, he turned Odette to face him. "Now, you're going back to bed," Grayson stated. "Doctor's orders. I'll check on you later."

From the corner of his eye, he saw movement in the foyer. It struck him odd, that Thorn hadn't got rid of Skylar already, but he didn't dwell on it. He bent down and pressed a chaste kiss on Odette's forehead.

Loud, frantic knocking drew him away from Odette. Bewildered, Grayson whipped his head around, staring at the large double doors incredulously. They rarely—if ever—had visitors. No one ever made it past the gate, it was always closed unless someone had called ahead or been invited.

No one moved. They all held their breath.

Another flurry of knocks sounded, louder than the first. The person on the other side of the door shouted something.

Odette moved trance-like towards the door, seeing no one was moving to get it. Grayson clamped his hand on her bicep, pulling her back.

"Stay back." Grayson wasn't angry, though. He swallowed hard, face wrinkling with concern. He should have had more time. He could feel his control slipping like sand through his fingers. He jerked his head at Thorn, who released Skylar. If he had to choose between getting rid of the boy and losing Thorn for a couple of hours, or hiding the boy; he'd take the latter.

"Go upstairs, take *him* with you," he ordered her.

But the knock persisted, keeping everyone cemented in their spots. It came repeatedly, hammering down on the thick wooden doors like the world would end if he didn't open up. *"Grayson Mages? This is the police."*

"The police?" Odette echoed.

He pushed her behind him, "Go upstairs, now."

Skylar rushed up the stairs to Odette's side, needing no further encouragement. Grayson passed him, heading straight for the door. His heart beat erratically with each step. He thought he had more time; but it didn't matter. They had arrived, and Grayson was certain they wouldn't go down without a fight.

Finally, he reached the door. It was shaking with each thump, like it might blow off its hinges. He opened it and schooled his face, preparing for the performance of his life. "Hello?"

He was face-to-face with potentially thirty policemen, each looking as crude as the last. Sheriff Landry led the herd, his face ruddy from the cold. They did not waste any time on his school-boy act and pushed inside, pouring into his home as an infestation of cockroaches would.

He was grabbed by one set of hands, then two, then— Grayson lost count. He was shoved to the ground, his knees slamming against the marble floor hard enough to bruise. Someone cuffed him.

Sheriff Landry stood in front of him and sneered. "Grayson Mages, you are under arrest for the murders of Bonnie McBride, Nadia Palit, and Greer Mages ..."

Somewhere above all the hubbub, he heard Odette exclaim in surprise. Poor, Odette, she must be so scared.

He grit his teeth together, glaring up at the officer. "You're making a big mistake."

Landry scoffed, "We'll see about that, *boy*."

Grayson looked up to the second floor landing and caught sight of Odette and Skylar, who were hiding behind a pillar. He wanted to shout at her, order her to hide in her room like he told her to.

A female officer noticed and followed his gaze, spotting the two immediately. She approached the steps cautiously. "Are you Mrs. Odette Mages."

Odette's eyes widened and she slowly stepped around the pillar, her hand rested protectively over her stomach. "I am."

Grayson hated how scared and weak she sounded. *Don't worry, you'll be safe soon.* He struggled against the handcuffs, but the officer behind him shoved his back so his face rested against the floor.

The woman started climbing the stairs. "And you?" Skylar, however, wouldn't budge, choosing to stay tucked behind the pillar. But, the cop recognized him, her breath stuttering to a halt. "Skylar Fraser?"

"Yes," he whispered. He looked between the cop and Odette. She extended her hand to him for comfort, and he crept closer to her, cowering behind her.

"There are a lot of people looking for you, Skylar," said the cop.

To this, Skylar flinched. Odette took control of the conversation. "What … what's happening here?"

"We want to talk with you, Odette. Is that okay?"

Breathlessly, she laughed. "Of course. Anything."

"*Odette!*" Grayson's roar broke her trance, and reality came crashing down. The policemen hauled him upright, and no matter how hard he twisted, they would not let him go. "You have got it all wrong. Get off! *Odette!* You aren't taking me anywhere—*Odette!*"

The color drained from her face, watching as they tried to force him from the home. Though he was the fly caught in the spider's web, he didn't act like it. No, he had that dangerous look in his eye, like a predator about to pounce.

She swallowed hard and stepped back, "It doesn't matter."

The officer furrowed her eyebrows. "I'm sorry?"

"It doesn't matter if I help you, he's going to get out. You've screwed us all by coming here." Skylar squeezed her hand, which had gone clammy. A cold sweat dripped down her neck. "You can't hold him. He'll get out and … and he'll come for us."

"You don't need to worry about that, Odette." The woman was on the landing with her now. "We can keep you safe from him, I promise."

"No, you can't!" All at once, a dam within her broke and all the secrets she had left inside of her poured forth. "None of you can protect us, do you know why? Because you never have! You're under his thumb whether you know it or not.

You don't have the power to protect us, you don't have any *power* at all."

The woman raised her hands as if she were trying to calm a wild animal. "I need you to relax, Odette."

"I'm not going to relax! Where were you when people were dying? Nowhere! And do you want to know why? Because there's no escaping the influence Grayson has on you. He's so deeply ingrained in your mind, I'm surprised you got this far!"

Grayson called out to her again, his voice full of warning. His message was clear, shut up or else. It would only be a matter of time before those cuffs were off of him. Why bother talking at all? Because nothing mattered anymore. So what if Grayson snapped? So what if he escaped again, this time she had obviously gone too far and there was no way he'd let her *live*.

"Are you saying that you've witnessed Grayson commit multiple murders?"

"And *kidnapping*," Odette nodded.

Grayson snapped. His reality fragmented, the one thing he loved most in the world had delivered him a devastating blow. His rage, which he'd tried so hard to stifle, exploded within his chest, burning him from the inside out. The air hummed around him. His amulet sparked to life, fueled by his ire.

Odette knew she'd overstepped. Her eyes widened knowingly, terrified of him. She turned away and buried her face in Skylar's chest, like she had accepted her fate.

"No one told me we were having a party."

That voice.

"Can anyone fill me in on what's happening here?"

It can't be.

Everyone around them stopped, all looking to the newcomer, bemused.

Grayson went slack jawed, his legs giving out beneath him. Luckily he was being held up by the officer behind him, or he would've fallen.

It wasn't possible. Thorn said the dead couldn't come back, but there in front of her was irrefutable proof the dead could live again.

"*Greer,*" Skylar breathed.

Though she stood there, very much alive, she looked like a corpse. Her face pale and gaunt, with bloodless cuts and green bruises decorating her face, looking like she physically fought her way back to life. Her hair framed her face in thin stringy, greasy clumps. Her lips were pale, and a small gash crossed her lower lip.

There was no scabbing, no bleeding, no nothing. She was *undead.*

Greer walked into the foyer, commanding the attention of the room. All around her, people parted, trying not to touch her. When she stopped, she was center stage; she whirled around curiously, eyeing everyone with intrigue. Her gaze then fell on Skylar.

"Puppy? What on Earth are you doing out here?"

"Greer Mages?" asked an officer. "You're supposed to be *dead.*"

She laughed a little too loud at that. "Do I look dead to you?"

"You *were*," said Odette, her voice hollow. "I watched it happen."

The officer beside her exclaimed softly at this. Greer shot Odette a withering glare. "You'll have to forgive my sister-in-law, she was diagnosed with antenatal depression and has a hard time differentiating between what is *real*, and what is *fake*." Her words cut through Odette like a knife. "No, I'm fine. I took a small vacation."

Again she laughed and waved her hand, as though she were physically clearing the air of any misunderstanding. No one else laughed with her.

"You're lying," Odette insisted. Her voice shook, forcing herself to continue. "You were impaled. I saw it go through your stomach. I saw the blood. You fell into the water ... The house burned down ... How are you here?"

"Oh?" She laughed bitterly, her pale tongue wetting her lips. "What a morbid little tale you've woven. How can you prove it?"

That was just the issue, wasn't it? Grayson wouldn't admit to it—it would implicate him in far more than the triple (well, now it was double, wasn't it?) homicide. Skylar hadn't been there at the time, so he was out of the question. The only other person who might be able to corroborate her story was Thorn, but he had vanished sometime after the police entered. Besides, he wouldn't help her even if she begged. She needed something else, something solid.

Then, it came to her.

"Lift up your shirt," Odette said.

Greer was taken aback. "Excuse me?"

If Thorn had healed her—*somehow*—it would've left a scar. Like he had said before, magic was no substitute for medical care. "Lift up your shirt and show us your stomach."

Greer's eye twitched. Smugly, Odette thought, *I've got you now.*

Reluctantly she reached for the hem of her shirt. Ever so slowly, she began to lift it, revealing a sliver of skin to the room.

However, Greer dropped her shirt almost as soon as it came up; from within her coat pockets she withdrew a knife.

The next series of events happened so fast, it was a blink-and-you-miss-it moment. Odette just caught the glint of Greer's knife before bodies began to drop, smashing onto the floor with a sickening smack.

Odette screamed and dropped to the floor to avoid the knife's war path. Skylar leapt to the side and hid behind the pillar once more. The woman dropped as well, crushing Odette's legs in the process.

It didn't take Odette long to realize the officer hadn't fallen voluntarily. A large gash going from one side of her neck to the other began spraying blood. It spilled onto her jeans and shoes as the woman convulsed, before stopping completely.

"Odette!" Skylar crawled out from his hiding space and helped her out from beneath the dying woman. "Are you hurt?"

She shook her head, words caught in her throat.

Skylar laid his hands over her face. She hadn't realized how badly she was shaking until that moment. "There's got to be another way out."

"There is." She turned to look over her shoulder at the staircase. "But, we have to go down. Behind the stairs, there's an exit to the pool."

"We won't make it ..."

Odette nodded. They had no chance of avoiding Greer and that wicked knife of hers. Even if they did avoid it, there was Grayson.

"We could go through a window," she said. "In one of the rooms—the study, there's a pipe outside the window. I-I don't know if it would even hold us."

"We can try."

They stood on their feet, Odette taking Skylar by the hand before they bolted. The sudden movement of the two did not go unnoticed. Below, Grayson had broken free of his handcuffs—melting the metal with his fire— when he spotted them. His left hand came alive with fire, blue flame burning like a halo around his knuckles. Sheriff Landry tried to attack him, but Grayson set him on fire before he had the chance.

Grayson realized they were too far away for him to chase them down. Instead, he turned to magic. He tossed the flame, which encircled his fist, and it went soaring. The flame caught the banisher and a brilliant blue wall of fire stopped them from getting any further. Grayson reeled back and threw another, this time aiming for them.

Odette saw the firebolt coming and shoved Skylar to the side. He fell to the ground hard, just as the firebolt struck where his head had been a moment before. The second was airborne, its path dead on for her.

She winced, shutting her eyes. The ball was mere feet away, the heat of it singing the hairs on her face, and then ... *nothing*.

Slowly, she opened her eyes, unsure what she might see, but she certainly didn't expect a large flaming fireball. She yelped, jumping back, but the fire never came any closer, nor did it recede. It just floated.

She wasn't dead—*how*? Odette opened her mouth, an unasked question on the tip of her tongue; as she turned, she was greeted by Skylar. He too just stared at her, open mouthed and unblinking. She waited, but he never moved. He was ... frozen.

Everything around her was frozen.

Odette sidestepped the fire bolt, which still crackled mid-air despite its petrified state. In the foyer, it was the same. Those who were still standing might as well have been statues; those who were on the ground weren't moving.

Puddles of blood surrounded the fallen. From this point of view, Odette couldn't tell who was dead and who was dying. Everyone was motionless, everyone was shell shocked. It was all too surreal.

There was movement out of the corner of her eye, startling her away from the railing. She expected Thorn—he always pulled something like this—but it wasn't the angel.

Grayson carefully maneuvered through the field of bodies until he found a clear-enough spot. He too, was just as confused as to what had occurred. Knowing it probably had something to do with Thorn, though, kept him somewhat at ease.

Off to the side, Greer waved her hand in front of an officer's face, trying to determine if they were responsive or not.

Thorn popped into the room so suddenly it was startling. He jogged down the stairs towards Greer and Grayson. "I need you to listen to me. We don't have much time."

"I could have handled this," Greer interjected.

Thorn shook his head, his tone grave. "You would have only made things worse. I have seen the future, and I wouldn't intervene unless I knew this would lead to great peril for the Mages bloodline."

"Speaking of 'great peril'," said Grayson. He turned to his sister, "Where the hell have you been?"

"Do you think healing yourself is easy?" Greer raised her eyebrows accusingly. "Luckily, I managed just fine, no thanks to you."

Thorn huffed impatiently, "Time is running out."

"Then what are you suggesting?" Greer motioned towards the room where less than a third of the officers were left standing. "It's a little too late to do anything about *this*."

"Untrue. Some of these humans are at the brink of death but I can bring them back. Though, when they come to, they'll remember everything about the event and their case about you. They'll remember what you can do."

"So it's a waste of time." Greer crossed her arms over her chest. "Why not let us fight our way out of this, Thorn? I can handle it."

"If you do, there will be grave consequences."

"Then ... we could alter their memories," said Grayson.

Thorn nodded. "My thoughts exactly. Altering these peoples' state of mind is the only way to ensure they won't come after you again. I should not have to go too far with it. The last week at most. All you have to do is lay low for a while so as to not trigger their memory."

"But what about their injuries?" asked Grayson. "They'll still have them. And the people who are already dead—altering their memories will only go so far. People will wonder why half of the sheriff's department is dead."

"We can make it so they remember a drug bust gone wrong." Thorn wrung his hands together. "Sometimes the simplest answer is the best."

"Sounds too good to be true." But Greer was smiling. She twirled her knife between her fingers giddily, staring at some far off point in the distance.

"If you can really do this, Thorn ..." Grayson looked up to the second floor landing and met Odette's gaze. "Then I want you to wipe *her* mind, too."

Greer looked at her from the side of her eye, tapping her chin with the knife. "I think that's a pretty good idea."

"No!" Though, Odette's protest fell on deaf ears.

Thorn wouldn't agree to that, Odette consoled herself, he *couldn't*. He might have been loyal to them, but she was still a member of the family. She had *some* sway. Moreover, Thorn had said he needed her for some kind of plot; he couldn't put her in harm's way if he needed her ...

But, as Thorn turned to face her, there was no trace of loyalty in his eye. No trace of the friend he had once been.

"You can't ..." Odette backed away slowly, hoping if anything the firebolt might come back to life and engulf her before they try anything. "Thorn ..."

Thorn shut his eye, as if deciding that the mere sight of her brought on pain. His shoulders sagged and he turned away, facing the twins once more. Their pale faces were illuminated by some unknown source; they seemed like devils to her, the sharp contours of their faces elongated to the point they were no longer human.

Odette couldn't stand to look at them anymore, so she ran; but the mansion was becoming brighter and elongating like the twins' faces. She bypassed the firebolt, lingering by Skylar before ducking into the next hallway.

This isn't real, Odette repeated to herself, *this is all a dream*. She made it to the end of the hall and tried to open one of the doors, but for some strange reason it remained locked. She tried the next, but it was just the same. Locked.

She turned around and found Thorn standing not a foot away. She wanted to beg him not to, but her tongue would not cooperate. A lump formed in her throat. One look from him told her everything she needed to know: Thorn had made up his mind.

Thorn lifted his hand and snapped his fingers; the crack striking her to her very core.

Her vision went white.

Hannah Boggs

EPILOGUE

MARCH

Odette shot upright, gasping at the air greedily. Her hand found her chest, landing right above her heart. She clutched it painfully hard, her nails digging into her t-shirt, ready to tear through it at any moment.

"Princess?"

Her head snapped towards Grayson. His voice had obviously startled her, a bewildered expression written all across her face. For several seconds, Odette stared at him as though she didn't know him, as though he were a different person all together. There wasn't a hint of recognition.

Slowly, he approached her with his hands raised to show he meant no harm. "Are you okay? How are you feeling?"

"I ..." She licked her lips, her eyes darting all around the room drinking in everything. "I don't know. I think I had a nightmare."

Grayson sat at the foot of her bed, careful to keep his hands folded in his lap. "What's the last thing you remember?"

She pursed her lips, frowning. What *was* the last thing she remembered? Frantic, Odette shut her eyes, but her memories came up blank.

"I don't know."

"It's okay." He reached out to pat her, but stopped when he saw the fear in her eyes. "You hurt yourself, Odette. It was terrifying. I thought I lost you."

A spark of recognition crossed her face. "Oh."

Grayson leaned forward, tears that would remain unshed gathered in the corners of his eyes. He hadn't cried this far—he wouldn't cry now. "You can't do that again, do you understand? Never. I know you're upset. I know you're struggling, but this isn't just about you anymore. You have to think of our son."

"Our son." She tightened her grip on her protruding stomach. "Yeah."

Grayson bit his lip, grounding himself. "I love you, princess. I think you need some more rest, okay? You don't seem like you're all here yet."

"I feel a little out of it," she agreed.

Grayson bent down to kiss her, but she didn't lean into him, leaving his lips to meet her forehead. He tried to fight the swell of disappointment. Everything was going to be okay—everything was getting better. His Odette was getting better. He smoothed his hand over her forehead, lingering a moment longer, before finally tearing himself away and leaving her to rest alone.

Greer waited for him outside of the room. She pushed off of the wall, getting only a moment's glimpse before he shut the door completely.

"How is she?"

Grayson stuffed his hands in his pants pockets. "She's getting there. Slowly. Thorn did say it would be a process."

The two of them began to walk side-by-side, their strides in time with one another. Greer glanced at him out of the corner of her eye. "Do you think she bought it?"

"I think she's slowly convincing herself," Grayson said. "I need more time to really sell it. It's amazing, Greer. When I'm in there with her, it's almost like I have the old Odette back."

His sister grunted, but Grayson was too preoccupied to care. It would only be a matter of time. Thorn said it would work and it had. He might have been a slimy weasel, but he really pulled through.

Pretty soon, Grayson would have the family he always dreamed of.

Acknowledgments

Okay, so I didn't get to do this with my first book which I seriously regret; but, it's okay! I published another one so I get to thank all the wonderful people who helped with the first AND second book in permanent ink.

First of all, thank you, the readers who have read book one and are back for more. Thank you for all the great reviews and for showing up for book signings and events. You guys honestly don't know how much it means to me knowing you enjoyed the book.

I want to give the BIGGEST thank you to Rebekah Coster for donating her time (and her face) as my model for the cover of these books.

Thank you to Kevin West for his guidance through the self-publishing industry.

To Lenny Schafer from Ohio Council of Community Schools, and Angela Gunderson and Mark Rickel from Ohio Connections Academy: Thank you for all of your amazing support with *Violent Delights*!

And a special thanks again to my Mom and Dad. They are my editing team, marketing team, cover designers, and everything in between. Without them this book would not be finished.

Also by Hannah Boggs:
Her debut novel & book one of the trilogy, and winner of
IndiesToday.com 2019 Best Paranormal Book!

VIOLENT DELIGHTS

Up Next ...

VIOLENT ENDS

For more information visit ...
www.HannahBoggsBooks.com
Facebook @HannahBoggsAuthor
Instagram @han.boggs

www.ingramcontent.com/pod-product-compliance
Lightning Source LLC
Chambersburg PA
CBHW070931100726
47908CB00001B/173